THE
POISON
TREE

F. M. O'Rourke

SIMON & SCHUSTER
NEW YORK • LONDON • TORONTO
SYDNEY • TOKYO • SINGAPORE

SIMON & SCHUSTER
Rockefeller Center
1230 Avenue of the Americas
New York, NY 10020

Copyright © 1996 by F. M. O'Rourke

SIMON & SCHUSTER and colophon are
registered trademarks of Simon & Schuster Inc.
Designed by Edith Fowler
Manufactured in the United States of America

10 9 8 7 6 5 4 3 2 1

Library of Congress Cataloging-in-Publication Data
O'Rourke, F. M. (F. Michael), date.
The poison tree / F. M. O'Rourke.
p.   cm.
1. Irish—Travel—California—Los Angeles—Fiction.
2. Terrorism—California—Los Angeles—Fiction.
3. Hollywood (Los Angeles, Calif.)—Fiction. I. Title.
PS3565.R64P6   1996
813'.54—dc20   95-26719 CIP
ISBN 0-684-80214-7

ACKNOWLEDGMENTS

I would like to extend my sincere gratitude to the many people in Ireland and the United Kingdom who shared with me their personal opinions, experiences and understanding of the complex history and politics underlying the ongoing debate over the future of Northern Ireland. Special thanks are due to former Los Angeles police lieutenant Fred Reno for his invaluable guidance in matters relating to weapons, tactics and security measures portrayed in *The Poison Tree*; to agent David Smith for his unflagging belief in the project; and to my wife and manager Sally Smith for the endless hours of research, travel and review that she has lavished upon this labor of love.

THIS BOOK IS DEDICATED
TO ALL THE INNOCENT CHILDREN,
WHO DREAM ONLY OF
LAUGHING AND PLAYING IN THE SUN.

A Poison Tree

I was angry with my friend:
I told my wrath, my wrath did end.
I was angry with my foe:
I told it not, my wrath did grow.

And I water'd it in fears,
Night & morning with my tears;
And I sunned it with smiles,
And with soft deceitful wiles.

And it grew both day and night,
Till it bore an apple bright;
And my foe beheld it shine,
And he knew that it was mine,

And into my garden stole
When the night had veil'd the pole:
In the morning glad I see
My foe outstretch'd beneath the tree.

WILLIAM BLAKE

PROLOGUE

Derry Road, Belfast, Northern Ireland, July 1985

IT WAS A RARE warm Saturday morning and the young man walking down the street with the wide-eyed little boy tagging along, comically trying to match his strides, was feeling particularly good. He had money in his pocket, his son at his side and the whole long summer weekend was ahead of him.

The man was tall and fair, his long blond hair tied loosely in a ponytail that fell across the back of his soft Italian leather jacket, giving him the vaguely familiar look of a handsome rock star whose name one couldn't quite place. The boy taking giant steps alongside had the same good looks as his father. His hair was, if anything, a shade lighter, cut in a soft fall of golden curls that framed his pink-cheeked face so that he looked like one of the cherubs that surrounded the altar in the cathedral at the other end of the town, where he had been baptized some six years earlier. From time to time he would look up adoringly at the man towering at his side, squinting against the bright summer sun, proud that his da was so big and strong.

The father and son were out after blue jeans this morning, specifically, a special pair of the shamefully expensive American Levi's that were to be a birthday present for the boy's mother, and it was for that reason they had ventured into this strange part of the city, far from their own West Belfast Catholic neighborhood. The young man had heard of a particular shop on this street where the desired garment could be had at a relatively reasonable cost, for even though he had recently found employment in the shipyard, and thus could afford the Levi's, he was far from rich and still had to watch his purchases.

The boy slowed after a while, his short legs tired from having matched his father's pace for so many blocks, and the man halted and smiled down at him. "All worn out now?" he asked.

The child shyly shook his head, reluctant to admit that he would really like to sit down and rest for a bit or, better yet, be picked up and carried on his father's shoulder: Now that he was a big boy he would not dream of asking for such a carry. Not in public at any rate.

Sensing the boy's dilemma, his father reached into the pocket of his faded denims and extracted a coin. "Look," he said, pointing to a tiny shop just a few steps farther down the street. A sign on the sidewalk beside a cluster of little white metal tables advertised that ice cream was available on the premises.

"How would you like a bit of ice cream and a sit-down?" asked the father.

The boy's blue eyes sparkled, and he nodded enthusiastically. "Very well," said his father, pressing the warm coin into his little hand and settling himself on a wire-framed chair at one of the tables. "You go and get your sweet while I sit here and have a smoke." He removed a packet of Marlboros from his jacket and fiddled in another pocket for matches as the youngster ran into the shop.

THE GREEN VOLKSWAGEN GOLF that had been shadowing the pair since they had stepped onto an omnibus in their own Falls Road neighborhood nearly an hour earlier was pulled up to the curb a few doors past the shop. The man behind the wheel, a mild, clerkly type wearing wire-rimmed spectacles beneath a tweed workman's cap, squinted into the rearview mirror. "Now here's a bit of luck," he said, watching as the fair-haired man at the table lit his cigarette and blew out a cloud of smoke. "He's sent the kid into the shop."

His companion, a darkly complected fellow whose stubbled features were twisted into a perpetual scowl, turned to look back down the street. Seeing that there was no one else about, he nodded and reached into the rear seat for the paper-wrapped parcel lying on the floorboards, and quickly unwrapped it. The man at the wheel watched as he checked the magazine of the squat black machine pistol, snapped off the safety and pumped a round into the chamber. "Hurry it up, then," he whispered, his eyes flicking back to the mirror.

"Don't wait for me," growled his companion. He lifted the weapon's muzzle to a point just below the sill of his window as the other put the shifter into reverse and backed out into the street.

THE YOUNG MAN at the table took another drag of his cigarette, savoring the expensive imported smoke and wondering if he should just peek into the shop and see if the boy was all right. He decided to wait a minute longer, proud that the kid had the self-confidence to make his own purchase and determined to let him conduct the transaction on his own. He looked up at the whine of the green Volks backing swiftly down the street toward him, wondering where the fool thought he was going. As the car drew alongside of him, he thought he recognized the face of the dark man at the passenger window.

The man in the car made eye contact, a grudging smile of recognition breaking the unshaven expanse of his stern jaw. "Quinn, isn't it, from the yards?" he said in a low, familiar grumble.

"Well, hello there," called the young man, crushing out his cigarette and standing to approach the stopped car.

LITTLE BILLY QUINN stepped through the doorway of the shop, a towering vanilla cone balanced carefully in his fist. His mouth was smeared white with a residue of the soft cream, and there was a dab on his nose, as well, the result of his first delicious plunge into the freezing confection. He grinned proudly at his father, who he saw was halfway across the walk to the green car on the street.

He was on the verge of calling out when the dark man inside the car raised something black and shiny into the window. The man's smile turned strange, his thin lips moving over his clenched yellow teeth as he said something the boy could not make out. Then a sparkling tongue of blue fire leapt from the end of the black object in his hand, and a thin rattle of sound echoed through the morning air.

The rattling noise continued as the boy's father stood shuddering like a marionette, and for a moment the boy thought his da must be playing some sort of grown-up game with the men in the car. Then the street abruptly went silent.

The boy realized with sudden horror that while watching the strange scene on the sidewalk he had let his hand tilt forward and the ice cream was tumbling out. He looked down as the swirled column hit the stoop with a soft plop. Hot tears welled up in his eyes, and he looked up to see if his father had noticed his clumsy blunder, anticipating the sharp reprimand that was sure to follow.

His father was sinking slowly to the sidewalk, turning to look up at him as he fell, mouthing words that the child could not hear. The whine of a racing engine filled the air, and little Billy Quinn swung his head slowly round in time to see the green car disappearing around a corner. A woman's scream sounded behind him, and he looked up to see the jolly fat lady who had sold him the ice cream staring out into the street, her chubby pink hands clutched into fists at the sides of her round cheeks. She reached for him, but he ducked from beneath her grasp and stumbled to his father's side, slipping in the thick, dark pool growing across the sidewalk. "Da!" he screamed, crawling on all fours through the hot, sticky blood and clutching his father's face in his tiny hands. Looking into the empty, staring blue eyes, he saw that something was horribly, terribly wrong.

"Da?" he cried again as a small circle of strangers began to gather on the sidewalk about him. He looked up into their grim faces, waiting for one of them to come to his aid.

Not one of them moved.

BOOK ONE

Hands Across the Water

I am troubled, I'm dissatisfied, I'm Irish.

MARIANNE MOORE

CHAPTER ONE

Monaghan
Republic of Ireland, March 1997

IT WAS RAINING, of course. A cold, splashing Irish rain of the sort guaranteed to make the arthritic pensioners in the out-of-the way pubs bank up the peat in their back room fires and cast longing glances at the RTE documentary films playing on the tellies above the bars, extolling the joys of winter visits to Spain and Majorca and other such warm places with sun-washed beaches and golden sunsets.

The blue Ford Orion, a year-old model belonging to the commercial representative for a Japanese electronics firm, had been stolen the previous night from the long-term parking facility at the Dublin airport. Still sparkling from its last wash and polish, it had been driven immediately to a small garage in a seaside village well to the north of the Irish Republic's capital city, where its number plates had been changed to match the registration of a nearly identical vehicle owned by a prominent member of the Royal Ulster Constabulary, Northern Ireland's state police force.

In addition to the false number plates, the Orion had undergone a number of mechanical and electronic revisions that had involved the removal and replacement of major components of its fuel, exhaust and rear suspension systems. The resultant modifications—which had been accomplished with an alacrity that would have astounded the service manager at the Dublin Ford agency garage where the car was normally taken for service—had left the vehicle's appearance virtually unchanged, although the loss of nearly three inches of travel from its rear suspension had drastically altered its normally unexceptional handling qualities from moderately firm to exceedingly harsh. The little Ford now rode more like a wooden-wheeled dogcart than a modern passenger car, a characteristic violently impressed upon its present occupants within minutes of their having taken delivery of the vehicle and started north via a circuitous route that was deliberately calculated to bring them to their chosen border cross-

ing into the separate, British ruled country of Northern Ireland a few minutes after dark.

The gray light was already fading from the western sky as the balky vehicle splashed down a potholed farm road less than ten miles from the border.
The young driver switched on the yellow quartz driving lights and fought
against the ache in his arms caused by the vibrations of the madly jerking
steering wheel, wishing for the night that had not yet begun, to be over. He
reached for the radio controls by force of habit, halting his hand just inches
from the switch. Christ, he thought, that was all he needed now, to turn on
the fucking radio. He glanced worriedly across the darkened interior of the
lurching Ford, wondering if his near-fatal blunder had been noticed.

The man in the passenger seat surprised him by breaking the silence he
had maintained for more than three hours. "It's a damned tricky thing,
this," Kileen said wryly, "and I don't like it at all." He gazed pointedly at the
radio. "Not at all," he added unnecessarily. He then leaned forward and
swiped at the mist obscuring his darkening view of hedgerows and
drenched fields. The wavering glow of the Orion's shuddering instrument
lights threw the ridge of white scar tissue along his jaw into sharp relief, further heightening the ever-present aura of menace that exuded from his
sharply edged features.

The tired youngster sighed inwardly and tightened his grip on the wheel,
reluctant to reveal his nervous impatience with his companion's grumbling.
Michael Kileen was after all a living legend, a veteran of nearly twenty-five
years of tireless campaigning against the British occupation of the North,
and the man on whose head MI-5 had maintained a standing hundred-
thousand-pound reward these five years past—ever since the Harrods
Christmas bombing that had killed a dozen London holiday shoppers and
left scores more injured. Kileen's exploits, the boy knew, were gleefully
whispered about in the back rooms of pubs from Belfast to Boston, an ongoing wellspring of hope and morale among the faithful. Songs had been
written glorifying the old man's brilliantly executed assaults on the hated
enemy, and it was common knowledge that his masterful tactics had been
integrated into the curricula of half a dozen terrorist and counterterrorist
organizations around the world.

The Orion's driver, a fair-haired teenager with piercing blue eyes and the
striking good looks of a magazine model, looked away from the dark road
long enough to cast another glance at the living legend riding beside him.
Having uttered his cryptic pronouncement, Kileen was leaning back against
the cushion again, his ruined face lost in shadow. He might well have been

asleep, but the young driver knew better. It was said that Michael Kileen slept as an ocean shark slept: which was not at all. And, the boy reminded himself, after twenty-five years the Brits had never so much as laid a finger on the old bastard.

Fucking amazing.

Still, he hadn't expected the great man to be so skittish about their scheme. He had, in fact, been more than a little disappointed at Kileen's dour assessment of the meticulous planning and execution that had gone into this entire operation. If he and his mates had expected at least some praise from the old master for their cleverness, it had not been forthcoming.

"Might work," was all Kileen had said of the plan when they had explained it to him over cups of bitter coffee at the safe house in the fishing village the previous evening.

Might work! Fuck-all, what did the man expect of them? The call had been put out for a foolproof means of delivering a compact, high-grade explosive punch to specific enemy locations. Gone now were the days when the lads could simply park a lorry filled with a ton or so of explosives down the road from an outpost and be content that the resulting blast would surely kill a few of the occupiers, along with whatever other poor sods might happen to be in the neighborhood, as well. Now, with the useless peace talks still dragging on, it was all public relations. All well and good to blow up a lot of bystanders on a London street corner in the old days, but you couldn't do that anymore. Surgical precision was what they wanted nowadays; clean strikes guaranteed to harm none but the hated oppressors who, despite the politicians' endless predictions of justice and democracy for Northern Ireland, still ruled the streets of Belfast with their armored cars and their attack helicopters.

Ruled with their superior technology.

Well, the call had gone out to meet that technology head-on, and he and his mates—one of them an older lad, a university engineering student—had answered with a plan that was, in the boy's opinion at least, nothing short of brilliant. Then the high-and-mighty Mr. Michael Kileen had showed up to put his personal stamp of approval on it, announcing that he himself would go along on the first trial run to be sure it worked properly, treating them all like a bunch of idiots in the bargain.

Jesus! The balls of the man . . . Of course it would fucking work properly. It had to work.

"You see," said Kileen, interrupting the driver's angry reverie, "it's the electronics of the thing that have got me worried."

The startled youngster swerved to miss a large pothole in the road and glanced into the deep shadows surrounding the passenger seat. Kileen's black eyes burned like coals in the reflection of the instrument lights. "The electronics are fucking brilliant!" countered the boy at the wheel. "Taiwanese!"

"Taiwanese, is it?" Kileen nodded thoughtfully. "Well then, they might be all right at that. It was the old Soviet stuff that would blow up in our own faces more often than not, the last time we were after trying a stunt like this."

"The last time?" The youngster's face fell. "You mean something like this has been done before?"

Kileen laughed, a short, ugly sound, twisted as it was around the scarred remains of his vocal cords. "Not done, *tried.* Sure it's been tried, the last time just after the cease-fire failed back in '79, when your mother's milk was still dribbling down your little chin."

"What happened?" The youngster deliberately ignored the insult, the tone of his voice suddenly devoid of most of its usual cockiness.

"Boom!" Kileen rolled his eyes skyward. "Three fine lads, a Limerick fishmonger's VW mini and eighteen kilos of Khadaffi's best Semtex explosive, all spread across the Falls Road in a thin red layer like so much strawberry jam." He closed his eyes, shaking his head. "Christ what a fuck-all that was." The black eyes clicked open, catching the boy in their gaze like a rabbit in oncoming headlights. "It was the electronics, you see. Soviet surplus sent direct to us via Cuba, via Syria, via the fucking PLO." He laughed again. "Hell, the Prime Minister might as well have sent it direct to us via Number Ten fucking Downing Street for all the good that lot did The Cause. MI-5 are still laughing about it."

"Shit," whispered the youngster, a sudden graphic vision of the careening blue Orion blowing sky-high at the next pothole filling his mind.

"It was shit, all right," said Kileen. "Let's only hope your Taiwanese wiring is better made than that lot. " He shifted his gaze to the streaked windscreen, focusing on a blur of light beyond a distant line of trees. "Better start slowing now," he cautioned. "The crossing is just ahead."

"These electronics are good," said the boy at the wheel with more confidence than he actually felt. He downshifted into third gear and reached for the radio, fingering the special button his mates had installed back at the garage. "All solid-state components with a computer-chip timer," he mumbled to make himself feel better.

"Ah, a computer chip!" Kileen laughed and straightened the lapels of his respectable blue business suit as the floodlights of the approaching border crossing filled the interior of the muddy car. "Then I don't see how we can miss. Now if you'll just wipe that panic-stricken look off your face and put on your handsome new hat, Billy Quinn, we'll see whether your little stunt works . . . or blows us both back to our Maker."

CHAPTER TWO

Pacific Academy High
Pacific Palisades, California

"OH MY GOD, how gross!" shrieked Kelly Huston. The grayish corpse of a fat bullfrog flopped limply into the plastic dissecting tray, splattering her pale blue silk shirt with droplets of pinkish embalming fluid. Kelly backed away from the black-topped lab table, knocking over the tall stool on which she had been perched while she took her biology notes.

"Hey, I'm really sorry," stammered Stanley Kinsella, her gangly lab partner. He pushed his thick glasses back up onto the bridge of his nose and began clumsily dabbing at the spots over her breasts with a dirty handkerchief from the pocket of his baggy corduroys. "I was just trying to get a better look at the heart," he explained.

"Stop it, Stanley!" hissed Kelly. She slapped his red-knuckled hand away and looked up to the sound of giggles. The entire class was staring at the two of them. She flushed to the roots of her dark blond hair, embarrassed and irritated at being the center of unwanted attention. The new shirt, which she had literally had to beg her mother to buy, was probably ruined now, and to make matters worse, her more than somewhat geekish lab partner was standing there feeling her up in front of the whole class.

"It just sort of slipped," murmured Stanley. His acned face was now even redder than hers, as he leaned over the countertop sink, running water on the dirty handkerchief. He turned and offered the sopping cloth to her. "Maybe you can rinse it off," he said miserably.

"Hey, Kelly," whispered Brenda Gaynor from the table just ahead of hers, "what are you and Stanley doing back there, having an affair?"

Kelly smiled sweetly and wrinkled her nose at the malicious jibe. "Up yours, Brenda," she replied. The slender redhead shot her a condescending look and turned away to whisper something into the ear of Thad August, her muscular lab partner. Thad shook his head and gave Kelly an amused look.

What a nightmare, Kelly thought. Brenda had been trying to worm her way back into Thad's good graces ever since he had started to notice Kelly a few weeks earlier, even stooping to bribery, getting Samantha Simms—who was going steady with a guy from UCLA anyway—to trade biology lab partners with her in exchange for tickets to the MTV Awards. That way Brenda ended up with Thad, and Kelly was stuck with the pathetic Stanley.

"Kelly, you okay?" She looked around to see Samantha peering at her from the next table over, her enormous brown eyes filled with concern.

"No thanks to you," Kelly hissed angrily, bending to pick up the fallen stool. Stanley saw what she was doing and beat her to it, setting the stool noisily on its legs and stepping hurriedly back, as though his touch might contaminate her.

Her ears burning, Kelly found her purse and rummaged through it for a tissue, dabbing at the spots on her blouse which, thankfully, already were beginning to disappear of their own accord. She managed to get back onto her stool as the door to the classroom opened and Miss Wyeth, the heavy-set biology teacher, clomped back into the room in her orthopedic shoes and began issuing instructions for removing the frogs' lungs. Kelly watched glumly as Stanley deftly excised the flabby gray organs from their specimen with a scalpel and proudly displayed them for her to sketch. In the row ahead, Brenda wriggled closer to Thad, pretending to be fascinated with the clumsy hash he was making of his frog, brushing her slim body against his at every opportunity.

Kelly bit her lip, resisting a sudden urge to climb over the lab table and wring the other girl's neck. She was convinced that no jury in the world would ever find her guilty. For, not only was Brenda Gaynor a first-class bitch, but with her flawless skin, deep blue eyes and shiny red hair, she was movie-star gorgeous. To top it all off, Brenda's father was the president of Grammy Records in Hollywood, which empowered Brenda to invite anyone she chose to any number of to-die-for concerts, music awards shows and private recording industry parties, a fact that, despite her bitchy temperament and total disdain for anyone else, kept her at the top of everybody's popularity list. Even Kelly's best friend, Samantha, hadn't been immune when it came down to choosing between her loyalty to Kelly and front-row seats at the MTV Awards.

It just wasn't fair, Kelly thought. Thad August had been close to asking her for a date for weeks now, and Brenda was deliberately trying to ruin everything.

The ten-minute bell rang, shattering her homicidal fantasies, which had progressed from mere strangulation to a full scale dissection of Brenda's liver. In her daydream, the hideous Stanley wielded his rusty scalpel at her cruel direction while a terrified Brenda wailed for mercy . . . .

"I'm really sorry about your blouse, Kelly."

She looked up to see Stanley standing before her, wringing his knobby hands.

"That's okay, Stanley," she said casually, "accidents happen." He shuffled away as she glanced down again at the silk shirt. She was relieved to see that the stains were barely noticeable, and gave silent thanks that she wouldn't have to explain to her mother how she had managed to ruin the wildly expensive garment, which she was not even technically supposed to be wearing yet anyway. Katherine Huston had bought the fabulous shirt on the express condition that it was to be saved for her stepfather's upcoming surprise birthday dinner at Le Dôme next week. But Katherine had left early this morning for Palm Springs with one of her clients, and the sight of the gorgeous new shirt hanging in the closet had been too much for Kelly to resist.

Reminding herself to be extra careful until she got home and changed, Kelly threw a towel over the disgusting remains of the sacrificial frog and hurried out into the broad echoing corridors of Pacific Academy High. Just walking down the polished floor with the bright California sunshine pouring in through the high arched windows lightened her mood, and she thanked the powers that be that her family had moved here from Boston six months ago. Even if they weren't as wealthy as Brenda's family, it didn't matter. Kelly knew lots of kids even richer. One of the things she loved about Pacific Academy was that, even though it was rumored to be the ritziest private high school in the country, nobody seemed to care very much. In fact, nobody at Pacific Academy seemed to care much about anything. They didn't really have to.

Every now and then, just to keep touch with reality, she reminded herself that somewhere in the world there were still people who cared passionately about things like poverty and politics and social problems. Once upon a time—before she came here—she had been one of them herself.

Funny how things like that didn't seem so important when you suddenly had everything you wanted. Well, almost everything.

Kelly Huston shook her head, feeling a twinge of guilt over being a child of privilege, and feeling vaguely sorry for everybody who didn't know what that was like.

CHAPTER THREE

The Border

THE FLOODLIT BORDER CROSSING, which straddled a minor junction of back roads some forty miles southwest of Belfast, was manned by two uniformed members of the Royal Ulster Constabulary. Both were wearing glistening rain slickers against the steady downpour that had begun in earnest a few minutes earlier. A bit back from the road, and made the more conspicuous by the presence of their armored personnel carrier, its windscreen and firing ports protected against stones and Molotov cocktails by heavy wire mesh, six young British troopers in full battle dress and armed with deadly automatic weapons looked convincingly, if somewhat self-consciously, menacing huddled beneath their camouflage canvas awning.

The troops and fortifications at the border were a strange admixture of pretense and the deadly serious business attending the continued British occupation of Northern Ireland. For while their ostensible purpose—to prevent the flow of illegal weapons and explosives into the North from the sympathetic haven of the independent Irish Republic—was still real enough, despite the ongoing cease-fire, no one really expected a gang of IRA renegades to arrive by road in a lorry filled with rocket launchers and grenades from the massive stores that were rumored to be cached in the South; not when Ulster's rugged coastline offered a hundred unguarded coves where a fast boat could unload the same amount of ordnance in half the time with absolutely no danger whatsoever.

By the same token, however, the show of force at the border had to be vigilantly maintained or the bloody radical liberationists who considered the peace talks a sham and a sellout *would* be hauling their guns into the country in laundry vans. As it was, nothing but civilian traffic moved through the heavily guarded crossing, and the greatest risk was to the constables and the nervous young Tommies, all of whom were the constant targets of obscene catcalls from local Catholic teenagers on the road by day, and the occasional sniper potting off a shot at them from the fields after dark.

The dull, mind-numbing work of guarding the remote crossing was nonetheless nerve shattering to all, none more so than Tommy Barnett, the twenty-three-year-old RUC constable who was junior man on duty this evening. Together with his partner, Harry Smith, a nearly useless veteran who had lost two sons in one of the last pub explosions in Londonderry two years previously, and who now dreamed only of retiring to his farm in the far North, Barnett had spent the previous eight hours quizzing insolent travelers from the South as to their destinations and their business in Northern Ireland, examining the muddy undersides of lorries loaded with produce by means of a mirror attached to the end of an aluminum rod and, occasionally, running his electronic sniffer—a newly operational device festooned with blinking lights and buzzers, on which he had received special training just two months earlier—over crates of beer and bales of stinking hides in the forlorn hope of detecting hidden explosives within. Although he knew the device was next to useless in the rain, he broke it out from time to time anyway, as he had been ordered. All part of the show for the fucking Paddies.

Tommy Barnett was cold and tired and wanted nothing more than for his relief to arrive so that he could go home and luxuriate in a warm bath until it was time to pick up his girlfriend, whom he had promised to take to the opening of the new Arnold Schwarzenegger film in the town later in the evening. He sneaked a glance at his wristwatch beneath the sleeve of his dripping mackintosh and was relieved to see that there were fewer than five minutes remaining of his shift.

"Oh sweet mother of God," moaned Smith from his protected perch beneath the tin roof of the guardhouse, "will ye look at what's coming down the road. Just at the shift change too," whined the older man, running out into the rain to join his partner at the crossing. "The bugger'll have us out here half the night now. He's a right bastard, that one."

Barnett turned and raised his eyes toward the oncoming vehicle splashing toward them, spotting the familiar number plate and the regulation cap of the uniformed driver at the wheel before the car had even rolled to a complete stop. "Christ, it's the superintendent himself," he murmured, hurrying forward to pull the spiked barrier out of the road. "What do you suppose he's been doing on the other side?"

"Bugger what he's been doing over there," growled the older man as the Orion's lights flashed impatiently behind the barrier. "They probably sent him down to Dublin to kiss the papist bastards' arses in hopes they'll tell him where the IRA have buried all their fucking bombs. Just move the bleedin' barrier before he decides to stop awhile and take it out on us."

Barnett hurriedly complied, jerking on the cold, wet chains to drag the steel tire trap aside and waving the waiting vehicle through. The engine roared, and the compact blue Ford leapt forward, flashing through the checkpoint and past the rank of watching soldiers without slowing. As it passed the soldiers' awning, something metallic clanked in the road and a long, cylindrical object bounded through the air, landing in a puddle beside the guardhouse. "Will ye look at that," Smith howled gleefully, "now the bastard's gone and lost his exhaust pipe, muffler and all . . ." He strode back toward the shack to examine the lost muffler, joining the three curious soldiers who were already gathering to stare down at it.

"Oh Jesus!" moaned Tommy, the sudden realization of what was about to happen dawning in his brain. "Get away from it!" he screamed. He heard the words tumbling from his mouth in a spray of spittle as he threw himself flat onto the ground.

Harry Smith, father of two sons killed in an IRA bombing as they'd toasted the winner of a televised snooker match two days before the '94 cease-fire, turned to stare at him as the world turned white hot.

Something wet and hideous slapped into Tommy Barnett's face, and he screamed for his mother.

CHAPTER FOUR

Encounter

THAD AUGUST was leaning against Kelly's yellow Mustang convertible—a seventeenth-birthday gift from Chuck Huston, her stepfather—in the school parking lot, the bright afternoon sunlight glinting off his sun-bleached hair. "Hi," he grinned, flashing his perfect teeth at her. His faded Levi's were carelessly ripped in just the right places, and the worn black polo shirt stretched across his broad chest was actually dark gray from the many repeated launderings it had endured before he had begun to wear it.

"Hi, yourself." Kelly tossed her things into the car, hoping her casual expression masked her lingering rage over having had to watch Brenda Gaynor climbing all over him in biology lab.

"Wanna grab a bite down at the club?" he asked.

Kelly's heart pounded a little faster. Samantha had told her that Thad's family belonged to the California Yacht Club at Marina del Rey and that he sailed competitively there, racing the small, sleek single-design boats that were rumored to have earned him an invitation to try out for the next Olympic team. Although Kelly had accompanied another boy, the son of one of Chuck's business associates, to a Christmas dance at the club shortly after they had moved to L.A., she had never been invited there during the day before. She grinned inwardly, gloating over this unexpected turn of events. So much for snotty little Brenda and her MTV tickets.

Kelly's shrug implied that such invitations were an everyday occurrence. "Don't you have to sail or something today?" she asked.

"My boat's hauled this week," he replied, as if that explained everything, "so I thought you might like to just, you know, come down and hang out for a while."

"Oh." She nodded, pretending to understand perfectly what his boat being hauled meant. "Well, I sort of promised Sam I'd go to the Galleria to help her look for some shoes . . ."

"So call her up and tell her you got a better offer." Thad grinned, producing a tiny cellular phone from the back pocket of his Levi's.

"How do I know it's better?" she teased.

"Guy at the club makes these great tuna sandwiches." He smiled, holding a thumb and forefinger three inches apart. "Stacks 'em this high with sprouts and fresh avocado."

"Mmmm." Kelly licked her lips appreciatively. "I do like fresh avocados."

"Cracked whole wheat bread," he added. "Home baked fresh every day."

"I don't see how I can resist," she laughed.

"Great, let's go." Thad vaulted lightly into the Mustang's passenger seat and propped his sockless Top-Siders on the dashboard. "You drive."

Kelly looked down at him, puzzled. "What about your BMW?" she asked.

Thad shrugged amiably and began fiddling with the dials on her radio. "The Beemer's kaput," he said.

Her eyes widened. "You had a wreck?"

"Worse than that," he answered without looking up. "The Old Man lifted my keys."

"Oh," she said, opening the door and slipping in behind the wheel. "Why?"

"The usual bullshit," he replied, making a small circle in the air with his free hand. "He found my stash in the glove compartment."

"Oh." Kelly started the engine, suddenly not quite sure she was doing the right thing.

Thad looked up from the radio, sensing the uncertainty in her voice. "Hey, it's no big deal," he smiled. "I mean it was just a little coke, not like hard drugs or anything."

She smiled tightly and backed the Mustang out of its parking place, wondering now if he had invited her to lunch just because he needed a ride to the club. "So, how have you been getting around without your car?" she asked, approaching the question as obliquely as possible.

Thad August flexed his heavily muscled shoulders without looking at her. "Well, you know, something always turns up . . . Yo, what's the number for K-Rock?"

CHAPTER FIVE

Λfτεr

"WELL NOW, that was a lovely explosion, if I must say so." Kileen stood in a thin copse of trees atop a hillock half a mile beyond the darkened border crossing, watching the ambulances scream down the road below.

"It was fucking brilliant," breathed Billy Quinn. He shrugged out of the constable's uniform he had been wearing over his street clothes, tossing it into the petrol-soaked interior of the blue Ford Orion, then leaning in through the open driver's door to fiddle with a bundle of wires hidden beneath the instrument panel.

"Mind now you don't blow us both to kingdom come," cautioned Kileen. He scrutinized the boy's actions as he carefully adjusted the dials of the Ford's radio and ever so gently shut the car door, completing an electrical circuit the manufacturers had never intended to be there.

"Won't the fuckers have another big surprise when they open up this little package?" grinned the lad. He stepped away from the car and turned to see Kileen smiling at him.

"Indeed," said the great man, clapping him on the shoulder with a scarred and mottled hand.

"We can start building another right away if you like," said the youngster, uncovering the rusted motorbike that lay artfully concealed in the wet bushes, beneath a sheet of green polypropylene, and passing a battered cyclist's helmet to the older man. Placing an identical helmet on his own head, he set the bike upright, straddled it and wheeled backward out of the trees, where he started the engine, all the while waiting for the other to reply.

Kileen finally nodded his affirmation. "Yes, perhaps we'll do another of these sometime. But we'll let the lads take care of the next one," he said, climbing gracefully onto the pillion behind the boy. "I've something else in mind for you, if you're agreeable."

Billy twisted around to look at him, raising the faceplate on his helmet to peer into the glittering black eyes. "Something else?"

Kileen smiled again. "Something a bit more exotic than this lot," he said, raising his chin to indicate the bleak landscape down the hill. "Tell me, have you got the true Irishman's yen for travel?"

The boy nodded excitedly.

"Fine," said Kileen, tapping him on the shoulder to indicate that it was time for them to go.

The youngster pushed off on his left foot, twisting the throttle and releasing the clutch. The motorbike wobbled off down the muddy path, its tiny engine whining beneath the weight of the two of them.

"No lights, now," cautioned Kileen as they splashed out onto a narrow cattle track heading south through the fields. "The army will have helicopters about in a few minutes."

"Where will you be sending me?" called the excited youngster over the noise of the bike and the rushing wind about his helmet.

"Oh, it'll be someplace fine and wonderful," laughed Kileen, "a place so grand you've only ever seen its like in the moving pictures."

CHAPTER SIX

Heartthrob

THE TUNA SANDWICHES were good. No, Kelly decided. They were great. Great tuna sandwiches. She and Thad August sat at a redwood table beneath a blue umbrella on the wooden deck overlooking the busy yacht harbor at Marina del Rey, with its thousands of gleaming vessels, laughing at the clumsy antics of a group of kids trying to learn to sail the funny little square boats he called Penguins and tossing bits of bread over the railing to the wheeling seagulls.

Her earlier misgivings about Thad had evaporated in the safe, friendly atmosphere of the exclusive yacht club. Here, surrounded by running children and beautiful women being served by smiling waiters, he seemed like another person. He was attentive and witty, patiently explaining to her the relative merits of the different kinds of boats sailing past in the channel and telling her funny stories about his sailing experiences, most of which centered on some incredibly dumb mistake he'd somehow managed to survive through sheer good luck. Smiling people kept waving to him from the decks of boats, and a jolly fat man had stopped by their table to ask his advice on an expensive piece of new navigational equipment that he was thinking about purchasing for his oceangoing cruiser.

"Well," he said when the fat man finally left and the white-jacketed waiter had cleared their table, "what do you think of this place?"

"I like it a lot." Kelly smiled, glancing at the bright green Swatch on her wrist. It was nearly four, and she really did want to get home and out of the forbidden silk shirt before Katherine returned from Palm Springs.

"Do you have time to see the boat now?" he asked, looking pointedly at the watch.

"I thought you said it was . . . hauled," she replied, still uncertain if that would prevent it from being seen.

"Not *my* boat." Thad laughed delightedly. "That isn't very much to look at anyway. I meant the Old Man's."

"Oh, sure," she replied, chiding herself for being so stupid. Of course his father would have a boat here. Probably one of the big ones if he was an important member, as everyone's treatment of Thad seemed to indicate must be the case.

"Great," he said, taking her hand in his and leading her down a flight of wooden steps to a maze of floating docks lined with gleaming white hulls, upon which their owners had emblazoned fanciful names: The yacht club moorings were a veritable parking lot of *Sea Princesses, Northwinds,* *Sea Sixes,* and *Six S's.*

"There are so many of them," marveled Kelly, gazing up at the towering superstructures of large motor cruisers and long sailboats with masts as tall as telephone poles.

"Yeah, and most of them are junk," Thad confided.

"Pretty expensive junk," she said.

"Most of the people who own these boats never even take them out of the harbor," he told her. "They like to come down here to the club for cocktails so they can wear their little blazers and yachting caps and impress their friends, or they use them for other things, but they're not really sailors."

Kelly frowned. "What kind of other things could you use a yacht for?" she asked.

Thad pointed to a huge cruiser with the name *Pacifica* etched in gold on the transom. "See that one? It belongs to a Chinese electronics manufacturer who uses it as his L.A. headquarters. It cost him three million to build, but if business or the government ever gets bad in California like it has in Hong Kong, he can just untie it again and move to New York or London. Anyplace. Three million sounds like a lot of money, but it's cheaper than an office building, and you can't take a building with you."

Kelly nodded, impressed with Thad's knowledge. He really seemed to know what he was talking about, and she decided that maybe he wasn't such an airhead after all and that the thing in the car about the cocaine had just been, well, a thing. None of her classmates in Boston had ever talked about international business or government. But then, she was still getting used to the way the kids at Pacific Academy High thought and acted, like they had their own private set of rules, rules that just naturally assumed they would all be every bit as wealthy and successful as their wealthy and successful parents.

Before her mother had married Chuck Huston, a successful producer of television movies, they had lived in a quiet middle-class Boston suburb. Katherine had worked in a small interior-design studio and Kelly had gone to school and that was about it. While they hadn't been exactly poor, none

of her friends at Franklin High had had their own cellular phones, much less their own Porsches and BMWs. She still had a lot to learn about wealth and privilege, and she suddenly realized that she was beginning to enjoy it. "So how can you tell the real sailors from the phonies and the business guys?" she asked, eager to know more.

"That's easy," Thad replied. "First of all, only serious sailors own serious boats."

Kelly laughed. "Ohhh, *serious* boats. And what's a serious boat?"

He led her to the end of the dock where a sleek, black-hulled sailboat with a triple set of masts lay tied to the concrete pilings, looking as though it might break loose and sail away on its own at any moment. "That," he said, pointing, "is a serious boat. You could sail her anywhere in the world in any kind of weather and you'd always know she'd bring you home again."

"She's beautiful," breathed Kelly, moving farther along the dock to examine the name of the boat, which was carved into a teak board on the stern and trimmed in scarlet. "*Force Ten,*" she read aloud. "I wonder what it means?"

"That's the designation the weather service gives to the strongest storms at sea," he explained, stepping lightly onto the deck. "Want to come aboard?"

"This is *your* boat?"

Thad August grinned, and his sharp green eyes took on a faraway look she hadn't seen before. "Don't I wish," he sighed. "Too bad she belongs to the Old Man. If she were mine, I'd be out of here so fast it'd make your head spin." He held out his hand. "Come on. You're just about to fall madly in love."

Kelly hesitated on the dock, looking up into his eyes.

"With the boat, of course," he smiled. "What did you think I meant?"

Kelly blushed and took his hand, allowing him to haul her up onto the polished deck.

CHAPTER SEVEN

Chosen

"YOU CAN'T MEAN IT," breathed the youngster, staring across the scarred wooden table at Kileen.

The great man stared back at him, saying nothing. It was late, and they were safely back in the Irish Republic, seated in a dark corner of a second-story Grafton Street hamburger palace called Little America, an ersatz atmosphere joint purporting, by virtue of a few strategically hung street signs, baseball memorabilia and the like, to be a little slice of the good old U.S. of A., right in the heart of Dublin.

Kileen had chosen the place as much for the nonstop blare of fifties rock music that blasted from the giant Seeberg jukebox in the opposite corner as for the fact that the proprietors' interpretation of the classic American hamburger and fries was not too bad, although their insistence upon referring to the ketchup as "tomahto sauce" and the fact that the All-American Double Burger listed on the menu came with a fried egg as standard equipment lent the food a decidedly un-American tilt.

"I mean, how would it work, a thing like that?" stammered the boy across the table. He sipped nervously at his coffee and leaned closer to Kileen. "Wouldn't they *know* straightaway?" he asked in a hoarse whisper.

Kileen shook his head in amusement and took a swallow of the pale "genuine American draft beer" from the tall glass before him. "They will know exactly what we want them to know," he replied without hesitation. "Everything about you will be absolutely authentic." He paused to take another sip of the cold brew, letting the golden liquid bathe the tender tissues of his surgically reconstructed throat.

After a moment, he swallowed, dabbing at his scarred lips with a New York Yankees napkin. "Everything," he repeated for emphasis.

"But how?" the youngster insisted.

"Now how do you think?" Kileen snapped.

"Christ!" whispered the boy. He leaned back in his chair, feeling suddenly queasy from the combined effects of the two greasy burgers he had just downed, and the thought of the distasteful things that would have to be done in order to carry out the astounding scheme the grizzled warrior had just laid out for him.

Kileen leaned forward, placing a disfigured hand on top of the youth's slightly trembling one. "You don't think we like doing such things, do you?" he growled.

The boy shook his head uncertainly.

The older man kept his horrible hand in place, the shiny tissue on its back gleaming white beneath the flourescent glare of the overhead lights as he squeezed the youngster's hand with bone-crushing force. "Absolute freedom demands great sacrifices," he said, "sacrifices not always of our own choosing, but which must be made nonetheless. Don't you know that yet?"

The youngster nodded, grimacing at the dull pain radiating up his arm in waves from the captive hand. A tumble of thoughts raced through his brain as he attempted to consider whether he was even capable of doing what the other was asking. "When would I have to begin?" he asked.

Kileen grinned, glints of surgical steel showing above his teeth where they had screwed and plated and wired the remains of his shattered jaw back together. "You have already begun," he said, releasing the boy's hand. "You kept your head tonight in a tight situation. You know their ways and manners, and you fit the description well enough." He paused, the black eyes seeming to burn into the boy's. "Your knack with the electronics shows you're a quick learner, as well," he added. The black eyes narrowed and a wry smile twisted the corners of his lips. "And, of course, now that you have been given the preliminary details of the plan, there can be no question of your turning back anyway."

Billy Quinn stared at him, the frightened realization of the other's meaning striking him like a hammer blow, for though he was barely seventeen and not yet through school, a life spent among hard-core revolutionaries had taught him the meaning of certain phrases. "You would have killed me, then . . . if I'd refused to go?"

The old revolutionary nodded sadly. "Regrettably," he said. "Another sacrifice to The Cause. You understand."

The boy nodded. He did understand, had grown up understanding that no compromises were allowable when it came to The Cause, certainly not to spare the life of one lowly foot soldier. There was far too much at stake for that kind of cheap sentimentality. He had been schooled to believe that if, ultimately, they were to win, they had to be hard, harder even than the murderous bastards who had gunned down his da on that long-ago Belfast morning, an ever-present image that was an incurable festering on his soul.

But he had also been taught that their resolve to win must be tempered with mercy, where mercy did not compromise their goals. For if they lacked mercy, then they were no better than their hated enemies, the smirking, deceitful bastards who, even now, toyed with the sincere but deluded representatives of Sinn Fein at the peace table, piling one unreasonable demand upon another, insisting that his side disarm themselves, even as their own hated troops patrolled the shell-pocked Belfast streets, flaunting their vastly superior weapons—tanks and helicopters—keeping his people prisoners in their own land.

"Can I ask you one more thing?" he finally said, looking around the nearly empty restaurant to be certain that no one was near enough to overhear.

Kileen waited.

"What will you do with him? The other?"

"Do?"

"I mean," said the boy, dropping his eyes to the table and lowering his voice to a whisper, "it's to be a straight-out kidnapping, you won't kill him or anything? After all, he hasn't done anything, has he?" He jerked his chin toward the North, where the two of them had lately done their night's bloody work. "Not like the bastards on the border."

Kileen smiled patiently. "He's one of Them," he said, "and isn't that reason enough to kill him?"

He studied the boy's shocked expression for a moment, then shook his head slowly. "But no, nothing will happen to him," he assured the youngster. "In fact, by keeping him all safe and in good condition, we'll have a valuable bargaining chip should anything go wrong at your end." Kileen lifted his glass and took a measured swallow. "We don't waste lives unnecessarily," he said.

The boy nodded, setting aside his misgivings about the plan. He had seen a great deal of blood spilled in his brief and violent life, a fair proportion of it the direct result of his own deliberate actions. But he had long ago managed to convince himself that the only victims of his aggression were the oppressors of his people. Even then, it was sometimes hard for him, for he was not an evil person. But whenever he felt himself shrinking from the work he had only to summon up that vision of his da, dead in the Belfast street at the age of twenty-eight. Dead for having committed the unpardonable sin of taking a Protestant shipfitter's job; a job that They felt rightly belonged to Them.

That was what it was really all about in his mind: What They had done to his da.

He grimaced at the omnipresent memory—himself as a snot-nosed six-year-old, sitting in the street beside Da, not yet understanding what had happened, and Them standing there staring down at him, coming out of Their shops and houses to whisper and point at the squalling brat in the gutter beside the dead man, until some of the lads—friends of Da's, he later learned—had come along, braving the dangerous mob of Them, and rescued him, picking him up and taking him into a nearby house, bundling him in warm blankets . . . taking care of their own.

He snuffled a bit too loudly, fixing Kileen's black eyes in his own steely gaze. If it was killing they wanted, then it was killing they'd get. He wasn't a helpless squalling brat now. He was a hardened fighter. "What do I have to do, then?" he asked.

Kileen reached into the pocket of his coat and produced a square of cheap white bond paper filled on both sides with rows of single-spaced typing. "You'll begin by memorizing this," he said.

The youngster scanned the contents of the page. Names, dates, addresses, bits of personal information. He nodded and started to slip the paper into his pocket. The scarred hand shot out and pinned his wrist to the table.

"Now," said Kileen.

The boy stared at him in disbelief. "What, this entire lot? It'll take me hours."

The great man stared back. "I've plenty of time," he said, raising an arm for the waiter. "You'll be wanting more coffee."

"Fuck-all," murmured the boy, bending to study the tightly packed information on the page.

"And mind your language from now on." Kileen laughed. "Remember, you're soon to be a proper young gentleman from a fine old school."

CHAPTER EIGHT

Force Ten

"THAD, DON'T!" Kelly sat up, annoyed, and looked at herself in the mirrored doors facing the king-size bed in the yacht's low-ceilinged main cabin. Her face was flushed, and the top three buttons of the new shirt were open. "I didn't come here to have sex with you," she said, fastening the buttons and getting clumsily to her feet. Actually, she wasn't quite sure how she had ended up lying on the burgundy velour bedspread with Thad's hands inside her blouse. They had been walking through the yacht's spacious salon and the chart room, where he had explained the workings of various pieces of nautical equipment. Then he had led her down a narrow corridor to the master stateroom, and they were suddenly kissing. "I'd like to go now," she said, tucking the loose tails of the blouse into her shorts.

"That's cool," he said, folding his hands behind his head and dropping back onto the pillows. "I'll catch a ride home with one of the sailing instructors."

She looked at him in astonishment. "Aren't you even going to walk me back to my car?"

Thad shrugged and fumbled in a cubby beside the headboard for a pack of cigarettes. "What for?" He shook a cigarette from the pack and lit it with elaborate casualness. "Don't you remember where you left it?"

Kelly shook her head. "Can I ask you a question?"

"Sure. What?"

"Do you treat every girl you go out with like this?"

"Hey," he said, sitting up and scratching his chest through the faded polo shirt, "in the first place, we're not *out*. I mean, this isn't exactly a date to the prom or anything." He smiled and regarded the glowing tip of the cigarette with his hard green eyes. "And in the second place, I didn't *treat* you any particular way. You gave me a ride, I bought you a sandwich and felt your tits. What do you want, an engagement ring and a big church wedding?"

"You arrogant . . . prick!" She snatched up her purse and stomped out of the stateroom, trying to remember how to get back to the steep stairway they'd come down. Thad August's laughter echoed in the narrow passageway behind her. "Hey, Kelly," he called, "this doesn't mean we can't still be best friends."

"Screw you," she yelled, spotting the stairs at the entrance to the salon and hurrying toward them.

"Only if you help," he shouted.

The sun was still shining as Kelly jumped onto the dock and hurried toward the parking lot behind the clubhouse. The fresh afternoon breeze snapped the little gaily colored triangular pennants flying from the sterns of the moored boats and cheerily rattled dozens of brightly plated metal shroud fasteners against their masts, making her feel as if she were in a bad dream. She suddenly wished she was back in the cozy refuge of her bedroom in the old frame house on their quiet tree-lined street in Boston, watching the rain streak her window. They'd been in Los Angeles for six months now, and it had never rained once.

"I fucking *hate* it here!" she fumed out loud.

THE DIGITAL CLOCK on the Mustang's dash was showing nearly five o'-clock by the time Kelly maneuvered her way through the angry snarl of late afternoon traffic on the San Diego Freeway, then fought her way down Sunset to the mouth of the winding canyon road leading to the breezy Mediterranean-style home that her stepfather had moved them into within a few weeks of their arrival from Boston. The place had been so new then that the empty rooms had reeked of paint and carpet adhesive, odors that had still not quite dissipated, even though the spacious living room was now filled with much of the comfortable and lovingly restored antique furniture that Katherine had shipped West.

With sweeping ocean and city views from her bedroom windows and the blue-tiled swimming pool beside the covered patio, Kelly had not yet gotten over the feeling that she was living on a movie set, a feeling that was frequently fortified by the presence around the pool of one or more of Chuck's studio friends, a succession of the famous and not-so-famous actors, directors and producers with whom her gregarious stepfather was forever "packaging" the vapid disease-or-tragedy-of-the-week TV movies he produced from his offices at Paramount.

Kelly guided the Mustang up into the circular driveway before the house, offering a silent prayer of thanks as the empty parking area came into view beside the triple garage. Katherine was not yet home, which meant that Kelly had plenty of time to run inside and change before her mother arrived and saw her wearing the forbidden shirt. She parked the car, got out and walked quickly to the shady front entryway of the house, fumbling with the coded electronic keypad that simultaneously unlocked the front door and deactivated the alarm system—if you punched in the proper combination.

As usual, she got the numbers wrong the first time and had to wait thirty seconds for the system to reset itself, or risk triggering the loud alarms scattered throughout the house. She glanced down the driveway, expecting to see Katherine's gray BMW appear at any second. Why in the hell, she wondered, couldn't they just have a key to their front door like everybody else in the world had?

While she waited for the alarm to do its thing, she stepped into the splash of bright sunlight painting the forward edge of the tiled entryway, looking down and examining the fabric of the blouse for damage. The stain from biology class seemed mostly to have disappeared, but she discovered to her horror that the topmost button was hanging by a thread from the corner of a small triangular rip in the blue silk.

"Damn!" Her face flushed angrily at the humiliating memory of Thad August's probing hands pulling carelessly at the sheer fabric, and she wanted nothing more than to get to her room and hang the blouse in the closet where she didn't have to see it until she could figure out how she was going to explain the ruined garment. "Bastard!" she whispered.

"I beg your pardon?"

Kelly looked up to see a cadaverous figure in dark clothing hovering over her. She squeaked in fright and stepped back into the shade covering the entryway, nearly tripping over one of Katherine's pastel painted Southwestern planters in her haste.

The man in the driveway, his features obscured by the dazzle of sunlight at his back, remained frozen in place, looking down at her. He cleared his throat noisily and raised one fluttering hand in a gesture of peace. "So very sorry, didn't mean to startle you." The voice was soft and cultured with a distinctive British accent.

Regaining her composure, Kelly turned away and punched in the correct code on the keypad by the door, heard the reassuring click of the lock opening. "I didn't expect anyone," she said, opening the door and slipping inside, then turning to peer back out through a narrow crack. When the man made no move to follow her, she scanned the long, empty drive beyond him, wondering where he had come from.

"Oh my dear," he said, genuinely distressed, "I'm afraid I did startle you. I *knew* I should have called first."

He stepped into the shade of the latticed entryway and she saw that he was elderly, a flowing mane of silvery hair curling about the slightly rounded shoulders of his dark, tailored suit. His handsome face was filled with concern, and for a moment she thought she knew him. "You see," he continued, pointing back toward the thick profusion of greenery at the far edge of the circular drive—a "privacy screen" Chuck's landscape architect had called it—"I live in the house just up the way. I would have rung before coming, but it seems your telephone isn't listed."

Kelly relaxed slightly, realizing that she *had* seen the old man before, walking down the steep canyon road in baggy khaki shorts and a comical tropical sun helmet. She thought she remembered having heard her mother once say that he lived in the old house hidden behind the rusting iron gates and massive stand of eucalyptus trees at the top of the road. He was the mysterious and eccentric neighbor Katherine and Chuck sometimes laughed about over cocktails.

Still keeping the door firmly between herself and the visitor, she managed a polite smile. "My . . . stepfather works in television," she explained. "We'd have a regular phone number, but he says that strange people are always trying to call him up with their story ideas, or to tell him about some show they didn't like."

The old man squinted at her with his watery blue eyes, and for a moment she was afraid she had said the wrong thing. What if *he* was one of those crazy people Chuck was always complaining about, the disturbed television fans who thought the stupid TV plots were real and who sometimes sought out the actors or producers in search of revenge? The old man suddenly frowned, and she inched back behind the door, realizing that he was scrutinizing her expression.

Then he began to laugh, a full, rich, baritone sound that echoed off the walls of the narrow entryway. "I see," he chuckled after a moment, lifting a gnarled hand to brush a tear from the corner of his eye. "Strange people. That's quite good. Yes, my dear, I can certainly appreciate your stepfather's concern for strange people in these strange and violent times."

He smiled warmly, revealing a mouthful of perfect white teeth, and executed a courtly little bow. "However, you have nothing to fear from me, dear lady. I assure you."

"Oh, I didn't mean—" she began.

He raised his hand, stifling her apology. "Quite correct of you to be wary," he said. "Shouldn't have blundered in on you unannounced like this." He chuckled again, mumbling to himself and wagging his handsome head. "Strange people! Wonderful."

"My stepfather isn't home yet," she said, looking nervously down the driveway and still dreading the imminent arrival of Katherine's BMW.

"Oh but it's you I came to see, young lady," said the visitor.

"Me?"

"Yes, my dear." He smiled again, and extended his hand to her. "First, however, allow me to introduce myself. I am Major James Queally-Smythe, late of His Majesty's Own Royal Gurkha Regiment."

Kelly wasn't certain what she was supposed to say. She took the proffered hand instead, finding it surprisingly soft and gentle. "I . . . I'm Kelly," she stammered. "Kelly Huston."

"Kelly," beamed the old man, "lovely name, lovely . . ." His bushy eyebrows moved closer together as he wrinkled his brow in thought. "Huston? Now you wouldn't by any chance be related to the Fairleigh-Hustons of County Wexford? Young chap in my regiment was a Fairleigh-Huston, I believe . . . Let me see now, that would have been back in '42—last days of the Raj, you know . . . Of course my lot were all down in Rangoon waiting for the Jappos then—"

"I'm sorry, I really don't know," Kelly interrupted. "Huston is really my stepfather's name . . ." *Which he and Katherine both decided I should share, without bothering to ask how I felt,* she thought bitterly. She glanced again at the drive, wishing the strange old man would just go back where he had come from. Her head was beginning to ache.

The old man's face reddened and he spluttered into a blue silk handkerchief he dug from the depths of the plum-colored vest he wore beneath his suit jacket. "Listen to me, an old fool, just nattering on, wasting your valuable time," he chided himself.

"Oh no, I'm sure it's very interesting," she lied. "It's just that I've got some homework to do for school."

"School!" The major's face suddenly brightened and he tucked the blue handkerchief away in his vest. "Now that's precisely what I wanted to speak to you about, my dear. Won't take a moment."

"You see," he continued, "I've seen you about with your friends, schoolbooks and whatnot, and I wondered if I might impose upon you to do me a favor."

Kelly stared at him, wondering what kind of favor she could possibly do for the blustering old Englishman.

"My only grandson will be coming to live with me very soon, you see," he explained. "Young fellow just about your age, I expect, and I wondered if . . . well, if I might impose upon the kindness of yourself and your young friends to perhaps come to tea one afternoon. Make him feel at home before he begins school here. I've enrolled him at Pacific Academy, which they tell me is the best in the area. I know it's a great deal to ask, but the lad's had a difficult time of it . . ." His voice trailed off apologetically.

"Your . . . grandson?" Kelly was intrigued. She drew a quick mental picture in her mind, a teenage version of his grandfather, in a three-piece suit. "Is he English too?" She blurted out the stupid question without thinking. Of course he would be English.

"English?" The Major laughed uneasily, retrieving the blue handkerchief and dabbing at his brow. "Good heavens, no," he said. "Seems m'daughter, rest her soul, took it into her head to marry an Irish fellow." He paused, seemingly considering his next words carefully. "Oh, a fine young man, you understand, a landed Derry man. Excellent family. Excellent." He sniffed loudly. "Still, a moneyed Derry man, and therefore a target, you see . . ."

Kelly was confused. What did the old man's son-in-law being a dairy farmer have to do with anything, and why did that make him a target? "Well, she said uneasily, I'd be happy to show your grandson . . ."

"Brian," said the old man. "The lad's name is Brian."

She smiled. "I go to Pacific Academy. I'd be happy to show Brian around the school and introduce him to some of my friends."

Major Queally-Smythe beamed. "Tea first. That's the ticket!" he insisted. "I'll have you all round for tea. Bless you, my girl! Wouldn't ask the favor, but the lad's had a rough go of it, losing both his parents and all."

"Both of his parents are dead?" Kelly's voice dropped to a whisper.

The Major's placid face darkened. "Yes, quite!" His voice was tinged with barely suppressed rage. "Damned republican bomb blast, you see. Horrible thing!" His frail body seemed to wilt before her, and she was suddenly overcome with pity for the old man standing there in the heat in his ridiculous heavy woolen suit and high starched collar. "Horrible," he muttered again.

"I'm so sorry," Kelly said. Having grown up in Boston, she understood now that he was referring to Irish terrorist politics, a topic she and her friends had always avoided discussing with the few dark and brooding Irish kids at school—refugees from the terror in Northern Ireland, who had been sent to stay with American relatives—and she realized that she wasn't quite sure which side the republicans were on, Catholic or Protestant. Besides, she had thought the trouble there was over, certain she had heard there was a peace treaty of some kind.

The old man was swaying heavily in the late afternoon sun, and she was suddenly afraid that he might faint. "Would you like to come in for a glass of water or something?" She impulsively blurted out the invitation, moving away from the door and holding it open.

The Major shook his regal head, dabbing at his perspiring brow and seeming to regain his composure. "No, thank you, m'dear. I've taken up quite enough of your time for one afternoon," he said. "I shall call round when the lad arrives, if I may." He smiled again, showing his teeth. "Have you and your friends over to tea. Sugar cakes, lemon squash and whatnot."

"I'd like that very much, Major." Kelly smiled. "We'll all try to make Brian feel at home."

"Bless you, dear girl." The old man raised his right hand in a jaunty little military salute, then turned and strode away down the drive.

Kelly closed the door and hurried to her room, the afternoon's humiliation with Thad August nearly forgotten as she pondered the tragic story of the teenage boy whose parents had been killed in a terrorist bomb blast.

Brian. Her earlier image of a miniature Queally-Smythe had evaporated, and she wondered if he would be dark haired and handsome.

CHAPTER NINE

Marching Orders

"But he's got black hair," Billy Quinn said too loudly, staring down at the color passport photograph on the table between them.

Kileen's black eyes darted warily around the nearly empty cafe. A couple of late-night filmgoers lingered over their coffee by the windows overlooking the street. The jukebox had been turned off, and, at the far end of the room, a pretty, freckled waitress in too-tight jeans was helping a stooped old fellow in a long white apron, who was cleaning the floor. The girl moved ahead of the old man as he mopped, lifting chairs onto the tops of tables just before he swabbed the patches of checked linoleum beneath.

No one in the place seemed to have taken any notice of the boy's outburst, and, letting his eyes linger on the firm contours of the girl's buttocks for just a moment longer, Kileen scooped up the photo and secreted it in the same breast pocket to which he'd returned the printed sheet. "Hair color's an easy thing to change," he said in his low, gravelly voice. "All the important things, your eyes, age, general height and weight, are close enough to pass."

The youngster nodded wearily. His head was swimming with trivia: the names of supposed cousins, uncles and schoolmates, dates and descriptions of places he'd never been, things he'd never done. "I don't see how it can ever work," he sighed.

Kileen smiled his unnatural plastic smile, the ridge of scar tissue curving along his jaw. "You've only to convince one doddering old man who last saw you when you were five, Brian," he said, speaking to the boy as though he had already adopted his new identity. "You've got few enough relatives as it is. It's unlikely you'll be running into any of them way across the ocean in California." The great man pushed away from the table and lifted his raincoat from the back of an empty chair, preparing to leave.

The teenager was incredulous. So far he had learned nothing of what he was to do, only who he was supposed to be: Brian O'Malley, son of the late Charles and Victoria O'Malley, wealthy Protestants from Derry who had been killed four months previously when their silver Jaguar ran over a land mine intended for a British army personnel carrier.

Young Brian had been away at his exclusive boarding school at the time of the accident. Following a brief visit home for the double funeral, which had been heavily attended by family friends and Ulster politicians—but no relatives, most of whom lived in England and were still afraid to come to Northern Ireland, peace talks or no peace talks—he had returned to his studies, growing increasingly withdrawn and depressed over the deaths of his parents. This latter fact had been duly reported to the family solicitor, who had in turn informed Brian O'Malley's grandfather. Shortly thereafter, the decision had been made to send the boy to California.

And that was where Billy came in: Kileen and his people were going to kidnap Brian O'Malley and send Billy Quinn to California in his place.

The whole thing was daft.

Kileen was already on his feet, draping the raincoat over his arm, picking up the bill and digging in his pocket for money. The boy grabbed his arm. The great man glared down at him as if he were becoming an annoyance. "And just exactly what is it that I'm supposed to do when I get to California?" he whispered.

Kileen twisted his body slightly, effortlessly slipping from the youngster's grasp, skillfully finding a grip of his own at the junction of the boy's neck and shoulder, pressing an iron finger against the thick nerve bundle there, an agonizing hold that was nonetheless invisible to the other occupants of the cafe. "Why you'll go to high school, just like the other lads, and be a credit to your old gramps, Brian me bucko," he said grinning so that glints of polished steel showed behind his teeth.

The boy grunted, stifling the urge to cry out at the sudden jolts of fire radiating from his shoulder. "But what if the old man catches on?" he breathed.

Kileen arched his eyebrows in unspoken reply to the stupid question, his shining black eyes seeming to drill into the other's very soul. "You know, Brian," he said in a pleasant conversational tone, "it took a great deal of convincing to persuade the others you were the lad for this mission. Now, it would reflect very badly indeed on me if it turned out I'd been mistaken in my judgment." He increased the pressure on the nerve, watching the boy's blue eyes for some sign that only he could read. Waiting for the teenager to betray his weakness.

"You made no mistake in choosing me," the boy groaned through clenched teeth.

The old warrior straightened, instantly releasing the pressure. "Good," he said, patting the youngster's cheek affectionately. "Take care of whatever odds and ends you must tonight. You'll be picked up outside your rooms at half-ten sharp in the morning by two lads in a blue Escort. They're fresh in from London, so you won't know their faces, but the driver will be wearing a red plaid scarf, the other a green hat, and they'll know you. Do exactly as they tell you." He reached into his pocket and withdrew a thick envelope, dropping it onto the table under cover of the folded raincoat. "That's for your mother," he said, watching approvingly as the boy swiftly palmed the envelope and slipped it into his own pocket without looking down. "Stay here and have another coffee before you leave," he instructed.

The boy looked up at his superior. "Won't I see you again, then?" he asked.

Kileen laughed, a low, throaty sound. "As sure as there's orange juice in California," he said.

"I *will* do the job," said the youngster.

"I know you will," said Kileen. "Else I'd not have chosen you for it, young Brian O'Malley. Now then, let me see how you'll do before I go."

The boy grinned, then frowned fiercely and fixed his eyes on the wreck of a man standing before him. "Here, you," he said, looking the other's cheap clothing over with a critical eye and pushing his voice up and into his nose in perfect imitation of the privileged rich boys in whose elegant houses he had grown up, "why are you loitering about, my man? Go over there and inform the serving girl that I require another coffee immediately, and be damned quick about it."

Kileen's laughter filled the cafe, causing the other patrons to look around. He clapped the teenager firmly on the shoulder and strode to the counter where he paid the bill, then pointed out the table and whispered something to the freckled waitress before slipping out the door.

The girl deposited Kileen's money in her till, then she peered at the boy and sauntered brazenly over to him, swinging her hips angrily, stopping before his table and glaring insolently down at him. Her pretty face was flushed, the freckles standing out against her fine, pale skin, and her arms were folded tightly over her nicely shaped breasts. "Are you the 'young gentleman' who 'requires' another coffee 'immediately'?" she demanded.

"Sorry, my love. I'm afraid my old uncle was simply having you on," said Billy. He laughed as though the whole thing had been an elaborate joke—

which in a way it was—maintaining his new upper class identity with careful inflection and intonation, practicing the precise grammar the sadistic Jesuits at St. Brendan's had whipped into him, and realizing for the first time that he just might pull this thing off.

Whatever it was to be.

The girl relaxed slightly, her frown softening to a tentative smile. "Will you have the coffee, then?"

He smiled his most charming and condescending wealthy schoolboy smile. "Please, may I?"

"I haven't seen you around here before, have I?" she asked, scrutinizing his smooth, handsome features with interest and making no move to get his coffee.

"Just down from school for a few days," he said, casually scanning the room and noticing that the remaining patrons were beginning to gather up their things. "I say, you're not getting ready to close up, are you?" He tried to look pained.

"Ten minutes," she said meaningfully, then adding on impulse, "... but I know of a little after-hours club just down the street that's open much later."

He smiled easily. "Perhaps I could buy you a coffee then . . . to make up for the old man."

She flushed again, squeezing her ample breasts together behind her folded arms. "I don't even know your name," she giggled.

"Brian," he said.

She wrinkled her nose prettily. "Mine's Moira. Just let me get rid of that lot over by the window, Brian," she said, hurrying away to the counter to take their money.

The youngster watched the promising sway of her hips as she crossed the room, deciding he'd treat himself—and Moira, if she'd let him—to a farewell fling before he left old Ireland. He leaned back in his seat, lighting a cigarette and wondering as he puffed on it if the old bugger . . . correction, his distinguished *grandfather* in America, would be so easily fooled.

CHAPTER TEN

The Folks

"JAMES QUEALLY-SMYTHE?" Chuck Huston sat at the head of the black lacquered dining room table, a forkful of pasta frozen halfway on its journey to his fleshy lips. "*The* James Queally-Smythe invited you to *tea?*"

Kelly toyed with the tomato-and-basil-drenched bowtie noodles on her plate, unsure whether her stepfather's expression of astonishment was indicative of a positive or negative response to her news. Sometimes she couldn't tell with Chuck. "His grandson is coming to live with him," she explained carefully. "From Northern Ireland."

"Damn! James Queally-Smythe!" Chuck let his loaded fork drop back to his plate with a small clink and twisted around in his chair to peer through the arched opening dividing the large dining room from the even larger kitchen. "Honey, did you hear what your daughter has just come up with?" he called.

Katherine Huston swept through from the kitchen, balancing a glazed ceramic coffeepot and three delicately flowered china cups on a tray. "Kelly," she asked, placing the tray on an unused expanse of the long table and swiping her mass of long, coppery hair back away from her perfectly made-up face in a familiar gesture of complete exasperation, "was Rosa still here when you got home?"

Kelly shook her head, hoping her mother wasn't about to launch into another of her tirades against the hapless Mexican maid. Rosa, who lived in Hollywood with her five children and unemployed husband, was fat and jolly, a great cook and, best of all in Kelly's view, the single predictably cheerful presence in the Huston household.

"Honestly, Chuck," sighed Katherine, walking around the table and taking her seat opposite Kelly, "that woman cannot remember to do a simple thing like running the dishwasher before she leaves. I don't know how many times I've asked her." She raised one crimson-nailed hand and examined it critically. "I had to wash all the coffee things by hand before I could even bring them out—"

"Honey, honey," Chuck interrupted, "did you hear what I just said?"

Katherine turned to him, planting her elbows on the corner of the table and resting her chin on her clenched fists. "I'm sorry, darling," she pouted. "It's just so upsetting not to have things nice for you when you come home." She mouthed an airborne kiss in his direction. "Now what was it that you wanted to tell me?"

Chuck raised his fork, pointing it meaningfully at Kelly. "James Queally-Smythe, *the* James Queally-Smythe, has invited *our* daughter to tea."

Kelly grimaced. *I'm not* your *daughter, Chuck,* she thought bitterly. *I'm John Kovac's daughter, something even my own mother seems to have forgotten in her rush to "go Hollywood."* Her stomach hurt like it always did when she was forced to watch Katherine pretending to fawn over her stepfather, and she felt the familiar lonely ache of longing for her father. Without him, California was nothing.

When they had still been back in Boston, Daddy had come to pick her up every Saturday morning like clockwork, arriving in his battered old contractor's truck like a blue-collar Prince Charming, carrying her away from Katherine's demanding tantrums to inspect the progress on his latest building site before the two of them embarked on some great adventure with his gruff working-class friends; sailing on the James in summer or boiling lobsters on the beach, ice skating in winter or, when the weather was too bad, just huddling over bowls of popcorn in his big, drafty Charlestown apartment and watching old movies on TV . . . She gave her mother a baleful look. Blaming her. Again.

Katherine had turned her beautiful green-eyed gaze onto her daughter now, and her mouth was formed into a pretty O, a clear sign that she was about to start gushing over something. "Really, darling?" she breathed. "Queally-Smythe? That's incredible. How on earth . . . ?"

Kelly stared at the pair of strangers across the shiny, overpriced table. They were both hanging over their plates like hungry carnivorous animals, awaiting her reply. "I don't understand why you're getting so excited," she finally said. "He's just that very nice old man who happens to live up the road."

Chuck guffawed aloud, dropping a bowtie onto the front of his yellow knit shirt, and Kelly wondered again why on earth her mother had married this coarse, balding producer ten years her senior, when Kelly's own father was so handsome. Of course, she *knew* why. Chuck had money. Daddy didn't. She stopped herself. That wasn't really fair. Katherine hadn't even known Chuck when she and Kelly's father had divorced. Had not met him, in fact, for three more years.

"The old man in the *pith helmet?* That's James Queally-Smythe?" Katherine stared at her daughter in disbelief.

"Nice old man," Chuck was gurgling.

"Darling," said Katherine, reaching across the table to dab with her napkin at the pale red stain on Chuck's shirt without removing her eyes from Kelly, "Mr. Queally-Smythe is a very famous man."

"Famous?" Chuck lifted his crystal goblet of North Country zinfandel to his lips and took a long, noisy swallow. "Honey, the man's a *legend!*"

"Why, who is he?" Kelly looked at them quizzically, thinking it was at least fortunate that Chuck, despite his being a complete slob, was really sort of nice in his own way. It hurt her to know that he would never even consider slapping her mother as Daddy used to do, frequently, whenever he'd been drinking and Katherine's acid temper had led her to say all those awful things to him.

"Queally-Smythe," Katherine explained confidently—she had recently completed a UCLA extension crash course in film appreciation, a "necessary requirement" for her successful Beverly Hills interior-design business—"is a *major* motion-picture director and screenwriter, Kelly. He won Academy Awards for *A Perfect English Summer* and his musical about the American Revolution called *Keep Your Damn Colonies.*"

"He did *Colonies?*" Kelly was suddenly interested. The old Technicolor musical comedy was one of her very favorite films. She and her father had watched it over and over again on video, pointing out the Boston locations to each other.

"That and about two dozen other *big* movies," said Chuck. "Man, what a break, you meeting him. I've wanted to talk to the old guy for years, but they say he eats producers for lunch."

"His temper is legendary," Katherine added, authoritatively. "I've heard that he once drove Joan Crawford to a nervous breakdown. Imagine—"

"He's really very nice," Kelly said defensively.

". . . Imagine that funny old eccentric who lives up at the top of our canyon being Queally-Smythe, and us not even *suspecting*," breathed Katherine, ignoring her. Her green eyes darted to Chuck, and a truly angelic smile curved the bow of her vermilion lips. "Just think what this does to the value of our *property*," she whispered.

Chuck lifted his glass to the light, swirling the ruby-colored wine around and around within the crystal bowl. "You know," he said thoughtfully, "I bet if I could get the old guy to sit still for a few minutes, I could talk him into doing a miniseries or something."

Kelly rolled her eyes. "Maybe *you'd* like to give him the tour of Academy High too, Chuck," she murmured, "that way I wouldn't have to do anything."

Katherine shot her a serious warning glance, then refocused her attention on Chuck, who seemed not to have heard his stepdaughter's sarcastic remark, freezing him in her green-eyed gaze like a sluggish swamp creature trapped in the beam of a hunter's spotlight. "Darling," she purred, "Queally-Smythe isn't going to do *television.* That would be an insult to an *artiste* of his stature."

"Yeah, I guess you're right." Chuck stared glumly at his glass, then drained it in a single gargantuan swallow. "Still, with a heavyweight like that in my corner I could name my own next project with the studio."

Katherine reached across the table, her slender fingers clutching his pudgy chin and forcing his flat brown eyes back to hers. "Not television, a *film,*" she whispered, her silken voice caressing him like a lover, "an *important* film . . . Well, it's what you've always wanted to do anyway. Really. Isn't it?"

Chuck's round face lit up as if a three-hundred-watt cartoon light bulb had just been switched on above his shiny scalp. "Yeah," he said excitedly, "something big and classy. Maybe with him directing Meryl Streep or Jodie Foster . . ."

"Jodie Foster *is* a director," said Kelly.

"Whatever," said Chuck, watching mesmerized as Katherine poured more wine for him, dipping a pale index finger into the zinfandel, then sensually licking the tip of her glossy painted nail before passing the glass back to him.

"Streisand?" Katherine queried.

"Another director," Kelly offered helpfully.

"Sweetheart, don't you have some really important homework or something?" Katherine's voice was a barely disguised hiss.

"Right, Mom!" Kelly pushed her plate back, got up from the table and walked out of the room without looking back. Katherine hated it when she called her Mom.

"Costner," said Chuck. "Maybe some kind of big historical thing from public domain."

From the far side of the house, Kelly heard the throaty tinkle of Katherine's delighted laughter, her small porcelain hands applauding Chuck's stupid idea.

"That's brilliant, darling. Of course. James Queally-Smythe directing Kevin Costner!"

"He's a director too, you dope," Kelly whispered to her empty room.

CHAPTER ELEVEN

So Long and Farewell

"I'VE GOT TO GO," said the boy. He leaned over the edge of the sagging mattress and held his cheap plastic wristwatch up to the spill of gray light filtering in through the dirty, rain-streaked window.

Half-six.

Moira Devlin, her thick red hair trailing across the pale expanse of her long back, moaned sleepily and eased her soft, warm buttocks tight against his thigh. "Mmmm, not yet, Brian."

"Sorry, love." He pushed aside the cozy coverlet and jumped onto the icy floorboards, squinting in the half-light for some sign of his clothes. He found them with hers, in an untidy pile beside an old dresser she'd painted a pale shade of blue, and bent self-consciously to untangle his underpants from the delicate black lace of her bra.

The girl sat up, propping his pillow behind her own and reaching for the packet of Marlboros he had left on the scarred nightstand. She lit one of the cigarettes and watched him silently as he dressed. "Didn't you like me, then?" Her voice was filled with hurt.

The boy turned and looked at her, the denim shirt he was pulling on hanging loose from one arm. The rumpled sheets were gathered about her narrow waist, and even with the cigarette dangling unattractively from her lips, she looked like a painting in the cold, soft light, the tangled ends of fair red hair curled about the smooth curve of her full breasts and white skin contrasting vividly with the dark wood of the old-fashioned headboard at her back. He felt a sudden wave of tenderness for her. "I like you very much," he murmured shyly, crossing the room to the bed. He gently took the cigarette from her lips and kissed her softly. "But I've got to go now."

He turned away to avoid looking at her, afraid that if he did, he would crawl back into her warm bed and lose himself in her soft, sweet flesh, and to hell with Kileen and his insane fucking scheme.

Although he had slept with two women before this, both had been sympathizers of The Cause, scraggly adventure groupies in dirty sweatshirts, both of them far older than he, each doing her grunting, hasty bit for the lads in the darkened back of a van full of contraband, their dull hair smelling vaguely of chemicals and damp canvas. Never before had he met a girl so near his own age, nor, for that matter, gone out on a proper date with one, as he had with Moira the night before.

To his amazement, he had found everything about her intoxicating; the way she had wrinkled her nose and whispered into his ear over the blare of the noisy band in the tiny underground club she'd taken him to, the way she'd leaned against him in the rain, her hand tightly squeezing his as they'd hurried to her flat afterwards, the silky black underwear she wore beneath her tight jeans . . .

He closed his eyes, remembering the look of her naked body above him in the soft blue light of the small lamp by her bed, the feel of her skin beneath his hands, her warm breath on his throat. Later, she had whispered the painfully ordinary story of her life to him, telling him how she'd bravely fled to Dublin from her little country town in the West, where she'd been expected to marry and have five babies in five years. How she'd taken the waitress job at Little America, where she made more in tips from American tourists in a week than her father made in a month on his little patch of rocky farmland, living in the tiny flat and spending her money on books for the computer courses she was taking at the extended university . . . How she'd never before brought a stranger into her bed.

He thought perhaps he could love her without very much trouble at all, and he wanted to stay.

Instead, he finished buttoning his shirt and tucked it into the waistband of his jeans.

"Will I see you again?" Her voice was bitter now, devoid of hope, and he was painfully aware of what she must be thinking. *Rich prick down from his high-and-mighty school picks up a nice girl, has himself a quick screw and disappears, leaving her alone.*

"It isn't what you think," he said, going back to sit on the edge of the bed and taking her hand in his.

She smiled knowingly. "And how would you know what I'm thinking?"

"Because I know," he said, raising her hand to his lips and smelling the scent of her skin. "It's just that I can't stay just now . . . I've got to . . . go away."

"Where?" She brushed her fingers lightly across his lips. "Where to, Brian?"

"To America, to see my grandfather." He blurted it out without thinking, desperate for her to believe him.

Her eyes widened in the pale light. "America? Where in America?"

"California," he said, looking at his watch. *Jesus, what was he thinking? If Kileen knew what he was saying he'd have the two of them shot.* "Look," he said, "I've got to go now."

"Can I write to you, then, Brian?" She was leaning over the nightstand, rummaging for something in the tiny drawer. She came up with a small pad of pink notepaper and a little gold pencil.

"I . . . I don't think that's a good idea," he stammered. "I mean, I'm not sure of the address . . ."

Moira Devlin giggled. "I could always ask your old uncle," she teased. "He often comes into the cafe."

"No!" He shouted out the word without intending to. Saw the tears beginning to well up at the corners of her eyes. Christ, what a fuck-all mess! He never meant to hurt her.

"I'm sorry," he said, forcing the panic out of his voice and returning to sit beside her. "I'm afraid Uncle is a bit of a bastard, you see . . ."

She looked at him with uncomprehending eyes.

"Look," he said, taking the little pad and pencil from her hands, "I'll make a deal with you. I'll give you the address, if you'll promise me never to speak to Uncle should you see him again."

Understanding filled her open, trusting face. "He'd think I wasn't good enough for you and try to put an end to it, wouldn't he?"

He nodded agreement with her explanation, scrawling the Los Angeles address he'd memorized from Kileen's typewritten sheet on a square of the pink paper. "I told you he was a right bastard," he said.

She took the pad from him and squeezed it to her breast, then leaned over and kissed him. "Do you want to know what the other girls in the cafe think of him?" she giggled.

The boy looked at her.

"They think he's some sort of a mysterious freedom fighter," she confided. "They're all frightened to death of him."

The boy laughed with as much conviction as he could muster. "Uncle? That's really very funny. The poor old boy wouldn't harm a fly. He's just a terrible blabbermouth."

She shuddered. "Sometimes I feel sorry for him. How did his face get so horribly scarred?"

"An accident," said the boy, kissing her again, then getting to his feet and pulling on his jacket. "Got to run now, love."

Moira pulled the sheet up to her neck and waggled her fingers at him. "I'll write to you, Brian," she said.

He nodded and stepped through the door into the cluttered hallway.

"MA?"

The frail figure seemed lost among the stiff, white sheets of the high, iron hospital bed, her damp hair spread fanlike across the pillow. For a moment he feared that she had died in her sleep and that he had come too late. Then the thin chest rose, and she emitted a small sound that might have been a sigh.

"It's early for her to be waking up," said the starched nursing sister at the boy's shoulder. She bustled past him in her thick white shoes and crossed to the bed, reaching beneath the sheets and exposing the skeletal wrist of her patient. The sister held the wrist up for a few seconds, glancing disapprovingly at the big, no-nonsense watch on her own beefy wrist, then replacing the frail arm where she had found it and smoothing the sheets. "Missus," she whispered, stroking the pale forehead of the woman in the bed. "Can you hear me?"

The pale, veined lids fluttered open, and Allison Quinn looked up into the sister's round face. "Is it time for my medicine?" she asked.

The sister smiled, the stern countenance with which she had intimidated the boy a moment before magically transforming into an angelic smile. "Not yet, dear," she said, stepping aside and turning her gaze onto the youngster. "But look who's come to see you."

His mother raised her head from the pillow, and her drawn face filled with light. "Billy," she cried. "You've come." She turned to the sister and grinned defiantly. "I told you my boy would come," she said. "I told you."

"So you did." The sister smiled, then turned to cast a withering look at the boy. "Though he might've waited until proper visiting hours."

"Sorry, Sister," he murmured.

"Just don't you tire her," warned the sister, moving back and motioning him to the bedside. She looked meaningfully at her wristwatch. "I'll be back in ten minutes, and then its out with you, and no arguments." She hurried out of the room, leaving him alone with the sick woman.

"She's really a dear," said his mother, grasping his hand and squeezing it fiercely in her bony grasp.

"How are you, Ma?" He bent to kiss her sunken cheek, recoiling at the clammy feel of her skin against his lips.

"Not as bad as they make me out to be." She smiled, raising her head, and he propped the pillows behind her, noticing that her long hair was still just as golden and lustrous as it had been when he was a child and she had still been beautiful. He forced himself to remember that, despite her deathly appearance, she was still young, barely forty.

"Oh, it's so good to see you, Billy." She sighed again, her thin arms appearing from beneath the sheets to enfold him.

"I'm sorry I didn't come sooner, Ma. I just heard—"

"Shush," she whispered into his hair. "I knew what to expect when I gave you over to The Cause. You're doing a man's work . . . important work, Billy. Your da would be so proud of you . . ."

The boy gently disengaged himself from her embrace, pulling back to look into her gentle gray eyes. Her belief in The Cause was all-consuming, having become the single driving force in her life on the long-ago day when They had murdered his father. It was The Cause that had driven her to stay in the North instead of returning to her relatives here in the Irish Republic. For that she'd sacrificed her beauty and her youth in the series of low-paid jobs she'd taken as a maid in the homes of a succession of Northern Ireland's powerful Protestant business and political leaders, living in the shabby downstairs rooms They provided for the help, spying on Them when they thought no one was looking, rifling through the papers in Their paneled studies when They were away at Their villas in Spain, or gone to Their important meetings in London.

Allison Quinn and Billy, the pretty little blond parlor maid and her snot-nosed Paddy whelp. She smiling obediently as they ordered her to do Their fetching and cleaning. He hiding back by the kitchen stairs with the dogs, staying out of Their way, lest he annoy Them. Eating Their leftovers. Putting up with the taunts and jeers of Their privileged, spoiled, pasty-faced brats. Wearing Their hand-me-downs.

Jesus! He wanted to kill them all, the smug bastards.

"Are you going to get better now, Ma?" He asked the question with no real hope of hearing the truth from her. The truth that was etched on her face so plain an idiot could see it.

She smiled dreamily, gazing upon him as if Jesus himself had taken time out from his busy schedule and descended from heaven expressly to see her. "Doctor says I'll be out of here in no time," she cheerfully replied. "He thinks they got all the cancer."

"Where will you go, then, back to Kilkee?"

She nodded. "Your Aunt Min says they're all dying to have me back, to help out with the new baby and all."

He smiled encouragingly, feeding her fantasy while at the same time picturing in his mind his aunt's overcrowded cottage with its interminable supply of squalling babes, his uncle coming in drunk from the pub after a bad day of fishing, hollering for his supper, then dragging Aunt Min off early to bed, going to work in the next room with an animalistic grunt and the squeal of tired bedsprings on yet another squalling bundle of joy.

"You don't have to go back there if you don't want to, Ma," he said, pressing the envelope Kileen had given him into her hand. "You can get a nice little flat of your own right here in Dublin." He squeezed her hand. "Someplace with big sunny windows and a garden."

She held up the envelope, lifting the gummed flap and peeking at the thick sheaf of notes inside. "You're going away, then," she said. It was not a question.

"Maybe I wouldn't have to go, Ma," he offered. "I could talk to them. Explain about the cancer . . . Your health is more important than—"

She slapped him sharply across the mouth. "Don't you talk like that," she said, some of the old fire coming back into her voice. "Don't you ever talk like that. Nothing's more important than The Cause. Nothing!"

"But the peace talks are on," he said lamely. "Some say there's no need to fight anymore . . ."

Allison Quinn pushed herself up on her bony elbows and bright spots of fire flared in the hollows of her sunken cheeks. "They don't want peace, you fool," she hissed. "They only say that so they can take away our guns. There'll be no peace without the guns, only more slavery. Are you too thick to see that?"

Billy bowed his head. "No, Ma," he whispered. "I only thought that now . . ."

She fell back onto the pillows, exhausted, beads of perspiration glittering against the pallid skin of her forehead. The lids fell shut over her bulging, luminous eyes, and she whimpered against the relentless pain that he knew was gnawing away somewhere deep within her tortured body. "Just remember what They did to your father," she said in a voice so faint he had to lean forward to hear. "Don't you ever forget that, Billy Quinn. Not ever."

"No, Ma," he said, brushing his lips across her damp cheek. "I won't forget."

CHAPTER TWELVE

Blue-eyed Envy

"Tea?" Brenda Gaynor stared at Kelly in astonishment. "We're invited for *tea?* I *gag* on tea."

Kelly sighed, wondering what on earth had ever possessed her to divulge James Queally-Smythe's invitation to a complete airhead like Brenda. School was out for the day, and she was sitting cross-legged on a redwood deck chair beside the pool behind the canyon house, trying to enhance her tan while explaining her encounter of the previous afternoon to Brenda and Samantha.

Sam, who lay stretched out on a Snoopy beach towel at Kelly's feet, raised her dark glasses and looked up at Brenda, who was sitting in a chaise lounge. "It doesn't really mean *tea*, Brenda," she explained patiently. "The English have afternoon snacks, like cake and things, and they just call it tea."

Brenda curled her lip distastefully. "Sounds positively weird," she sniffed, holding her hands out before her to examine her freshly polished nails. "So what does this English guy look like?" she asked, sounding bored by the whole discussion.

Kelly sighed. "I told you, he's Irish, not English."

Brenda craned her neck to peer at her left shoulder, risking a freshly painted nail to flip the strap of her nearly transparent Lycra swimsuit down about her arm. "Whatever," she yawned. "Is he good looking?"

"How am I supposed to know?" said Kelly. "I talked to his grandfather, for God's sake."

"I met this English guy two years ago, when my parents took me to Cannes," Samantha offered. She rolled over onto her stomach and unsnapped the top of her bikini, dropping her large breasts onto Snoopy's grinning face. "One night we went skinny-dipping in the pool at my father's villa while everyone else was at the *Palais*." She grinned. "He had the biggest pair of balls I've ever seen," she added casually.

"I think you're disgusting," said Brenda. She gazed self-consciously at Samantha's full, dark breasts, which were spilling over the Snoopy towel.

Kelly, who suspected that Sam had undone her top only to remind Brenda of her own dismal near-flat-chestedness, fought to suppress a wicked grin. "We didn't come here to talk about guys' balls," she said.

"You're right," said Samantha, sitting up and raising her arms lazily over her head like a stretching cat. "Besides, I guess it's really pretty crude to call them balls . . . I think nuts is a much nicer term, don't you?"

Even Brenda began to laugh.

"All right, you two. Get serious," Kelly giggled. "Are you going to come to tea with me or not?"

Samantha, who was still stretching, did not answer, and Kelly glanced worriedly over her shoulder, certain that Chuck would have an instant brain seizure if he should come home and find his stepdaughter's gorgeous best friend doing topless exercises on his pool deck. "Sam," she pleaded.

"I'll come only on the condition that he lets me see his balls," grinned Sam. "I'm thinking about writing a term paper."

"Well, I'll come on the condition that he falls madly in love with me, if he's a hunk," said Brenda.

"Great, you're both coming, then," said Kelly. "Now, should we invite anybody else?"

They both stared at her. "Are you insane? There's already three of us," Brenda whined.

Kelly rolled her eyes. "I meant other *guys,* Brenda. I did tell his grandfather I'd introduce him to some *people* from school."

"What are we," asked Sam, twisting energetically from the waist, "alien life forms?"

"You know what I mean. *People* usually means guys too."

Brenda tossed her long, red curls decisively. "No other guys," she said. "If he turns out to be a hunk, they'll all just be jealous of him."

"And if he doesn't turn out to be a hunk?" Kelly awaited her reply with genuine interest.

Brenda gave her the thin-lipped smile she usually reserved for complete idiots. "Well, for God's sake, Kelly, then who is going to *care* anyway?"

Kelly snorted angrily. "Thanks a lot, Brenda, you're a genuine human being. We're supposed to be making this poor guy feel at home. He just lost his parents."

Brenda shrugged. "Well, I'm sure that's too bad, but I'm certainly not going to hang out with him if he looks like the elephant man," she said, pressing a finger experimentally against the reddening skin of her right arm. "Oh my God, I'm burning. Have you got any sunblock?"

"Don't need it." Kelly smiled viciously and looked down at Samantha.

"Don't look at me. I never burn." Sam smirked. She pulled up her top and stood, raising her glasses onto her forehead and pretending to scrutinize Brenda's fair skin. "But I wouldn't worry about it if I were you, Bren. You look really good in red."

Brenda leaped to her feet, covering her shoulders with a towel. "You're not a very nice person, Samantha Simms."

Samantha nodded agreeably. "Right. Well, you're not exactly Mother Teresa yourself, Bren."

Brenda glared at her. "What in the hell is that supposed to mean?"

Sam rolled her eyes in Kelly's direction. "Forget it, I couldn't explain it to you."

MAJOR JAMES QUEALLY-SMYTHE, late of His Majesty's Royal Gurkha Regiment, sat on the small, leafy veranda overlooking the formal expanse of neatly clipped green lawn rolling down to the hedge at the gates of his property. The sun was going down, and Ranjee, his servant, had just brought out the large crystal tumbler of single-malt scotch the old man permitted himself at the end of each day. Inside, in his tall, paneled study, the manuscript detailing his history of the British armed forces in India lay nearly complete beside the stacks and boxes of personal correspondence, diaries, collections of memoirs and faded government documents that made up the bulk of his research materials, but he had no stomach for the usually fascinating work this evening.

This evening, he must decide how he was going to rearrange his affairs in order to accommodate the young man he had reluctantly invited into his strictly ordered life.

The Major—for that is the way he always thought of himself, even though he had been gently mustered out of service following the war, his time in the Japanese prisoner of war camp having left him with what the doctors referred to as a "delicate constitution"—had turned to writing during his long recuperation from the various tropical diseases he had contracted as a POW.

His collection of short stories about the valor of the brown men with whom he had served in those dark days had, surprisingly, won him a coveted literary award, and an old friend from school days who had gone on to head the Pinewood Studios outside London had come calling with a proposal to turn the stories into a film glorifying the brave soldiers about whom he had written.

Unable to entrust the work to any but his own hand, the invalid had thrown himself into a study of cinema techniques and, ultimately, he had written the screenplay on his own. In the process, he had learned a great deal about the way motion pictures are made, reasoning that it was all simply a matter of organization and details, and foolishly convincing himself that no director could put the story to film better than himself.

Somehow he had managed to convince his friend at Pinewood and, to his everlasting amazement, he had found himself at the helm of a huge film production, which he had attacked with all the enthusiasm of a full-frontal infantry assault. Within a few weeks the massive project had been on the verge of foundering disastrously. Then, fortunately, his cinematographer and two assistant directors had locked him into a London hotel room and managed to talk him into letting them walk him through the bewildering process of directing his first motion picture.

The film, *Honour & Glory,* had become an international sensation, and James Queally-Smythe had soon found himself besieged with offers from Hollywood, which was then still immersed in an orgy of serious films about the war. He had made three more such pictures before tiring of the genre and turning his talents to lighter fare with his history-based musical comedy *Keep Your Damn Colonies.*

Returning briefly to England in the early 1950s, he had married a quiet and withdrawn girl ten years his junior, lost her in a scandalous divorce a few years after the birth of their only child, a headstrong daughter who had grown up in England with her mother after Queally-Smythe had forsaken his native land for the gentler—and less critical—climes of California.

Dina, his ex-wife, who was a devoted horsewoman, had died in a riding accident a few years after the girl left school, and Queally-Smythe had lost track of his daughter. He learned from the *London Times*—to which he remained a loyal lifelong subscriber—that she had married a wealthy Irishman she met on holiday in Barbados, not even bothering to invite her expatriate father to the wedding.

Now the issue of that marriage, seventeen-year-old Brian O'Malley—whom the Major had seen but once in his life, when the boy was not much more than a toddler—was suddenly and tragically being dumped into his lap. He cringed again over not having attended the funeral of his daughter and son-in-law, trusting the boy would understand that the authorities in

Northern Ireland had not even managed to track him down to inform him of the deaths until nearly a fortnight after the fact.

The old man's face reddened in the fading light as he thought about the heartless Catholic bastards who would place a deadly mine in the middle of a public road where anyone was liable to run over it. It was a tactic he had seen many times while he was in the East, before the war, but one practiced then only by the godless heathens set on ejecting the British from India—for, despite all the attendant publicity, and as his new book would make perfectly clear, not all the wogs had been followers of the nonviolent Gandhi. "We knew how to deal with barbarians in my day," he snorted aloud. "Line the bastards up against a wall and shoot 'em."

The sound of his own voice snapped him out of his bitter recollection, and he tried to turn his mind back to the far more pressing subject at hand. The boy would be arriving tomorrow.

Queally-Smythe, who had remained a confirmed bachelor since the disastrous marriage to Dina more than forty years previously, was not quite certain how he would cope. He knew nothing of youngsters or their ways. To make matters worse, since settling permanently in Southern California, a place that prided itself on the strangeness and individuality of its inhabitants, he had deliberately steeped himself in the trappings of an extinct lifestyle that provoked fond memories of his prewar days in India and that had once charitably been characterized by a newspaper columnist as The-British-Gentleman-Abroad.

The columnist had been an ignorant man, however. James Queally-Smythe was fully aware of the fact that he was an anachronism and that no one in England, much less a seventeen-year-old schoolboy, lived as he did anymore. Here in California, his eccentricities were tolerated as the quirks of a brilliant film director, but he feared that his grandson would see him as a comical figure, and he wished that there had been some alternative to sending for the boy.

But then what was he to do? The troubled boy obviously needed someone, and his daughter's only child had no other living blood relatives besides himself.

He sighed heavily, sniffing the delicious odor of Ranjee's lamb curry on the soft evening air. Queally-Smythe had grown quite fond of curry during his years in India, but he somehow doubted very much that young Brian would like it. At least not in the quantities and frequency with which he himself consumed the fiery concoction.

He made a mental note to find out what the boy might like to eat and lay in a supply of preferred foodstuffs. It was just one more item on the long list of things he must remember to remind Ranjee to attend to.

He sipped his scotch slowly, ticking off the many things he had so far done to try to make the lad's stay with him as comfortable and pleasant as possible: Ranjee had been instructed to clear and paint the guest suite, a breezy upstairs garret that had become in recent years a catchall for the voluminous overflow of his research materials.

When the walls of the room were gleaming beneath a fresh coat of white paint, he had personally accompanied the Indian servant on a shopping expedition for sheets and curtains—he chose a bright, masculine plaid—for the room, which was situated, along with its own private bath and a balcony with an outside entrance, atop an airy tower at the opposite end of the fanciful old Spanish-style house from his own rooms. And, of course, he had made arrangements with the headmaster to have the boy enrolled as a senior at the exclusive Pacific Academy High School, which had come highly recommended and was nearby.

He supposed he would have to purchase some sort of motorcar for the lad as well—for all the local youngsters seemed to have them—but he decided to wait until Brian's arrival for that. He was not even sure if the boy drove. He would probably require some instruction, at any rate, to acquaint him with the perverse American habit of driving on the wrong side of the road. He thought briefly of presenting the lad with his own Jaguar roadster—which he hadn't driven since he had bought the automatic-shift Bentley some years before—but decided also to defer judgment on that matter until he saw what kind of driver the boy was. Queally-Smythe loved the old Jag, now stored beneath a tarp in the triple garage beside the house, and he didn't wish to see it damaged. Also, he suspected, the youngster would probably prefer to have one of those foolish new Japanese models that these days scooted up and down the freeways like so many enormous brightly colored Easter eggs.

The proliferation of the despicable Jappo cars was, in the old man's private view, one of the many things that was wrong with the world these days: There was no longer any appreciation for hand-worked craftsmanship. No sense of pride in things British, or even American for that matter. Everyone, but especially the younger generations, seemed more than willing to settle for mass-produced anonymity. The flash of chromium and the gleam of plastics. Disgusting.

Hopefully, he thought, the boy's exclusive boarding school near Belfast had drummed some solid British values into his head. After all, Northern

Ireland was rightly British too. Had been, in fact, for three hundred years or more; something the damned nationalist renegades who had been responsible for the death of his daughter pigheadedly refused to acknowledge even after their equally despicable IRA counterparts had seen the futility of continuing their terrorist acts and gone to the peace table.

The old man sighed wearily. He'd just have to do his best by the boy. Perhaps if he were able to mix with others his own age in this bright, sunny world . . .

Queally-Smythe peered over the edge of the veranda and down the canyon at the lights twinkling through the elaborate screen of decorative foliage surrounding the raw new house that had been built there less than a year earlier, a hideous thing of glass and stucco that seemed just right for television people.

Still, he reflected, the young girl with whom he had spoken yesterday had seemed pleasant enough, though her clothing had seemed something out of a clown's closet. One shouldn't be too hasty to make judgments, he supposed.

He smiled to himself and raised his glass in mock tribute to the ungraceful house below. At least he had arranged for his grandson to meet some local youngsters of his own age, including at least one pretty girl.

What more could a feeble old man be expected to do?

KELLY HUSTON sat in the center of her bed with her knees drawn up to her chin, thinking about the tragic story of Brian O'Malley and trying to imagine how she would feel if both her parents had been killed in a bomb blast. She wrapped her arms tightly about her, shivering in the cool Southern California evening. Wondering how it was even possible to imagine the unimaginable. Her parents might be divorced now, Daddy thousands of miles away from her, but at least they were both alive and well.

God, it was so awful.

Her heart went out to the lonely Irish boy, and she vowed to make herself his friend, even if he turned out to be a bigger geek than Stanley Kinsella, who, she fairly reasoned, couldn't help being what he was.

She smiled to herself, remembering the grateful expression on poor Stanley's ravaged face this afternoon when she had gone out of her way to tell him how much she appreciated his performing the gruesome chores of cutting up all the specimens in biology. Of course, Brenda had been watching her, making faces and snickering into Thad August's ear the whole time . . . Thad had turned around once to flash his smug, handsome grin at Kelly, and she had been delighted to discover that she hadn't even cared.

Kelly was gradually coming to understand that the old Englishman's story of the day before had touched her far more deeply than she had realized at the time. In fact, it had kept her awake most of last night, and forced her to reassess the glossy veneer of life at Academy High in an entirely new light today.

The obvious pain in the old man's voice as he had spoken of his orphaned grandson had reminded her just how much real suffering there was in the cruel world that lay out there just beyond the glittering, artificially insulated bubble in which she lived. Even within the fragile confines of the bubble, she realized, people could be hurt.

Kelly didn't want to hurt anyone if she could help it. *Wouldn't,* she had resolved, ever deliberately hurt anybody. Thus her kinder attitude toward the bumbling Stanley today, and even her charitable last minute offer to include the vile Brenda in the Major's invitation to tea, although that had obviously turned out to be a mistake.

She stared out through the big window by her bed now, mesmerized by the twinkling lights of an airliner approaching the runways of Los Angeles International Airport a few miles down the coast, and daydreaming about the boy who would soon be arriving there. In her mind's eye, the Major's grandson had become a tragic, brooding figure, a tall, handsome guy with flashing blue eyes who bore a vague resemblance to the strong, silent heroes depicted on the lurid covers of the romance novels that Katherine always left scattered about on her bedroom floor.

Like the dashing figures in the cover paintings, Kelly imagined that Brian O'Malley's hair would be long and dark, his chest broad. And like them too, when she offered him her profound understanding and compassion, she knew he would take her into his strong arms and weep softly on her breast, like a little boy . . .

"You idiot!" Kelly laughed aloud at her foolish daydream and fell back among the soft pillows piled on her bed, blushing furiously at the impossible romantic image she had just conjured up for herself. She grinned, pulling the warm down comforter over her. *If I'm really, really lucky, he'll at least have the long dark hair.*

CHAPTER THIRTEEN

Change of Face

BLACK HAIR.

Black and glossy.

Billy Quinn stood in the cramped confines of the British Airways 747's vibrating forward lavatory, staring at himself in the mirror. Gone was the longish blond hair that had framed his smooth, somewhat soft features for all of his life. Gone, along with his familiar denim trousers, his old black plastic diver's watch and navy turtleneck sweater, and every other time-worn vestige of his personal identity.

All gone.

The face that looked back at him from the mirror now was dominated by the slightly wild mop of black curling hair—the result of a hastily done coloring, haircut and perm, all courtesy of one of Kileen's groupies, a London hairdresser named Maxine. The black hair was shorter than he had worn it before, but still long enough to touch the collar of the soft white shirt he now wore with a distinctive striped tie beneath a Kelly green blazer bearing an embroidered school crest worked with threads of silver.

As he examined himself in the mirror, he noted with surprise that the shining black hair made his blue eyes stand out more prominently against his face, a face that seemed to have taken on added character and dimension.

Fucking amazing!

In his pockets he now carried Brian O'Malley's British passport, along with the other boy's soft leather wallet, which contained, besides his plane tickets, the other's driving licence and school identity card, a gold Barclays Bank credit card and a hundred and forty pounds in cash. Tucked into a separate pocket was the permanent U.S. residence visa that O'Malley's influential grandfather had obtained some weeks earlier, and on his wrist he wore the engraved stainless-steel Rolex given to the other boy by his father on the occasion of his sixteenth birthday.

Somewhere below, in the airplane's massive cargo hold, a set of matched leather luggage contained an expensive assortment of clothing, personal belongings and books, all of which Kileen's lads had insisted he examine again before they had driven him back to Heathrow.

"You *are* Brian O'Malley," Billy Quinn said to the face in the mirror. "You fucking *are* him!"

The unfamiliar face looked back skeptically.

"Sod you," sneered Billy Quinn from behind the mask. He flushed the chemical toilet, unlocked the narrow lavatory door to admit a sweating fat man, who glared at him—probably over the inordinate amount of time he had been locked inside thinking things over—and made his way back to his first-class seat.

The sky was already growing light outside his window, illuminating a vast gray expanse of ocean thirty-six thousand feet below. The sight made him feel small and inadequate, and he tried to marshal his thoughts for the ordeal he was soon to face. The events of the past eighteen hours skittered through his addled brain like bits and pieces from a poorly remembered movie, making it hard to think clearly.

Kileen's lads in the Escort had picked him up from the rainy Dublin sidewalk exactly as promised, the two of them driving him straight to the airport outside the city and hustling him wordlessly onto a jammed British Airways flight to Belfast, where they had been met by a third man driving an old Opel Senator that belched clouds of thick black smoke whenever the throttle was opened.

He had been taken directly to a falling-down farmhouse, several miles out in the country to the north of the brooding industrial city, and hurried inside for a brief conference with Kileen's men on the scene. Then they had hustled him up a narrow staircase to a drafty upstairs room.

Brian O'Malley, a large, ugly bruise spreading down the right side of his handsome face, lay bound hand and foot in his underclothes on a dirty mattress in a dark corner of the room, his wide blue eyes darting in terror from the peeling walls of his drab surroundings to the hard, unforgiving faces of his armed captors.

Before they let Billy into the room, the two men had ordered him to carefully examine the captive's hair style and the little finger of his left hand, which they said had been broken in a school rugby game the year before, and which therefore projected slightly away from the other fingers. Kileen's men had moved away then, huddling by the door for a whispered conversation of their own as Billy had knelt beside the shivering boy, bending close and trying to keep his features neutral, even though the other's helplessness pricked at his conscience. It bothered him that Brian O'Malley was guilty of nothing more than having a relative in the States.

The prisoner must have read the concern in his eyes, because he raised his head slightly, first glancing to the door to be certain the others were not looking, then whispering to him in a hoarse, frightened voice, "Look here, can you help me? There's been some horrible mistake, but that lot over there won't listen to me. I haven't done anything . . ."

Billy Quinn had drawn back in surprise, staring at the helpless boy on the mattress, wanting to hate him but instead noticing the angry red welts along his rib cage, where someone had obviously kicked him.

Recovering from his surprise, Billy had winked confidentially at O'Malley while he bent and examined his hands. In contrast to his own ragged nails, Brian O'Malley's were clean and neatly clipped, and he made a mental note to clean the grease from beneath his fingernails. "They won't hurt you, if you'll just cooperate," he confided in a low, encouraging voice. "They'll just keep you here for a few weeks at most, and then they'll let you go."

Instead of receiving the news with grateful relief, as Billy had expected him to do, the other boy had let out a long, pitiful moan and buried his face in the dirty striped ticking of the mattress. "Weeks . . . I don't think I can bear it here for weeks," he had sobbed. "It's filthy here, and the smells are nauseating me . . ."

Billy Quinn had felt his heart grow cold at the sound of the other's whimpering complaint. "Our lads in Long Kesh Prison endure worse than this for years on end," he said bitterly. "You've got to take it like a man."

O'Malley sniffled loudly and looked up at him with pleading eyes. "Money," he whispered. "I could get you money if you'll help me. Lots and lots of it . . ."

"I don't want your fucking money, you whining little cocksucker," Billy spat. "You can't buy your way out of this." He swung his head around, aware that the guards by the door had stopped talking and were turning to stare at the pair of them. "You're damned lucky that these brave men aren't set on killing you instead of holding you as a prisoner of war," he said. "Now don't say another word to me or I'll kick your pasty face in myself."

He had heard Kileen's men laughing and applauding, and then, strangely, he felt the ache of hot tears beginning to well up in his own throat as Brian O'Malley flopped over on his filthy mattress and began to sob as though his heart were breaking. Instantly regretting the unnecessary cruelty of his threat, Billy touched the prisoner's shoulder and squeezed it encouragingly. "I didn't mean that," he whispered. "But you've got to be brave if you're going to make it through this." He leaned closer, chancing a glance at the door. The guards had turned away again, engrossed once more in conversation. "Don't let them see you cry," he warned. "And don't ask them any questions. It'll just go harder for you."

Brian O'Malley had rolled back onto his side and looked up at him then, swiping at his reddened eyes with crossed wrists. "I'm sorry," he whispered. "Of course you're right."

"You'll be okay," said Billy. "I give you my word on it."

O'Malley sniffled noisily and managed a grim smile. "I believe you," he whispered.

"Good." Billy had punched him lightly on the shoulder then, and got up and crossed the room to examine the contents of Brian O'Malley's expensive luggage, which lay open on the floor awaiting his inspection. When he had thoroughly examined the contents, one of the guards came over, and Billy was made to discard every stitch of his own clothing and to dress in the clothes of the frightened boy on the mattress, who had looked on silently.

In less than ten minutes he was wearing the unfamiliar new clothes and ready to go. One of the guards instructed him to close up the cases and report back downstairs with them. He did as he was told, picking up the heavy luggage and starting to the door. Casting a final glance at the trussed-up prisoner, he saw that O'Malley had curled into a fetal ball and was shivering against the near-freezing temperature in the room. Dropping the cases, he searched the room until he found a stained army blanket, which he shook out before walking back and bending to gently drape it over O'-Malley's shivering body.

"Thank you," said Brian O'Malley. "I won't forget this."

"Remember," said Billy, "you have my word."

Walking past the smirking guards, Billy Quinn had left the room and gone downstairs where he was hustled into a nondescript black taxi along with the expensive luggage. During the twenty-minute ride back to the Belfast airport, it was explained to him by the taxi's bearded driver that his flight to Los Angeles connected through London's Heathrow Airport, and that he would have exactly three hours there, which time would be used to complete his physical transformation into Brian O'Malley.

Another man in a similarly nondescript black taxi met him outside Terminal 3 at Heathrow and sped him through the early afternoon traffic to an empty warehouse in one of the sprawling industrial estates near the airport.

There his hair was changed and he was instructed how to pass through U.S. Customs and what to say to the immigration officers who would question him. That done, he was clapped gruffly on the shoulder and hustled back to the British Airways terminal in plenty of time to board the fourteen-hour nonstop transatlantic flight to California.

Among the many pieces of advice that Billy Quinn—who had until this day never been farther from the alleyways of West Belfast than his aunt's cottage, less than two hundred miles away in the Irish Republic to the south—had been given during the course of the day, the one that remained seated most firmly in his mind had come from one of the two men who had picked him up in Dublin, then accompanied him on the short flight to Belfast.

The man, a puckish little fellow in a red plaid scarf, claimed to have used many false and borrowed identities in the course of his fifteen years as a nationalist freedom fighter, never having been found out and rarely even suspected in all that time. "The trick of it," he had confided as the overworked Boeing 737 had passed out of Irish airspace and dived for the relative safety of its low-level landing approach to Belfast, "is never to volunteer anything about yourself that's not absolutely necessary. If somebody starts asking a lot of personal questions, you've got to look offended, like they've no right to be prying, you see. Most of 'em'll take the hint and leave you be."

The little man had laughed, swallowing the last of his vodka and orange juice as the bedraggled BA air hostess had struggled up the sloping aisle of the crowded commuter plane, collecting plastic glasses in a little bin. "The second best way to avoid embarrassing questions," he had chuckled, "is to pretend to be drunk or asleep, depending on the circumstances, of course. That works with women, as well," he had added humorously.

Billy Quinn had laughed weakly, but he had not forgotten the little man's advice. The dangerous blunder of giving Moira Devlin his California address had been an object lesson in the desirability of keeping things to himself until this mission—which Kileen had promised would last a month or two at the most—was over.

Turning wearily away from the airliner window, he closed his eyes, trying to imagine what it was going to be like to live in California among the palm trees. He thought he knew a lot about the place from what he'd seen in films and on the telly. The frightened eyes and battered face of Brian O'-Malley intruded to disturb his vision of shining freeways filled with Cadillacs and Thunderbirds, and beautiful tan girls in bikinis.

CHAPTER FOURTEEN

The Pawn

THE BOY ON THE MATTRESS had finally fallen into an exhausted sleep beneath the ragged army blanket. His captors had awakened him once, to feed him a cup of sour cabbage soup and let him up to relieve himself in a bucket. Now he lay tossing restlessly on the thin mattress while his new guard, a skinny youth not very much older than himself, leaned against the faded wallpaper on a straight-backed chair by the room's only door.

The young guard, whose name was Dermot Tumelty, had grown up hurling rocks at British commandos in the streets and alleyways of West Belfast, and he felt little sympathy for the weepy sod across the room, who he had only been told was a valuable political prisoner.

Tumelty, who had once envisioned himself as a bass guitarist in a famous rock-and-roll band, had lost the use of his right hand at the age of nine, when a gas grenade fired by a frightened British soldier had hit his thin wrist at point-blank range as young Dermot had crept around the corner of a brick wall in defiance of the curfew. The resulting impact had shattered the fragile wrist bones beyond all hope of repair, leaving the hand below no more useful than the twisted claw it now resembled.

For a brief period following the incident—when, due to infection, it seemed he might have to lose the hand altogether—young Dermot's prospects had brightened. A sympathetic American family had brought the boy to New York for emergency medical treatment at the Albert Einstein Medical Center, and the time he had spent in their pleasant Long Island home during his recuperation from the surgery that had saved his hand from being amputated had been the happiest and most secure period of his entire brief life.

In those weeks, Dermot Tumelty had watched Saturday morning cartoons on television with the family's other children, learned a hundred fascinating words; words like "barf" and "glom" and "humongous," and become deliriously addicted to undreamed of and uniquely strange and wonderful American foods like Froot Loops and Twinkies. He had run and played and swum in the parklike grounds surrounding the family's spacious home, and, before twelve weeks had passed, he had changed from a withdrawn, frightened loner who woke screaming in the night at the sound of trucks rolling down the street, to a happy, outgoing child with an uncanny knack for predicting the outcome of major league baseball games.

Then his medical visa had run out, and Dermot had been sent back to the mean and deadly streets of Belfast. For a few weeks, he had cowered before the telly in his mother's shabby row house, refusing to go outside at all, his waking hours spent relentlessly searching the grim BBC and RTE channels for shows about America.

In time, though, he had returned to the old familiar streets and alleyways, and he was soon running with his old mates. His anger over the loss of the earthly paradise that had been dangled briefly before him and then rudely snatched away again had ultimately driven him into the waiting arms of the rebels, and he had by the age of fourteen become the trusted courier of a militant nationalist splinter group, a swift, wiry slip of a boy able to pass undetected through the most daunting arrays of razor wire to deliver his messages, grinning and smoking cigarettes afterwards as the tough street soldiers slapped him on the back and stood him to pints almost bigger than himself.

Although he'd gladly volunteered for more than his share of offensive operations against the hated occupying troops, his crippling disability had largely prevented him from engaging in any of the group's more dangerous actions.

Nowadays, Dermot Tumelty spent all of his free time writing his rock-and-roll music, clumsily scrawling the notes on ragged sheets of lined school paper with his left hand, filling the space beneath the notes with angry lyrics having mostly to do with injustice and the need to be free.

He was writing such a song now, working by the weak glow of a battered tin lantern that provided the only light in the unheated room. The ancient, Chinese-manufactured AK47 rifle which he had been given to guard Brian O'Malley was propped against the wall beside his chair.

Tumelty looked up at the sound of movement from the corner, not much concerned about his prisoner attempting to escape. Besides the fact that, when he was unconscious, the boy on the mattress was tightly bound hand and foot—a job he had seen to himself after earlier getting the prisoner up and feeding him—he had marked O'Malley as a wanker from the moment he had jumped into the back of the taxi that Michael Kileen had organized when the call had come through to an accomplice in the taxi company dispatcher's office to collect the wealthy boy from his exclusive private school outside the city for a trip to the airport.

Not far from the school, the taxi had slowed at a road junction, and Dermot Tumelty had pulled open the door and flung himself inside. In that first startled moment, the captive had gazed at the scruffy intruder's crippled hand, snottily demanding to know how he had dared enter his cab. His false, upper-class bravado had dissolved instantly into tears of pain and astonishment when Tumelty had slammed his good fist into the side of the boy's head.

Now Brian O'Malley was nothing more in the dim light than a dark shape beneath the old blanket in the corner of the cold room.

A cellular phone beeped softly somewhere in the downstairs of the farmhouse, and Dermot Tumelty heard the sound of one of the lads talking. After a moment, footsteps sounded on the stair. Giving the prisoner another quick glance, he carefully folded his sheet of music and tucked it away into the pocket of his dark jacket, bending to pick up the AK47 and cradling it across his lap just as the door opened. "What's up?" he enquired of Duffy, the man Michael Kileen had placed in charge of the Belfast end of the extraordinary operation.

"Orders," said Duffy, his closely shaved head gleaming in the glow from the lantern. He inclined his chin toward the prisoner. "The little snot awake yet?"

Tumelty shook his head, letting his chair fall forward onto its front legs and getting to his feet. Although there wasn't much the young fighter feared, Francis Duffy, who had spent six years in an English prison and who had a well-deserved reputation as a psychopath, was high up on Dermot Tumelty's short list. He knew full well that it never hurt to show respect before such a man as Duffy. "Sleeping like a babe," he smiled, trying to sound tough.

Duffy lifted the lantern and crossed the room to the sleeping prisoner. "Get up, you," he ordered, prodding O'Malley's ribs with the toe of one muddy boot, then dropping to a predatory crouch beside him.

The boy on the mattress moaned, and after a moment he struggled to a sitting position, blinking up at the fierce, hulking figure above him. His eyes widened in fright as Duffy snapped open a large folding knife with a white bone handle and pointed the gleaming blade directly at his heart. "Oh Christ, please don't kill me," he screamed, throwing his bound hands up before his face.

Duffy lunged forward with the knife, slashing at the tough nylon cords holding the boy's wrists together. O'Malley's hands fell apart, exposing his frightened eyes, and the sharp stink of ammonia filled the air. "Sweet Jesus, will you look at this now, exclaimed Duffy, rocking back on his heels, "the poor little boy has gone and pissed all over himself."

Tumelty swallowed hard, feeling his stomach turn over. For a heart-stopping moment, he had been as certain as O'Malley that the mad Duffy was about to kill his charge. The thought frightened and disturbed him, for in all his years of involvement with the struggle to free his country, he had never seen a bound and helpless man murdered in cold blood, although he knew full well that Francis Duffy was more than capable of such an act.

Tumelty managed a grim smile, but said nothing, curious now to know why the prisoner was being freed.

"I've just had a telephone call," said Duffy, bending to cut the boy's feet free. "There's been a terrible mistake, and we're to let you go at once." He slashed at the bonds holding Brian O'Malley's ankles together, then straightened and looked into the boy's eyes, his rasping voice lowering to a soothing, deferential tone. "I've been asked by the organization to offer our sincere apologies, and to obtain your word that you'll say nothing of what has happened, nor take any action that would bring the police down on us."

O'Malley sat on the soggy mattress, rubbing his chafed wrists in dumb amazement, his eyes darting from the faces of the men who, just moments before, he had been certain were set on murdering him. "I, uh," he stammered. "That is, if it's all been a mistake, then certainly . . ."

Duffy suddenly turned his red-rimmed gaze on Dermot Tumelty. "Well, don't just stand there like an idiot," he barked. "Go fetch this poor lad some of that hot coffee your ma sent over with you."

Shocked by the unexpected instruction, Tumelty stumbled backward, searching the room for the thermos he had brought with him. He found it on the floor beside his chair, retrieved it and returned to find Duffy helping the boy to his feet.

Snatching the bottle from the astonished young man, the psychopath screwed off the cap, poured a measure of steaming liquid into the little red plastic cup that fit over the top of the thermos and pressed it into Brian O'Malley's trembling hands. "Here, drink this," he urged.

The youngster took a long swallow and looked up into Duffy's flat, gray eyes. "You're really going to let me go?" he asked. "I mean, this isn't some kind of a republican trick?"

Duffy somehow managed to look hurt. "Well, if you don't want to believe it—" he began.

"No! I mean, I do believe you," protested the boy, anxious not to offend the monster before him. "It's just that . . ." A great, wracking sob shuddered through his body, and for a moment Tumelty thought the poor sod might collapse onto the littered floor.

"I know, I know." Duffy draped a huge, tattooed arm around the sobbing youngster's heaving shoulders. "We gave you a hard time of it. But we've been in a war, you see . . . These things sometimes happen in a war." He paused, as if he'd just remembered something. "Oh Christ, your clothes and things—"

"Don't worry about them," croaked the frightened youngster. "They're only things."

"Look here," said Duffy, leading him across the room to a table on which Billy Quinn's belongings were neatly piled, "we'll try to get them back to you. You see," he explained, "the lad who took your clothes needed to pass for a well-off sort like yourself, and we picked you out at random because you were about his size and had a lot of luggage and things with you. But it was all a mistake . . . They say there'll be a real peace soon and we'll get all your things back to you straightaway."

"It's all right," said O'Malley. "Really."

"Then we can have your word of honor you won't go to the police?" Duffy persisted.

The boy shook his head up and down vigorously, and Duffy looked at Tumelty as if to ask his opinion—like he ever would care what a crippled messenger thought.

"Well, if we have his word," said Tumelty, playing along with Duffy and wondering what in the hell the big man was thinking of. Was it really possible that Michael Kileen was going to throw in with the others who had resigned themselves to joining in the ongoing peace talks with the hated British? He couldn't imagine such a thing.

"It's all settled then," said Duffy. He pointed to the table containing Quinn's things. "Look, why don't you just take the other lad's clothes for now." He laughed heartily. "Can't let you go out completely starkers, can we?"

Brian O'Malley gratefully attacked the pile of rough clothing on the table, shrugging quickly into Quinn's wrinkled denims and turtleneck and hurriedly pulling on the other's socks and shoes as well.

"NOW DO YOU THINK you could find your way back to Belfast City on your own from here?"

The three of them were standing in the overgrown yard of the farmhouse, shoulders hunched against the cold, steady rain that had been falling all day. Brian O'Malley—whose head had been held down against the muddy floor of the taxi throughout the long, circuitous ride to the farm— looked at the unfamiliar outlines of the black countryside about them. "I, uh, I think so."

"The thing is," said Duffy, moving closer to him and lowering his voice to a confidential tone. "We wouldn't like to be seen driving you back there . . . Not that we don't trust you . . ."

"No, I understand," said the boy. He was still shivering in spite of the warm clothes, and he wanted nothing more than to be away from this frightening place.

"It's easy enough to find your way," Duffy said encouragingly. He pointed to a muddy track running past the gate. "You just follow this road about a mile down to the junction. Go right there, until you come to the Belfast road. The town's not more than another ten miles on."

"I'll find it," said O'Malley, starting for the gate.

His heart lurched in his chest as Duffy laughed, grabbing him by the sleeve. "Not so fast! You don't think we'd make you walk all that way in the rain?"

The boy looked confused. "But I thought you said—"

"Come here," said Duffy. He crossed the yard to the wall of the house and pointed to a red Japanese motorcycle parked beneath the eaves. "Take this. You can ride, can't you?"

Brian O'Malley nodded eagerly. "How will I get it back to you?"

Duffy laughed again. "I'm afraid it's borrowed, just like your clothes. You might leave it someplace where the owner's likely to find it tomorrow."

The boy nodded, anxious to be off. "I can go, then?" he asked meekly.

Duffy clapped him on the back. "With our apologies," he said remorse-fully. "We'll send your things back to you by post." He pointed to the mo-torcycle's ignition key. "You just turn that switch there to start it."

Brian O'Malley picked up the black plastic helmet from the seat, put it on his head and straddled the bike. He reached for the ignition switch, hesi-tated.

"Here," said Duffy, reaching over to turn the key for him. The motorcy-cle's powerful engine roared to life between the youngster's trembling legs. The big terrorist turned another switch and the headlight came on, a hard white beam stabbing out into the rainy blackness of the yard.

"Off you go," said Duffy, slapping him on the shoulder. "Mind the wet, now." He stepped back and crossed his arms, watching as the red motorcycle lurched forward, then turned onto the muddy track and splashed away into the night. "Remember," yelled Duffy, "if the coppers ask you what happened, you don't know us!"

The boy on the motorcycle made no answer but gunned the machine down the track. When it was gone, Dermot Tumelty stepped out into the yard and stared after the receding taillight. "Jesus," he breathed. "Why did we let him go? Is Kileen giving up and going into the peace talks with the IRA and all the others, then?"

Duffy glared down, passing a huge hand over his shorn head, squeegeeing the water beaded there down onto his thick neck. "Jesus, you can be daft," he grunted, turning back toward the house. "Let's get the fuck out of here."

"Yeah, but what if he goes to the cops?" said Tumelty. "I mean, he's seen our faces, hasn't he?"

"That's not for you to worry about," said the psychopath. "Not where you'll be going."

Dermot Tumelty stopped in the doorway to stare at him. "I'm going someplace?" he asked.

Duffy grinned, a row of jagged yellow teeth showing in the dim light filtering out through the farmhouse door. "Didn't Kileen tell you, then?"

"Nobody ever tells me fuck-all," Tumelty complained in a rare show of protest at his unappreciated status within the tiny organization.

"Well, you're going back to paradise, lad. It's off to California for you."

Tumelty stared at him in disbelief.

"And haven't I got our passports and tickets right here in my pocket this minute?" said Duffy, reaching into the depths of his great black coat and withdrawing a thick white envelope emblazoned with the blue-and-green logo of a well-known firm of travel agents.

"What are we going to do there?" asked the stunned youth, sudden visions of Saturday morning cartoons and boxes of Froot Loops dancing unreasonably through his head.

Duffy's grin widened into an obscene jack-o'-lantern leer. "Why we're going over there to fuck all of them gorgeous Hollywood movie stars in their wee little bikinis, of course," he laughed.

BRIAN O'MALLEY guided the red motorcycle out onto the Belfast road, gunning the engine and turning south, feeling the rear tire slip dangerously sideways on the wet pavement. He quickly recovered from the skid and swiveled his helmeted head around, looking back down the unlighted country lane he had just exited, seeking any sign that his kidnappers were pursuing him.

The road was dark.

He twisted the throttle toward him, letting the machine speed up easily through its six gears, intent on putting as much distance as possible between himself and the frightening Catholic bastards who had kidnapped him.

Cold rain splattered against the clear plastic faceplate of the battered black helmet they had given him, hard, pelletlike drops exploding before his eyes and restricting his forward vision to the narrow cone of black tarmac and rushing, white-painted lane dividers delineated in the quartz-bright beam of the headlight, and adding to the din of the exhaust cones roaring in his ears.

The cheap clothes he had been forced to don were soaked through, the cold, wet fabric reeking faintly of dirt and sweat. The sweat of that other fellow, the one who had come into the room around noon and knelt over him, with something that had looked like pity showing in his hard, blue eyes. The one who had given him his word. The word of a thief and a rebel.

"Cheeky, sodding, Paddy bastard!" The sound of his own bitter words echoed faintly over the roar of the speeding motorcycle. Well, he remembered the bastard's face. Remembered all their faces.

Christ! What had they been after?

He looked into the fogged mirror affixed to the handlebar by his left hand, fully expecting to see the lights of a pursuing vehicle. He *knew* who they were. IRA renegades. One of the confusing array of radical nationalist splinter groups that had split off on their own after the '94 cease-fire, determined to carry on with their murderous terror campaign despite the fact that their cause was already lost; desperate killers operating with even fewer constraints than the damned IRA provos at their worst.

The group whose bomb had killed his parents?

Them or another just like them.

It didn't matter to Brian O'Malley what they called themselves. They were all the same in his eyes: ragged, bloody Paddy nationalists. Thugs and murderers every one.

But they had had him in their grasp. Their knives and automatic weapons literally at his throat.

And then they had let him go.

His heart pounded in his chest, and he thought he might pass out. Either that or vomit into the stinking plastic foam padding of the black helmet.

They had let him go.

Brian O'Malley had lived in Northern Ireland for the whole of his life, and he knew as well as he knew his own name that they never let anyone go.

Never.

Which meant they were only toying with him.

You don't know us! He remembered the last shouted words of the evil giant who had cut him free, had him dress in the other boy's clothes, then put him on the motorcycle and sent him on his way alone.

What were they playing at?

Freezing rain pelted against his unprotected knuckles, driving the sensation out of his fingers. He thrust one numb hand into the front of the wet jacket, keeping it there until the fevered heat of his body brought the stinging sensation back to his fingers. Removing the hand from its temporary shelter, he swiped at the streaked faceplate, saw the lights of the approaching city glowing against the low clouds.

You don't know us! Rage was building in him like a solid black wall. He had whined before them, peed his pants in fright like a two-year-old. The sodding bastards had blown up his parents, kidnapped, beaten and terrorized him. *Laughed at his helplessness.*

They were so smug. So certain of themselves and their dumb Paddy belief that his country belonged to them. Them with their sacred Cause. Certain too, he was sure, that he wouldn't dare go to the police or the army. That he'd cringe at the very thought of angering them, lie awake nights in a cold sweat, fearing their reprisal.

"Bastards!" He'd show them, by God. He'd see every one of their smirking, loutish faces up before a magistrate. Let them laugh that off.

After another fifteen minutes of hard riding, he entered the outskirts of the city, driving toward the town center. The rain was letting up, and he slowed the bike to a safer speed, pushing up the plastic faceplate and letting the cold droplets bathe his feverish face. The blue lights of an RUC police station glowed before a heavily fortified concrcte building to his right, and he slowed the motorcycle to a crawl, guiding it between a car with wire mesh over the windows and an armored lorry, cruising slowly up a short brick drive to the front steps of the station and stopping before the fogged glass doors.

Inside, he saw a figure in a dark blue constable's uniform, sitting at a desk and working with a computer. The man stopped what he was doing and peered out at Brian suspiciously, then turned away, and the boy could see his lips moving silently behind the glass, the shadows of other men hurrying forward from someplace beyond the field of his vision.

Then suddenly, the glass doors were flung open, and two constables in heavy flak jackets and armed with squat, black machine pistols were hurrying down the steps toward him. Two others stood above, peering out through the doors. "You, on the motorcycle," shouted one of the constables on the steps. "What do you want here?"

Brian O'Malley grinned with relief, reaching up to pull off the helmet so they could see him. "It's all right, Constable," he called over the sound of the engine, dropping his eyes to the unfamiliar controls of the motorcycle and searching for the kill switch. He spotted it, a round, chrome ring with a silvery key protruding from it.

The footsteps of the constables were louder, hard, black leather slapping on the wet bricks of the steps. Brian O'Malley looked up reassuringly, saw the dull black muzzle of the nearest constable's machine pistol swinging up toward his head as he fumbled with cold-numbed fingers for the switch. "It's all right," he said again, "An unbelievable thing has happened to me . . ."

His fingers found the wet bit of metal, slipped as he tried for a grip on it.

His blue eyes darted sideways, surprised to see the constables splitting up, six of them now, moving warily around him, front and back, their thumbs touching the sides of their deadly weapons, flicking little levers that moved with loud, metallic clicks.

He grasped the key between the thumb and forefinger of his frozen right hand, anxious to shut off the noisy engine, feeling the tension of the spring-loaded switch against his sluggish muscles as he twisted it anti-clockwise, toward the kill position.

The *kill* position!

His eyes dropped to his hand in astonishment as the import of his action registered in some distant part of his agile brain. Mindless now of the machine pistols trained on him, he watched with growing horror as his own fingers continued to turn the shining key, the hand moving of its own volition, like a glass that you've just seen fall from a shelf but know you can never catch.

The kill switch!!!

And for a brief fraction of a second, Brian O'Malley knew with crystal-clear certainty exactly why the bastards had let him go on his way. Sent him driving off into the cold, rainy night, absolutely certain beyond a shadow of a doubt that he would do precisely what they had made him promise he would not, driving their explosives-packed motorcycle straight to the nearest police station.

You don't know us!

The hateful, mocking words boomed inside his head as he tried to will his hand from its deadly course.

CHAPTER FIFTEEN

Geneva

MICHAEL KILEEN sat in a comfortable leather and chromium chair in the spacious and tastefully appointed waiting room on the third floor of a modern office building in the financial district gazing out through the frameless, floor-to-ceiling plate-glass windows at the gray waters of Lake Geneva a few blocks away.

He unfolded the late edition of the English-language newspaper he had picked up at an airport kiosk during his brief layover in Zurich, bending to reread the brief page-two article sandwiched in as a last-minute lead in the International News column:

FIVE DIE AS SUICIDE BOMB
ROCKS BELFAST POLICE STATION

Belfast, Northern Ireland. A powerful bomb blast shattered the fragile peace of recent months, killing at least five persons, including the bomber, when a motorcycle packed with explosives blew up a Royal Ulster Constabulary station in the heart of the city early today. The bomb was thought to have been detonated by the unidentified cyclist, who is said to have drawn at least eight police constables outside to investigate. An anonymous telephone call received shortly before the blast warned of an impending terrorist attack on the station. No group has yet taken credit for the explosion, and officials presiding over the Joint Irish Peace Negotiations were quick to issue a statement denying that the attack signaled any breakdown in the ongoing talks, blaming the blast on one of several militant groups opposed to any compromise in Ireland.

"Mr. Jameson?"

Kileen folded the newspaper back into his raincoat pocket and smiled up at the tall, attractive receptionist standing before him.

"Doctor will see you now."

"Thank you very much," he said, giving her a small appreciative smile. He got to his feet and followed her through a vaultlike metal door and down a tiled corridor decorated with valuable hunting prints.

The striking brunette stopped before a door and held it open for him. "Please to make yourself comfortable," she smiled. "Doctor will be right with you."

Kileen thanked her, watching appreciatively as she walked away, her hips swaying seductively beneath her pale pink smock, and he considered asking her to join him for dinner at his hotel this evening. By now she would have peeked into his file and discovered that he was a wealthy American businessman who had been tragically disfigured in an explosion that had occurred during an inspection tour of the North Sea oil platform he had been visiting on behalf of the large investment firm he headed.

He had dated another of the doctor's receptionists—all of whom seemed to have been selected on the basis of some formula that placed a premium on long legs, flawless complexion and lustrous hair—on a previous visit to Geneva, and he had been highly pleased with the outcome, which had culminated in the king-size bed in his luxury hotel room.

The door opened, and the doctor, a short, youngish man in an exquisitely cut blue suit entered and shook his hand warmly. "Mr. Jameson," he smiled. "So good to see you again. Please do be seated."

Kileen sat in a black leather chair, making no protest when the doctor took his scarred and mottled hands in his own beautifully manicured ones, turning them over to examine first the palms, then the backs. "Yes," he nodded. "They are coming along quite nicely. I think with additional split-thickness grafting, and perhaps the new collagen treatments as well, we can make a major improvement here."

"What about my face, Doctor?" There was genuine emotion in the terrorist's voice as he raised his black eyes to the surgeon's pale, calm ones.

The doctor, whose success with burn victims was unmatched in Europe, sat on the edge of a narrow chart table and looked thoughtfully at Kileen's scars for a long while, reaching out to touch the thick, white ridges about his jaw, then cupping his own soft chin in his fingers. "Yes," he finally nodded. "The grafts I did in July have healed well, with less of the keloid than I would have expected." He prodded the heavy rope of scar tissue below the Irishman's ear again. "You see, it is this heavy scarring that gives me some concern. There is no blood supply here, which accounts for the white, shiny texture. It is the frequent problem we encounter with a fair skin such as yours." He smiled at some private recollection. "Though I might observe that very dark Negroid skin exhibits many of the very same keloid tendencies. Ironic, is it not?"

"What can be done, then?" asked Kileen, ignoring the surgeon's attempt to lead him into a discussion of his fascinating studies of human skin types, a topic on which he frequently lectured before international medical groups.

The doctor's smooth face creased in a disappointed smile. "Ah, well," he said, adjusting his glasses and tracing a delicate double line down the borders of the heavy ridge of scar tissue with the tips of his gentle fingers. "Since the first corrective operation to lay in those large sections of grafted skin has healed so well, I can now excise this great, unsightly section of thickened scar tissue, approximating the edges with healthy skin, which will then have a good blood supply. Of course," he added, "in order for it to be done properly and ensure that there will be no recurrence of the heavy scarring, the incision must be closed with hundreds of tiny sutures. A very laborious and time-consuming procedure . . ."

"And very expensive as well?" Kileen interrupted.

The little surgeon smiled and shrugged helplessly.

"When would you like to operate?" asked Kileen, reaching for his wallet, which contained a bank draft from one of Zurich's most respected financial institutions.

"Perhaps tomorrow afternoon, at my suburban clinic by the lake," smiled the surgeon.

Kileen nodded, passing him the draft. The doctor pocketed it without bothering to look at the row of zeros behind the first number. "You should plan on staying at the clinic for a few days afterwards," he said. "I think you'll find the time not too painful, and we can offer a number of diversions to make your stay more pleasant. We have an excellent new chef now, you know."

Kileen raised his eyebrows appreciatively. "I'll look forward to it," he said. "And speaking of diversions . . ." He glanced meaningfully in the direction of the reception room beyond the closed door.

"Her name is Annette," said the surgeon, part of whose excellent reputation came from his recognition of the fact that *all* the needs of his wealthy patients required attending to. "She is twenty-six, from a small village in the Alps, university educated . . . Perhaps you would care to have her dine with you this evening?"

"That would be very pleasant," said Kileen. "Thank you for thinking of it."

The surgeon stood, straightening the crease in his trousers. "The nurse will be in to draw some blood samples in a moment," he said. "And I shall ask Annette to speak with you on your way out." He extended his small, soft hand to Kileen. "Until tomorrow then, Mr. Jameson."

"Just one more question," said the Irishman. "What will I look like after this surgery?"

The little man smiled. "Far better than you do now, I promise you." The smile broadened. "I'm afraid you'll have to have a new photo for your passport, however." He reached up once more, caressing the line of Kileen's jaw, running his fingers up to the cheekbones, across to the crooked bridge of the nose. "I think you shall be a very handsome fellow. But far different than you are now."

Kileen smiled, revealing the stainless-steel screws at the edges of his gums. "Well," he said, "I imagine many of the people who know me well will sleep better because of that anyway."

The Swiss surgeon laughed nervously, not quite certain what his strange American patient meant by the odd remark.

BOOK TWO

City of Angels

With drums and guns, and guns and drums
The enemy nearly slew ye.
My darling dear, you look so queer,
Oh, Johnny, I hardly knew ye.

IRISH FOLK SONG

CHAPTER ONE

Tea & Sympathy

"OH MY GOD, he's beautiful!" Samantha whispered.

Kelly stood beneath the arch of James Queally-Smythe's old-fashioned front doorway, gazing down a long, dimly lit corridor that cut straight through the house to a pair of open French doors leading out to a sunlit veranda on the other end. A tall, dark-haired young man wearing a green blazer stood framed in the doors at the back of the house. He was leaning nervously against a black wrought-iron railing looking at something beyond her field of vision.

Kelly felt Samantha nudging her from behind, her stage whisper louder than before. "Did you hear what I just said, Kelly?"

"I heard you," hissed Kelly. "Now shut up." The two of them had just arrived at the old tile-roofed house, having walked up the Major's curving drive from the canyon road below, and stepped into a recessed porch—which was filled with planters shaped like elephants and hanging decorations of hammered brass that might have been wind chimes—to find the front door standing open.

"I think I'm going to pee my pants," Samantha sighed. "Do you think we should just go in, or what?"

The handsome boy on the veranda at the other end of the house smiled at something, still not looking their way, and Kelly felt her heart beginning to pound. "I think we'd better ring first," she said, examining the elaborately carved door frame for a bell. If there was one, she couldn't find it, and she raised her hand to knock instead.

A shadow moved within the house, and a short, brown-skinned man wearing a white jacket and an elaborate turban appeared from a doorway halfway along the corridor. He spotted Kelly and Samantha on the porch and hurried to the front door to greet them.

"Good afternoon, misses," he said in a melodious voice. "I am very sorry. I did not hear you ring."

Kelly smiled, feeling slightly foolish, and said, "We didn't . . ."

"We couldn't find anything to ring," confessed Samantha.

"Ah, that often happens!" The Indian servant sighed dramatically, then stepped out onto the porch and pointed up to a large brass bell hidden among the wind chimes.

"We saw that, but we didn't know if we were really supposed to ring it," said Samantha.

"Exactly so." The little man rolled his eyes in exasperation. "I am telling the Major repeatedly that we must purchase an electric bell, but he will not hear of it."

Samantha giggled. "Why not?"

Kelly elbowed her to silence. "We were, uh, invited," she said. "For tea."

The servant looked up at Samantha, who stood a good foot taller than he in the heels she wore with her yellow sundress. "The Major likes the sound of the old bell, even though visitors will seldom ring it," he explained before turning to Kelly and bowing his head slightly. "Of course you dear ladies are most eagerly expected. If you will please to follow me." He turned on his heel and walked away down the corridor with surprising speed.

Kelly and Samantha looked at each other, then followed him, hurrying to keep up, and peering off into a succession of side rooms filled with massive pieces of dark, carved furniture. "Except that there's no cobwebs, this place looks like the Haunted Mansion at Disneyland," Samantha whispered. "Just look at all that old junk."

Kelly, who had spent the better part of her childhood prowling the art and antiques markets of the East Coast with Katherine, said nothing. She recognized the distinctive shape of a Chippendale settee in a room that also contained what appeared to be a graceful eighteenth-century spinet. In another room, a painting of dancers hung above a massive fireplace; a Degas, she thought.

They reached the French doors, and the Indian servant stood aside to let them pass onto the veranda. The young man in the green blazer turned and regarded them with piercing blue eyes. "Hello," he said, extending his hand and taking a halting step toward them. "I'm Brian."

Samantha nearly knocked Kelly over in her haste to grab his hand. "I'm Samantha Simms," she gushed, hanging on to him with both hands and letting her eyes drift up to the top of his head, which was more than three inches above her own, despite her heels. "I want to be the first to welcome you to Pacific Palisades."

"Sorry, Sam, you'll have to be the second," called a familiar voice.

The handsome boy looked around in obvious embarrassment, and Sam followed his gaze to Brenda Gaynor. She was sitting in a low patio chair, most of her long legs showing beneath the skirt of the short green dress she was wearing. Beside her sat the old major, who looked very British in a navy blue blazer with a silk ascot at the throat. "I'm afraid she's got you there, my girl," laughed the old man, hoisting himself up out of his chair and striding across the flagstones to greet the new arrivals. "So good of you both to come."

"I'm happy to meet you, Samantha," said the handsome boy, avoiding her liquid brown eyes, and, Kelly noted with a sinking heart, fixing his gaze on Sam's magnificent, and not-too-well-concealed, cleavage.

The Major smiled his perfect white-toothed smile at Kelly, and his watery blue eyes twinkled beneath his fierce, bushy eyebrows. "You both look delightful, my dears," he said. "What a pleasure for an old man to be surrounded by such loveliness in his own home."

Kelly smiled at the flowery compliment, letting him pump her hand, and glancing over at Sam and Brian. Her voluptuous friend was saying something that Kelly couldn't make out over the Major's jolly chatter. Brian was smiling uneasily and nodding back at her.

Then, suddenly, the Major had dropped Kelly's hand, sidestepping gracefully over to Sam and nudging his grandson gently aside, and Brian O'Malley was standing before Kelly, gazing down into her soul with those incredible blue eyes. "I, uh, understand I've got you to thank for this little party," he said, shyly extending his hand. "Thanks."

Kelly's eyes darted over to Sam. Her friend winked and turned back to the Major, who, Kelly noticed, was just as fascinated with Sam's cleavage as Brian had been. "It was actually the Major's idea," said Kelly, looking back up into Brian's eyes and feeling the warmth from his hand radiating sparks of chemical energy up her arm and through her body. She tore her eyes away from his, looking past him to Brenda, who sat in her chair, sipping something from a tall glass and aiming her crossed legs provocatively at Brian. "All I did was invite a couple of friends along," said Kelly, hating herself for having included the treacherous little redhead.

"Well, it was very kind of you all the same," said the boy, as though he were reciting a difficult speech he had memorized for school. "Is it true that you live just down the road from my grandfather?"

Kelly laughed and said, "I'm just the girl next door." He wrinkled his brow, and she wondered if he was familiar with the American phrase.

Brian's frown disappeared, and he flashed her a little smile. "Judy Garland," he said. "*Meet Me in St. Louis.*"

She stared at him.

"The BBC showed it on the telly . . . on television . . . last Christmas. It's one of me . . . my mother's favorites . . ."

The Major's white head swung around to look at him, the watery blue eyes narrowing. The boy's face flushed and he lowered his eyes to the flagstones. "That is, it was . . ." he murmured. "She passed away recently."

Kelly squeezed his hand, which had suddenly gone damp in hers. "I know," she said awkwardly. "The Major told me. I'm so sorry, Brian."

The Major stepped up to them, his concern of the moment before seemingly forgotten. He beamed at the young couple, spreading his arms wide to touch both their shoulders. "Well now," he boomed in a loud, cheery voice, "enough of this idle chitchat. What do you young folks say we all settle down and have some tea, eh?"

Kelly looked away from Brian's tortured face as the old man offered Samantha his arm and led the way toward the far end of the veranda, where a large table was laid with linen and crystal. "Ranjee," he bellowed, "bring the tea!"

"STUPID SODDING BASTARD!"

Billy Quinn stood before the mirror in his private bathroom—Brian O'Malley's private bathroom—glaring at his reflection. He had very nearly blown Kileen's entire bloody setup this afternoon with his tongue-tied performance. And as if that hadn't been bad enough, he'd made that daft remark about the old Judy Garland movie being his mum's—Brian O'Malley's mum's—favorite, talking about the Major's daughter in the present tense, as though she were still alive. "Your mum is supposed to be dead, you damned fool," he growled, "killed by a nationalist bomb."

"Jesus!"

He turned away from the mirror in disgust, padding barefoot into the large, brightly decorated bedroom the old man had prepared especially for him and stepping out onto a small balcony overlooking the vast, unbroken carpet of lights to the south. Lights running so far away they disappeared at the horizon.

L.A.

Christ, the size of the place!

Thank God he wasn't supposed to know anything about Los Angeles except what he'd seen in the films—most of which, he had gathered during the course of the afternoon, was untrue anyway. Kelly had said there were no palm trees on the beaches, and the others had all agreed that the legendary Hollywood district was no more than a dirty and dangerous slum neighborhood where you were more likely to be killed for your wallet than see a movie star, and that most of the films these days were really made in a place called Burbank—or Canada—anyhow.

Hollywood, it seemed, was made of lies.

In a way, Billy, who'd spent his whole life living with lies—loyalist lies about the Catholic nationalists, and the nationalists' own lies about the Protestants and their British guardians—liked that. He thought it helped to explain why everyone he'd so far met here in California was so eager to accept him as Brian O'Malley.

Perhaps Kileen had been right. Maybe he could pull it off. After all, he didn't really have to *be* Brian O'Malley. He only had to be what they *wanted* Brian O'Malley to be. As in a Hollywood film, he was beginning to discover, his role as the Major's wealthy grandson had little to do with reality.

A quick, painful flash of Brian O'Malley—the *genuine* Brian O'Malley—filled his mind, and he wondered guiltily how the other boy was holding up under his harsh captivity. Driving the image of the hapless prisoner from his thoughts, Billy dropped into a metal and plastic chair, propping his feet on the iron balcony railing and attempting to assess how he was pulling off his masquerade so far. The old man—O'Malley's grandfather, with whom Billy had expected to encounter the most difficulty—had been pathetically easy to convince. At first, he had thought, almost too easy.

From the moment the old duffer had clapped eyes on him at the airport yesterday afternoon, James Queally-Smythe—"Call me Major, my boy. All my friends do"—had swallowed Billy's transparent act without question. Clasping the startled teenager to his bony breast and staining his green school blazer with his great, greasy tears, the old fellow had wheezed out his grief over the loss of Brian's "dear parents," promising to provide him a warm and loving home and to look after him as if he were Brian's own dear father.

Although Billy had quickly come to realize that the old man was acting more out of grief and, perhaps, guilt at having stepped out of his daughter's life long before her death, Billy had been uneasy over the whole encounter. His stomach after the fourteen-hour jet flight, already queasy with the anticipation of having to face the old fellow, had threatened to turn over on him as Queally-Smythe had tearfully poured out half a lifetime of regrets to the stranger he'd naturally assumed was his grandson.

At some point during the emotional airport reunion, Billy remembered that he had abruptly pulled away from the Major, casting his eyes down at his shoes and muttering a string of halfhearted one-word replies to the other's endless daft queries about his health, the length of the flight from London, whether or not he'd eaten yet . . . His brain had gone numb with the torrent of sentimental words pouring out of the old man, and he hadn't been certain what he was supposed to do or say. Nothing Kileen told him had prepared him for that.

Evidently, he had played it just right, however, for at the sight of his obvious discomfiture, the old man had suddenly stopped his maudlin snuffling, pausing to blow his nose into his silk handkerchief and drying his eyes in embarrassment, then quickly launching into a windy apology for having distressed his grandson with such talk.

Together they had moved through the vast airport terminal while the little Indian fellow had collected Billy's luggage and hurried ahead to pack it all into the cavernous boot of the Major's great silver Bentley, which he had brazenly parked right before the front doors.

Then they had driven out of the airport, following a ramp up onto a ten-lane concrete freeway, melding into a gleaming river of cars, speeding silently along in the Bentley, and eventually turning off into the hills above the city—passing so many green-lawned mansions on the way that the counting of them had made Billy's head spin—finally entering a steep canyon road, slowing at the top to drive through a pair of tall iron gates and up a long private road to the old man's own mansion, a sprawling Spanish castle of a place set high on a hilltop and overlooking the entire coastline.

Since then, no effort had been spared to see to the creature comforts of Billy Quinn.

Christ, but the old boy must be loaded with money, he reflected now: Billy had spent enough years in the houses of his mother's rich employers to know high-quality goods when he saw them, but he had never seen the like of the furnishings in Queally-Smythe's house. He had roamed through the huge place several times following his arrival the day before, wandering aimlessly from room to room like a country farmer in a grand museum, trying hard not to be seen gawking at the fine paintings, the lovingly polished silverware, the thick Oriental carpets on the floors.

Even the room they had prepared for him—nearly as big on its own as his Aunt Min's entire cottage in Kilkee, and taking up one whole end of the mansion's topmost floor—was far more luxurious than any room belonging to any of the rich brats of the families his mother had worked for.

Billy Quinn wished they could all see him now; all those pale, snotty Percivals and Quentins whose cruel childhood taunts he had endured. Him

with his very own personal Sony color television set and VCR, his own battery-powered portable telephone, and his very own bath with both a tub
and a separate glass-walled showerbath, both in the same bleeding room, if
you could even believe that.

And, according to the Major, he was soon to have his own car as well,
some priceless old Jag the old fellow had kept going on and on about over
their late supper tonight. Or, if he, Billy, preferred, a shiny new sports convertible of his own choosing. He was to decide for himself tomorrow.

Billy Quinn grinned, leaning back in the chair and letting the cool night
air bathe his naked chest. He saw it as proof of his acceptance that the old
boy had gone all out for him after having had the chance to look him over
for a day, even arranging the little tea with the three smashing California
girls for this afternoon.

And, God, but weren't they something?

Brenda, the little redhead, who was, he suspected, a right little bitch
when she wasn't flashing that movie-star smile of hers, had been all over
him from the moment she'd come in, rubbing up against him at first, then
dropping her little arse into that low, low chair, deliberately letting him look
up her dress, and right in front of the old man himself. Billy squeezed his
legs together at the very thought of her, the sensible part of his brain telling
him to stay well away from her kind unless he wanted to get himself in really big trouble, fast.

Then the other two girls had arrived. Samantha, the tall, sultry one, with
her flowing dark curls and great round boobs, and the shy, pretty blonde
from down the hill . . . Kelly. Quiet but beautiful, and emanating a warmth
that had nearly taken his breath away.

She was the one who had got him so tongue-tied that he'd almost blown
his cover this afternoon, making the potentially deadly mistake of embroi-
dering something he'd done with his own living mother into the vague fantasy he'd conjured of Brian O'Malley's mother . . .

Billy had seen the old man's shaggy head snap around at the mention of
his dead daughter. Realized instantly he'd screwed up. Christ, how was he
to have known? Perhaps the dead woman had hated that old movie he'd
said she loved. Perhaps she never even watched the telly, or was stone deaf
or something. Billy Quinn had no way of knowing, for the personal details
Kileen had given him to memorize about Brian O'Malley's parents were
thin; a cold collection of dates and facts and names. Not enough.

Not nearly enough to maintain his clumsy impersonation for very long.

Billy suddenly remembered the advice of the little freedom fighter who had accompanied him on the flight from Dublin to Belfast. *Never volunteer any information.* Advice he intended to follow in future.

Still, he thought, he had gotten away with that blunder too, just as he had at the airport the day before, by pretending to look grieved when what he had really been feeling was blind panic. He couldn't count on that kind of luck a third time, though. He'd just have to be far more careful of what he said from now on.

He let his mind drift back to the blond girl. Kelly, the girl next door, had looked good enough to eat in her flouncy pink dress, and he was glad he was going to be seeing her again. Tomorrow was Saturday—no school— and she'd invited him to come for a swim at her house down the road. On Monday, she'd promised to drive him to the high school in her convertible.

Billy Quinn's grin broadened, and he wondered how long Kileen planned for him to live this posh life before contacting him to explain what in the hell he was supposed to be playing at here. He hoped the scarred old free-dom fighter would hold off for a few days at least. He was beginning to en-joy California immensely, and he wanted to be here long enough to see a bit of Los Angeles.

The stark image of Brian O'Malley lying trussed up and weeping on his dirty mattress returned, and Billy guiltily remembered that however long he stayed here enjoying the sweet life was how long the other boy would be confined to the drafty upstairs room in the cold, cheerless farmhouse north of Belfast.

The thought lasted no more than a moment, and he drove it away this time by reasoning that Brian O'Malley had a whole lifetime of California girls and shiny convertibles ahead of him, while Billy Quinn would never in his life have such an opportunity again. Besides, Billy reminded himself, Brian O'Malley was a spoiled little Protestant prick who had a measure of suffering coming to him, for the insult he'd delivered by trying to bribe Billy, if for nothing else.

And after all, it wasn't as if the lads were going to really hurt him.

He snatched a Marlboro—a genuine, honest-to-God American Marlboro, not the poor imitations they made in West Germany and shipped through-out Europe disguised as the real thing—from behind his ear, lit it with a match from a book on the tiny round table beside his chair and took a deep, satisfying drag.

Despite the fact he'd read that Brian O'Malley was not known to smoke, Billy had decided that the cigarettes—which he had purchased in the duty free on board the airliner, and to which he had been firmly addicted ever since he had been old enough to cadge small items from the shelves of Belfast shopkeepers—were no more than a minor risk to his cover, although, this morning, he had noted that little Indian fellow looking at him strangely when he had walked unexpectedly into Billy's bedroom with a stack of towels and seen him smoking.

Well, fuck him, thought Billy. Kileen himself had admitted when asked that nobody really knew if the real Brian O'Malley had ever smoked or not. If it turned out that he hadn't, Billy could always say he'd picked up the habit after the deaths of his "dear parents." And if that little wanker of a Hindu servant didn't like it, he could get stuffed.

All in all, Billy decided—except for the remark about his mum's favorite film, which he'd managed to cover instantly—he'd so far done a first-rate job of being Brian O'Malley. He closed his eyes, and took another deep drag of the wonderful American cigarette, trying to imagine what Kelly Huston would look like in her swimming costume tomorrow.

JAMES QUEALLY-SMYTHE sat at his massive oak desk—the desk taken from the set of the lavish Revolutionary War musical comedy he had directed; the comical British Prime Minister's desk, now jammed into his crowded, book-lined study—sipping his nightly scotch.

He had come into the study after supper to work on his military history, as was his nightly habit, but again the research papers and the unfinished pages of his manuscript lay undisturbed to one side of the desk, and he was gazing instead at a small photograph in a silver frame.

The photo, which he had taken down from a shelf filled with framed awards and autographed pictures of film stars, showed a young, dark-haired woman with a child on her hip. The woman, her back against a white rail fence enclosing a green pasture, was squinting sourly into bright sunlight, the raven-haired child gazing off at something just beyond the range of the camera.

Queally-Smythe had taken the photo of his daughter and grandchild himself, and only he knew that the boy was looking down the road at his father, who was leading a lathered polo pony back toward the pair, following the hard-won practice match he had just completed. He lifted the photo into the light of the Tiffany reading lamp, squinting intently at the faces of mother and child.

The occasion of the photograph had been the old man's one and only visit to his daughter's home, a handsome Georgian estate set like a jewel among the rolling green hills east of Londonderry.

That had been twelve years ago.

Queally-Smythe had been up in Scotland for the summer, struggling with the final draft of a ponderous medieval costume drama, when the telephone in his rented lakeside cottage had rung one afternoon.

The voice on the other end of the line—which he hadn't at first recognized—had been Victoria's. His daughter, sounding quite grown up, and every bit as cool as her aristocratic mother had always been, had heard that he was filming in Scotland and wondered if he'd like to fly over at the weekend to see his grandson.

He had gone over to Northern Ireland filled with the joy of expectation of a tearful reunion with Victoria, learning only after his arrival that the visit had been the idea of Charles O'Malley, the son-in-law he'd never met. Orphaned himself at an early age, O'Malley, it seemed, had wanted his young son to know at least one of his grandparents, and so he had insisted that Victoria extend the invitation.

The weekend had been chilly and awkward, Victoria regarding her estranged father with polite if undisguised contempt while Charles, a decent enough young chap as it had turned out, had filled the embarrassing silences between father and daughter with friendly talk of horses and bitter commentary on the adverse economic effects of the tiny nation's political troubles.

Throughout the ordeal, Queally-Smythe—whose temper was legend among his peers in the film community—had meekly endured Victoria's livid glances and barely civil remarks, in return for the opportunity of spending a few precious hours with his only grandchild. Together, laughing child and doting grandfather had tramped the green fields, shouted themselves hoarse at the thrilling sight of Charles displaying his not inconsiderable skills at polo, shared a solitary picnic by a rushing stream . . . Happy hours. Hours Queally-Smythe, now nearing seventy-five, had never thought it possible to recapture.

He wondered if the boy remembered any of it. Probably not. Little Brian had been going on six at the time. Or was it only five? He couldn't rightly recall.

He had gone back to his film location in Scotland at the end of the weekend, hoping for another invitation before he returned to America. When, after a couple of weeks, it had not been forthcoming, he had issued one of his own, asking them to bring the boy down to watch him film a magnificent action sequence, replete with mounted knights in armor and the scaling of a castle wall. Irresistible enticements to a small boy, he remembered having thought at the time.

Charles had called a few days later with an apologetic refusal, saying the boy had come down with bronchitis shortly after his grandfather's visit and was unable to travel . . . An illness Queally-Smythe had no doubt that his bitter daughter had blamed on him.

And that had been the end of it. Afterwards, he had sent birthday cards and holiday gifts to the child for a while. Never receiving a reply, he had stopped sending the greetings when the anticipation of the continued rejection had become too painful for him to bear.

The old man sighed and pushed the picture away, leaning back in his leather chair and sipping thoughtfully at his scotch. He had another chance with the boy now, and he didn't intend to let it pass.

He smiled, thinking of the way the girls had looked at young Brian this afternoon, all three of them vying openly for the attention of the handsome lad with his raven hair and serious mien. He'd have to warn the boy about female wiles, he happily reflected, else he'd soon be something more than a grandfather.

He was especially proud of the way the boy had handled himself in what might have been a difficult social situation. There had been one especially awkward moment, when the subject of Brian's mother had popped up, and Queally-Smythe had seen for the first time the depth of the grief etched on his grandson's handsome face and cursed himself for having pushed the youngster too soon into attending the well-intentioned but nonetheless silly tea party, realizing in that moment that he had only devised the afternoon's entertainment for his own selfish ends, wanting to show the boy off.

The awkward moment had passed quickly, however, young Brian recovering nicely and going on to table, where he had shyly questioned the girls about their school, American football, films and a host of similar subjects, dividing his attention equally among the three of them like a proper gentleman, even if his gaze had never strayed too far from the serious little blond girl from down the road, with whom he had obviously been much taken.

For all of that, the boy had given each of the others their fair share of smiles too, listening closely to their silly, breathless comments, making them feel at ease, when it was all too obvious that he himself had been uneasy. The ability to comport oneself socially among strangers was a difficult skill that could not be learned, reflected Queally-Smythe, one that came only after generations of good breeding. Good breeding that had been pleasantly evident in Brian O'Malley's bearing this afternoon.

And, the old man admitted to himself, he had thoroughly enjoyed hosting the little get-together, listening closely to the conversation of the young people and interjecting remarks of his own into the few awkward silences.

Queally-Smythe flushed with pleasure as he remembered the soft touch of the girls' smooth hands in his own wrinkled ones, the exquisite curve of their limbs beneath their bright party dresses in the afternoon sunshine, the delightful sound of their feminine laughter on the warm breeze. And it occurred to him that having the boy around was not going to be nearly the burden he had originally envisioned.

Things were actually turning out splendidly.

Better than splendidly.

He took another thoughtful sip of his drink, then opened the center drawer of the desk and reverently lifted out the heavy, cream-colored envelope that had arrived by messenger this very morning. Turning back the flap, he slipped out the engraved announcement card within, scanning the smaller personal notice enclosed, which requested the favour of his reply.

He let his weak eyes savor each of the elaborately scripted and composed words on the card, wondering again who on earth had been responsible for this, and deciding to save the momentous news contained in the announcement until Monday, when he could call the proper parties to officially confirm that his newly arrived grandson might be included, as well.

Major James Queally-Smythe still couldn't believe the great good fortune that had brought him the announcement.

Especially after all these years!

He sensed a familiar presence in the room and turned to see Ranjee hovering in the doorway. No telling how long the little beggar had been standing there silently watching him. "Yes, Ranjee?" he said, slipping the cards back into the center drawer of his desk and speaking impatiently, somewhat resentful of the unexpected intrusion.

"I will retire now, if there is nothing else, Major," said the servant.

The old man nodded curtly. He had not yet even told Ranjee the astonishing news. Though the servant had been with him for years, had, in fact, been his "native boy" when he had served in India, he was, after all, still a servant.

No, he decided, this news must be withheld until it could be properly shared with young Brian. Blood thicker than water and all that. His brow creased, the fierce, bushy eyebrows coming together in studied concentration. He wasn't yet finding it that easy to converse with the boy. Hadn't, for instance, been able to get more than a few monosyllabic replies out of him at supper tonight. Still, he supposed that was natural, considering the circumstances. Certainly Victoria hadn't spoken kindly to Brian about the father whom she felt had deserted her—had possibly even berated him to his grandson. He felt again a deep pang of regret over not having taken the time to know his daughter better when she had still been a girl. Sighed. Spilt milk and all that. He was sure the boy's almost frightened reserve before him now was something that would pass in time.

Queally-Smythe looked up somewhat guiltily to see the Indian still standing in the doorway, his dark eyes gleaming out from the mask of his dusky face, a sure sign that there was something on his mind. "Well, is there something else?"

Ranjee inclined his head slightly. "It is a thing of no great consequence," he said nervously. "I hesitate to speak of it . . ."

"Out with it, you bloody heathen," barked the Major in the same gruff, good-natured military tone he had been using with the servant since the day he had picked him up as a starving ten-year-old, crouched half naked at the edge of a teeming Calcutta gutter.

"It is about the young man," Ranjee began.

"My grandson," Queally-Smythe corrected. "You are henceforth always to refer to the boy as either my grandson, or as Master Brian."

"Young Master Brian," said Ranjee a bit peevishly. "I have seen him smoking cigarettes in his room."

The old man leaned back in his chair, staring at the Indian in mild astonishment. "Cigarettes, eh? Mmmm, can't say I like that very much," he said after a long moment. "Not good for a youngster to get into the habit too soon."

"I have discovered this quite by accident," Ranjee apologized, and the Major realized that the little fellow was quite genuinely distressed over the matter, "however, I felt it my duty to advise you."

"Quite right," said Queally-Smythe, suppressing a small grin at the servant's exaggerated concern over what was in fact a small problem. Still and all, he knew that Ranjee, a strict Hindu, meant well. No point in offending him by pointing out that it was not really his business to criticize the boy.

"Not saying I want you spying on him, you understand—nothing of the sort—but this does involve the boy's health, after all, so you were correct to come to me with it." The Major cleared his throat noisily. "You may retire now, Ranjee. I shall speak to young Brian about the cigarettes myself."

Relieved, the servant bowed his head and slipped silently away into the depths of the house. When he had gone, Queally-Smythe sipped his scotch, considering the small speech he would make to his grandson at breakfast, and remembering how he and a schoolmate had nipped off behind the school chapel at around the age of twelve in order to experiment with the joys of tobacco—their chosen material being two of the headmaster's finest Havana cigars, "borrowed" direct from the old boy's humidor, as he recalled.

He chuckled softly to himself, draining off the last of the scotch and surprised to discover that he was quite enjoying his new role as mentor to the handsome youngster. Such small difficulties as had just arisen were bound to pop up from time to time, he supposed, difficulties that he would have to manage with fairness and common sense, just as he had done with the young, homesick troops he had commanded in his army days.

It seemed to the Major that a breath of fresh air had suddenly swept into his rather stuffy life.

CHAPTER TWO

California Dreaming

EARLY MORNING RAIN.

Cold rain.

A rain to chill your soul.

He slithered forward another few feet on his stomach, the cold, viscous mud oozing down the front of his trousers, settling uncomfortably against the naked skin of his crotch. Ahead, something moved, and he froze where he was.

"What the fuck are you doing? Go on!" He heard Tommy Mackay's panicked whisper behind him, felt the other boy prodding the bottom of his shoe with the muzzle of the ridiculous old shotgun he had insisted on bringing along with him, a rusty blunderbuss fit for nothing but shooting birds.

The two of them lay in the shadow of a broken wall at the edge of a deserted car park. Twenty yards away, at the front of the park, the olive drab bulk of an armored car sat facing out toward the street, clouds of white vapor rising into the slate-gray sky from the grumbling exhaust stack of its powerful diescl engine.

The armored vehicle's single heavy machine gun was trained on the intersection of the next street, guarding the nightmarish cage of iron and wire the bastards had stretched across the pavement the day before.

"Look at that shit," whispered Tommy, crawling up beside him and pointing to the cage.

Billy Quinn shrugged. He had seen such devices used to seal off troublesome parts of the Catholic districts before. "Security checkpoints," they called them. "I've got mud in my crotch," he complained.

"But don't you see what they're doing?" Tommy's voice was hoarse with emotion.

Billy watched as two middle-aged women with drooping shopping bags were escorted into the cage by the pair of British soldiers posted on the Catholic side. The wire gate closed behind them, trapping them inside, and another soldier dumped the meager contents of the bags onto the damp surface of a makeshift plywood table, then poked through the women's worn pocketbooks, questioning them sharply the whole time. After a few moments, the women were permitted to replace the articles in their shopping bags, and another gate was opened on the opposite side of the cage. A laughing soldier gestured with the muzzle of his automatic rifle, and the women were let out to proceed on their way. One of them looked back and yelled something at the soldiers as two more shoppers were admitted into the enclosure.

"My da says they got the idea for that from the Australians," said Tommy. "It's how they line their sheep up for the slaughter."

"They got it from the Nazis," Billy explained patiently, recalling a favorite theory he'd once heard his uncle propose.

"Who's that?" Tommy looked at him, the freckles standing out against his skin.

"Nazis. You know, the ones that gassed all the Jews in the war," said Billy. "My uncle says they used to herd Jews about like that in the part of Warsaw they'd set aside for them to live in."

"They gassed all the Jews?" Tommy was incredulous. "Then how'd those Jews come to own the sweet shop down in Meath Street?"

Billy was growing increasingly impatient with his dim friend's ignorance of the world. "They didn't gas *all* of the Jews, stupid, only the ones in Poland and places like that. Besides," he added, "the Nazis lost the war to the Americans and had to give up the gassing before they got them all."

He looked out at the cage again. The soldiers had an enraged old man before their table now, had him turning out his pockets onto the plywood. The old man was screaming obscenities at them.

The boys watched in silence until the pensioner was ejected into the street. Tears of rage streaming down his cheeks, he stumbled to the next corner and disappeared into a pub.

"My ma says we're like the Jews here," Billy observed bitterly. He backed into the shelter of the broken wall and regarded the soldiers. "And those are the Nazis. They'd just as soon kill us all as look at us," he said pointedly.

"Well, I don't care," said Tommy. "I'm gonna make the bastards pay for what they did."

"What, because some soldier felt up your sister in the cage?" Billy tried to make light of the routine outrage, which had taken place the previous evening when Sheila Mackay, a rather plain fifteen-year-old with big boobs and the same wiry red hair and freckles as Tommy, had been on her way home from shopping with her mother. He had heard of far worse things than that being done to Catholic girls by the soldiers and had only come along with Tommy this morning to try to show his friend the absolute impossibility of retaliating against machine guns and armored cars with his uncle's old gamekeeper's gun.

Tommy's face was white with rage. "They poked at her tits with their rifles and accused her of smuggling. And then they called her a great cow of a Paddy whore in front of our own mother," he said, his high, thin voice very close to breaking. "Now she's afraid to go out of the house and our ma lay up in bed, crying half the night."

"They'll just kill you like they did Tim Ryan when he tossed that brick at the police Land Rover last summer," Billy said matter-of-factly. "Then your ma'll be crying over your casket, won't she?"

"Fuck you, then, Quinn," sniffed Tommy, wiping his runny nose on his sleeve. "I thought we were mates."

Billy shook his head in frustration at the other's thickheadedness. However, his obligation to his friend was clear. "What do you want me to do?" he sighed.

Tommy reached into his woolen jacket, extracting a soda bottle filled with equal parts of petrol and washing powder and plugged off with a wad of damp cloth torn from one of his mother's old bedsheets. "Just go round and make a racket out in the street by the cage so the pricks in the armored car won't notice me creeping up on them," he said.

"If you'll leave the gun," said Billy, knowing that the mere sight of the weapon would be the only excuse the bastards would need to shoot his friend dead.

"I'll fuck-all leave the gun," Tommy protested. "My uncle'd have my balls."

Billy folded his arms resolutely. "We'll hide it here, just by the wall," he said reasonably. "We can come back and get it tonight."

Tommy looked dubious. "It'll get all wet."

"We'll clean it after." Billy's resolve was firm. "I'm not in unless you leave the gun."

Tommy grudgingly relented, pushing aside a mound of broken stones by the wall and carefully covering the precious gun with them.

Billy grinned and punched his mate's arm, knowing full well that the cowardly soldiers would hesitate to shoot a kid if they saw that he had no weapon. "Give me two minutes to get around front. And be sure to keep the petrol bomb hidden in your coat till you're right up there on their blind side," he counseled. "You sure you know where to put it?"

"Engine c . . . compartment?" Tommy's pale lips were blue with the cold.

"Right, 'cause if you put it on top, the fire won't get inside anyhow, and all you'll do is spoil the paint." Billy repeated the instruction he'd overheard from a group of men loitering outside Brennan's Pub weeks earlier. "But if you put it in the engine compartment, the flames will kill the motor. Then they'll be stuck, and the fire'll draw a mob." He grinned. "With any luck, the bastards'll have a proper riot on their hands." He winked at Tommy, backed around the corner of a wall and took off at a fast run down a narrow alleyway, intending to circle the block and create a diversion by hurling a few paving stones from the other side at the soldiers guarding the cage.

"All right, you! Where the fuck are you running to?"

The voice came booming out of the shadows at the far end of the alley, and Billy looked up to see two hulking nightmare figures—a pair of patrolling British troopers in full battle dress—blocking the way in front of him. Skidding to a stop, he turned, started back in the opposite direction. Back toward Tommy Mackay. His friend was down on his knees, scrabbling among the rocks.

"No, Tommy! For Jesus' sake!" Billy screamed.

"Look out! The one down the alley's got a gun!" The British trooper shouting in panic to his mate, the black paint smeared beneath his eyes making him look like a demon from hell. The muzzle of the trooper's huge automatic rifle slowly coming up as Tommy lifted the old shotgun free of the stones . . . Winking blue fire from the trooper's muzzle making a light show against the grimy bricks of the alley . . . An ear-shattering echo of gunfire an instant later.

WHOOMPH!!!!

Tommy Mackay exploding in a ball of superheated flame as the trooper's burst of armor-piercing automatic fire stitched his scrawny twelve-year-old chest, the bullets gutting him like a sacrificial lamb, striking the bottle of petrol he'd tucked back into his coat.

"Shit!" The stunned troopers staring openmouthed at the obscene orange apparition blossoming before them, filling the end of the narrow alley. Greasy flames consuming the small boy's body. The stink of charred meat drifting down on the damp wind.

Billy taking to his heels then. Running blindly past the stunned troopers. Hearing their shouted warning. The echo of more gunfire against the bricks, and himself screaming in the cold rain of a long-ago Belfast morning at the sudden fiery jolt of pain in his side . . .

"JESUS!"

Billy Quinn came awake. Eyes blinking rapidly. Heart pounding in his chest.

Sitting up among the tangled sheets of the king-size bed, he stared out at the bright California sunshine pouring through the open balcony doors, remembering where he was and feeling the horror of the old nightmare slowly beginning to subside.

The same nightmare he'd been having since he was eleven years old.

He got to his feet, fumbling on the nightstand for a cigarette. Stepped out onto the balcony and lit it, gazing out over the placid landscape at his feet. A few high, puffy clouds dotted the postcard-blue sky. Out beyond the brown hills dotted with blocks of red rooftops he could see the triangular white patches of sailboats etched against the darker blue of the sea. Nearer, the never-ending stream of autos moving up and down the broad white ribbon of a freeway. Lazy whine of a power mower somewhere down the hill. Faint smell of flowers in the air.

A perfect California day.

"Hullo there, Brian!"

He looked down to see the old man on the grass below, dressed in a flowered shirt and a pair of bush shorts that ended below his knobby knees. It took him a moment to remember who he was supposed to be. He forced a smile and raised his hand in greeting. The old man pointed to the veranda, where the Indian was setting a table. "Breakfast in ten minutes," the old man said cheerily.

Billy looked down at the cigarette in his hand, wondering if Queally-Smythe had noticed. If so, he didn't seem particularly disturbed. "Thank you, Major," he called out. "I'll just have a quick shower."

He ducked back into the bedroom, wondering if he was going to get a lecture on the evils of tobacco.

"MOTHER, what are you doing?"

Kelly was standing by the kitchen door in her old terry bathrobe, watching Katherine rummage through a bank of cabinets. The granite countertop was littered with plastic cups, paper plates and napkins.

"Oh, good morning, darling." Her mother, resplendent in white designer slacks and a shimmering green blouse looked up and beamed her a sunny smile. "I'm just seeing what we're going to need for lunch," she said. "I thought it might be fun if we barbecued, and I wanted to be sure we had enough picnic supplies.

"You're having a picnic?"

Katherine grinned and shook her head. "No, silly, *we're* having a picnic. All of us . . . Chuck is going to do chicken breasts on the grill, and I'm going to order some special deli things from Gelson's." She gnawed thoughtfully at a long fingernail. "Do you think Brian will like chicken, or should I get some cold meats and things just to be on the safe side?"

Kelly stared at her.

"Well, you did say he was coming by for a swim," said Katherine. "And we do want to make him feel at home . . ." She hesitated, evaluating her daughter's expression.

"I don't believe this," said Kelly. "Do you really think that fixing lunch for Brian is going to get Chuck a movie deal with his grandfather?" She shook her head and dropped onto a bar stool beside the counter. "I can hear it now," she said, dropping her voice to a poor approximation of the Major's hearty baritone. "'I say, Brian, what did you do today?'" "'Well, sir,'" she continued, changing over to imitate Brian, "'I went down the canyon to have a swim with the Hustons and they served me a terrific lunch of barbecued chicken. If you don't mind my saying so, sir, you should definitely consider doing a movie with those people . . .'"

"Very amusing," said Katherine. "But for your information, the Major will be coming to lunch too, and I might add that he thought it was perfectly charming of me to call and ask him."

"You called him?" Kelly was mortified. "Shit, Katherine, why did you do that?"

"I thought it would be a nice gesture to invite Brian's grandfather," Katherine said sweetly. "After all, we have been meaning to ask him over."

"Bullshit," Kelly spat. "You and Chuck have been making fun of that poor old man ever since the first time you saw him walking up the canyon in his funny hat."

Sparks flared in Katherine's eyes. "That is absolutely not true," she said.

Kelly rolled her eyes. "I don't believe this. The next thing you'll be doing is inviting Chuck's studio friends over for a piece of the action."

"Only the Kornfelds and the Andersons," Katherine said defensively.

"Well, I'm not going to be any part of it," said Kelly.

Katherine glared at her. "What is that supposed to mean?" she demanded. "This is *your* swimming party I'm going to all this trouble for, young lady!"

"My God, Mother . . . !" Kelly let her arms flop uselessly to her sides and walked away toward the back of the house.

"Where are you going?" Katherine called.

"To take lots of heavy drugs before I slash my throat, Mother," she yelled over her shoulder. "Please don't come into the bathroom. You know you can't stand the sight of blood."

"That is not in the slightest degree funny," screamed Katherine Huston.

"That's strange," Kelly fired back at her. "You thought it was hilarious when that bimbo actress said it in Chuck's last stupid TV movie."

"WELL, MY BOY, what do you think?" The Major stood at the far end of the garage beside the house, holding up the corner of a dusty tarp. A stray beam of sunlight from the open door picked out the exquisite curve of a glossy fender. Dark paint, a deep, deep shade of forest green, shone in the still, dark air.

"An XKE," breathed Billy. He took the corner of the tarp from the Major's wrinkled hand, carefully folding back the cloth to expose the long, gleaming bonnet, and then revealing the open cockpit with its deep buckets upholstered in leather the color of honey. "What's the matter with it?" he asked, running his hands across the shining paintwork. He leaned into the cockpit to touch the polished walnut steering wheel.

"The matter?" The Major sounded confused.

"Yes, I mean, why is she just sitting here idle?" Billy straightened and stood back away from the low-slung sports car. He couldn't remember ever having seen a piece of machinery quite so lovely.

The Major began to laugh. "My boy, I'm close to seventy-five years old," he said. "I drove this beauty until my damned back wouldn't let me get down into the seat anymore. Couldn't bear to part with the lovely beast, though. Just like to come down here and look at her from time to time. Ranjee takes her out for service once in a while."

He held out a set of keys, offering them to the boy. "Go ahead, start her up."

Billy Quinn opened the door, slipped into the butter-soft leather of the driver's seat. "Takes some getting used to, the American left-hand drive, you see," the old man said unnecessarily. He watched the boy insert the key into the ignition, heard the throaty rumble as the massive V-12 engine roared to life, then settled to a sweet, burbling idle through the four pipes jutting up from beneath the rear license plate. "Nothing can touch her for speed out on the open road," he said wistfully. "Not the Corvettes or even a big Mercedes. Nothing."

Queally-Smythe grinned, remembering the time twenty years earlier when the Jag had been new. "I once ran her full throttle across the Mojave Desert at night," he said in a faraway voice. "Touched one hundred and sixty miles per hour on the speedometer." He cleared his throat noisily and tried to look stern. "Damned foolish thing to do, of course . . . Expect you to have more sense than that . . . If you take her, that is."

Billy Quinn looked up at him in awe. "I can really have her?"

Queally-Smythe nodded. "Unless you'd prefer one of those new stamped-out contraptions. All paint and plastic, with their buzzing little engines . . ."

Billy shook his head vigorously. "No," he said. "This is the car I want."

The Major harrumphed loudly. "Well then, if you're sure that's your decision," he blustered, secretly delighted at the boy's wise choice. "I'll just ring up my agent about the insurance come Monday. Meanwhile, I'll have Ranjee run her down to the mechanic's for a check while you're at school, then perhaps he can take you out in the afternoon and get you used to the driving rules here."

Billy switched off the engine and sat for a moment, inhaling the rich fragrance of saddle soap and wood polish permeating the cockpit. For all his years of tinkering with cars, he'd never even sat in such a machine, let alone dreamed of driving one. He got out of the car and gently closed the door. "Thank you, Major," he said, feeling suddenly confused by the old man's generosity. For just a moment he wanted to clasp the old fellow's thin shoulders.

Then he remembered who he was. Where he was. "I promise to take proper care of her," was what he said. His brain was buzzing with visions of himself speeding down an empty California freeway—if indeed there was such a thing—in the beautiful green Jag. In his mind's eye, Kelly Huston was beside him, her long, blond hair flying back in the wind stream.

"BY GOD, will you just look at it all?" Dermot Tumelty, his good arm propped on the windowsill of the rented Toyota sedan, was happily gaping at the distant silhouettes of a dozen skyscrapers rising out of the haze of downtown Los Angeles, then peering down over the edge of the freeway at two, no, three levels of intersecting roadways carrying endless streams of traffic below them. "It looks like the city of the future, that," he said pointing with his crippled hand to the maze of soaring concrete structures supporting the multilevel interchange.

"City of shit," growled Duffy. He was trying to keep the yellow Toyota in a lane of speeding traffic while deciphering the multicolored map spread on the center console between them. He found the exit he was looking for and glanced over at the boy beside him. "You get down there among the blacks and Mexicans," he said, jerking his head toward the sprawl of low-rise industrial buildings stretching away to the brown hills in the east, "and you'll get a taste of the *real* city of the future."

"What do you mean?" Tumelty was peeling the cellophane from the package of Twinkies he had purchased in an airport snack bar several minutes earlier, while Duffy had been off renting the car. He lifted the sweet yellow cakes to his nose, breathing deeply.

"Anarchy," said Duffy. "That's where the blacks rebelled and started burning the city after the cops beat one of them on the video a few years back. Not many cops down there now," he said knowledgeably. "They say the buggers are afraid to go in because gangs of armed blacks set up ambushes for them. No law but the law of the gun. You go down in there today and they'll kill you straightaway."

"The blacks? What for?" asked Tumelty, not much caring to hear another of Duffy's addled revolutionary theories. The psychopath had expounded his peculiar views of the world without pause during the entire course of their cramped and bumpy economy-class charter flight from Amsterdam, and the younger man had had enough of it. At the moment, his mouth was filled with the exquisite taste of cake and cream, and he wished the other would simply leave off and allow him to enjoy it.

Duffy bit the end off a black cigar, clamping it between his yellow teeth. "What for?" he spat derisively. "For nothing at all, that's what for: Because you're a white man and they're not. Because they've got a gun and you haven't. Because they like your shoes or your watch, or maybe just for the sheer hell of it. That's what they'll kill you for down there."

Tumelty was looking at the big terrorist now, unaware of the glob of white cream hanging comically from the tip of his somewhat longish nose. "Go on with you," he said. "It's not all that bad . . . Is it?"

"No, it's not bad," said Duffy, touching a flaring match to the cigar. Blue smoke enveloped his glistening skull, reminding Tumelty of the drawing of an evil giant from one of his adventure comic books. "It's beautiful is what it is," Duffy declared after a pause. "It's what we ought to be doing back home ourselves." He paused to puff on the cigar, gazing out over the ragged sea of rooftops with his glittering eyes. "Pretty soon they'll rise up and take over completely. Then everything you see down there will belong to them, and that'll be your city of the future. See? We could learn a thing or two from these American blacks. Armed rebellion, that's the thing. War."

Dermot Tumelty nodded absently, unable to create in his mind a realistic vision of the madman's apocalyptic prediction. For though he mouthed the proper radical slogans from time to time, in his heart Tumelty cared nothing for the useless politics of war and rebellion anymore, and he had joined Kileen's group only because they wanted him and made him feel needed in the world. "Are we going to the hotel now?" he asked, anxious to know if the television stations still ran cartoons and horror films on the weekends.

Duffy peered disgustedly at his gentle young companion through the haze of cigar smoke, wondering what in the hell Kileen had been thinking when he'd insisted on sending him along. "Not just yet," he snorted. The big man glanced into his side mirror and guided the car off one crowded freeway, merging smoothly onto another, following the big green road signs pointing to Hollywood. "We're here on business. Or have you forgotten already?"

Tumelty shrugged and looked out the window at the shining glass-and-steel buildings growing on the horizon. Los Angeles still looked like the city of the future to him. It was the one place he had dreamed of visiting ever since he was a boy. L.A. was Disneyland and Malibu, surfers and movie stars. He watched the road signs with growing anticipation, secretly glad that they were turning toward the most fabled part of the magical city.

Hollywood. He couldn't believe his luck.

He wondered if he would see any movie stars.

CHAPTER THREE

Connections

SPARKLING WATER.

Sunlight rippling across the agitated surface.

A tremendous splash.

Katherine Huston stifled a little squeal of shock as a spray of cold droplets speckled her face, and she turned to look at the two teenagers cavorting in the swimming pool. "We don't usually use the pool at this time of year," she said, casting a furtive glance at her satiny blouse to see if any damage had been done.

"Beautiful weather for it, though." Queally-Smythe shaded his eyes to watch young Brian paddle to the opposite side of the pool, hoist himself up onto the sunny deck and drop onto his stomach. The old fellow was sitting in the midst of a rough semicircle of patio furniture, surrounded by Chuck and Katherine Huston and their studio friends. "Real treat for the boy," he murmured, reaching for the fresh drink being extended to him by Chuck. "Not much sunshine in the North of Ireland in March, I'm afraid. Very kind of you . . ."

"Nonsense, Major." Katherine put on her most winning smile, leaning forward to lay a reassuring hand on his bony knee. "We're just delighted to have the chance of meeting you at last . . ."

"You were telling us about your project dealing with the British army in India, Major." Sam Kornfeld, his thick, steel-rimmed glasses winking beneath the shining expanse of his pink forehead, pulled his chair closer. "We'd love to hear more about that."

There were enthusiastic murmurs of agreement from the others at the table.

"Oh, not much there to interest you television fellows," Queally-Smythe protested. "Pretty dry stuff actually, the ruminations of an old man, I'm afraid."

"Oh no, I think it's positively fascinating," said Ann Grantham-Kornfeld. She was a thin, fortyish blonde who wore a perpetually thoughtful look that went perfectly with her businesslike Liz Claiborne originals. "The romance and the exotic locations, the fabulous wealth and adventure . . . And just because we're doing television now doesn't necessarily mean we have to restrict our thinking to that particular medium," she added.

"I personally see it as a major theatrical feature," said Chuck Huston.

"Really?" The Major looked at him with new interest.

"Chuck was telling me over lunch that he thinks your book is far too grand for the small screen," said Katherine. "He's been searching for a project like this for years, you know."

"How very fascinating," said Queally-Smythe, settling back with his drink and warming up to his favorite subject. He had no idea that anyone other than a few military-history buffs might be interested in his work. "Well then, perhaps you'll be interested in something I stumbled across in the course of my research. It seems that one family—the Harts, I believe—sent five generations of officers out to India. Carried on from the earliest days of the Empire right through to independence . . ."

Katherine Huston clapped delightedly.

"*The Harts of India,* that's an absolutely perfect title," said Ann Grantham-Kornfeld.

The Major laughed. "Harts, hearts . . . Oh yes, I see. Terribly clever . . . India has many hearts, you know."

"You can get incredible below-the-line production deals from the Indians these days," Michael Anderson, a slender executive in a linen jacket, interjected.

"Really? I had no idea." Queally-Smythe's face was now flushed with excitement.

"Oh yes," Kornfeld assured him. "They have some of the finest studios in the world in Bombay. I believe David Lean worked with them on several occasions . . ."

"I'M REALLY SORRY about all of this."

Billy looked up from the deck where he had been lying for the past five minutes, letting the hot afternoon sun pound into his back. Kelly was kneeling over him, wet tendrils of her blond hair curling sensually about the top of her black two-piece suit, beads of sunstruck water glittering against her golden skin. He couldn't remember having ever had a better day in his life. "Sorry?"

She glanced across the pool to the knot of people surrounding the Major. "This wasn't supposed to turn into a studio circus," she said. "I just wanted you to come over for a swim."

He rolled over, propped himself up on one elbow and looked across the pool. They were all laughing at something the old man had just said.

"I don't mind," he said, gazing up into her clear, honest eyes. "They seem to be having a good enough time." He smiled. "And they're not really bothering us, are they?"

"I don't think you understand," said Kelly. "They're trying to talk your grandfather into making a film with them. That's why they're all here."

Brian sat up and looked again. "Really? What kind of a film?"

Kelly laughed bitterly. "Any kind of a film. They know the studio will give them millions of dollars, just as long as James Queally-Smythe is part of the deal."

Billy frowned. "Is he that important?"

She nodded. "They only used our swimming date as an excuse to get to him. My mother and I had a major fight over it this morning."

Billy scrutinized the group at the other side of the pool more closely. "Perhaps we ought to charge them a fee, then," he said frowning.

She gave him a strange look.

"That was a joke," he explained shyly.

"You're not angry?" The relief was evident in her voice.

"They say the Major is the toughest old bastard in the whole of the film industry," he told her, repeating something he'd memorized from Kileen's fact sheet. He lowered his voice to a conspiratorial whisper. "Frankly, I think they'll all be lucky if the old boy doesn't end up eating them alive."

Kelly laughed. "It would serve them right."

She looked down at his back, laid a soft hand on his skin. "Oh my God, you're burning up."

"Really?" He craned his neck, trying to see. The skin at the top of his shoulders did appear to be taking on a decidedly pinkish tinge. "What shall I do?"

She giggled. "You've got to get out of the sun, dummy." She grabbed his hand and pulled him to his feet. "Come on, we'll go into my room and listen to some music. I bet you like U2. I just got their latest album."

Billy started to reply that U2 was one of his favorite bands, prepared to inform her that the group's classic, "Sunday, Bloody Sunday," commemorated the darkest day in Irish history . . . then he remembered, for a change, who he was supposed to be, and stopped himself in time from saying anything. Instead, he forced his expression into an injured scowl.

Kelly saw his face and clapped her hand over her mouth. "Oh hell," she said. "They were on the other side, weren't they? I mean they wanted to free Northern Ireland from the British or something like that . . ."

"Northern Ireland *is* British," he said forcefully, repeating the Protestant government's standard justification for the armed occupation that continued to this day, despite all the talk of peace. "As British as England or Scotland or Wales. I am a British subject."

"I'm sorry," she said. "I don't think I really understand what's been going on over there. I mean, I know there was a lot of killing and things, but I'm not sure why. Maybe you could explain it to me."

He shook his head. "It's nothing to do with you," he said, panicking at the very thought of attempting to explain his people's rebellion from the point of view of the hated Protestant majority. How could any thinking person believe the bastards even *had* a point of view that justified the things they had done, for Christ's sake?

She looked hurt.

"It's just that it's rather hard for me to talk about all of that," he murmured, falling back on the same reliable old crutch he'd used before. Playing on her sympathy and, oddly, for the first time feeling guilty for doing it. She didn't know or understand any of it. How could she?

"Damn, what is wrong with me anyway?" Kelly lowered her head in shame. "I'm sorry, Brian. I'm not usually this stupid about things."

Billy lifted her chin with his fingers. "You're not stupid at all, Kelly," he said. "If everyone at home was as gentle and concerned as you, then there'd be no war." He was tempted to kiss her lips, but a sudden vision of Moira, the girl he'd been with that last night in Dublin, came unexpectedly into his mind, and it seemed like the wrong thing to do—to kiss her while he was thinking of someone else. He smiled instead.

"Come on," she said, taking his hand. "Let's get you in out of the sun. I've got some cream I can put on your back to keep it from peeling."

He followed wordlessly as she led him through the luxuriously furnished modern house and down a carpeted corridor to her room. "Don't look too closely," she said, as she opened the door. "I'm a terrible housekeeper."

He looked around the bright, airy room with its collection of stuffed animals on shelves above the rumpled bed, the stereo system in the corner, rock posters on the walls. It wasn't at all what he had expected for a wealthy American girl. "I like it," he said, thinking of Moira's shabby little flat with its one dirty window.

Kelly sat him in a chair before a desk equipped with a personal computer and stepped into the adjoining bathroom in search of the sunburn cream. He ran his fingers lovingly over the white plastic keyboard.

"You a computer freak?" she asked, reappearing in the doorway with a tube of cream.

"I'd like to learn something about them," he said, again without thinking. How was he to explain that he longed to have a computer like this one, but that someone as poor as he was could not even contemplate the awful expense?

"This is a pretty good one," she said, returning to the desk and leaning casually over his shoulder to switch on the machine. He felt the damp fabric of her swimsuit touch his flesh, the soft weight of her breast squeezing pleasantly against him. The computer screen flickered to life with a bright array of numbers and boxes. "It's an IBM," she explained, "a Pentium with CD ROM. Bigger than I need for my homework, but great for games and things."

He nodded, examining the legends written in the tiny icon boxes arrayed across the screen.

"I can teach you to use it if you want," she offered. "It's really easy with Windows." His body stiffened as she spread the cool white cream across his back. Even the fascination of the wonderful computer was no competition for what he was feeling. He closed his eyes, letting her hands massage his feverish skin. The pleasant sensation spread down his spine, and he looked down in horror to see the beginnings of an erection poking out at the thin fabric of his swim trunks. He dropped his hands into his lap, praying for it to go away. Looking around to see her hovering above him, he tried to decide if she had noticed.

She said nothing, but went on rubbing the cool cream into his back, soft hands moving lower. "What's this?" she asked, touching a shiny, triangular spot showing just at the point where the waistband of his trunks had slipped down on his hip. He groaned, lurching away from her probing fingertip in a sudden intense spasm of pain, his erection dissolving in an instant.

"I hurt you!" Her voice was filled with horror.

"It's nothing," he lied, getting to his feet and leaning heavily against the desk, waiting for the wave of pain to recede.

"I'm going to get your grandfather," she said, turning to leave the room. "You need a doctor."

"No!" he said it louder than he had intended, causing Kelly to freeze in her tracks. She turned back to face him and he saw the fright in her eyes.

"It's all right," he said as softly as he could manage, for his heart had begun pounding violently in his chest at the possibility of being discovered. "It's just a tender spot left over from an old injury. Honestly. I'm fine."

She looked at him skeptically. "What kind of injury?"

He shook his head. "Something that happened at school, a long time ago, playing football . . . "

"You're lying," she said, coming closer.

He stared at her.

"My father—not Chuck, my *real* father—was in Vietnam. He was wounded . . . a sniper's bullet." Kelly stepped suddenly behind him, bent to peer closely at the jagged wedge of scar tissue.

"What are you doing?" He spun around in near panic, grabbing her arms and forcing her to straighten.

"It looked just like that," she said calmly. "A bullet wound. Sometimes it still hurt him too."

"Oh Christ!" Billy Quinn sank into the chair before the colorful computer screen, his mind reeling as he tried desperately to think of something to tell her. Kelly knelt before him, took his hands in hers. "You don't want your grandfather to know. Is that it?"

He shook his head. "He's old," he said. "There's no need for him to worry." He looked into her eyes. "You can't breathe a word."

"You sure you're all right?"

He smiled. "As long as people don't go poking their fingers into me," he said.

Kelly Huston raised her shining eyes to his face and kissed him gently on the lips. "It'll be our little secret," she promised.

Billy felt relief sweeping over him as he tasted her lips on his. "Thank you, Kelly."

She pulled back and looked up at him. "How did it happen?" she whispered.

"YOU WANT WHAT?"

The obese biker, who Kileen had told them went by the name of Hog Mother, ran a dirty hand through his greasy, shoulder-length hair and laughed in their faces, his enormous belly quaking beneath the skintight fabric of his black Harley tee shirt. "What are you, fucking crazy?"

Francis Duffy took an ominous step forward, his enormous fists clenching and unclenching dangerously at his sides. Dermot Tumelty's eyes darted to the other bikers hovering near the partially open door of the cluttered garage. The taller of the two lifted a stout iron bar from a pile of tools and motorcycle parts on the floor, then let his arm drop, the eight- or nine-pound bludgeon swinging easily at his side, just in case.

"We were told you could provide us with ordnance," said Duffy to Hog Mother, his voice low and threatening.

Sensing the deadly purpose in the other man's eyes, the fat biker choked off his fit of laughter and raised his hands in a peaceful gesture. "No offense, dude. I got plenty of ordnance available," he said, "but things ain't the same as they was the last time we dealt with your pal. The riots and shit put the clamps on a lot of the stuff I used to be able to sell. There's some things I just can't get no more. Dig?"

Duffy said nothing, but some of the tension seemed to drain from his shoulders. From the corner of his eye he saw the bikers at the door relax slightly.

"Look, I wanta help you guys out," said Hog Mother, scratching his belly with a hairy fist emblazoned with blue prison tattoos that spelled out H-A-T-E across his knuckles. The old kitchen table on which he was sitting groaned as he lowered himself to the grease-encrusted floor and waddled around the mammoth skeleton of a disassembled Kawasaki 1100 to a workbench draped in dark cloth. "Guns, I got," he said, lifting the cloth to reveal an array of handguns and three or four automatic rifles. "You can take your pick."

He lifted a heavy caliber, chrome-plated automatic pistol, offered it butt-first to Duffy. "Look at this piece. Custom-built frame, laser sighting, fourteen-round mag. They don't come no nicer than that."

Duffy expertly popped the empty magazine from the gun, pulled the slide back and stuck his thumb into the chamber, peering briefly down through the muzzle at the light reflecting back from his nail. After a moment he grunted grudging approval. "It'll do. How much?" he asked, offering the piece back to the biker.

The fat man grinned, gently pushing it away. "Look closer, pal. That baby's clean as a whistle. Not a number on her anyplace. And they ain't been filed off, neither—the forensics dudes can bring up a filed-down number under an electron microscope now, ya know. The numbers on that piece is *wiped* off. Electronically peeled right out of the steel."

Duffy shrugged, unimpressed. He tossed the gun on the scarred top of the kitchen table and pulled a cigar from the breast pocket of the baggy brown suit in which he'd been traveling for the last thirty hours. "Serial numbers don't mean fuck-all," he grunted, lighting up. "The coppers catch you with the piece and they can trace it back to the bullet from the marks left by the rifling in the barrel. How much?"

Hog Mother's bearded face split into a toothy grin. "Eleven hundred," he said "but you don't get it, pal. Like they say in the TV commercials: Wait, there's more!" He opened a small pasteboard box at the rear of the work-bench and lifted a gleaming, red-nosed bullet into the light of a fly-specked fluorescent fixture hanging over the table.

Duffy leaned closer, the cigar clenched in the corner of his mouth. "What is it?"

"This, fellow criminals," said the fat biker, sounding like a Home Shop-ping Network pitchman, "is the technological breakthrough we've all been waiting for. An untraceable bullet to go with the untraceable gun."

"Shit!" Duffy snorted derisively, but he was clearly fascinated, as was Tumelty. The younger man crowded in beside Duffy, blinking against the thick stench of cigar smoke to stare at the red bullet.

"What you got here," said Hog Mother, scraping a grimy thumbnail down the side of the bullet and peeling away a thin strip of red plastic to reveal the bright sheen of the copper jacketing beneath, "is a bullet that's made slightly smaller than the barrel of your gun. Then it's coated with this here special plastic to bring it back up to size, so it fits in the barrel perfectly. When you fire, the plastic keeps the grooves in the barrel from making a mark on the bullet." The grin widened. "But the heat as it goes down the barrel melts the plastic away. Clean as a virgin's bathwater. Dig?"

"Jesus," breathed Dermot Tumelty, "that's fucking brilliant!"

Duffy cast him a murderous sidelong glance that said he should keep his mouth shut, and Tumelty melted warily back into the shadows. "I'll be wanting three of those, then," said the big man, reaching for a bulging leather wallet. He pointed to the workbench. "And a couple of the AK-47s like that one, with extra mags and fifteen-hundred rounds of ammo . . ."

Hog Mother scratched his head and leaned beneath the counter. He pulled a couple of dripping bottles of Corona beer from a battered ice chest and passed one to Duffy. "AK-47s are tough," he said, twisting the top off his beer and emptying the bottle in a single swallow. Duffy did likewise and glared defiantly at the fat man, who laughed and dug into the ice for two fresh beers. "Problem," he said, pausing to belch, "is most of that old Com-mie shit is junk, so nobody bothers with it anymore."

He gestured to one of the men by the door. The young biker skirted around him and dived into the ice chest, digging out three more beers. He handed one to Tumelty, then returned to his post, tossing a bottle to his companion with the iron bar and keeping the third for himself.

"Look," said Hog Mother, picking a well-worn AK-47 from the workbench and holding it up by its wooden stock. "This here's a 1960s Chinese model. Son of a bitch has probably had eight jillion rounds fired through it." He shook the weapon vigorously. "Lookit that," he laughed. "The fucking barrel's going north while the stock's going south. You couldn't hit a pregnant elephant at ten paces with the fucker. I'm tellin' ya, dude, even if I could find you two good ones, the AK's an obsolete piece of shit. Heavy, bulky and inaccurate, a triple threat." He laughed again and his belly shook. "And fifteen-hundred rounds of ammunition? Maybe in fucking Afghanistan."

Duffy belched, looking somber. "I never used nothing else but the AK," he confessed.

Hog Mother clamped an enormous arm around his thick shoulders. "Then friend, you're gonna think you done died and gone to heaven." He tossed the AK onto the table and snatched a tiny compact Uzi from the bench, pressing it into the terrorist's huge hands. "Feel that," he urged. "That's the latest model. Israeli design, South African manufacture. Weighs practically nothing, and you can blow the balls off a gnat at fifty yards, single fire or full auto."

Duffy tested the weight of the tiny weapon, stroked the smooth, black metal with his thick fingers as if it were the thigh of a beautiful woman. "How much for one of these, then?" he whispered, obviously in love.

Hog Mother laughed, dipping into the ice for two more Coronas. "Let's say fifteen hundred even, seein' as how you're already taking the three Magnums."

Duffy frowned, performing calculations in his head. "Extra magazines and ammo?"

Hog Mother thrust the fresh beer into his hand. "I'll throw 'em in for free," he said magnanimously.

Duffy grinned and tilted the bottom of his beer bottle to the rafters. "Done!" he said, slamming the empty back onto the table. He dug into his wallet, dropped a thick wad of bills down beside the bottle.

"Dude, I surely do like your style," laughed the biker, turning to point to one of the men by the door. "Wizard, bring these gentlemen's purchases up from the back."

The designated biker disappeared through the crack around the garage door. When he was gone, Duffy gave Hog Mother his best approximation of a smile. "Now you're sure you can't help us out with the other?" he said.

The fat man spread his arms helplessly. "Man, I only ever even *heard* of the shit you're talkin' about for the first time a couple of months ago," he said. "Besides, I got no call for anything like that around here, even if I did want to risk keeping it on hand, which I don't."

"But surely somebody must have some for sale," the terrorist persisted.

Hog Mother scratched his beard thoughtfully. "Back during the riots a few years ago there was a rumor going around about one of them gangs down in South Central making off with a Marine Corps Humvee and a trailer full of real special ordnance," he said. "After the cops cut and ran and buildings were burning down all the way from Hollywood to Long Beach, they say the military called in this special outfit from Camp Pendleton . . . There was talk of blasting all the freeway overpasses and creating a security zone up around Beverly Hills if the riots kept spreading."

The big belly began to shake. "Story is a bunch of them smart-ass niggers done went and stole the shit them marines were gonna do it with. Ain't that a pisser?"

Duffy nodded.

"Anyway," said the biker, "I've heard the dudes that took that Humvee might have what you want, but I gotta tell ya, they ain't gonna want to part with it. They say them crazy fuckers are savin' up to start themselves a real war down there." Hog Mother belched, and the big belly began to vibrate as another laugh welled up within him. "On the other hand," he gurgled, "I ain't sure those dumb niggers even know what they got when they stole that shit."

"Well, I'd like to talk with them," said Duffy. "Can you give me a name?"

Hog Mother glanced down at the wrinkled stack of currency on the table, which was only a small fraction of what he had seen in the Irishman's wallet. "Well now, dude," he said, stroking his scraggly beard. "I'd be taking a major risk . . . Those gang bangers are real bad actors, you understand."

"I see," said Duffy. He reached for the wallet and dropped an extra thousand onto the table.

Hog Mother's eyes shone. "Better make it two," he said encouragingly.

Duffy complied, and the biker moved to within a few inches of his face. "There's a liquor store at the corner of Eighty-fifth and Orange," he whispered. "You ask around out front for a dude named Slice; warlord of a gang called the Double Zeros. Bastard got him a face somebody cut in half with a razor while he was doin' time out in Chino. You can't miss him." Hog Mother grinned, showing a mouthful of rotting teeth. "And, dude, you be real careful down there with them Double Zeros. I'm here to tell you that's one mean bunch of niggers.

Duffy grinned, took a deep drag of his cigar and jammed the glowing end into the fat man's left eyeball, muffling Hog Mother's scream by clapping a great hand over his mouth. He deftly moved around behind the huge man, kicking at his knees from the back and simultaneously levering a forearm under the biker's sagging triple chin. Hog Mother fell forward like a dropped anvil, his neck snapping with a dull crunch under the weight of his own massive body.

Dermot Tumelty whirled to see the biker who had been guarding the door squinting dully across the garage, trying to figure out what had happened. The slight Irishman was on the man before his hand could touch the iron bar he had discarded on the junk pile. Tumelty smashed his beer bottle over the biker's head, then jammed the jagged neck of the bottle into his throat, jumping away to keep the bright jet of arterial blood from staining his white running shoes.

"Nice work," said Duffy, snatching up the heavy chrome automatic from the kitchen table, quickly loading it and chambering Hog Mother's sample bullet. He looked up at Tumelty, who stood frozen by the door, gazing down in amazement at the bloody remains of the man he had just killed.

"Here, Dermot, called Duffy. The youngster looked up in time to see the gun being tossed to him. He caught it with his good hand and stared questioningly at the madman. "Don't look so pained," smiled Duffy, who was unexpectedly pleased with his little companion's performance. "It's not the holy saints we're after killin' here." He winked encouragingly. "Now you kill the next one nice and quiet too, if you please," Duffy grinned, showing his yellow teeth, "and I'll treat you to a double helping of them Froot Loops you been going on about, whatever the hell they are!"

Tumelty nodded and jammed the pistol into his belt, then picked up the dead biker's beer bottle. He smashed it against a disabled Harley engine and, clutching the jagged neck in the fist of his good hand, moved to the door to await the return of the third biker with the rest of their guns and ammunition.

Duffy scooped his money from the table, then picked up the Uzi and stepped over Hog Mother's body, pausing to look down at the great heap of flesh on the floor. ""Let me give you a small piece of advice, *dude*," he said to the dead man. "Never be too greedy, and *never* call a black man Nigger. You see," he whispered confidentially, "it's the same thing as callin' an Irishman Paddy."

The big terrorist moved to the workbench and began loading the Uzi magazine from the box of ammunition he found there.

CHAPTER FOUR

Poinɀs of darkness

NIGHT AGAIN.

Billy Quinn gazed into the smoky interior of the falling-down warehouse that lay somewhere in the vast industrial sprawl of abandoned buildings lining the empty concrete ditch they called the Los Angeles River.

Orange neon glowed above him, and a violet laser made jagged sweeps across the rusting cross beams supporting the high ceiling, the combined light casting an eerie glow down onto a concrete floor teeming with the bodies of hundreds of teenagers. All of them were writhing more or less in time to the ear-shattering electronic riffs of a band called The Brain Donors.

He was sitting on a rough platform overlooking the dancers, watching from a tiny table made from a packing case as bikinied girls whirled and twisted in wire cages hung beneath ultraviolet lights that made the painted psychedelic designs on their skin glow bright against the backdrop of the black walls.

Club Retro.

Kelly had told him that the place, which purported to have revived the wild, anything-goes atmosphere of Los Angeles in the late 1960s, was the latest "flavor of the month" rage among L.A. teens, who gathered here in great mobs from all over the huge city to dance and mingle on the weekends.

He scanned the constantly surging crowd now for some sign of her, wondering whether it could really be taking this long for her to use "the little girls' room."

The two of them had sneaked away from the Huston house hours earlier, leaving the adults gathered in the gigantic living room, where they had gone after the sun had dropped behind the hills and a chill had crept into the air. They were still excitedly discussing *The Harts of India*—which they were now calling the Major's "project"—had been at it like that for the whole afternoon, sprinkling their conversation with unfamiliar terms like "above-the-line" and "*perri-passeu* points" and making lists of famous actors they might get to play this part or the other.

The adults had been talking about "sending out for Chinese" when Kelly had whispered into Brian's ear, then led him outside to her yellow Mustang.

"Aren't you afraid they'll miss us?" he had asked, looking back at the brightly lighted house and unsure whether the Major's grandson was expected to ask the old man's permission before driving away into the night with a beautiful girl.

She had laughed and started the engine, driving away down the canyon road, telling him he had obviously led a very sheltered life in his private boys' school and that it was time he saw L.A. She then informed him that she had decided it was her sacred duty to show him the ropes.

They had cruised east up Sunset Boulevard, tracing the course of the famous road inland through the wealthy suburbs of Brentwood and Beverly Hills, past the seventy-room mansions of Bel-Air and the tree-studded campus of UCLA and heading down along the Sunset Strip with its posh clubs and restaurants before plunging into the glittering, noisy environs of Hollywood, where the sidewalks were crowded and he heard a dozen different languages spoken on as many street corners, saw gleaming low riders bucking up and down on their tiny mag wheels to the raucous Latin rhythms blasting from blown-out stereos, neon light shows flaring beneath their wheels as grim-faced *cholos* in sleeveless tee shirts and bright suspenders glared their defiance at the world from behind steering wheels formed of welded chrome chains, while their sultry Latina girlfriends clung adoringly to their tattooed arms; saw blacks in shapeless, baggy overalls, their heads shaved with patterns of lines and zigzags and lightning bolts, carrying blaring, five-foot-long boom boxes on their shoulders, the hard, flat music rattling the windows of the dazzling storefronts with unintelligible strings of revolutionary rap lyrics as bewildered families of newly arrived Thais and Armenians and Filipinos wandered agape past open-fronted stands selling falafel and pizza and chorros and schwarma and Cuban sandwiches, while Arab and Chinese and Jewish merchants tempted them to enter the doorways of E-Z credit shops whose alarmed and barred windows displayed video players and Walkmans and Watchmans and imitation Rolex watches and naughty red underwear and pornographic magazines and fake vomit and live nude girls and num-chuks and chrome-bladed throwing stars, all beneath the omnipresent clatter of hovering LAPD helicopters that wheeled overhead like giant dragonflies, stopping now and then to stab blinding spotlights down at the whole bloody incredible show and for thirty seconds or so turning half a block or an alleyway brighter than the sun at high noon on the brightest summer day while ambulances and fire trucks and black-and-white police cars with screaming sirens and strobing red, white and blue lights wound their way up and down through endless parading streams of Cherokees and Beemers and Fords and Monster Trucks and Lexuses and Chevys and Harleys and Caddies and Mercedeses and Corvettes and open-topped Jeep Wranglers driven by butch lesbians who had jacked up their vehicles lighted suspensions on banks of spotless Monroe-matic shocks and giant-tired, sixty-inch off-road wheels.

Billy, whose previous experience in a city other than Belfast was limited to Dublin—a quiet place of stately old public buildings and green parks in the dripping rain, where a black tourist was an oddity and street crime was the occasional mugging—had stared wordlessly at the casual chaos that surrounded them on every side. He saw a middle-aged man in red, sequined panties, worn beneath a clear plastic raincoat, walking down the street, reading a newspaper; a giant police dog riding on the back of a powerful motorcycle driven by a beautiful woman with pink hair; a trio of skinheads in heavy boots wresting a shopping cart from a tiny old woman who sprayed them with oven cleaner.

His brain had been spinning on the verge of sensory overload by the time Kelly wheeled the yellow Mustang off the street and negotiated a steep spiral ramp onto the rooftop parking lot of a neon-etched, multilevel minimall, built to resemble the whitewashed façade of a Moorish fortress, and backed up to a blank concrete wall separating its shops from a dark cemetery filled with eighty-foot-tall royal palm trees and the white marble tombs of famous movie stars. "Well," she'd grinned mischievously, her tangled hair glowing in the garish reflections of the ice-blue neon strip pointing the way to a sixteen-kiosk specialty food fair, "what do you think so far?"

"Christ," he'd breathed, staring out over the low railing at the sparkling lights of the city and realizing he'd seen nothing but one miniscule slice of it, "how do they all live here together like this?"

As if in answer to his question, the unmistakable rattle of faraway automatic-weapons fire overlaid the noises from the street. Billy flinched reflexively, and she'd peered at him with concern.

"What's wrong?" she asked, her untrained ear obviously unable to distinguish the distant gunfire from the general racket on the street below.

He had looked out at the great city, listening for the sound again. "Didn't you hear that?"

She had listened. Shook her head.

On the sidewalk below, an argument had begun, strident voices rising in a language he'd never heard before. He'd looked down from the rooftop garage to see two men in identical white robes shaking their fists at each other.

She'd taken him into the mall, where they'd sat at a small table under the neon and eaten fiery burritos washed down with great quantities of Pepsi-Cola drunk from Day-Glo green plastic bicycle bottles, that they were allowed to keep.

She hadn't asked him again about the bullet wound—which he had told her he'd received as an innocent bystander to a gunfight between IRA terrorists and police—but had kept looking into his eyes in a way that made him feel uneasy for having told the lie and nervous that she might be tempted to blurt it out, and reaching across the table from time to time to squeeze his hand.

In an effort to lighten the mood, he had asked her if there was someplace they might go to hear some music and dance.

She had brought him to Club Retro.

The music stopped, and the sweating Brain Donors stepped off the back of the crude stage, dabbing at their soaked heads with towels and lighting cigarettes as they pushed their way through the crowd. A thin girl in skintight black vinyl stepped up to a microphone on the stage, adjusted the height while two longhairs fiddled with an electric bass and a keyboard. The longhairs began to play, and the overhead lighting settled into a misty purple hue as the girl started to sing a sad, sweet song about riding a motorcycle down an empty freeway in search of her lost lover.

Half the couples had drifted back toward the tables ringing the floor, while the rest clutched each other in dreamy ecstasy, pressing hips and chests close, wrapping arms about necks. Some just stood swaying lazily to the music, their tongues probing the insides of their partners' eager mouths.

Billy scanned the room again for some sign of Kelly. He saw her standing by a doorway near the stage, talking with a group of people.

"Brian, is that you?"

Billy heard the voice call out behind him, paying no attention until a hand fell onto his shoulder and he spun in his chair, nearly upsetting the plastic cup before him.

Brenda Gaynor, her spectacular legs encased in black Spandex under a loose blouse of some shimmering white material that showed off her long red hair, stood over him. There was a clear plastic cup of sparkling liquid in her hand, and her blue eyes were slightly glazed.

"Brenda!" Billy silently cursed himself for not having immediately answered to the name Brian, and jumped quickly to his feet. "How are you?"

"I'm wonderful," she sighed in a warm, husky voice. "Just wonderful, Brian." She stepped forward, pressing her slender body close, reaching up to kiss him softly on the cheek and grinding her hips against his. "You're looking stud," she whispered, raking her fingers through his hair. He pulled back, smelling the sweet odor on her breath and realizing that she was stoned on something.

"Well, it's good to see you, Brenda," he said, looking over her head for Kelly. The group near the stage had grown larger, and he could no longer see her.

Brenda swayed against him, splaying her long fingers against the thin fabric of the white cotton shirt he'd pulled on with a pair of khakis after changing out of his swimming trunks. "Love that music, huh?"

He nodded as she pressed her cheek against his shoulder and slid her free arm around his neck. "Wanna slow dance?"

Billy looked down to see her gazing up into his eyes. The tip of her pink tongue slid over her full, pouting lips. "Please?"

"Well, the thing is," he said nervously. "I was waiting for Kelly to come back from the W.C."

Brenda's eyes focused, and a tiny wrinkle creased her smooth forehead. "The what?"

He smiled at her befuddlement. "Never mind."

"Good." She placed her drink on the table and tugged at his hand, pulling him toward the dance floor. "Then we'll just dance until Kelly comes back from the . . . wherever, and that way we won't waste any time," she said.

Billy laughed at her tipsy logic and allowed himself to be led down to the dance floor.

KELLY HAD HAD TO WAIT for nearly twenty minutes before the crowd in the smoky restroom had thinned enough to allow her admittance. Another five minutes had passed inside while two badly dressed high school girls from Thousand Oaks stood threatening each other with knives before the only empty stall.

She had finally come back out into the club only to be grabbed by Samantha, who was waiting to get into the restroom. Sam had insisted on pointing out Brad, the gangly UCLA sophomore she was dating, who was standing nearby talking to a bunch of self-conscious preppies, then she immediately launched into a breathless description of the new Porsche his father had given him for his birthday.

"That's great," Kelly finally said when the other girl paused for breath, "but I've got to get back to Brian. I left the poor guy sitting all by himself up there on the other side of the room."

Sam winked approvingly. "You're moving fast, Huston," she said. "Think you'll be able to make it with him before he gets to Pacific Academy and all those party bitches get their hands on him?"

Kelly rolled her eyes heavenward. "Samantha, I am not trying to *make it* with him."

Sam's huge brown eyes widened in disbelief. "Why not, are you crazy? He's the best looking guy I've met in practically my entire life, and if it wasn't for the fact that you're my very best friend—and that Brad's father just gave him the Porsche—I'd have that stud muffin chasing me naked down the beach before sunup."

"You really are disgusting," laughed Kelly. She glanced over at the gangly sophomore, who was still huddling with the preppies. "Is that how you caught old Brad?"

Sam pretended to examine her lacquered nails. "Honey, Brad didn't take that much catching. In fact, I haven't actually let him do it yet." She grinned. "But I've got him drooling."

Kelly was familiar with Samantha's many alleged conquests, and there was more than a note of cynicism in her voice when she replied. "You know, Sam, sometimes I think you just like to shock people with all that dirty talk of yours."

Sam lowered her eyes contritely. "You're right, Kelly," she confessed. "Actually, I've never really done it with anyone before." Then her infectious giggle broke the solemn mood, and she added mischievously, "I'm a virgin and I'm saving myself for my third husband. He's going to be a disgusting little bald man with a potbelly, who owns a movie studio, and he'll have to give me a thirty-carat diamond before I'll put out. Happy now?"

Kelly laughed. "Well, for your information, Brian and I are just getting to know each other. If something happens between us, then it happens, but right now we're just enjoying being together."

"I think that's wonderful, Kelly. I really do." Sam nodded seriously, all the while looking over the top of her head at the swaying couples on the dance floor.

"You do? Really, Sam?" Kelly was surprised. At least to hear her talk, Sam firmly believed that there was no male-female relationship that wasn't based on pure lust . . . or greed.

"Sure," said Sam, who was staring now, "because that way you won't feel too bad when you find some horny slut wrapped around him trying to undo his belt buckle."

Kelly turned and followed her friend's gaze to the dance floor. The singer on the stage was just bringing her plaintive love song to an emotional, wailing climax as Brenda Gaynor wrapped her arms tightly around Brian O'-Malley's neck and pressed her lips to his.

THE MUSIC STOPPED, and Billy stood rooted to the spot, feeling the girl's hot, slick tongue expertly probing the roof of his mouth. One of her hands slipped down his back and beneath the waist of his trousers, and he could feel her cool fingers gently caressing the cleft at the top of his buttocks. *Jesus Christ, what was she doing down there?* He gasped and tore his lips away, looking down at her in confusion. Girls did not do things like this at home . . . At least not any of the girls he had ever known.

Brenda smiled up at him like a contented cat. "I liked that a lot," she whispered.

He found it hard to take his eyes off of her. God, but she was beautiful . . . and he instinctively knew that the touch of her lips and the feel of her soft thighs pressing against his had been a promise, not a tease. He nodded, tongue-tied.

The girl singer began a new number—something faster this time—and the other dancers jostled against them. "I'd, uh, better get back to the table," he stammered, looking desperately around the crowded room for Kelly.

"What's your hurry, Brian?" Brenda hooked her long fingers beneath his belt, pulling him playfully to her.

"BASTARD!" Kelly whispered the curse aloud, then stormed out of the club in a black rage, elbowing her way past a knot of ridiculously dressed retro-punks lounging by the front door.

"Hey, watch it bitch!" A combative girl in knee-high combat boots and an oversized leather jacket followed her out into the dimly lit parking lot. "I'll kick your ass!"

Kelly whirled on the girl, staring down at her shaved head and pierced eyebrows. She was fifteen at most, a pitiful gamin too young even to be allowed inside a place like Club Retro. Somebody's little sister from The Valley. "How'd you like your baby teeth shoved down your throat, kid?" Kelly growled.

The underage retro-punk flinched, then retreated. "Fuck you, bitch!" she yelled.

Kelly smiled despite her anger. Then she turned and walked quickly toward the far end of the crumbling parking lot, where she'd left the Mustang.

The lot, which had earlier been brightly lit by the headlights of arriving cars, was now a dark sea of empty vehicles. She briefly considered going back to the club, then she remembered the sight of Brian O'Malley kissing Brenda Gaynor. Her anger flared all over again and she stomped defiantly across the broken pavement in search of her car. *Brenda Gaynor. God! How could Brian humiliate me like that?* She had really thought he was different. A grim smile flickered across her lips, and she fumbled in her purse for her keys. *Well, if he liked Brenda Gaynor so much, let her give him a ride home.*

BILLY LOOKED DOWN at Brenda, wondering what in the hell he was doing. The thing was, he didn't even like her. The kiss had come so unexpectedly that he'd momentarily been swept away by it. The redhead stood swaying drunkenly in front of him now, her narrow hips moving suggestively in time to the music. "Let's go someplace dark," she whispered.

"Sorry," he said, disengaging himself from her grasp and starting across the floor. "I've got to find Kelly."

"Hey," Brenda yelled. "You're not going to leave me standing here alone." A couple of people turned to stare at her, and she glared back at them.

Billy shrugged apologetically, looking up at the seating area above the dance floor. He saw that the table was still empty and started toward the stage, heading for the place he had last seen Kelly. Someone grabbed him by the elbow, and he turned to see Brenda still angrily confronting him. "What's wrong with me?" she demanded in a loud voice.

Billy flushed. A number of teenagers had stopped dancing to watch the encounter. "There's nothing wrong with you, Brenda," he said quietly.

She stamped her foot like a spoiled two-year-old. "Then come back and dance with me," she pouted.

"Christ!" Billy shook his head in frustration. "I don't want to fucking dance with you anymore. Okay?" He turned quickly on his heel and walked away, disappearing into the crowd of dancers.

Brenda stood alone on the dance floor, watching him go. "You won't get away with this," she screamed over a sudden crescendo of electronic music. Then she dropped her head onto her chest and began to sob. Brenda Gaynor was not used to being humiliated.

"What's the matter, babe?"

Brenda looked up to see Thad August standing before her. The pulsing overhead lights were playing in his sun-bleached hair, and his loose, flowered aloha shirt was open, exposing his tanned chest. He held out a frosted glass and smiled sympathetically.

Brenda wiped her nose on her sleeve and took the glass, draining its contents in a long, noisy swallow. "Some asshole just humiliated me," she spat, scanning the crowd for some sign of Brian.

August's eyes darted over the dancers. "Just point him out and I'll kick his ass for you," he offered chivalrously.

Brenda scanned the swirling crowd and slowly shook her head. "I don't see him now."

"Come on," said August, taking her hand. "We'll just go and find him."

She sniffled gratefully and allowed him to lead her off the floor. Things were working out far better than she could have anticipated.

BILLY STEPPED OUT from between a row of cars, trying to remember exactly where in the darkened lot Kelly had parked the Mustang. Moments after leaving Brenda in the club, he had run into her tall friend, Samantha, who had smirkingly informed him that Kelly had left in a rage. He'd run outside to stop her, but now he couldn't find the car.

Headlights turned down the aisle behind him, and he ran back between a van and an old sedan in time to see the yellow Mustang bearing down on him. He stepped out in front of it, and it screeched to an abrupt halt inches from him. "Kelly," he called, running up to the driver's door. "Where are you going?"

Her face was streaked with tears, her eyes red from crying. "I'm going home. Now get out of my way, Brian." She revved the powerful engine threateningly.

"Look," he said lamely, "Brenda said she only wanted to dance until you came back to the table."

Kelly smiled. "I'm sure it's none of my business who you dance with, Brian." She engaged the clutch, rolling the car forward a few inches.

He stood away, hands on his hips, and cocked his head at the poorly lit parking lot. "So, are you just going to leave me here, then?"

"I thought you'd be going home with Brenda," Kelly replied snottily. She swiped at the tears on her cheeks and glared at him.

"Kelly, she was drunk," he explained.

"Oh well, then that explains how your tongue came to be stuck down her throat," she said angrily. The car inched slowly forward.

"She . . . took me by surprise," he said truthfully. "I just wasn't expecting anything like . . . like what she did." He forced a contrite smile. "It was you who said I'd led a sheltered life . . ."

Kelly searched his eyes for the lie behind his words, saw nothing there but remorse. "Next thing I suppose you're going to tell me they don't have girls like Brenda back home in Ireland."

Billy's face reddened. "Oh yes they do . . . I've just never met one of them before."

Kelly's anger was beginning to dissipate. She wasn't sure why Brenda's outrageous behavior had surprised her . . . after all, everybody knew she was a backstabbing little witch. She scrutinized Brian's pained expression, reading the genuine distress in his eyes. "Well," she said at last, "I guess I can't really leave you here without a way home, can I?"

He grinned, relieved. "I'd probably be massacred by the natives before I got a mile."

She smiled. "Okay, get in."

He had already started around the front of the car when a rock-hard fist came at him out of nowhere, propelled by a dark shape hidden in the glare of the headlights. Kelly called his name as he fell heavily onto the hood of the car and the dark figure leaped onto him.

Billy shook his head groggily. His jaw felt as though he'd been hit by a brick. He opened his eyes and saw the big man hovering over him, preparing to strike again. Metal glinted across the knuckles of his assailant's upraised fist. He heard Kelly's sharp scream and looked back to see her struggling with another attacker who was trying to pull her out of the car.

"Give me your money, motherfucker," growled the man above him, "and we won't kill you and your girlfriend. We just want the car and the money." The man with the brass knuckles pulled his fist back threateningly. "Now, fucker!"

Billy heard the threat through buzzing ears, realizing that they were being robbed. He nodded meekly, dropping his left hand toward his trouser pocket . . . Then, suddenly, reflexively, his right hand arced up from his body, clasping the mugger's upraised fist in his own, twisting it viciously around until he felt the muscle and cartilage of the other's arm begin to strain and pop. At the same time he brought his knee up into the big man's groin, solid bone crunching into soft, yielding tissue.

The man holding Kelly heard his partner's gasp of pain, saw him drop from sight below the hood of the car. The second assailant pulled the trembling girl closer to him, squinting into the vacant headlight beams and waving the knife in his hand menacingly before her terrified eyes. "I'll cut her, man," he threatened. "You hear me? I'll cut her!"

There was no response from the front of the car. The mugger leaned forward, trying to see over the open door. He called to his companion, "Wint, you okay?" Heard a soft groan from the ground beneath the Mustang's front bumper.

"You down there, you hear what I said?" he demanded, his voice breaking at the end of the sentence. This wasn't going as he had expected—*We'll just run on down to that new teen club on the L.A. River, knock over some of them candy-ass rich punks, get us some fine wheels, man* . . . He wished he'd never let that stupid son-of-a-bitch Wint talk him into this. Wished they'd just got on the bus back to Oklahoma City like he'd wanted to do all along, ever since they'd found out there wasn't really no shortage of stuntmen out here in California like they'd read about in that dumb-ass movie magazine. Shit, people had laughed right out loud at them . . . Two busted-down Okies in worn-out cowboy boots.

He heard someone slithering across the ground, and he moved the knife closer to the girl's throat. "I'm warnin' you . . ." he began without conviction. Something hard and fiery slashed at the spot where his shoulder met his neck and he dropped instantly to the rough pavement, his head cracking with a wet, hollow thud on the ground.

Suddenly free of the mugger's grip, Kelly Huston whirled around to see Brian O'Malley standing over her unconscious attacker, his right hand still held rigid from the devastating karate chop he'd delivered to the man's neck. Brian's white shirt was ripped and there was a bloody scratch down one cheek. His eyes flickered to her as he bent to pick up the man's knife, carefully laid the needle-sharp point alongside the mugger's throat . . .

"Brian, no!"

Billy Quinn looked up at the frightened blond girl. She was staring in terror at the knife, and he followed her gaze back down to his own hand: The hand that was about to plunge the shining six-inch blade into the robber's throat, to snuff out the bastard's worthless life, dealing with him as he had always been taught to deal with anyone and anything that threatened his mission.

The enemy you kill today / Never will your deed betray! The scrap of doggerel he'd seen scrawled on a broken wall somewhere in the Falls Road popped into Billy's mind, and he gripped the plastic handle of the cheap knife more tightly in his sweating fist. "*Bastard!*"

"No, Brian!"

He looked up again at the frightened girl. Heard the pleading in her voice. Nodding, he got shakily to his feet and gave her a tight little grimace. "You didn't think I was really going to kill him?"

She shook her head slowly. "How did you manage to get behind him?" she asked in a tremulous voice.

He showed her his scraped palms, the torn knees of his trousers. "On my hands and knees," he explained.

She looked fearfully toward the front of the car. "The other one?"

"Sleeping like a babe." He smiled, gently pushing her into the car. Sliding behind the wheel himself.

"Shouldn't we call the police or something?" she asked, her eyes darting nervously around the deserted lot.

He looked at her as though she were mad. "We don't actually need them now, do we?"

Kelly shook her head slowly, watching his face as he backed the car expertly up the aisle, catching a final glimpse of their would-be assailants lying motionless on the pavement before the sweep of the headlights consigned them to darkness. Wondering aloud at their plaid shirts and faded Levi's. "Cowboys!" She giggled on the verge of hysteria as he wheeled the Mustang around a pickup at the end of the aisle and sped out onto the street. "We were just mugged by two cowboys."

"DID YOU SEE what he did?" Brenda Gaynor stood in the shadows between two cars, gawking at the receding lights of the Mustang. She had led Thad August out into the parking lot a few minutes earlier, intent on having him teach Brian O'Malley a lesson. They had followed the sound of voices to the yellow Mustang, arriving at this hidden vantage point just as Brian had disabled the first mugger, then watched in silent awe as he had crept around the car on his stomach and gotten the drop on the second man.

August was standing behind her, staring at the two unconscious men spread-eagled on the ground. When he spoke, his voice was hoarse in her ear. "I thought you said this guy was some kind of an English pussy," he breathed.

"Irish," Brenda said absently, remembering the taste of Brian O'Malley's mouth and the feel of his hard, muscular body against hers, and determined now to have him for herself. "He's from Northern Ireland."

"I think I heard about those guys," whispered August, his voice filled with fear at the sudden realization of how close he had come to challenging the deadly stranger on behalf of Brenda Gaynor's somewhat dubious honor. "All they do is kill each other over there."

Thad August was sweating profusely after having witnessed the violent parking-lot encounter, seeing the gleaming knife blade at Kelly Huston's throat while Brenda's cushiony buttocks had been pressing back hard against his crotch and, now that the danger was past, he suddenly wanted the sexy redhead. He slipped a hand over her shoulder and down into the front of Brenda's loose blouse, finding the enticing mound of her small breast, squeezing her erect nipple between his thumb and forefinger.

"We'd better go back," she said, ducking hurriedly away from his rough caress, "before somebody calls the police."

"DO YOU WANT to tell me where you learned how to disarm muggers?" Kelly had curled her legs up beneath her and was gazing at him from the Mustang's passenger seat. They were sitting at the foot of the Major's driveway, having spoken no more than a few words on the drive back from the club.

Billy shrugged. "I studied some martial arts," he said evasively.

"In school, I suppose?"

He nodded.

She laughed. "That must be one hell of a school you went to, Brian. I'm afraid you're going to find Academy High pretty dull by comparison."

"I don't think so," he said, reaching across the car and taking her chin in his hand. "Not if you'll be there." He leaned forward, making an awkward attempt to kiss her, but she pulled away. "Is something wrong?" he asked, his face reddening at the rebuff.

She shook her head. "I was just wondering how I'd measure up to Brenda," she said, hating herself for having let the bitchy remark slip out. Still, she couldn't forget the image of the two of them kissing beneath the violet lights of Club Retro.

Billy threw his head back against the seat in frustration, unsure what she expected him to say. He had no experience with girls and their mercurial moods. He thought she'd already forgiven him for the scene on the dance floor. "I explained what happened," he said miserably.

"I know," she said. "I know you did. And I believe you."

He moved closer, touching her cheek with the tips of his fingers. "Give us a little kiss, then?"

She giggled at the strange turn of phrase. "You got a frog in your pocket?"

He frowned at her.

"You said, give *us* a kiss . . ."

He laughed, mentally cursing himself for having let himself slip back into his usual way of talking. "Will *you* kiss *me*, then?" he asked formally.

"Oh well, I suppose," she said, putting away her disturbing image of Brenda—which she was certain it had been the other girl's intention to provoke—"since you practically saved my life." She raised her lips to his and they shared a soft, lingering kiss.

He sighed, letting his hand caress her breast, and she felt the heat through the thin fabric of her blouse. The kiss grew more passionate, and she had a new vision: the wildly imaginative cover painting from one of Katherine's romance novels coming to life.

In a strange way, Kelly realized, Brian O'Malley really was the mysterious and vulnerable adventurer she had imagined in her silly daydreams. She ran her fingers through his thick, dark hair, urgently pressing her body closer to his in the cramped confines of the car. The hand on her breast grew bolder, fumbling to unbutton her blouse. If he wanted to make love to her now, Kelly knew she would not be able to say no . . . But not here, in the front seat of a parked car in his grandfather's driveway.

She was about to say something when the car was filled with a blaze of yellow light, and they looked up to see the twin lanterns flaring beside the Major's iron gates.

"Christ Almighty." Billy sat up, shielding his eyes against the sudden brightness.

A small figure walked down from the dark driveway and stopped beside the car. "Ah, it is you, Master Brian. I saw the strange auto in the street and thought perhaps there was some difficulty . . . " Ranjee, Queally-Smythe's sneaky little Indian servant, peered in through the open window.

"There's no *difficulty*," said Billy, barely managing to contain his irritation. "We were talking."

"I am most embarrassed to have so rudely disturbed you," Ranjee apologized, his dark eyes absorbing the details of the boy's torn shirt and scratched face, the girl's rumpled clothing. "If there is no problem, then I shall be wishing you good night."

"Good night," snapped Billy.

The servant bowed his head and left. A moment later the driveway lights were extinguished.

"Bloody little wanker." Billy dug in his shirt pocket for a cigarette, lit it and blew an angry cloud of smoke into the darkness. "Do y'know he told the bloody Major he'd caught me having a fag yesterday?"

Kelly looked over at Brian O'Malley in the darkness, wondering why his accent sounded so different when he was angry.

His anger frightened her, and there had been a moment tonight when she had actually thought he was going to kill the two men who had tried to rob them.

RANJEE LAY in his bed, listening to the sound of the yellow Mustang's engine starting up. A short time later, he heard footsteps in the corridor downstairs. He listened as the strange young man who had come to stay climbed the stairs at the rear of the house, heard the hiss of water running in the shower.

Ranjee fretted over the scene he had witnessed when he had gone down earlier to investigate the strange car at the foot of the drive. Young Master Brian had obviously been involved in some sort of misadventure this evening.

The servant did not relish the prospect of incurring the Major's displeasure by reporting this latest incident, but neither did he desire to let it go. Ranjee worshiped his difficult old employer, to whom he felt he owed his very life. For the Major had lifted him up from the unthinkable squalor of Calcutta, given him clean quarters, good food and a fine wage, which he was carefully saving for his retirement. Despite the Major's occasional bombastic outbursts, which Ranjee had long ago learned to cheerfully ignore, the Indian had found both his life and his work enjoyable and rewarding, until the arrival of young Master Brian just three days previously. Now . . .

Ranjee sighed and closed his eyes, wrestling with the difficult problem. Something was not right with young Master Brian. Something he could not yet quite pin down in his mind. In the course of his long service with the Major, Ranjee had spent more years than he cared to count looking after his employer's many wealthy British friends, and he knew their ways intimately.

On the surface, Brian O'Malley spoke and behaved as Ranjee had come to expect young men of privilege to speak and behave. In his personal habits, however, the boy's behavior more often resembled that of the workmen who came to do the gardening and plumbing and such about the house than a member of the upper class. At breakfast today, for instance, master Brian had picked up his bacon in his fingers and used the knife from the butter dish to spread jam on his toast . . . Aberrations that Ranjee found most disturbing.

"You are a foolish old man," he chided himself, remembering the glow in the Major's cheeks this evening when the old fellow had returned from the house down the road, bubbling over with enthusiasm for a new film project he had been discussing, smiling broadly and chuckling over his scotch when he had learned that the boy was not yet home, then winking and remarking proudly on the lad's good looks and the way the girls all looked at him.

"Master Brian has brought happiness to the Major," Ranjee whispered to the walls of his comfortable room, "and perhaps what you are now feeling is jealousy."

Ranjee determined that he had no right to interfere with the Major's happiness, reflecting that the world was an ever-changing place and that even the best schools might no longer teach boys the proper way of doing things. He allowed himself to drift off to sleep, vowing to remain silent on the subject of the orphaned boy's odd behavior. Beginning tomorrow, rather than being so critical of the young man, he would attempt to help Brian O'Malley live up to his grandfather's idealized image of him.

CHAPTER FIVE

Bloody Sunday

"WILL YOU LOOK at this fucking place!"

Dermot Tumelty was gaping wide-eyed through the window of the rented Toyota at the seemingly endless rows of clapboard houses, shabby blocks of flats and burned-out or boarded-up storefronts. Every available vertical surface was covered with bright, unreadable scrawls of spray paint, many of them simply X-ing out a previous scrawl.

They'd been off the freeway for more than fifteen minutes now, and he had lost count of the blocks they had traversed. Alongside the street, black faces turned to stare at them from the gaps between junked cars, from the patches of scraped earth before the desolate blocks of flats, from broken sidewalks fronting the barred windows of liquor stores, and Tumelty felt uneasy, despite the heavy automatic pistol tucked in his belt. He had seen the television pictures of the Los Angeles riots years before—as he supposed everyone else in the world had—and he could easily imagine the tiny car being suddenly surrounded and overwhelmed by a howling mob of angry black men. Fat lot of good the guns would do them then. Even if you killed a dozen of them, they would just keep on coming until your clip was empty and your hammer snapped down on an empty chamber.

He looked over at Duffy, who drove silently, a long black cigar clenched in his teeth. Gone was the brown traveling suit. Now the psychopath looked more menacing than ever in his worn leather jacket. The L.A. Dodgers baseball cap he had bought from a street vendor near their seedy Hollywood hotel was pulled down over his bald head, and his red-rimmed eyes were shielded behind mirrored glasses.

The big man seemed to be taking no notice whatsoever of the angry looks they were getting from the street, even though it was he who had warned Tumelty of the dangers they might face in this no-man's-land south of the city. To the younger man, even Duffy's silence seemed fraught with danger on this bright, sunny afternoon.

"How many of them do you think there are, the blacks I mean?" Tumelty asked, mainly to break the silence.

Duffy snorted. "Thousands. Hundreds of thousands." He turned to look over at his frightened companion. "And they're all out there staring in at you, my lad. Hating you for your white skin and this nice shiny automobile you're riding in. How does that make you feel, Dermot?"

Tumelty shuddered. "Why did we have to come here, then?" he asked.

"For The Cause," Duffy laughed happily. "We do it all for The Cause." He turned his mirror-shaded eyes on Tumelty. "That's why we're the new heros of the Irish Nation, don't you see?"

Tumelty tried to smile at the joke. Today being Sunday and all, he'd thought they might have a day off. Perhaps go to Mass, then somewhere for a meal. Instead, Duffy had dragged him out of bed, ordering him to dress and to bring along his gun. And now this. He was sure they'd be killed by the black men.

"Don't you worry, young Dermot Tumelty," said the madman as though he had been reading Dermot's mind. "We are now in the territory of our fellow freedom fighters, and they will surely not harm us."

Tumelty gave him a dubious look.

"We are all part of the same brave revolutionary brotherhood, you see," Duffy assured him. He pointed toward something ahead, and Tumelty looked through the windshield.

At the next corner stood a low stucco building with barred windows, surmounted by a faded red sign that read OUTLAW'S LIQUOR—ICE COLD BEER, CHECKS CASHED. Between twenty and thirty black men, mostly young, many with shaven heads, stood around on the sidewalk or lounged against the flanks of rusting cars, drinking from cans and bottles wrapped in paper bags. "Our destination," said Duffy, swinging the Toyota in toward the curb. "I'll do all the talking."

THE BLACKS gathered before the liquor store stared sullenly at the jaunty little car with the two white men inside, casting knowing glances at one another as it pulled to a stop before them.

"Look at this shit," said a grinning sixteen-year-old in a satin KINGS jacket and two-hundred-dollar Air Jordan Nikes. "Some lost white folks. I gots to get me a piece of this . . ." He started toward the car and was immediately brought up short by a fierce look from a muscular older youth who was leaning against the wall of the store.

"Don't you do nothing," warned the older boy. His street name was Junior, and he was a three-time veteran of the California Youth Authority's Violent Repeat Offender Program. The other boy withered beneath his gaze and joined him against the wall. Junior leaned back against the scarred brown stucco, closely scrutinizing the intruders through hooded eyes.

The driver of the car, an enormous white man in rugged street clothes, was getting out, grinning at the black crowd from behind a huge cigar, and Junior smelled danger. Whatever the man was, he was no fucking tourist, and the prominent bulge in front of the baggy leather jacket he wore wasn't no loaf of bread neither. The other white, a scrawny, nervous-looking youth of about Junior's own age, was on the sidewalk behind the first man, an even more prominent bulge showing beneath the fabric of his flowered Hawaiian shirt.

"Good morning, gents," said the big man, grinning jovially and sounding like some kind of foreigner on the TV. None of the blacks answered him, and he curiosly scanned their angry faces. After a moment, he walked straight to Junior, causing the startled youth to straighten against the wall. "Have I said something wrong?"

Junior stared brazenly into the mirrored glasses. "You ain't said shit, yet, mister," he muttered.

"I beg your pardon," said the other, reaching up to remove the glasses and fixing Junior in his predatory gaze. "You see, I'm new in the area and I'm looking to transact a small bit of business."

Junior was suddenly wary. The big man didn't look or sound like any cop he'd ever seen, but what the hell else would he be doing down here in South Central, unless maybe he was just plain crazy? He looked into the flat, red-rimmed eyes again. Insane eyes. He'd seen lots of eyes like that in the slam.

"I don't know what you talkin' 'bout, mister," he said, keeping his voice low and neutral, playing it safe. In fact, Junior had thirty grams of prime crack hidden in the trunk of a burned-out Impala at the curb, but he wasn't eager to risk his stash or the hard time that might result from trying to make a sale to this fucker. His eyes darted involuntarily to the wrecked automobile.

The white man's eyes flicked to the Impala, and he shook his big bald head. "It's not drugs that I'm wanting today." He grinned around the cigar, turning to glance at the curious crowd of men hovering about them. "I'm after looking for a fella by the name of Slice," he said loudly.

Junior froze at the mention of the feared leader of the Double Zeros. "Don't know no Slice," he stammered unconvincingly. The other men in the crowd began to murmur among themselves, moving silently closer to form a loose half circle around the two whites. Junior dropped his voice to a whisper, thinking vaguely of the consequences of being involved in the killing of white foreigners. "You better get your ass out of here, mister. Slice don't never do no business with whitey."

"Not even when whitey does him a favor?" growled the big man, pressing in so close Junior could smell the reek of his stale breath.

"Don't know what the fuck you're talkin' about, motherfucker," said Junior.

The white man grinned around his cigar, showing his crooked yellow teeth, and pressed something into Junior's unwilling hand. Junior looked down at a wadded up scrap of rusty black material. "What's this shit?" he asked, trying to keep his voice from cracking.

"My calling card. Look at it," said the other, letting the front of his leather jacket fall open to expose the butt of the chrome automatic in his belt. "Look real close now."

Junior opened the wad of cloth, exposing the bloodstained image of a Harley eagle printed on a roughly cut square of black cotton fabric—tee-shirt fabric—smelling the stink of cigar smoke in his nostrils and suddenly feeling the sausage and eggs he'd had for breakfast rising into his throat. "What the fuck is it?" he screeched, dropping the filthy thing onto the sidewalk.

"Same as this one," said the grinning, crazy white man, slapping another wad of blood-soaked cloth into his hand. "And this one."

Junior turned to the wall, retching. "Go to Slice," he gasped to the wide-eyed sixteen-year-old beside him. "Tell him the man want to see him."

The younger boy stared at the gore-encrusted trophies cut from the shirts of Hog Mother and his boys, and took to his heels, vaulting a small wall at the side of the store and disappearing down a narrow alleyway.

"Thank you very kindly," said Francis Duffy, smiling. He puffed his foul-smelling cigar and turned to the crowd of wary black men surrounding him. "Now, can I stand any of you gentlemen to a drink while we're waiting?" he asked.

"THAT WAS a very dangerous way for you to announce yourself, friend."

The black man they called Slice sat behind a table at the end of a large hall that might have been a church except for the huge pair of interlocked black circles painted on the wall at his back. Duffy recognized the enigmatic symbol of an international black unity cadre, known to the uninitiated here in the States as the Double Zeroes, from a PLO sponsored training course he had attended in Algeria some years earlier, and he knew he had come to exactly the right place.

Like Duffy, the man at the table wore heavy mirrored sunglasses. In his case, however, the squarish reflective lenses served not to disguise, but rather to accentuate the lopsided effect of his horribly mutilated face.

In contrast to the brightly colored tee shirts and satin jackets of the youths on the street, Slice, who was not much over twenty-five—if his otherwise unlined skin was any indication of age—wore a somber black suit over a collarless white shirt buttoned to the throat. Two identically dressed bodyguards in dark glasses stood behind him at opposite ends of the table.

"We live in dangerous times," said Duffy, gazing unflinchingly into the other's terrible face. "Revolutionary work is never without risk."

The black man nodded. "That is true. But why have you come to us?" He turned his head slightly left, then right, indicating the grimly expressionless bodyguards at his back. "We were of the impression that your struggle was coming to an end. That an agreement was being written . . ."

"It will only end when the English invaders leave my country," Duffy replied. "Until that day, the war goes on, and the troops of our enemy still walk our streets to remind us that we are a captive people." He jerked his chin toward Tumelty, who stood silently at his shoulder. "Take this poor lad, for example, maimed at the age of nine by the cruel bastards occupying our land, and for no greater reason than that he'd slipped into the street to fetch a bit of milk for his poor old mum . . . Do you think they can make us forget a thing like that by writing some words on a paper?"

Slice looked at Tumelty's mangled hand, absently reaching up to massage the massive scar running from the top of his own head to beneath his chin. "Yes," he said. "You are right about that." He turned his head to the guard on his right. "Bring a chair for my visitor."

A chair was brought, and Duffy sat, leaving Tumelty standing nervously at his back. When his own guard had resumed his position behind the table, Slice leaned forward. "Now," he said, "what is it that you desire from us?"

"It is a matter of a very specialized and extremely powerful explosive," said Duffy.

Slice smiled thinly. "I would be curious to learn who told you we possess such a thing," he said. "Rumors like that could be very dangerous to our group."

Duffy looked pained. "Alas," he said, "I heard the poor fellow that was spreading those rumors about you had met with a fatal accident."

The black man's smile broadened. "Perhaps we can do business together," he said.

CHAPTER SIX

School Days

"BRIAN O'MALLEY?"

Billy looked up from his seat in the center of the row of hard, tweed-covered waiting-room chairs to see the apple-cheeked blond secretary beaming at him from behind her counter.

"Doctor Hughes will see you in just a few minutes," she announced, gathering up the file containing all the forms he'd just filled out. Flashing him a warm smile, she left the desk and disappeared through a wood-paneled door at the rear of Pacific Academy's busy main office.

Billy mentally crossed himself, trying to remember the details he had read on Kileen's data sheet about Brian O'Malley's school background. He cursed his own stupidity for having wasted a good portion of Sunday fiddling around with the green Jag and lying about in his room thinking about Kelly Huston when he could have been preparing himself for today. Why hadn't he had the good sense to foresee the fact that the school authorities were going to want to interview him before simply admitting him to classes?

You're stupid and you're going to get caught, he told himself, watching the paneled door. It opened, and the blond secretary came out empty-handed, resuming her place behind the counter and bobbing her frizzy head encouragingly in his direction. "It shouldn't be long at all, Brian."

Shit! Everything had been going so well until now.

Yesterday he'd had a long, leisurely chat with the old man, absorbing far more information about O'Malley's parents and family background than Michael Kileen had probably ever dreamed of, picking up lots of intimate details—little things that would come in handy should anyone ever challenge his identity. And, too, he'd felt the Major warming up to him, telling him all about his career in films and his heroic exploits in Burma during the war, and hinting mysteriously that he would soon be revealing even more about that early part of his life; something that was bound to make his grandson very proud indeed.

Hard as he tried not to, Billy had found himself liking the old boy, despite the fact that the Major couldn't seem to help veering off from time to time to rant about the deaths of Brian's parents and the murdering Irish nationalists who had killed them.

It had felt strange, sitting out on the old man's veranda, sipping cold drinks with him in the warm California sunshine and biting his tongue in order to prevent himself from blurting out the bloody facts of his own da's cold-blooded murder by the same Protestant bastards the Major kept affectionately referring to as "the loyalists" and "your father's people," painting the heartless, murdering sons of bitches as hardworking, God-fearing British subjects who'd only had the great misfortune to live in a land of lawless and violent Catholic troublemakers who couldn't see reason.

Somehow, he had managed to keep his silence throughout, congratulating himself on having tolerated the Major's daft political rantings with never an outward sign of the churning emotions he was feeling, and grateful that the old fellow had not seemed to notice the faint scratch on his face from Saturday night's fracas with the car-park robbers.

Kelly Huston, looking fresh and beautiful in an amazing green dress worn over white stretch tights that accentuated her long legs, had arrived to pick him up this morning, smiling and offering him her cheek for a quick, friendly kiss, then chatting gaily about school and the classes they might expect to share. Saturday's unpleasantness with Brenda seemed to have been forgotten entirely, and Kelly had regaled him with a hilarious story of the horrible birthday dinner she'd had to attend at a posh restaurant with her parents on Sunday, both of whom she said had probed and prodded her the entire time, begging her to tell them more about "Queally-Smythe's handsome grandson," and insisting that she see "as much as possible of him."

"Well, you've already seen me in my swimming trunks," he had laughed, blushing. "How much more of me would they like you to see?"

Kelly, too, had blushed furiously, reaching over from behind the steering wheel to deliver a playful punch to his ribs, turning serious then and making him feel great by telling him she hoped he did want to see her again.

He had of course said he would like nothing better.

Then they had arrived at the school, driving into a great car park filled with expensive sports cars beside a sprawling complex of elegant Spanish-style buildings. He had gaped at the place as she'd taken his hand and led him across the lushly landscaped campus, pausing several times to exchange greetings with groups of students, and obviously proud to be seen with him.

When they reached the steps of the main building, she'd stood on tiptoe to kiss his cheek, promising to meet him at lunchtime.

Billy had floated up the broad stone steps on a cloud, entering the cathedrallike administration building and staring at the polished marble floors and frescoed ceilings that made the place look more like a great university than a high school. After a few minutes of wandering, he'd found the school office and gone inside, and his bubble had burst.

The frizzy blonde at the desk had greeted him warmly enough, passing him a sheaf of forms to be filled out and informing him that the principal—which was, he determined, some sort of headmaster—had asked to see him before he began classes, the way she said it indicating that such a meeting was quite unusual in this large school. Billy had stared at her in near panic.

Christ, why hadn't Kileen warned him this might happen? It was one thing to pass himself off as Brian O'Malley to a bunch of stupid kids and a misty-eyed old man, quite another to pass the scrutiny of some flinty school headmaster . . . and him a doctor of something or other at that. He had seriously considered bolting out the door, especially when, after a few minutes, a short, thick-shouldered, balding man in a severe dark suit had come into the office and leaned over the counter to hold a whispered conversation with the secretary. The man had turned to give Billy an appraising look, then had disappeared behind the paneled door.

Billy's mind had raced over the possibilities. *He could be a cop, or somebody from Immigration!* What if Brian O'Malley had somehow escaped from Kileen's people and gotten to the police, or if Kileen himself had been captured at long last? Convinced that the game was up, he got slowly to his feet and sauntered casually toward the glass doors leading out to the main lobby of the building. He stopped before a colorful bulletin board, pretending to read the notices about marching-band practice and something called Homecoming. He was just about to slip out through the doors when the secretary's voice rang out behind him.

"Doctor Hughes will see you now."

She was holding open a small wooden gate at the end of the counter, gesturing for him to enter. *If it was the cops or Immigration, they wouldn't have left me alone to walk away, would they? No. Shit, they'd have me cuffed and on my way to a police station by now . . . So it can't be that.*

Billy Quinn took a deep breath, wiped his damp palms on the legs of his trousers and smiled weakly at the secretary, then walked to the wooden gate and stepped through, feeling like a mouse that has just wandered into the jaws of a trap too cleverly constructed for him to comprehend. "You may go right in," she said, pointing to the paneled door.

He slowly crossed the office to the indicated door and placed his hand on the ornate brass knob, wondering as he turned it what Kileen would do to him if he was found out. He drove the frightening thought from his mind, opened the door and stepped through.

BIOLOGY LAB.

Kelly sat gazing dreamily at her lab notebook, heedless of Stanley Kinsella's zealous efforts to isolate something disgusting from the frog corpse on the table before them. She was writing Brian's name inside the back cover of her book, tracing the letters over and over in blue pen, adding fanciful curlicues and exclamations.

"Mmmm, cute. I haven't written a guy's name in my notebook since I was in the eighth grade."

Kelly felt her face reddening as she slammed her notebook shut and looked up to see Samantha Simms peering over her shoulder.

"Next thing you'll be doing is writing your name over his in a big red heart," Sam smirked.

"You're not funny," whispered Kelly, looking around the room and noticing that Miss Wyeth was gone. Several of the students had gotten up from their places and were wandering around visiting one another.

"Kelly, I think we'd better try to complete the central nervous system before the end of class . . ." Stanley Kinsella looked up nervously from his gruesome task, his weak eyes blinking owlishly behind thick lenses.

"Stanley, be a darling and play with your little frog alone for a minute while Kelly and I discuss something really important." Samantha flashed him a dazzling smile, and he turned meekly away, hunching over his dissection tray.

"Okay," said Sam, returning her attention to Kelly. "I've been dying to talk to you but Brad and I drove up to Santa Barbara to his parents' place yesterday and we didn't get back until late. What's with you and Brian? After that scene Saturday night I figured you two were history."

Kelly smiled sweetly. "Why, whatever gave you that idea, Sam?"

Sam stared at her. "Excuse me, weren't you the one who ran out of Club Retro the other night while Brenda Gaynor was polishing your boyfriend's tonsils with her little forked tongue?" She looked across the room at Brenda's lab table. Thad August was bent over the dissecting tray by himself. "And where is Brenda today, by the way? I haven't seen her all morning."

Kelly followed her gaze to August's broad back and shrugged. "How am I supposed to know where she is, for God's sake? And as far as what happened with Brian the other night, that was all Brenda's doing. Brian said she was drunk and that she practically attacked him."

"Whoa, you really have got it bad." Sam patted her shoulder sympathetically. "I didn't notice Brian exactly throwing hammerlocks on her to make her stop."

"Well, he went home with me," Kelly said defensively. "After we got back to his house we sat in the car and talked for a long time . . ."

Sam raised a professionally plucked eyebrow. "You talked? Now let me get this straight, you're alone in a parked car with the winner of the Tom Cruise look-alike contest and you *talked?*" She placed a hand on Kelly's forehead. "I knew it, you're sick."

"Sam, cut it out!" Kelly was growing increasingly irritated at Sam's refusal to ever take anything seriously.

"Okay," Sam scrunched her shoulders, looking hurt. "If you don't want to tell me all the gory details . . ."

Kelly nodded curtly, turning back to the lab table and forcing herself to look at the mess in the dissecting tray.

"Stanley, I have a confession to make. I love you more than words can say," whispered Sam, leaning over to brush her breasts against him. The nerd's head abruptly snapped up from his work and he followed her with his eyes as she sashayed back to her own table.

"Don't pay any attention to her, Stanley," said Kelly. "She doesn't mean anything when she acts like that."

Stanley pushed his glasses up on his nose and smiled wearily. "It's okay," he said. "I mean, I got used to people treating me like that a long time ago. It doesn't bother me anymore."

Kelly frowned. "It *should* bother you, Stanley. You should get angry or something. Stand up for yourself. They've got no right to treat you like that." She lowered her eyes. "And if I've treated you that way, I want to apologize for it now."

He stared at her. "Kelly, you don't have to—"

"No," she said, cutting him off. "You've always been nice to me and I've treated you like crap. I'm sorry." She leaned over and kissed his cheek. "Forgive me?"

Stanley Kinsella's pale eyes misted over behind his thick glasses, and for a moment Kelly was afraid he was going to cry. She watched him helplessly, then placed her hand on his shoulder. "Come on, Stanley," she pleaded. "Tell me what we're supposed to be doing to this poor dead frog."

BILLY QUINN was beginning to relax.

He sat in a deep, comfortable chair across from Dr. Hughes's desk, flashing his best British schoolboy smile. His nervousness over the unanticipated interview with the scholarly principal had dissipated almost immediately upon his having entered Hughes's well-appointed office several minutes earlier.

Instead of the sharp grilling he had expected, the meticulously tailored, gray-haired educator had fairly leaped up from behind his broad desk, hurrying around to grasp both of Billy's hands in his, clasping them tightly and making a little speech he had obviously prepared in advance. "Pacific Academy is honored," he had intoned, "honored to have James Queally-Smythe's grandson joining our little academic community . . ." There had been more, all having to do with Hughes hoping the school would live up to Billy's academic expectations and reasserting the *personal* assurance he had given to James Queally-Smythe to assist in whatever way possible in easing his grandson's transition to the "less structured educational environment here at Pacific Academy."

Suddenly understanding the special treatment being accorded him, Billy had allowed himself to be guided to the comfy chair, where he had listened with his mouth hanging open as Hughes returned to his desk and began fussing over Brian O'Malley's school transcripts. "An excellent student! Head of his house at St. Stephen's School. University material!" Hughes had ticked off the list of O'Malley's accomplishments as though they were battlefield commendations. And all the while the thick-shouldered man in the dark suit had sat in a chair off to one side, oohing and aahing, but saying nothing else.

Billy could think of nothing to do but nod modestly, answering the principal's few questions with polite yessirs, nossirs and I'll-do-my-best-sirs.

When at last he had run out of adulatory steam, Hughes got up and hooked his thumbs under the red suspenders he wore beneath his lightweight gray suit, looking for all the world like the nineteenth-century explorer that Billy had once seen posing over the carcass of a dead rhinoceros in a faded photo.

"Now that I've made my little welcoming address," he said, looking immensely pleased with himself, "I'm certain you're anxious to get on with your studies." Hughes lifted a pink card from a file on his desk. "I've taken the liberty of preparing your schedule myself, based on your transcripts from St. Stephen's," he said, handing over the card. His eyes twinkled behind his wire rimmed-spectacles. "Hopefully, you won't find it too dull."

Billy stood and accepted the schedule, running his eyes down the list of courses, and groaning inwardly at the sight of Advanced Calculus—whatever the hell that was—and Third Year Biology. He smiled up at Hughes and started to back out of the office, grateful, at least, that he would probably not be around Pacific Academy High long enough to have to sit their exams. He was nearly to the safety of the door when the man in the dark suit cleared his throat loudly, and Hughes turned around to look at him.

"Oh my, I nearly forgot," said the principal. "Our Mr. Gianelli has been dying to meet you. I alerted him that you would be joining us, as soon as I received your transcripts."

The short man grinned and got to his feet, advancing on Billy with his hand extended. "Welcome aboard, son," he said, grasping Billy's hand in a bone-crushing grip and pumping vigorously.

"Thank you very much, Mr. . . . Gianelli." Billy looked down on Gianelli, noticing for the first time that the top of his scalp was sunburned.

"I can tell you I'm really charged up over the prospect of having you on my team," said Gianelli. He winked conspiratorially. "And you can forget that Mr. Gianelli stuff with me. All of my boys just call me Coach."

Billy looked at him in utter confusion. "Team? I don't think I understand."

Hughes and Gianelli exchanged amused glances. "No need for modesty, Brian," said the principal. "Your reputation has preceded you."

Billy gurgled, "It has?"

Gianelli grinned, showing lots of teeth. "It's all there in your record, son. All-British Schoolboy Champ two years running. Jeez, Coach Fulton over at University High is gonna crap his pants when I trot you out at our next meet."

The sinking feeling in Billy's stomach was turning into a leaden ball. Kileen's notes had contained nothing about Brian O'Malley playing any sports, much less his being All-British Schoolboy Champion of anything. The two men before him were waiting for him to say something and he didn't even know what the hell sport he was supposed to be champion of. Then it hit him. Rugby! Kileen had instructed him to examine the small finger on O'Malley's left hand.

The finger he had broken playing Rugby!

Thank God it was the one sport he knew well, had, in fact, grown up playing and watching. Billy Quinn could debate Rugby strategies and plays all day long without pausing for breath . . . He grinned as one of his favorite slogans popped into his head: Rugby Players Eat Their Dead. He hadn't even known the Americans played the rough-and-tumble game.

The men were still waiting for him to say something. He started to tell them he couldn't wait to get out on the pitch with the other lads . . . Then he hesitated. Kileen had told him he must remain available for his mission. What if the Pacific Academy team traveled away to games, or required late practices?

Billy shook his head and held up his left hand, showing them the crooked little finger. "Don't know how much use I'd be to you, Coach," he said remorsefully. "I'm afraid this finger has never healed properly since it was injured during a rather rough match at St. Stephen's last year."

Hughes and Gianelli stared at the crooked finger for a long moment. Then they both began to laugh in unison. "Now that is funny, son," said Gianelli, clapping Billy on the back and running his fingers over his pink scalp. "Glad to see you've got a sense of humor."

Hughes dabbed at his eyes with a handkerchief. "Very good. I must remember that," he chuckled. "Tell us, how on earth did you manage to break your finger in a cross-country run, Brian?"

"Yeah," Gianelli wheezed, "I heard you Britishers took your running seriously, but broken fingers? What happened, you trip and fall?"

Billy swallowed hard. "Yes, I, uh, stumbled," he muttered.

"Well, I hope it didn't knock too many seconds off that record time of yours," the coach grinned. "See you on the track, son." He and Hughes were still laughing as Billy slipped out of the principal's office.

Long-distance running! Jesus, he'd never run track in his life. Didn't know the slightest thing about it, except what he'd seen on the telly when they'd showed the Olympics. *Now you are truly fucked, my lad,* he told himself, not even bothering to return the frizzy-haired secretary's cheery smile. He hoped Kileen burned in hell forever for putting him in this impossible situation.

"Brian!"

Billy looked up to see a smiling Brenda Gaynor standing demurely by the door leading out into the lobby. Groaned. *Jesus Christ, what now?* he wondered angrily. Forced himself to smile back, remembering her rage when he'd left her standing on the dance floor.

"Brenda, hello," he said warily. *What in the name of God was she doing here, grinning at him like a damned hungry crocodile?*

"I just wanted to apologize for Saturday," she said, pushing out her lower lip and batting her eyelashes at him. She cast a furtive glance at the blond secretary, whose head was bent over a stack of computer printouts. "I guess I'd had a little too much nitrous," she whispered.

Billy tried to squeeze past her. "It's all right," he said absently. "There was no harm done . . ." He looked down at the pink card in his hand. According to the schedule, he was supposed to attend a class called Geog II in ten minutes. "Well, I'd better be going," he said, pushing on the glass doors. "Nice seeing you."

Brenda grinned and linked her arm through his, guiding him out into the marble lobby. "You'll be seeing a lot of me today," she said mysteriously.

He looked at her, confused. Held up the pink card. "I've got a class now . . ."

She wrinkled her nose prettily, leaning over to peer at the schedule. "Yuck, geography. Well come on, we'd better hurry. It's all the way over in the DeMille building on the other side of campus."

"You have this same class at ten-fifteen?"

Brenda laughed. "No, silly. I'm your orientation guide. That means I'm supposed to show you where everything is today." She squeezed his arm and pulled him toward the building entrance. "I volunteered." She looked up into his eyes. "To make up for being such a bitch the other night."

Billy sighed and stopped walking. "Brenda, you don't have to do this," he said.

She tugged on his arm. "But I wanted to, Brian," she insisted. "Besides, Doctor Hughes made it official and told me to ditch all of my classes today. Come on now or you're going to be late."

"DON'T SAY anything, please."

Billy was standing over Kelly's table on the sunlit patio outside the school cafeteria. They watched Brenda disappear into a restroom, and he dropped wearily onto a picnic bench. "She got the bloody principal to appoint her my 'orientation guide,'" he said. "She's been hanging onto me like a fu— like a leech all morning."

"Isn't love wonderful," Samantha observed, spearing a slice of raw zucchini on the tip of her plastic fork. He cringed and looked helplessly at Kelly.

"Sam, shut up," snapped Kelly. She turned back to Billy and patted his hand. "Don't worry about it, Brian. You need someone to show you where everything is, and they would have appointed somebody."

"Wish it had been you, then," he said, shyly squeezing her hand.

She smiled and offered him half of her tuna sandwich.

"Just watch yourself around that tongue of hers," Samantha advised. "The last guy Brenda got a good tongue lock on needed emergency surgery to have it removed."

Billy stared at her in amazement, sure she was joking but uncertain whether a reply was called for. "Hey, my father's a doctor, I know about this stuff," said Sam.

They all began to laugh.

THAD AUGUST leaned against a palm tree at the edge of the patio, glaring at the dark-haired Irish asshole sitting with the two girls. He hadn't even met Brian O'Malley and he already hated his guts.

It had started with Brenda on Saturday night. Good old Brenda, who had until a few days ago worshiped Thad's ass, and who was always more than willing to do whatever he wanted. The other night, though, she had skittered away from him like some kind of a goddamn virgin when he had just wanted a little screw. Then it had happened again yesterday. His parents had left to spend the week at their place in Aspen and he had called Brenda immediately, giving her the chance to drive over to his house and spend the whole day in bed with him, drinking his father's booze and snorting a little coke the old fart hadn't found.

And the little bitch had turned him down.

He couldn't fucking believe it!

Then he had finally started to understand this morning. First she hadn't shown up for biology lab. And later, she'd come bouncing into geography, hanging onto the asshole, whispering into his ear and giggling at everything he said.

Now, while old Brenda had ducked into the crapper, the bastard was sitting with Kelly Huston and *she* was falling all over him, looking like she'd happily climb right up onto that picnic table and let him do it to her in front of the whole school if he felt like it.

Thad August's rage was growing. Christ, Kelly Huston! Last week on his father's boat the stupid bitch had practically screamed rape when all he'd done was grab a little tit.

He watched sullenly as Brenda came out of the girls' room and waved. Brian O'Malley got up and crossed the patio, and she latched onto him again like a goddamn magnet. The two of them walked off together,

Brenda, her long, coppery hair glowing in the sunlight, slipping her arm around the asshole's waist and laughing hilariously at something he said.

The high, clear sound of her laughter reached his ears, and August felt a sudden longing for her, closing his eyes at the memory of that fiery mass of hair splayed across his naked chest, her warm, excited breath tickling his skin as he lay sprawled on the big bed in the main cabin of his father's sailboat with Brenda's long, perfect legs straddling him.

He had to do something to get her back.

Something that did not involve his actually tangling with the murderous Irish kid.

CHAPTER SEVEN

Expendables

"YES . . . NO PROBLEMS."

Francis Duffy sat on the end of his sagging mattress in the double room on the fourth floor of the Hollywood Sunset Hotel, clenching a black cigar in his teeth and gazing out through the open window at the continuously shifting mosaic of prostitutes and drug dealers gathered by the taco stand across the street. The terrorist had the receiver of an ancient Princess phone pressed tightly to his ear and was straining to hear the faint voice on the other end of the line above the racket of the television set at the opposite side of the room. "Hold the line a moment," he shouted, reaching down by the bed for a shoe. He took aim at the back of Dermot Tumelty's bushy head and threw the shoe, catching the younger man on the shoulder and knocking over a bottle of grape soda on the cheap coffee table. Tumelty, his trance broken, whirled to face him.

"Turn that fucking thing down, or I'll put me fucking foot through it," growled Duffy. Tumelty scrambled across the coffee table, lowering the volume on the monster-movie marathon he was watching, then turning back to stare at the big man.

Duffy glared at him, raising the phone to his ear. "Now give me that last bit again, to be certain I've understood." He listened carefully, his big head nodding, the fleshy lips silently moving as he memorized the instructions. "Got it," he said when the voice on the other end had finished. He replaced the Princess phone on the bedside table and sat motionless on the bed.

"Who was that, then?" asked Tumelty, who was busily mopping up the grape soda with a worn hotel bath towel.

Duffy's great bald head slowly swung around, and he regarded his young companion through murderous red-rimmed eyes. "Now who the fuck do you think it was, you dim little beezer, Her Royal Majesty asking us to high fucking tea at the palace?"

Tumelty cringed. Although he himself was delighted to have nothing more to do than eat fast food and watch the telly, Duffy had become increasingly irritable during the time they'd been forced to wait in the cramped confines of their small room for Kileen's call. The giant maniac disapproved of everything Tumelty did, and the little fellow was beginning to seriously worry for his safety if they had to wait much longer. "I didn't hear it ring," he began lamely, as if that somehow explained his present confusion. "Who was it?"

"Well now think hard, Dermot. Who knows we're here?"

"Nobody," said Tumelty, "except . . ." His mouth fell open and he left the sentence unfinished.

Duffy nodded like a stern schoolmaster who has just pried a correct answer from the class imbecile. "Himself," he said.

"Did you tell him we got all the stuff?" Tumelty was suddenly interested in the phone call, anxious to have Kileen know that the two of them together had succeeded in obtaining the weapons and the exotic explosives their volatile leader had ordered, although he knew he would never have been able to carry it off on his own. It had really all been Duffy's doing.

Duffy shook his head in disgust. "Sure, I shouted it out to him over an open international telephone line, Dermot, just in case the CIA or MI-5 happened to be listening in." He touched a match to the cold cigar, filling the room with a cloud of stinking smoke and shaking his head at the other's stupidity.

Dermot's face fell, and he returned to mopping up the grape soda. Seeing the crestfallen expression on the youngster's face, Duffy reflected that, despite his annoying chatter and daft childish addictions, the little bugger had stood up with him before the motorcyclists and the dangerous mob of blacks, and that he had remained completely loyal to both Kileen and The Cause when most of their former comrades had sold out many months ago. Maybe he was being too hard on the lad.

"Kileen knows, Dermot, my boy," he finally said in a softer tone, somewhat mollified by the thought that they were finally free to leave the claustrophobic confines of the hotel room. After his six years in Brixton prison, Duffy could no longer stand the inside of any room for very long. "I told him you did well enough too . . ." He grinned and added, "though I'm still liable to tear off your head and shit down your scrawny neck if you don't leave off with that fucking telly!"

Dermot Tumelty's face lit up like a cheap Christmas display. "Will he be coming soon, then?"

Duffy nodded. "Soon enough. Now what do you say to getting out of this shithole for a while? We'll have us a little holiday for a couple of days, until Kileen gets here."

Tumelty grinned, producing a stack of glossy adverts he'd torn from the in-flight magazine during the course of their long plane ride to L.A. "That would be grand, Francis. There's Disneyland, and the film studios at Universal . . ."

Duffy rolled his eyes to the cracked ceiling. "Dermot, my boy, I am dry and I am horny. I want to get drunk, and then I want to get fucked, and then drunk again. Now can I do all that at Disneyland?"

Disappointed, Dermot Tumelty slowly shook his head. "I don't . . . think so, Francis."

Francis Duffy's howl of laughter rolled out through the open window, causing a bored hooker on the street below to look up. "You don't fucking *think* so?"

MICHAEL KILEEN stepped out of the public telephone booth and stared up at the sodden Dublin sky. It had been raining when he had left Zurich too, but somehow the Irish rain had always seemed unique to him, as did the faint gaseous smell of burning peat in the air, overlaid with the sharp, metallic odors of decaying seaweed and salt.

The skin surrounding the nearly invisible latticework of fine incisions tucked away beneath his hairline and the overhang of his strong jaw were itching madly—the result of slowly healing tissue about the hundreds of hairlike sutures the Geneva scalpel artist had threaded beneath his skin to approximate the fresh-cut edges after the disfiguring scar tissue had been cut away with the needle-fine tip of his argon laser.

Thanks to the surgeon's exclusive collagen dressings—developed, so he'd been told, to speed the healing process among film stars and politicians who were not desirous of walking around for weeks bearing the distinctive signs of recent plastic surgery—the postoperative swelling and redness that had, just a few days previously, given his face and the freshly grafted skin on the tops of his hands the appearance of overripe tomatoes were all but gone, and now he looked no worse than a man recovering from a bad sunburn—a circumstance to which he had artfully adapted by booking his flight back to Dublin via the Spanish sun coast, where he had spent twenty-four hours in a villa belonging to a wealthy nationalist sympathizer in exile, who had also seen to it that he was provided with the flawless American and British passports, credit cards and other identity papers that he now carried.

All in all, thought Michael Kileen, things were progressing quite satisfactorily. The two expendables he had sent ahead to Los Angeles had actually managed to obtain the specialized ordnance he had ordered, and his deep-cover contact there had assured him that the eager youngster he had planted in the home of James Queally-Smythe, one of Great Britain's most fiercely loyal and vocal expatriates, was, so far, passing scrutiny.

Kileen stopped to admire his new face in a shop window, then crossed Grafton Street to the familiar cafe where he planned to have a coffee and something to eat before retiring to his hotel. In the morning, he would take care of the one remaining detail he had left hanging here in Dublin. Then it would be off to the airport for the circuitous journey to Los Angeles via Mexico City and Acapulco.

He opened the downstairs street door to Little America, heard the blast of the jukebox playing "Hotel California," an old favorite by the Eagles. Halfway up the steep stairs he paused to listen to the song, softly singing the familiar lyric—"You can check in anytime you want, but you can never, ever leave . . ." Despite his pain, he smiled at the irony of the song, thinking how perfectly the strange words described the dangerous life he lived. He and all the recruits he had lately enlisted: Duffy and Tumelty and young Billy Quinn, and all the others before them.

Like himself, they could never, ever leave The Cause. For the life of an Irish freedom fighter was like a virulent cancer, jumping from generation to generation, taking young men's souls and eating them alive. Taking all their lives in the end, one way or another.

Kileen stood there in the narrow stairwell, his head suddenly splitting with the racket above, reliving the night more than twenty-five years ago when the life had got him. It had been in Belfast, in the second year of the British occupation, in a noisy pub filled with university students.

"WE JUST WANT a word in private, if you please." The man in the badly scuffed leather coat was tall and thick about the shoulders, with the crooked-nosed look of a failed prizefighter gone to fat. His broken face, which had seemed jolly and good natured in the pub just minutes earlier, was now sinister in the stark shadows cast by the single naked bulb lighting the alleyway.

"Nothing for you to worry about," said the other man, stepping stiff-legged from the shadows and leaning heavily on his stout black crutch to squint at the youth they had hustled out through the back way. "We only want to know where you stand, Michael Kileen."

The second speaker was smaller than his companion, and older too, with a thatch of graying brown hair showing beneath the greasy brim of his tweed workingman's cap. When he opened his mouth to speak, the mixed odors of strong tobacco and stale Guinness filled the close confines of the alley, making their young captive feel slightly queasy.

"I stand for a united Ireland," Michael Kileen whispered, wishing that he were safely back inside the warm, smoky pub with his university mates, and that he'd kept his impassioned opinions to himself about what ought to be done to the British soldiers who'd settled down to patrolling the Catholic districts in their screened, armored vehicles and manning the steel barricades with which they'd lately ringed the city. But he had seen the bastards harrassing a tearful young woman in the road this very afternoon and, fearful of what they might do to him with their lead-weighted truncheons and their machine pistols if he dared to intervene, he had turned away in shame, hurrying down a side street with their crude laughter ringing in his ears.

Then, this evening in the pub, with the incident still burning in his guts and the half dozen pints he'd consumed fueling his fervor, he'd begun loudly boasting about the lesson he'd like to teach the bastards. Too late he'd noticed the sinister pair watching him.

Kileen had fallen silent at the sight of the men, and though there'd been cheers around the bar for his speech, and his university mates were all slapping his back, he'd retreated sheepishly to a corner booth by the smouldering peat fire, averting his eyes from the watchers by pretending to fix his attention on the fresh pint in his hand. But of course the damage had already been done. Someone at the bar had produced a guitar, and the other students had all begun to sing "Four Green Fields" in brazen defiance of the British occupation, shouting out the words of the inflammatory revolutionary ballad at the tops of their lungs, making him proud to be one of them, but making him wonder, too, what they would have thought if they'd seen him scurrying away from the swaggering group of uniformed Tommies scarcely four hours before.

The song was just winding up when the reek of harsh tobacco wafted across his table and he felt the ancient dark wood of the fireside booth groan beside him. Looking up, he'd found himself trapped between the two grim-faced men.

Indicating with subtle though unmistakable gestures that he was to follow, they had led him out into the dark alley behind the pub, and now they were both standing there in the harsh light, scrutinizing him.

And young Michael Kileen was suddenly very, very frightened. Because he knew who these men were, had known of them and others just like them—men like his father—for his whole life. And he knew that they wanted something from him. Something that it was beyond his power to deny them. Not if he wanted to live, at any rate.

The cripple—rumored to have lost the better part of his foot to a British bullet in the ambush of a street patrol the week the occupation had begun more than a year earlier—had been a great friend of Kileen's father, an activist steamfitter in the Belfast shipyards who had drunk himself to death after his position had been made redundant in retaliation for his participation in a strike aimed at forcing the hiring of more Catholic workers in the skilled union trades.

The man's name was Whalen, and his boy, Jimmy, who had been at St. Brendan's School with Kileen when they were both sixteen, had been taken away by the soldiers in the sixth month of the occupation. Jimmy Whalen was a patriot.

"So, have you had any news of Jimmy, then?" Kileen asked uneasily, though in fact he had never cared for Whalen's son, a dim, bullying brute of a boy who had been forever telling the hapless nuns at St. Brendan's to "get stuffed" and thus making life perpetually miserable for his classmates.

At the mention of his son's name, the elder Whalen snatched the ragged cap from his head, dropping his stubbled chin reverently onto his chest. And despite his fear, Kileen felt himself suppressing a smirk, for the old fool was behaving as though he had just heard the holy name of Jesus uttered, rather than that of his dimwitted son.

"They say our Jimmy's been moved down to Newgate Prison with the Cohan brothers," mumbled the old man. "Tried and convicted of sedition."

"Shit!" said Kileen, truly shocked by Whalen's revelation. Of course he'd heard of the Cohan brothers: The pair had been arrested for half killing an off-duty Tommy after they'd claimed he raped their sister during a midnight weapons search of the family's Bogside flat. It was common knowledge on the street that the brothers had been held by the Brits without charge for nearly a year. But he'd heard nothing of any trials and said as much.

"Haven't you heard, the fuckers don't have to hold public trials anymore," growled the brute in the scuffed leather coat, whose name Kileen could not remember. "Not for the likes of Paddy."

"They've issued a special judicial order, just for our people," Whalen continued bitterly. "Like as if we're different from them. Less than human . . ."

The old man snuffled loudly into his sleeve. "The fuckers!"

Kileen shook his head sympathetically, casting a longing glance toward the pub door. Inside, he could hear his mates launching into another loud protest song, their drunken young voices rising discordantly above the clatter of glasses and the drone of the BBC announcer reading the news on the telly above the bar. "Christ, I'm sorry," he said, trying to think of some excuse to get back in out of the cold. He was shivering in his thin sweater, and it had just occurred to him that if an army patrol happened along and discovered him here in the alley with the two old firebrands he'd be arrested right along with them, and to hell with the reason.

"I was always fond of your Jimmy," Kileen said lamely.

Whalen raised his bloodshot eyes to the youth and sniffled. "My Jimmy was never no scholar like yourself," he said, laying a dirty hand on Kileen's sleeve, "but he's a good lad, Michael . . . Now his poor mother's heart has been broken."

Kileen nodded soberly. In his opinion, Jimmy Whalen, who he suddenly remembered had once been caught pissing in the holy-water font by a red-faced Jesuit who'd beaten him senseless before the entire school, was a fucking idiot who had probably done something incredibly stupid in order to land himself in British hands . . . Not that that gave the fuckers any right to take him away from his home for some cocked-up secret trial. Still, Kileen felt there were plenty of ways to protest the occupation without landing in gaol. Ways he had himself taken an active part in.

Whalen was snuffling softly to himself now, and Kileen thought he at last understood why the old man had sought him out. He breathed a deep sigh of relief at the realization that the crippled patriot had simply wanted the commiseration of someone who'd been at school with his lamented son.

"Let's go back inside," he offered solicitously. "We'll drink Jimmy's health and curse the rotten bastards who've imprisoned him."

Whalen seemed on the verge of moving, but the great oaf in the leather coat stepped forward, blocking the way. "You say you're for a united Ireland," he demanded in his gutteral prizefighter's voice. "But will you stand for her?"

Kileen's eyes darted nervously about the alleyway. Though nothing specifically treasonous had actually been said yet, this was dangerous talk. For he knew exactly what the brute was demanding of him; a pledge of loyalty to Whalen and his violent compatriots. "I do stand for Ireland reunited," he repeated evenly. He lowered his voice and stepped closer to the big man. "And for Sinn Fein."

A crooked smile crossed the ogre's battered face at the mention of Northern Ireland's outlawed political party, and his black eyes glittered in the glow of the naked bulb above the door. "And your mates as well?" he enquired, tilting his lopsided head in the direction of the singing voices, which had at some point transitioned into another song, a mournful litany of the centuries-old British cruelties to the Irish.

Kileen hesitated, because now it was clear to him that, after all, the desperadoes wanted something more from him than a few kind words about Jimmy Whalen.

Both men glared suspiciously, awaiting his answer, and Kileen saw the big fellow's right hand slip into the bulging pocket of his leather coat.

"My friends as well," Kileen carefully replied in a frightened voice.

The two men exchanged triumphant glances, and the brute rewarded Kileen with a gruesome grin. "Then you'll all do us a small favor, for the good of The Cause?"

Kileen nodded slowly. "If we can," he said warily.

"It's a little thing." Whalen smiled encouragingly. "A matter of showing the colors, so to speak."

Back on familiar ground at last, Kileen, a veteran of more than a few illegal student protests since the beginning of the armed occupation, nodded affirmatively. "We can put three hundred student demonstrators in the streets," he offered importantly, suddenly excited at the dangerous prospect of working in direct concert with these hard-core freedom fighters. Such a thing had not to his knowledge been openly organized before, but he had no doubt it would attract international attention, if it could really be brought off.

"We'll prepare banners stating our message, and there'll be bullhorns for speaking to the crowd, trained marshals to keep order—"

A sneer twisted Whalen's thin lips. "What are you saying?" he hissed, abruptly cutting the younger man off. "We don't want you to organize a fucking hippie parade."

Kileen stared at the cripple, confused. "I don't understand, then," he stammered. "Passive resistance has been shown to be a highly effective tool for political change . . ."

The big man spat at his feet and dug deep into the pocket of his cracked leather overcoat. "No, laddie," he growled, "that's all just so much shit for the television." He withdrew a heavy object from his pocket and thrust it forward into the light. "*This* is the only 'highly effective tool for political change.' The only one those brutal English bastards respect, at any rate."

Michael Kileen, twenty-two-year-old student activist and secret coward, stared down at the giant's proffered hand. Atop the massive pink palm lay a dull gray automatic pistol, the checkered pattern etched into its black plastic grips glittering like the big man's eyes in the yellow light of the naked bulb. "Take it," ordered the monster.

Kileen took the gun, the unexpected weight of it causing his hand to sink involuntarily to his side. He felt his bladder threatening to let go at the touch of cold metal against his skin, for even to possess such a weapon in this time and this place, he knew, was good for twenty years or more of harsh British justice.

"What am I supposed to do with this?" he whispered through lips suddenly gone dry as ashes.

Whalen's crafty red eyes darted about the deserted alley. "There's a killing to be done," he whispered. "You see, Michael, most of our best young lads are in prison or being watched, so it'll have to be done by somebody who's not considered a threat." The big man's eyes settled on the closed door of the pub. "Somebody with mates he can depend on, mates who'll swear he was someplace else with them at the time."

"You want me to kill somebody?" Kileen felt as if he might faint at any second.

"Don't you worry now, lad!" The big fellow grinned down at him, showing his mouthful of crooked brown teeth. "It's only to be a small killing," he crooned, leaning forward until their noses were nearly touching, "nobody important at all." The awful grin widened and Kileen smelled the sweetish reek of raw whiskey on the brute's breath. "And you'll never be found out."

"Who?" asked Kileen, his voice a ragged whisper. "Who do you want me to kill?"

Whalen shrugged noncommittally. "That hasn't been decided yet."

Kileen looked at him in amazement. "What do you mean?"

The hulk playfully clapped him on the back, then took the gun from Kileen's trembling hand, gently tucked it into Kileen's belt and pulled his sweater down over the bulge. "It's a matter of policy, you see," he explained, nudging the shivering student back toward the door of the pub. "Time for another of the bastards to die as a show of our resolve to fight on. It doesn't really matter which one of them we kill, does it? We'll let you know the name in good time."

He pushed the scarred wooden door open, and the warm, beery atmosphere of the noisy pub spilled out to mingle with the cold night air. "Now let's all go inside and drink young Jimmy Whalen's health, shall we?" He laughed, shoving the bewildered Kileen ahead of him.

"Jimmy'll be proud of ye, Michael," whispered Whalen, touching him affectionately on the shoulder from behind. "He always looked up to you, did my Jimmy."

Michael Kileen halted in his tracks and turned to stare back in genuine surprise at the cripple. "He did?"

Whalen's old head bobbed up and down. "It's God's own truth," he affirmed solemnly. "'Da, he's a scholar, that Michael Kileen,' Jimmy told me. 'Smart as a whip. When you've got a job that calls for brains, then Kileen's your boy-o.'" The old man smiled sweetly, stepping through the door and pulling it shut behind him.

It was amazing, thought the stunned Kileen as the odd trio pushed their way back up front into the noisy barroom. He had always been convinced in school that Jimmy Whalen had hated his guts.

The flat, cold alloy of the slab-sided automatic pistol in his belt chafed uncomfortably against the soft skin of his belly, and Kileen wondered how in the hell he was going to talk his way out of this mess. Someone called to him from the bar, and he waved, then turned back to say something more to Whalen. To his surprise, the cripple was no longer following him. He spun around to see the broad back of the brute's scuffed leather coat disappearing through the door.

"Well, I'm not going to kill some poor fucker on the say-so of those two old wankers," he mumbled aloud, elbowing his way up to the bar and waving for a whiskey, silently vowing never to be so stupid as to use the gun in one of their daft murders, no matter what they threatened.

But of course he had used it. That very same night, in fact. And the two old revolutionaries hadn't even had to provide him with a name.

That was just the way of it.

"PARDON US, SIR. Could you let us get by."

Michael Kileen looked up in momentary confusion, the memories of twenty-five years ago dissolving in an instant. A smart young couple wearing identical black leather jackets stood impatiently on the narrow stairs above him, waiting to come down, and he realized he was blocking their way. Overhead, in the cafe, Little America's giant Seeberg jukebox was belting out another golden oldie.

Kileen moved aside and the young couple, a boy and a girl not much older than Billy Quinn, hurried past, giving him a curious look, then pushed out through the door leading into the rainy street.

When they had gone, Kileen climbed wearily the rest of the way up to Little America and stepped into the noisy cafe, peeling off his raincoat against the stifling heat and marveling that his remembrance of that night in Belfast still remained so clear. Of course, he'd had his doubts about the rightness of his actions back then. Doubts that had long since been scoured clean by the years.

Now, as he had forcefully reminded the boy he had sent off to California to implement the final critical stage of his meticulously engineered scheme, no sacrifice was too great. Not when that sacrifice would snatch complete and total victory from the crumbling diplomatic defeat he saw in the uneasy peace that had left Northern Ireland firmly in British hands.

CHAPTER EIGHT
Fools For Love

BILLY QUINN trudged slowly up the long driveway leading to the Major's house. His head was down, and he was thinking about the ever-growing tangle of lies and deceits he must keep up with if he were even to last out the week at Pacific Academy. For, aside from somehow muddling his way through the baffling array of class assignments—many involving subjects about which he knew absolutely nothing—he must also somehow become at least conversant with the rules of long distance running, in order to avoid seeming the utter fool before the eager track coach.

The more he thought about it, the more impossible it seemed to maintain the charade he was carrying on, and he realized that although he had been given no timetable for the old freedom fighter's arrival, Kileen would have to come very soon now, if Billy was not to be found out.

And then there was Kelly Huston.

Billy had sat quietly in the passenger seat of her yellow Mustang all during the ride home from school, watching the way the wind whipped strands of golden hair about her pretty face, listening to her tell a funny story about something that had happened to her when she was just a little girl in Boston. And all the while he had longed to reach out and caress her soft cheek, to confess that his dreams were filled with confusing images of her. He longed to hold her close to him, to touch her soft breast, as he had two nights before, to see her every day of his life.

But, of course, that was completely daft. He didn't even know her. Not really. He didn't know what to do, wanting to be near her, but afraid he might hurt her.

Billy Quinn had never been in love before, else he might have recognized the ache in his throat and the tight, longing sensation in his chest for what they were and seen the true danger of someone in his position harboring such emotions. He only knew that he wanted desperately to be with

Kelly Huston. And so, just minutes earlier, when she had slowed the Mustang before the gates at the foot of the Major's drive, smiling at him and suggesting that they could see each other later, if he wished, and maybe drive out to her favorite beach to watch the sunset together, he had gladly agreed. For in the brief moment that he had weighed his guilty misgivings against the joy his youthful heart had felt at the unexpected invitation, he had discovered that he was completely incapable of saying no to her.

Something flashed in the sunlight at the top of the drive, and he looked up to see the green Jaguar parked before the front door of the house. The gorgeous bodywork had been freshly washed and polished and the green paint gleamed like an emerald in the light. The boy stopped before the car, his concerns of the moment retreating temporarily to a far corner of his mind.

He gazed down at his reflection in the dark, glassy finish of the bonnet, enjoying the momentary illusion of looking into a bottomless pool of cool, green water. Reaching out to touch the surface, he gently stroked the sleek metal with his fingers. *Beautiful!*

"Beautiful, is it not?"

He looked up to see Ranjee standing in the shadows of the front porch. The little servant was smiling at him, a ring of silvery keys glinting against the dark skin of his upraised hand.

Billy nodded his silent agreement, and Ranjee stepped out of the shade to join him by the car. "The mechanic has said it is perfectly tuned," said Ranjee, "and your grandfather has this morning added your name to his insurance policy, although you must obtain a California driving license within thirty days." He handed Billy the keys. "I have had these new keys made for you."

Billy accepted the car keys, then looked questioningly at the big house. Somehow he had expected the old boy to be here himself to give him the car.

Ranjee followed his gaze. "The Major has gone to meet with the television people at their studio and then to dine with them," he said, "and so he will be quite late. He has told me to convey his apologies. Although he could not be here, he felt you would be anxious to have the automobile, and he did not wish to delay your driving lessons."

Billy stared at him.

"Would you care now to go for a small spin, as they say?" Ranjee opened a door and dropped comfortably into the Jag's low-slung passenger seat.

"I already know how to drive, thanks anyway," said Billy, opening the passenger door and waiting for the servant to get out.

Ranjee nodded solemnly and folded his arms firmly across his chest. "Nonetheless," he insisted, "the Major has most specifically instructed me to acquaint you with the driving regulations peculiar to California."

Billy sighed, walking around the front of the car and getting into the driver's seat. He supposed the little wanker was only doing what he'd been told, after all. "Very well, teacher," he said sarcastically, "now what should I do first, in California, that is?"

"First you must start the engine," Ranjee instructed, either ignoring or having altogether missed the sarcasm.

"Your wish is my command!" Billy laughed and twisted the key in the ignition. The throaty roar of the Jag's V-12 filled the air. "Jolly good," the Indian shouted above the din, again closing his door. "Now kindly make a right turning onto the driveway and you may take me to the market to shop for your supper."

The heavy sports car wheeled around in the parking area and rocketed away down the steep drive, with Ranjee clutching at his turban in the wind. "That was a most excellent turning!" he shouted. "However, please try to remain on the right side of the road at all times."

Billy complied tolerantly, turning onto the canyon road and craning his head around in hopes of glimpsing Kelly Huston's yellow Mustang as they flew past her parents' house. Chuck Huston's thick "privacy screen" of flowering shrubs made it impossible to see the front of the house, and he turned his eyes back to the windscreen just in time to see an elderly Cadillac sedan lumbering toward him in the center of the narrow road. Ranjee squealed a frightened warning as Billy expertly tapped the brakes, slipping the speeding Jag onto the dusty shoulder and passing the huge American car in a cloud of brown dust, then regaining the pavement in time to plunge into the next curve.

Three minutes later, he brought the car to an abrupt halt at the foot of the canyon road and looked across to see Ranjee fearfully regarding him from the passenger seat. "Did I do all right on that bit, then?" he asked the Indian.

Ranjee slowly nodded. Though he drove much too fast for the servant's liking, the youngster had, in fact, handled the heavy roadster like a professional race driver. Still, the idea that something was wrong with young Master Brian continued to nag at him. Even now, he was convinced that the boy's flushed features and nervous demeanor hinted at something deeper than the excitement of driving. To Ranjee, who had spent a lifetime anticipating the needs of others, the Major's handsome grandson seemed constantly preoccupied with some great problem; a problem beyond his tender years. Perhaps, he thought, the boy's grief over the recent deaths of his parents still weighed upon his mind.

"You are doing very well with the driving," Ranjee finally admitted. Then he took a deep breath and added, "But, Master Brian, if there is some way I can be of service to you . . . some difficulty with which I may assist . . ."

The boy gave him a quick, forced smile and inclined his head toward the busy cross street ahead of the Jaguar's gleaming bonnet. "Well, you can start by telling me which way this market of yours is," he replied.

THE DRIVER of the battered Cadillac pulled to a stop at the iron gates leading up to the old Spanish-style house on the hill. She had recognized the boy, whom she had observed on two previous occasions—the first as he had arrived at Los Angeles International Airport five days previously, then again today on the grounds of the high school—as he had raced down the hill with Queally-Smythe's Indian servant just moments before, and although she had not planned on entering the house today but merely observing, it occurred to her that the place might well be empty now. Picking up a compact cellular phone from the seat beside her, she dialed Queally-Smythe's unlisted telephone number, which she had memorized.

When there was no answer after ten rings, she guided the big car up through the narrow gates. At the top of the drive, she opened the voluminous trunk, exposing the array of window-washing tools that were all the cover she needed in this exclusive neighborhood where no one ever cut their own lawns—if they even had lawns—or cleaned their own pools, and where the servants did not do windows.

She knew from her previous visits that the house had no alarm system, and so it was an easy matter to gain entrance. Slipping the simple dead bolt on the front door with a locksmith's tool, she quickly entered the darkened house and looked down the long corridor leading to the main rooms.

She walked directly to the old man's study and switched on the exquisite Tiffany desk lamp, pausing to admire it for a moment before starting her meticulous sweep of the papers arrayed on the desk's leather-cornered blotter. She made a mental note to remember the lamp, which she knew would easily fetch upwards of fifteen-thousand dollars at one of the upscale auction houses in Beverly Hills, and which an unscrupulous antiques dealer for whom she often "located" such items would pay at least three thousand, cash, with no questions asked—for while Michael Kileen paid her well, he was certainly not the primary source of her income, and his money was not the reason she occasionally worked for him.

Finished with her search of the desktop, she opened the unlocked center drawer. The heavy, cream-colored envelope she had sought on her previous visits was lying on top this time, and she quickly removed the cards inside, scrutinizing the spidery formal script with a practiced eye. When she was certain that she had memorized the date, times and other essential details contained in the announcement, she slipped it back into its envelope, closed the drawer and switched off the lovely lamp.

Three minutes later she had let herself out of the house, locking the door behind her, and was on her way back down the hill, smiling to herself over having finally obtained the crucial information contained in the envelope.

She desperately hoped that Michael Kileen would be pleased enough with her to show his gratitude in more than a fiscal way.

KILEEN SAT AT A TABLE overlooking the rain-swept street of shuttered Dublin tourist shops. It was late, and except for a noisy group of Irish-American conventioneers occupying a large booth in the rear, Little America was deserted.

The same red-haired waitress with whom he had briefly spoken the night he had started Billy Quinn on his journey to California was serving the Americans, one of whom was demanding to know why all the pubs closed at the uncivilized hour of eleven, forcing honest men to come to places like this and drink coffee. She finished with them, squealing as another reached out to furtively pat her nicely rounded buttocks, and hurried over to Kileen. Her face was flushed, and she stuck out her lower lip and blew a wisp of hair out of her eyes.

Pulling a pad from the little black apron she wore over her tight jeans, she flipped back a fresh page and cast an annoyed glance at the Americans, who had launched into a noisy and slightly obscene version of "Paddy Dear" that was threatening to drown the music on the jukebox. "Can I take your order, sir?" She asked the question of Kileen without looking directly at him.

"Yeah, I'd like a cuppa coffee and a double burger with fries," said Kileen, trying out the accent that went with his new American passport, which showed his name as Joseph Green of Jamaica, Queens, New York.

The girl wrote the order on her pad, then looked down at him, her freckled forehead wrinkling. "Haven't I seen you in here before?" she asked.

Kileen shook his head, delighted that she hadn't recognized his gravelly voice, crediting her confusion to the accent he'd been practicing at odd moments over the past several weeks. "If ya did, it musta been my twin brudder, honey, 'cuz I just got in from Miami dis afternoon."

He jerked his head in the direction of the rain-streaked window. "Jeez, lookit all dat rain out dere, willya. I coulda just gone back to Noo Yawk. Does it always rain like dis here?"

She smiled at last, and he noticed for the first time how pretty she really was. "I'm afraid so," she said. "I'll get your coffee."

Kileen watched her walk away, admiring the motion of her hips. The too-tight jeans and the cheap perfume he had smelled as she had leaned close to take his order had stirred something within him, and he glanced down at the stainless-steel Rolex on his wrist. He had a long wait before he could take care of his Dublin business, and the idea of asking the girl back to his hotel room suddenly occurred to him. For although the tall receptionist in Geneva had been a cool and practiced sexual partner, bedding her had been little more than an unexciting clinical exercise. By contrast, he was enormously excited by the look and the scent of this earthy Irish girl.

Kileen smiled at the thought. For, given a preference, he was invariably attracted to such women. Women with the same soft, ripe bodies and coarse mannerisms of this waitress. It was the one weakness he recognized in himself, and one to which he gladly succumbed whenever possible. Hopefully, he reflected, peering out into the rainy night, his liasons would be more easily accomplished now that he no longer resembled a movie monster.

The girl returned with his coffee and caught him smiling. "You're looking quite happy for a man who's just come in out of the rain," she said, looking at his reddened skin. "Did you get sunburned like that in Miami?"

He looked up at her, raising a hand to stroke the side of his face. "Yeah, ain't this a bitch? Two freakin' hours I'm out in the sun and I get fried. Can you believe it?"

She nodded sympathetically. "The same thing happened to me when I went on holiday to Majorca with my girlfriend two years ago," she said. "I burned everywhere."

Kileen raised his eyebrows. "Everywhere, huh?"

Moira Devlin's face turned nearly as red as his own. "Well, everywhere my swimsuit didn't cover . . . I had to lie in a bath of cool water afterwards, to take the heat down."

"Mmmm, wisht I coulda seen that," he teased.

"You Americans, always making jokes. I'd better see about your sandwich," Moira walked back toward the kitchen, feeling his lustful gaze upon her. She smiled for the first time in days, secretly flattered by the handsome American's attentions. She had been moping around ever since the night she'd spent with the boy she'd taken back to her flat.

Brian.

Moira reached the window to the kitchen and peered in at the cook, even though she knew it was far too soon to pick up the food the American had ordered, then turned and found that he was still observing her. He was awfully good looking, despite the sunburn and that horrible accent, and she wondered how old he was. Thirty-five or forty at least. She wondered too what it would be like to be with a man that old?

The thought reminded her guiltily of the thick letter in her handbag. She had spent hours composing it, painfully writing out the tender, hopeful words in her small, uneven hand on sheets of the delicate pink notepaper she'd received as a Christmas present from her married sister last year, using up nearly the whole box before she'd got it right. She had been carrying the letter with her for three days now, all properly addressed to Mr. Brian O'Malley in Pacific Palisades, California, U.S.A., and already stamped with the correct postage, thinking to send it to him every time she passed a postal box, but then always hesitating at the last moment, lest he think the things she had written to him were foolish and far too intimate coming from someone he barely knew, afraid, too, that he would not bother to reply, or, worse, that he might not even remember the night they had spent together in her tiny rented flat.

The more she thought about him, the worse it made her feel, for she was coming to realize that it had been stupid of her to think she would ever see the handsome and wealthy boy again. She looked up, surprised to see that the prosperous American was still watching her, and so, putting on her brightest smile, she went over to his table to talk with him.

CHAPTER NINE

Discoveries

THE PACIFIC COAST HIGHWAY running north from L.A. was wide and straight, and after they got through the miles-long congestion of storefronts and stoplights and precariously hung hillside villas, beachside shacks and condos and the walled mansions of Pacific Palisades and Malibu, surprisingly free of traffic in the light of the sinking afternoon sun.

The easy, rumbling note of the Jaguar's quadruple exhaust tubes throbbed capably beneath the boom of rock and roll blasting from the stereo, creating the illusion that the car and its occupants were wrapped in a timeless bubble of their own making, a secure cocoon that nothing bad could ever penetrate.

From time to time, when he wasn't gawking at the endless sparkling vista of the blue ocean on one side of the car, or the rolling brown hills on the other, Billy would sneak a glance at Kelly, who was curled contentedly in the leather passenger seat with her feet tucked up under her long, tanned legs, rummaging in the big canvas bag she had brought along. She was wearing brief blue shorts and a loose white shirt that billowed in the wind, and her blond hair was a lovely tangle beneath the old red baseball cap she'd pulled down tightly about her ears.

The exhilarating feeling of having her beside him in the speeding car was as close to perfection as Billy Quinn had ever experienced, and at some point after the road had stretched out into empty countryside he realized with a start that he was actually living out a little piece of his fantasy dream of the night before.

After a bit, Kelly found the comb she had been searching for and looked up to catch him gazing at her.

"What?" She reached for the console between the seats and lowered the volume on the radio.

He grinned sheepishly. "Nothing. That is, I wish we could just go on driving like this." He stammered out more words in a clumsy attempt to verbalize the idyllic, half-formed vision he had imagined, of driving on and on along beside the blue ocean with her at his side, driving northwards until the road ran out.

She laughed. "Well, that would take us all the way up into Canada somewhere. Kind of a long drive for our second date, don't you think?"

Billy's face reddened. He was embarrassed at having given voice to his innermost thoughts, and he angrily reminded himself that there was really nothing between them to suggest that Kelly Huston felt as he did.

"Besides," she said, touching his arm and pointing ahead through the windshield, "we're almost there now."

Squinting through the glass into the lowering orange ball of the dying sun, he saw a narrow dirt track leading down to the sea at a point where the highway curved sharply away toward the hills. "Turn off there," she commanded.

He did as she instructed, slowing the Jag to a labored crawl and driving off onto the bumpy dirt road and down a hill surrounded on either side by tall, wheat-colored grasses. The highway disappeared from view behind them as he carefully guided the low-slung roadster around a massive outcropping of rock. After they had gone a hundred yards or so, a tiny cove fringed by a perfect half-moon of white sand appeared before them. Away in the distance, beyond the stony point at the farthest edge of the cove, rank after rank of mist-shrouded mountains ran down to a headland jutting indistinctly into the placid blue sea.

Billy switched off the engine. The thrumming of the Jag's exhausts was instantly replaced by the sounds of lapping waves and screeching seagulls. "What is this place?" he asked, his voice a reverent whisper.

Kelly removed the red hat, stowing it in a pocket on the door and shaking out her golden hair. She ran the comb through the careless tangle and leaned back to drink in the marvelous view. "I don't know its name," she said quietly. "Maybe it doesn't have a name . . . I think it's much too beautiful to have a name, don't you?"

He thrilled to the feel of her soft hand slipping into his. "Let's go down to the water. The sun is almost gone." Billy turned to see the huge glowing orb slipping behind the horizon, then let her lead him out of the car and down among the growing shadows to the beach.

They sat side by side on the warm sand, holding hands and saying nothing until the sky above them turned from gold to deepest blue and the only illumination in the rocky cove came from the phosphorescent glitter of millions of microscopic marine organisms riding in on the tops of the small waves breaking at their feet, and the dull orange glow lighting the haze above the great city to the south.

After a long while, he felt her squeeze his hand, and he turned to see her peering intently at him in the gloom. Their lips brushed lightly and something seemed to melt inside him. Swiveling clumsily about, he put his arms around her and kissed her harder, felt the tip of her tongue flicking against his teeth, her hand behind his neck, pulling him closer, the silken fingers of her free hand resting lightly on his bare leg, almost touching the aching, embarrassing hardness trapped within the thin cotton fabric of his tennis shorts, the sheer intensity of all those sensations wracking his hormone-charged young body with tremors so pleasurable he feared he might lose control of himself at any second.

The kiss finally ended and they pulled slightly away from each other, panting for breath in the rapidly cooling evening air. "I have a confession to make," she said in a small, husky voice. He gazed at her face, which was lost in shadow, trying to see into her eyes and unable to imagine what she could possibly have to confess to him.

"I've dreamed . . . about you," she whispered.

His voice was hoarse with emotion, and he was barely able to form the single word, uncertain he had heard her correctly. "What?"

She reached out in the darkness and touched his lips. "Dreamed . . . about us . . . together." There was a long pause during which something splashed into the surf a few feet from where they sat, and he heard the fear and hesitation in her voice when at last she continued. "I think, well, I really care about you a lot, Brian."

"I . . . care . . . for you too, Kelly." He repeated the bland, careful phrase, cursing it and his own halting inadequacy to express the feelings surging in his breast, even as the words tumbled from his lips. He wanted to shout aloud that he loved her. No, worshiped her, to make her understand that he adored her beauty and her kindness and her funny stories and her compassion and, most of all, the way she made him feel with her slightest touch.

In that moment too he wanted to tell her about himself; to confess who he was, and what he was, and to beg her to drive away with him, to let him take her someplace far away from the likes of Michael Kileen and his bloody terrorists, from her grasping parents, from all that was familiar to both of them.

He wished with all his heart they could go somewhere new and clean, to a fresh and innocent place where he might have a chance to live a normal life and where he would never again have to think about lies or deceits or the hopelessly hate-filled politics of his accursed homeland.

But of course that was all just another hazy daydream he played out in his mind from time to time, one in which Kelly Huston had only recently become a player. In fact, Billy Quinn knew it could never be anything more than a fantasy. Because if she knew who he really was, she would certainly not care for him, would more than likely despise him for what he was and the things he had done.

Nor would she ever understand.

Just one day spent in the sheltered environs of Pacific Academy High had convinced him that Kelly and her friends, with all their petty rivalries and their false concerns, could not ever even begin to imagine what it was like to deeply and truly hate; to hate so passionately that you would gladly risk your own life for the sheer pleasure of seeing the object of your hatred humbled and destroyed, even though you yourself might be destroyed in the process.

Though the politicians at the fund rallies and the tipsy old men in the pubs always layered it over with eloquent phrases and noble motives when they made their high-and-mighty speeches about freedom and oppression and equal opportunity, Billy Quinn knew what drove them all and kept them faithful to The Cause. It was, he suspected, the same thing that kept the Protestant bastards on the other side going as well; the thing that had been born in him on that long ago Saturday morning in Belfast when he had sat on the bloody sidewalk beside the body of his slain da.

It was always the hate.

And he knew that no matter how many peace conferences and cease-fires and grand treaties they made before the television cameras, that none of them, not the Protestants, nor the nationalists, the Catholics nor the loy-alists—but especially not Billy Quinn—could ever stop doing the things they did, because the hate inside would not let them go. For in the end, he believed, the hate was stronger than all of them, and they could no more control it than the beating of their hearts.

Sitting on the perfect beach with the beautiful girl in all her golden-haired innocence, Billy realized all of this, and it broke his heart, because he knew that the scarred and pitiless Michael Kileen would soon come to give him his orders and they would go to carry out their mission and Billy Quinn would vanish from her life forever, without ever even having told her so much as his real name.

And Kelly Huston would know nothing more about him than that he had lied to her. That every word he had ever spoken to her was a lie.

He felt her trembling in his arms, and her warm breath seemed to glow against his cheek as she snuggled closer in the night. "I lied to you before," she whispered into his ear. "What I was really trying to say is that I love you."

"Oh Jesus," Billy moaned as if she'd plunged a dagger into him, pulling her closer, clinging to her like a drowning man. "Please don't say that," he begged. "You don't know what that means."

"Yes," she said. "I do, Brian. I've never said it before to anyone else, but I do know."

Her lips found his this time, and they sank back into the yielding, sun-warmed sand together, their hard young bodies urgently entwined. When he lifted his head he saw that her loose shirt had come open. Kelly smiled and pulled his face down to her exposed breast, and as he tenderly kissed it he felt her hand slip softly to his bare leg, reaching beneath the edge of his thin shorts to boldly touch his burning flesh.

Billy Quinn groaned in ecstasy, wishing all the while that he'd never been born.

"WELL, HOW ARE you getting on, my boy? Ranjee tells me you handled the Jag like an old master today."

Billy, who had entered his room through the balcony door just moments before, looked up from the math book he had snatched when he'd heard the old man laboring up the steps from the floor below to see James Queally-Smythe standing in the doorway in his dressing gown. "I'm doing fine, sir," he said, dropping his feet from the top of his desk.

"Now, you must call me Major, or Grandfather, I insist," chided the old man. His face was pleasantly flushed, and the faint iodine aroma of scotch wafted through the room. "May I come in?" he asked.

"Of course," said Billy, jumping quickly to his feet and pulling another chair up beside the desk.

"Won't stay a moment," said the Major. "Just came from dinner with that Huston fellow and his wife. May do a film with them next year. India and all that."

"That's wonderful," said Billy, trying hard to sound enthusiastic. He wished desperately that the old man would go away and leave him in peace so he could think about his problem and what had happened between him and Kelly on the beach. He could still feel the imprint of her body beneath his, hear the things they'd whispered to one another afterwards. The sweet promises made. The lies he'd told . . .

The Major harrumphed, dismissing his remark about the film with a tremulous hand. "Can't say I care too much for the people," he grumped. "All the same, in Hollywood, these producers, you know. Promise you anything, give you a sharp stick in the eye . . . But I'd certainly love to do one truly good film in India . . . God, to capture the light there and the textures, the teeming, dusty masses . . . " His voice trailed off and he looked at the boy. "But of course that's all just an old man's dream . . ."

"No, I think it sounds very exciting," said Billy. "Really." He suddenly remembered what Kelly had told him about her parents and their friends. "That is, if you think the . . . studio people will treat you fairly," he added diplomatically. "I mean, you oughtn't allow them to take advantage of you, sir."

The Major snorted derisively. "That lot? Good God, boy, I've been dealing with greedy sods of their sort since they were all just gleams in their fathers' eyes." He chuckled happily. "I may let 'em think they've talked me into something now, but it'll be my film that's done my way in the end, you see. That's precisely the way one must deal with them. First let 'em get the funding for the film, then to hell with the lot of them. Exactly the way I've always done it."

Billy smiled, whatever concerns he might have had for the old fellow's welfare allayed. For all his bumbling, it seemed that Brian O'Malley's gramps was a tough old bastard who could look out for himself.

"At any rate," said the Major, "not the reason I've come up so late. Just wanted to ask if you'd care to attend a small, um, social function with me."

Billy nodded agreeably. "Of course . . . Major . . ."

"Good, good." Queally-Smythe blustered, fumbling in the pocket of his dressing gown and producing a heavy square envelope that he passed to Billy. "It'll mean getting fitted out with formal attire, I'm afraid," he said, "rather stuffy these affairs . . ." He fell silent, eagerly watching the boy's expression as he opened the envelope and read the flamboyantly inscribed announcement inside.

"What does this mean?" asked Billy after he had read it through twice. He was unable to tear his eyes from the engraved gold crest dominating the top of the card. He scanned the unfamiliar words again. "Brigadier? It calls you Brigadier-General Queally-Smythe!"

The Major cleared his throat noisily. He could tell from young Brian's startled expression that the boy was far more impressed with the belated honors being accorded him than he had dared to hope, and his old heart pounded joyously in his chest. "Nothing to get too excited about, Brian," he said as calmly as he could. "It's what we used to call in the army a graveyard promotion. Strictly ceremonial, of course."

"B . . . but why are they doing it?" stammered Billy. "I mean, why now?" His palms were beginning to perspire, and he thought he might be ill. For with the few ornately scripted words on the card, Kileen's whole, exquisitely worked out plan was suddenly brilliantly clear to him: Kileen, the clever, devious, murderous bastard!

He was barely aware that the old man was suddenly talking again, as though a valve had been turned somewhere within his frail, scrawny body, opening a floodgate to release an excited torrent of words that had been bottled up inside for half a century.

"It was 1945 . . . Bad show back then, you see . . . wartime and all . . . took ill and was mustered out without the proper recognition . . . Everyone said so . . . Time at last to give the old boy his due, I suppose, for having saved a few blokes, organized an escape . . . Simply convenient to coincide with the state visit . . . They'll want us both in full mufti, of course, black tie and all . . . Must see to that . . ."

Queally-Smythe finally paused for breath. Billy stared at him, blinking, unable to think what to say.

"Quite an opportunity for you too, my boy," the old man continued, his watery blue eyes shining with pride. "Had the devil of a time making arrangements for another guest through our consulate here on such short notice—what with security concerns these days—but I managed it with a few well-placed calls . . . Friends in high places and all that." He smiled broadly, clapping the boy heartily on the back. "Waited to tell you until it had all been properly organized."

He waited for the boy to say something, and when he did not, Queally-Smythe went on. "Suppose your new schoolmates will all be green with envy when they hear you're to be presented to Her Royal Majesty right here in California, eh?" He retrieved the card and envelope from the desk, tucking them safely back into the pocket of his burgundy dressing gown.

"It's . . . brilliant!" whispered Billy.

The Major seemed embarrassed by the obvious emotion in his grandson's voice. "Well, I'll let you get on with your studies now, Brian," he said, hoisting himself to his feet and tottering toward the door. "Just wanted to give you a bit of advance notice. Nothing to worry about. Plenty of time to make the necessary arrangements . . ."

Billy nodded dumbly as the old man went out. He sat at the desk, listening to Queally-Smythe descend the steep wooden steps, one at a time.

When the Major had gone, the boy stepped onto the balcony and lit a cigarette with trembling hands. He gazed out over the vast, twinkling carpet of lights stretching away to the southern horizon without really seeing them.

Her Royal Majesty!

The Queen of fucking England!

Surely Kileen meant to kill her. There could be no other possible explanation for the elaborate preparations he had made. It was why Brian O'-Malley had been kidnapped. Why Billy Quinn had been sent here in his place.

A sudden horrible thought flashed into his mind. What if Kileen meant for him to do it?

Billy's knees went rubbery beneath him, and he dropped into the metal chair with a thump.

Assassinate the bloody Queen!

A helpless, unarmed old woman!

For all the British blood he had shed in the name of Irish freedom, never in his young life had Billy Quinn considered the possibility of doing such a terrible thing.

He looked down the hill at the wavering reflections of the lights on the swimming pool at the Huston house.

And what about Kelly? What in the bloody hell was he supposed to do about her now?

BOOK THREE

Northstar

Let this be your motto—Rely on yourself!
For, whether the prize be a ribbon or a throne,
The victor is he who can go it alone!

JOHN GODFREY SAXE

CHAPTER ONE

Kileen

RAIN AGAIN.

He stood on the wet stone steps in the gray Dublin morning, looking up and down the narrow street of brick buildings. Half a block away, a young woman in a red plastic slicker ran clumsily for the shelter of a storefront as a sudden torrent of fresh rain swept the shining black pavement. The woman paused long enough to open a bright umbrella, then splashed away in her heeled boots and disappeared around the next corner. Farther down the street, a blue grocer's van started up and pulled out from the curb, its tires whirring briefly as they grabbed for traction.

Then nothing. Except the soft sound of the steady Dublin rain striking the sidewalk.

Kileen looked both ways, then turned and walked quickly away in the direction of the river Liffey a few streets beyond. As he walked, he reflected on the luck of having gone to the cafe the night before, of having met the young waitress with the red hair.

The girl who had called herself Moira Devlin.

At first, she had agreed only to go with him for a drink. Presenting, he thought, an opportunity for him to talk her into going back to his hotel with him. She had obviously been intrigued and flattered by the attentions of the well-dressed American, and he had let her suggest the smoky after-hours club, where he had bought her a bottle of outrageously overpriced wine and started in on her. He had complimented her looks and her refinement, wondering aloud why an intelligent girl like herself was working as a waitress when she surely might have had any number of jobs in a building society or bank office.

She had seemed to warm to his approach, drinking glass after glass of the undistinguished chardonnay while pouring out her banal story of having come to the city to better herself. The underground club's 2:00 A.M. closing time was fast approaching when he had reached for her hand, mentioning his hotel and the excellent bottle of wine he kept there.

He had felt her pull away immediately, fussing with her cheap coat and making noises about getting home. Experience had taught him it was time to back off before she refused him outright, and so he had smiled indulgently, offering to take her home in a taxi instead. She had relaxed then, finishing her wine and apologizing. Explaining that she had recently met someone with whom she thought she might be in love. Someone who was far away in the States.

They had ridden together to the street of old brick buildings where she lived, he enquiring solicitously about her faraway friend and, later, reaching over to take her hand and reassure her of her own worth as she'd tearfully confessed that the boy was from a wealthy family that would never approve of her.

By the time they'd reached her door, she was clinging possessively to him. He had, of course, insisted on seeing her inside, been surprised at the ferocity of her passion as she'd raised her tear-streaked face to his, enveloping his lips in a hot, salty kiss, angrily challenging him to prove that she was indeed desirable and worthy of being loved.

Kileen, who no longer cared anything for love, had whispered the meaningless words he knew she wished to hear, pressing her back onto the soft coverlet of her lonely bed, losing himself in the exquisite curves of her fine, smooth flesh.

And there it might have ended.

Except for luck.

Hours later, she had turned on a shaded lamp, then padded barefoot into the small bath adjoining her room as he lay exhausted among the tangled covers, watching fat drops of rain sliding down the outside of her window, looking around at the shabby furnishings in the dim light and wondering whether to go back to his hotel, which would surely be locked at that hour—it was then nearly five in the morning—or to simply stay the night, sleeping in the warmth of her bed, for she had already told him she did not wish to be alone.

Propping himself up on one elbow, he had cadged a rare cigarette from a nearly empty pack of Marlboros on the bedside table, thinking it strange that he hadn't seen her smoke for the entire evening. Shrugging off the oddity, he had searched for a match and, unable to find one, stuck his hand into her open handbag, which lay on the floor beside the bed. He had picked up the thick pink envelope, intending to set it aside . . . glanced curiously at the address in the dim light of the shaded lamp.

She had returned shyly to the bedroom minutes later to find him propped among the pillows, smoking one of the cigarettes. Climbing in beside him, she'd snuggled beneath the covers, laying her head on his shoulder and replying quietly when he had asked her to tell him more about her friend in far-off California, the one whose leaving had made her so sad, the one who had left the cigarettes on her nightstand.

She'd told him everything—anyway, all that she could remember, he believed—about the gentle schoolboy with the golden hair, while Kileen lay there feeling her warm breath upon his chest and weighing the decision of whether or not to kill her.

It had not been an easy decision.

On the one hand, that little idiot Billy Quinn had given her only the name Brian O'Malley and the address of the grandfather with whom he was to be living in the States. And, while that information was harmless enough at the moment, soon the names of Brian O'Malley and James Queally-Smythe would be appearing on the front pages of newspapers round the world.

On the other hand, the girl was sweet and innocent, the daughter, as it turned out, of a lifelong activist in The Cause; a man, in fact, whom Kileen had once met, and whom he knew had sheltered and fed fugitives in the loft of his barn some years ago, following an aborted bombing attack on a British Saracen armored car across the border.

He had casually queried her about that incident, claiming to be an avid American supporter of Irish reunification, learned that if she knew anything she wasn't talking.

In the end, Kileen had determined that she ought to die, given the gravity of the mission upon which he was embarking and the terrible consequences that were certain to follow if anything went wrong. For not only had Moira Devlin seen Billy Quinn's face—a face that was not Brian O'-Malley's—she had seen Kileen's as well. His new face, the face unknown to anyone. And that posed an additional risk to his own safety. The two of them had been seen together; in Little America, in the after-hours club, in the taxi . . .

But still he had not killed her.

Rather, he had left her sleeping in her bed.

Dressing silently in the gray morning light, he had taken the letter from her handbag, placing it in his pocket. In its place—on a piece of her own pink notepaper—he had printed a brief note, telling her what a fine girl she was and cautioning her against contacting the boy she had known as Brian O'Malley, who had been, he explained, an agent of British military intelligence seeking evidence with which to incriminate her father and his friends.

He thought that would do the trick.

Even at that, the decision to let her live had been a dangerous one. One that completely defied the cold and calculating logic with which Michael Kileen routinely conducted his deadly business.

But how could he have killed her when she reminded him so very much of Ginnie Keenan? Ginnie, the sweet and innocent girl who had been the reason he had forsaken a normal life on that cold Belfast night some twenty-five years before; the same night that the two old revolutionaries had forced him to take the gun.

YOUNG MICHAEL KILEEN was leaning against the bar in the Belfast pub, drinking his whiskey, oblivious to the din of the rowdy students about him. The weight of the heavy automatic pistol the two men had forced upon him hung like a death warrant in the waist of his trousers. *A small killing, they had said. Nothing to worry about. Showing the colors.* What was it to them, thought Kileen, if he got killed for their bloody stupid colors? For Jimmy fucking Whalen?

"Bastards! Stupid, sodding bastards!" The frightened Kileen hurled the bitter curse into his glass.

"Talking to yourself now, is it, Michael?"

Kileen turned to see Ginnie Keenan regarding him curiously, her bare navel winking lewdly in the gap between her short pink sweater and the tight, hip-hugging French jeans that had only recently become acceptable street wear among Belfast girls.

Ginnie moved closer to him, deliberately brushing his sleeve with her cushiony, melon-shaped breasts, and pushed her pretty red lips into a sweet little pout. "I've been looking for you everywhere," she complained, holding up her glass to show that it was empty. A soft, lightly freckled hand slid up to caress his cheek, and her huge green eyes widened in surprise. "Why you're cold as a corpse!" she exclaimed. "Where have you been, you naughty boy?"

Kileen shrugged away from her hand, annoyed. "Just out back for a breath of air," he lied, taking the empty glass and leaning over to make a show of sniffing at her breath. "How many of these have you had?"

Ginnie tossed her pretty head abruptly, whipping his face with her luxuriant fall of scented auburn curls. "Enough that you're starting to look very good to me, my lad." She teased wickedly, touching his lips with the rosy nail of her index finger. "But not quite enough that I'm ready to do anything about it yet."

An electric tingle surged straight down from the tip of her finger to his crotch, and Kileen felt himself growing hard. Unaccountably, the weight of the heavy pistol the brute had stuck in his waistband seemed only to fortify his desire, and he realized with sudden horror that the blunt muzzle of the deadly weapon was pointing directly at his genitals. He shifted nervously around toward the bar, intending to reposition the gun to a less dangerous angle, but Ginnie deftly interjected herself into the narrow space, pressing her flat stomach tightly against his and smiling up into his eyes. "Is that a machine gun in your knickers, or are you just glad to see me?" she giggled.

"Jesus, Gin!" croaked Kileen, his eyes darting apprehensively around the crowded bar. "Watch what you're saying." He took her by the arms and slipped her aside, pressing himself close to the bar and hollering for two whiskeys. Ginnie's arm snaked around his neck, and he felt her hot breath tickling his ear. "I'm sorry, love," she whispered, "for embarrassing you in public." She lowered her eyes. "You know I'm no slut, Michael . . . It's just that I thought you wanted to . . . you know. To do it with me."

Kileen, who had been trying in vain for months to coax the eminently desirable Ginnie into his bed, stared down at her, dumbfounded. Tonight of all nights . . . tonight when his entire world was threatening to collapse about his ears, she had finally decided to cooperate. He muttered something incoherent, which she seemed not to hear anyway.

"I love you, Michael," she continued in a tiny little-girl voice that was nearly lost amid the general clamor of the pub. Her cheeks reddened, and she bit her lower lip engagingly. "Everyone agrees that it's no sin to do it with someone you really love. You do love me too, don't you?"

He nodded stupidly.

Ginnie smiled brightly, standing on tiptoe to peck him on the cheek. "There, then, it's all settled. I'll go home with you tonight and we'll make love."

Kileen was just not prepared for this. "What about your mum?" he stammered. For unlike most of the girls at her business college, who shared flats and were free to come and go as they pleased, Ginnie Keenan lived in a somber row house with her devout mother, a sour-faced widow who dressed only in black and was forever fingering her shiny rosary beads while mumbling prayers for the soul of her dear departed husband.

"I told Ma I was spending the weekend with Celeste," Ginnie said, indicating her pretty friend sitting at a table across the room. The other girl, who was obviously quite drunk, was surrounded by several males of Kileen's acquaintance, all of whom were openly intent on monopolizing her attention and spiriting her away into the night.

"We're supposed to be visiting her family down in the country until Sunday." Ginnie's wicked laughter tinkled in his ears. "Going down to ride the horses, I told Ma."

The whiskey arrived at last, and Kileen downed his neat, all thoughts of the sinister revolutionaries replaced by the insistent yearning in his loins. Fuck the loony buggers, he decided as the fiery liquor slid down to join the inferno already raging in his belly. He might never get another opportunity like this one. Tonight he was going to lose himself entirely in the lovely and willing Ginnie Keenan.

He'd just have to worry about the two old men and their daft plot tomorrow.

Ginnie sipped her whiskey, then reached up to nuzzle his ear, her wet, pink tongue like cold velvet against the lobe, and he took a moment's pause to consider the fact that, despite what he had let her believe, he did not love her at all—did not, in fact, even like her very much. For though they excited him beyond reason, he considered her revealing clothes and cloying perfume to be cheap and tasteless, her way of speaking coarse and low bred; all characteristics reminiscent of the big-bellied slatterns he'd grown up watching, all of them endlessly pushing their prams of squalling brats up and down the cracked sidewalks of the working-class neighborhood he had escaped in order to attend Queens University. In his mind, they were women who had turned overnight from bright young girls like Ginnie Keenan to dull-eyed hags, as if they had all somehow fallen under the evil spell of some malevolent fairy godmother.

No, he decided, Ginnie Keenan was not to be the love of Michael Kileen's life. Not the dreamland princess he had sweated through a hundred grueling school exams to end his hopes and his days with. Kileen wanted nothing more from pretty Ginnie than a few leisurely hours in which to fuck her. A little time to revel in that still-fresh, beautiful body of hers. To feel the weight of her huge, firm breasts resting for a while upon his naked chest.

Then it was on to better things for him.

Wrestling ever so briefly with those guilty thoughts, Kileen took the tipsy girl by the arm and experimentally pulled her closer. Ginnie sighed contentedly, nestling her head deeper into the hollow of his throat, and whatever lingering doubts he might have entertained about the morality of his lie were instantly dispelled by the feel of her warm and pliable body molding like hot wax to his own.

Grinning into her maddeningly perfumed hair, he coldly reflected that her love for him would just have to do for the both of them.

Michael Kileen's true love was still somewhere out in the wide world, waiting for him to discover her. In less than a year now, armed with the engineering degree that would guarantee him a position of substance with a major company, he would go forth to find her.

Tonight, though, he would be Ginnie Keenan's true love.

Their whiskeys finished, he found her fake-fur coat among a pile of garments by the door, bundled her up and led her giggling into the street. She stumbled awkwardly in her tall vinyl boots with their silly high heels, and gently taking her elbow to hurry her along, he guided her toward his rooms two streets away.

Minutes later, Ginnie was leaning lopsidedly against the wall at the top of the steps outside the dun-colored block of flats where he lived, laughing at him as he fumbled for his key and ducked like a blind man into the tiny unlit alcove by the doorway, from which someone had days before either stolen or smashed the feeble light bulb.

Without warning, a powerful beam of light stabbed out from the street, illuminating the girl like a laboratory specimen on a board, and a harsh voice ordered her to raise her hands and come down to the walk.

Ginnie squealed in confusion, throwing her hands up to shield her eyes from the blinding glare and peering down at the unseen voice in the light.

Kileen, his heart thundering in his chest, looked out from the shadowed alcove, acutely aware of the forbidden weapon he carried. "I said hands up, you Paddy bitch!" shouted the voice, and Kileen realized that he hadn't yet been seen. Praying that the frightened girl would go down to the street, he fumbled the weapon from his belt, intending to shove it through the big brass mail slot in the door.

"Michael!" Ginnie had turned away from the light and was looking in at him, the fear in her voice telling him she had become instantly sober.

"Hands up or I'll shoot!" The voice from the street hollered, the order ending with a peculiar squeak.

"Ginnie, for God's sake go down and talk to them!" Kileen pleaded, fumbling on the rough wood surface behind him for the mail slot. "I've got to get rid of something," he explained.

Ginnie's eyes widened with sudden understanding and she winked at Kileen and blew him a little kiss. "Don't worry, love, I'll charm the crap out of the bastards," she said, with no trace of fear left in her voice. Turning back to face the light, she calmly raised her arms over her head, allowing her cheap fur to fall open, and turning back to the bright light to give them a good look at her bare stomach. "You shouldn't go about frightening people like that," she called down to the street, sounding angry.

"Come down slowly now," the voice demanded.

Kileen, his hand on the mail slot, allowed himself a small breath as she started to move, vowing to chuck the goddamned gun into the sea if he got out of this fuck-all mess, and to hell with Whalen and his trained gorilla.

Astounded by her sudden courage, Kileen watched mesmerized as Ginnie placed her foot on the first step. "You're not afraid of little me, are you?" she called bravely into the street, and her infectious giggle echoed against the cold stones. "I'm just a little black sheep that's lost her wa—"

Ginnie screamed as the heel of her ridiculous vinyl boot caught on the edge of the next step and she tumbled headlong into the light. A strangled "Halt!" was shouted from below, and a burst of blue fire simultaneously exploded from the muzzles of two automatic rifles, the obscene, flatulent eruption shattering the still night and echoing down among the dark, dingy streets.

Kileen smelled the stink of cordite on the wind, edged forward to peer down at the two helmeted troopers examining the sad, broken body on the walk.

"What the fuck did you do that for, you stupid fuck?" asked a thickset figure swaddled in body armor. He was standing over another trooper—the one who had been manning the light—his face obscured beneath a thick layer of black grease paint, and in his strong Midlands accent the shocked Kileen noticed that the word fuck sounded comically as though he were saying *fook*. Frightened faces were peeking out of windows up and down the street, no one daring to come out.

"I didn't mean to shoot her, did I? She just come at me." The soldier with the spotlight—his accent unmistakably North London—was kneeling at Ginnie's side. He looked up at his mate, and Kileen saw that he was young, barely out of his teens, his scrawny neck sticking out of the top of his flak jacket like the neck of a chicken in a butcher's window. "You shot her too, didn't you?" he accused his mate *sotto voce*. "Why'd you shoot her, then?"

"You stupid fuck," muttered the other, prodding cautiously at Ginnie's pitiful bare midriff with the toe of his muddy boot. "She tripped on the step. Good-looking bit too," he said regretfully. "What a fucking waste." He looked down the street at the sound of a fast-approaching vehicle. "Shit, the sarge'll have our balls for this. Better get our story straight while we can. She came at you and you thought you saw a gun. Got that?"

The boy on the ground nodded eagerly. "That's the way it happened. She come at me and—" He never finished the sentence, for Michael Kileen, the heavy automatic pistol in his hand, came charging down the short flight of steps like an avenging angel. Screaming his rage into the freezing night, he shot the scrawny boy point-blank in the face three times before his companion could raise the muzzle of his own weapon, delivered two more dead center shots into the standing trooper's head, then ran for his life.

Executions!

The dead men crumpled onto Ginnie Keenan's body, making a grotesque little pyramid of corpses on the walk, a few seconds before an armored personnel carrier and a heavily screened and shielded Land Rover, their lights ablaze, slid into the street. Michael Kileen, his heart threatening to burst in his rage and his fright, dove into the shadows of a doorway half a block away as the first of a dozen arriving armored troopers piled out of the APC to stare down at the carnage he had wrought.

Then a door silently opened behind him, and someone who had seen what had happened from a window dragged him weeping to safety, prying the hot pistol from his frozen grasp and dispatching it out a back door in the hands of a child as two others silently stripped off Kileen's gore-spattered clothes, doused his underwear and hair with raw whiskey and placed him beneath the covers in an untidy bed with an extraordinarily fat girl, instructing him to feign unconsciousness.

Michael Kileen had laid there among the smells of whiskey and sweat and sex, waiting for the soldiers to kick down the door, silently weeping for the lost innocence of poor Ginnie Keenan, whom he had wanted only to fuck.

Weeping for his own life, which could never again be what he had imagined or planned for it to be.

For Michael Kileen knew then that there was no way back for him, and he saw himself, henceforth and for the rest of his life, creeping about in filthy alleys with the old men of the revolution.

THE RAIN had slackened a little by the time Kileen reached his comfortable hotel at an exclusive Dublin address across the way from the American embassy. He went directly up to his room and luxuriated in a long, hot bath before presenting himself at the elegant dining room, where he sat at a window table and consumed a full Irish breakfast of black and white puddings, eggs and grilled tomatoes served on fine bone china, complemented by sparkling crystal and snowy linen. It still surprised him that his rebel's life had not turned out to be nearly as mean or uncomfortable as he had once supposed it would.

"I'M VERY SORRY, Mrs. Quinn."

The invalid was sitting in a wheelchair, her wasted body shuddering beneath the bright-colored blanket in which they'd tucked her up before wheeling her into the joyless, gray solarium. Heavy rain drummed onto the sooty skylights, masking the sounds of her grief, and her quiet sobs were lost among the ceilings of the tall, drafty room.

After a few moments, she looked up from the handkerchief into which she'd been crying, turning her luminous gray eyes upon her visitor, searching the smooth, handsome face for confirmation of her worst fear. "It was him died in that Belfast police station bombing last week, wasn't it?" Her voice was a harsh whisper.

Kileen's nod was barely perceptible. He held out the envelope filled with money, watching as her bulging eyes scanned the room for possible eavesdroppers. "He wasn't supposed to have been harmed," he whispered. "It just went wrong somehow." It was a familiar enough story to anyone who had regularly followed the clumsy antics of would-be bombers in Northern Ireland over the past twenty-five years or so. Bombs were forever going off before they were supposed to, and she accepted the explanation without flinching.

"I knew it would probably be him when I saw it on the telly," she breathed when Kileen had finished.

Kileen raised his eyebrows questioningly.

She saw his expression, then smiled. "He came all the way down here to see me, just the day before," she explained.

Kileen relaxed. For a moment he had feared the young fool had told his mother something else, something that could force Kileen to make another life-or-death decision, when the whole point of his coming to see the Quinn woman had been merely to seal the transfer of identities from Billy Quinn to Brian O'Malley . . . to confirm that there no longer was a Billy Quinn.

"He's a hero, isn't he?" Allison Quinn asked hopefully. "My Billy?"

He nodded again, gently placing the envelope in her lap. She looked down at it, a wet tear splashing onto the brown manila. "I'd like to give him a proper Requiem Mass," she said, raising her eyes to his. "Would that be all right, do you think?"

Michael Kileen squeezed her emaciated shoulder. "Yes, Mrs. Quinn," he said. "They can't hurt your Billy anymore."

He turned and walked away through the empty solarium as she bowed her head and began to pray.

THREE HOURS LATER, Kileen was stepping out of a taxi on Wardour Street, a seedy alley of entertainment complexes just off Piccadilly Circus. He paid off the cabbie, who had driven him all the way in from London's second major airport, Gatwick, where the direct flight from Dublin had landed ninety minutes earlier.

He stepped beneath the awning of a peep show to check his watch—less than fifty minutes in which to obtain the items he'd come here for and get to Victoria station for the train trip out to Heathrow on the other side of the city, where his flight to Mexico was waiting.

The small shop was easy enough to find. A tiny, green-painted storefront with an anachronistic tinkling bell at the door, it was just down the street from where the cabbie had let him out, tucked away between a noisy game arcade and a "fully licensed" Indian restaurant.

Inside, the little shop proved to be a proper Victorian place, all dark wood paneling, and smelling of brass polish and leather. The proprietor, a paunchy, red-cheeked man in his sixties, sized up Kileen as he came through the door. "Afternoon, sir. May I help you?" he said, as he looked up from a spotless glass display case filled with his most impressive wares.

Kileen stepped up to the case, peering down at the rows of velvet-covered show cards on which the gleaming merchandise had been artfully arrayed. He folded his hands behind his back as he examined the cards. "I shall be needing one of those," he said, pointing to a card containing a pair of nearly identical items.

The proprietor opened the case, bending to extract the card, which he laid carefully on the case. "May I recommend you purchase the other as well, sir?" He raised his eyes to Kileen's, chuckling knowledgeably. "These are particularly difficult to come by, and if something should happen to the first one, I'm not sure I could get you a replacement any time soon."

Kileen nodded agreeably. "Suppose you're right. You had better put in the extra, then."

The old man's head bobbed happily up and down as he carefully removed the items from their card, wrapped each in a piece of white tissue, then bound the whole lot up in a neat packet of brown paper tied with string. He wrote up a bill by hand, made change from a battered tin box and bid Kileen a cheery good day.

Kileen smiled, then tucked the small packet into the pocket of his raincoat and hurried out into the street to hail another taxi.

THE AEROMEXICO FLIGHT direct from Heathrow to Mexico City was well out over the Atlantic before Kileen really began to relax. Sipping a fresh margarita, he felt the tortured tissues inside his mouth slowly going numb around the freezing liquid concoction.

Everything that could conceivably have been done in advance to assure the success of the assassination—the assassination that would surely go down in the history books alongside the killings of John Kennedy, Mohandas Gandhi and the Archduke Ferdinand—had now been done.

He leaned his head back against his pillow, mentally composing the revolutionary statement that he would issue when it had been accomplished, putting them all on notice—the bloody false aristocracy, the Parliament, the ruling Protestant majority in Northern Ireland—that his country must be unequivocally freed. That this time there would be no compromise, or he would continue to knock down their silly, useless comic-opera monarchs as long as they kept setting them up, and as easily as one would knock down targets in a fun-fair shooting gallery.

The aircraft's powerful Rolls-Royce engines shifted to a lower pitch as the jumbo jet settled in at its cruising altitude, and Kileen held up his empty glass to a passing flight attendant. She quickly refilled it from a frosted pitcher. He took another freezing swallow, wishing he might have the pleasure of seeing all their smug faces when he'd pulled it off.

Of course they'd all be outraged, the Ulster Defense League screaming for Catholic blood; the IRA and their would-be Sinn Fein peacemakers falling all over themselves to deny any involvement; the military intelligence establishments on both sides of the water casting blindly about and hauling in the lot of them in their frenzied quest for someone—anyone—to lay it all on.

His smile broadened into a grin, causing him pain and exposing the stainless steel bits that held both his lower jaw and maxillae together.

But there would be no one to blame.

No one at all.

He had seen to that with his new face.

Seen to it by carefully compartmentalizing his people. By deliberately choosing them not too smart, like Francis Duffy and Dermot Tumelty.

Or completely naive, like young Billy Quinn.

By telling none of them anything at all.

By setting it up so that by the time they knew exactly what they had done, they would all be dead.

As dead as Brian O'Malley.

Kileen raised his glass in tribute to the poor, dumb sods who, of unfortunate necessity, would have to die in order to give birth.

Birth to a new organization and a new way: An organization that would strike renewed terror into the hearts of all those who had dared to stand by while his people were oppressed. A way that would smash forever the empty and unsatisfactory diplomatic stalemate that still, for all the empty talk of peace and freedom in Northern Ireland, held his people in bondage to their British masters.

When he was done, he had no doubt, there would be a real war in Northern Ireland. A revolutionary war of national independence. But it would be a war that would be won this time, because it would be led by a new and shining terrorist organization so fierce and powerful in its determination that its enemies would crumble in fear at the very mention of its name.

He would call it Northstar.

"Northstar." He said it aloud, the magical name that had come to him as he had lain in hospital after the bloody stupid explosion, fighting the pain and despair that had nearly cost him both his sanity and his life. It was there—in the London hospital—that he had finally come to realize the utter futility of the old, tired ways. The ways that had traded a killing for a killing, a bombing for a bombing, a headline for a headline in a never-ending spiral of petty atrocities that had, in the end, made no difference at all. Had simply become a way of life, until the silly bastards on both sides had finally tired of the mindless carnage and sued for peace at any price.

Northstar.

He had been watching a BBC news report on the television bolted to the wall above his hospital bed when the idea had burst upon him like a bolt from the blue, driving away his pain and the daily horror of staring at the unrecognizable remains of his own face in the stained mirror of the bathroom he'd shared with the other three men on the cheerless ward.

The entire scheme had been prompted by a single image on the flickering blue telly screen: an image of the Queen on a state visit to New Zealand.

Lying there on his back, watching the ridiculous, overdressed symbol of all that he hated reviewing a platoon of spit-and-polish ceremonial troops, Kileen had let his rage run rampant, muttering curses under his breath—for the stupid sods who had brought him to the hospital had never even realized that the bomb that had destroyed his face had also been planted by him. Carrying him out of the rubble along with a half-dozen other "innocent victims" of the premature bomb blast he had caused, they had merely given the false identity papers in his pockets a cursory examination before shunting him off to have his life saved by dedicated British surgeons. The fools!

Michael Kileen had watched the droning news report of the Queen reviewing the New Zealand troops that day, wishing he'd been one of those silly parade-ground soldiers, thinking how ridiculously easy it would be for one of them to slip a bullet into his rifle, stick it under her weak royal chin. Send her bloody stupid hat spinning high into the air along with her addled brains . . .

And then she had come to the end of the line of ceremonial troops and moved on to stop before a rank of bent old men in outdated military uniforms—ANZACS from the Second World War, the BBC announcer had called them, intoning the strange acronym through his nose, as BBC news commentators always did—and begun pinning medals to their sunken chests, decorating them for forgotten heroics undertaken half a century earlier, to safeguard British interests in Asia from the Japanese. Now there was a laugh.

Kileen had turned his head away, bored with the all too familiar spectacle. He'd seen it before a thousand times, whenever she made a state visit . . . The Queen bestowing honors on the harmless old fools who'd given their all in the name of British colonialism. Still, he had thought, how wonderful it would be if one could simply wire up one of the old soldiers . . . Say, somehow rig him with a clever bomb that wouldn't be detected once he was inside her security net—for her normally airtight security was probably far looser than usual on these occasions, everyone anxious to dispose of the doddering old soldiers and get on to the inevitable glittering cocktail reception and dinner at the embassy, panting to bow and scrape and kiss the royal arse . . . And who would ever suspect an old patriot, anyway?

Kileen had sat upright in his bed then, wondering just how the honorees were notified. Wondering whether the lists of their names were published in advance, or somehow otherwise made available to the public. If their relatives were invited to the ceremonies . . .

And that was when the idea began to form in his mind. The idea of carrying out a single bold killing action so swift and unthinkable that it would shake the whole bloody world right out of its bored complacency over the alleged settlement of "The Irish Problem" with the unsatisfactory peace accord and its vague promise of someday allowing the Catholic minority in Northern Ireland to vote their way out of British dominion. Perhaps.

At first, the idea had been no more than a diversion from the unending pain and boredom of his days, a pleasant mental exercise to while away the dreadful hours between the hideous surgeries that were slowly but surely transforming his face and hands into something that once more resembled those of a human being. But as the days had passed and he had worried it from every conceivable angle—How to locate a proper old soldier? How to get close enough to him? What sort of explosive to use? How to plant it?—the simple idea had grown and flowered into a plan, a plan of such incredible complexity, and yet so beautifully simple in its essence, that it had finally come to occupy all his waking hours, until he had calculated every last detail, had known for a certainty that it could be done.

Northstar.

On the day he had been released from hospital, he had gone with his plan to the same wealthy exile who had supplied the papers he carried in his pockets now, an old patriot who had long since given up all hope of ever seeing his homeland free; an old, old man with unlimited money, who felt, as did Kileen, that the current peace in Northern Ireland was just another manifestation of the centuries-old British oppression.

Kileen had stated his proposition to the old patriot. Gotten the money on the understanding that he was entirely on his own, that he must recruit his own handpicked men with no assistance from any of the perpetually bickering nationalist groups, who would, if they ever found out, likely kill them all.

The old bastard had actually grinned as he'd given him the funds.

Northstar!

All the rest—the things he'd told Billy Quinn and the others—had been necessary lies.

Certainly he regretted the fact that the loyal followers he had recruited under the guise of striking a bold blow on American soil for Irish freedom—because it was, after all, the bloody Americans who had engineered the unsatisfactory peace in the first place, by cutting off the money and arms that were the lifeblood of the struggle—would die in bringing his dream to life. But what was that when compared to the freedom of an entire people?

Northstar.

The shining new name would begin and end the taped message that Michael Kileen intended to dispatch to the world's media as soon as the deed was done. In it, he would honor the names of those who would die as martyrs to The Cause.

Northstar!

Kileen himself would, of course, survive anonymously to head the powerful new organization, ensuring that the world paid heed to his demands.

CHAPTER TWO

Heartthrobs

"I LOVE YOU, KELLY."

Brian O'Malley sat in the driver's seat of the green Jaguar roadster, his sharp blue eyes shining in the moonlight.

Kelly said nothing, but stepped from the car and ran down the beach, feeling the sand, still warm from the late afternoon sun, between her bare toes. The Jag was parked on the curving strip of deserted seacoast north of Malibu, above the secluded beach she'd found on her own one afternoon as she'd walked the shore while Chuck and Katherine met with the architect who had been trying to talk them into building a house in the nearby Malibu Sunrise Colony.

She slowed to a walk, moving down a slight incline toward the water, drawn by the luminous tops of the endless lines of waves rolling in from the open sea to crash onto the sand. The sound of the surf grew louder in her ears as she approached, drowning out every other sound except for the mournful screech of a wheeling seagull overhead.

Her feet touched the cold wetness of hard-packed sand, and she stopped to look up as a huge breaker towered above her, tons of luminous green water seeming to hang for an eternity between herself and the rising moon, and she imagined she saw dark creatures moving within the glassy walls; predatory things with great shining teeth, gazing down on her with flat, hungry eyes.

The wave collapsed in a flash of wind-whipped foam that swirled up around her ankles, sending a cold chill through her entire body, and she wondered why she had not remembered to wear something warmer than the light sundress she had on.

It was always cold on the beach at night.

She sensed footsteps behind her, but she did not turn to look. For she knew it was Brian, still awaiting some reply to his declaration. He had told her that he loved her, and she knew in her heart that she loved him too, because when they had made love for the first time, on this very beach a few nights before, it had been perfect. But right now she was so terribly confused.

Confused and miserable.

For, since that magical interlude on the sand, she had hardly seen anything at all of Brian O'Malley. Except for the history class they shared—a class in which he sat on the opposite side of the room from her—she had caught only brief glimpses of him, as he sped past her house in the green Jaguar or ran past her on the playing field during P.E., or stood in a cafeteria line.

And, always, Brenda Gaynor had been hovering nearby. Brenda in her sexy short skirts, with her smug, pouting smiles . . . Brenda, touching Brian's fair face with her pale fingers, standing daintily on her tiptoes to whisper secret things into his ear.

How was Kelly supposed to believe that he loved her, after . . . After what she had seen? After what her imagination told her he and Brenda had been doing together since Monday night?

"Kelly!"

She spun around to see him standing there in the sand, looking at her, the moonlight casting blue highlights in his long, black hair. "I love you, Kelly." He said it again, his voice a dreamy whisper above the roar of the surf.

"I love you too, Brian." Kelly felt a sharp ache in her throat. "I just don't understand . . ."

"You have to trust me," he whispered, enfolding her in his arms. "I can explain everything . . ."

His lips touched hers, and Kelly felt her resistance draining away, all the bitter hurt and disappointment magically melting as though it had never been there. They sank slowly to their knees in the sand, and she pushed her tongue into his clean, warm mouth. Felt his hands on her shoulders, slipping down the straps of her sundress, felt him caressing her exposed breasts with his gentle hands . . . He moaned softly through the kiss, and she knew that in a moment they would be lying on the warm sand together, making sweet, tender love.

Her desire was growing, and she pressed her hips urgently against his, feeling the heat radiating from his hard body, feeling his strong hands sliding around to rest lightly on her buttocks.

"Well, well, isn't this romantic?"

Kelly jerked away from Brian at the sound of the mocking voice, staring up in amazement to see Brenda Gaynor silhouetted above them atop another towering wave of green seawater, her coppery hair ablaze in the moonlight. "Get away from him, you bitch!" Brenda snarled, revealing long, razor-sharp fangs. Kelly screamed.

"OH MY GOD!"

Kelly Huston came suddenly awake, blinking her eyes and looking around at the familiar outlines of her darkened room. The luminous hands of the old-fashioned alarm clock by the bed showed 5:45. It wouldn't be light for another half hour yet.

She grimaced at the ridiculous image of Brenda with her fangs hanging out, angrily punched her pillow with a balled-up fist, then rolled over and pulled the down comforter over her head. She had been dreaming about Brian again. Something she had vowed before going to sleep tonight that she would not do.

The familiar ache rose in her throat, and she angrily willed herself not to cry. Kelly had always prided herself on the fact that she never cried; not the time she had fallen down and cut her knee when she was seven and had to have stitches, not even when her favorite porcelain doll—the one Daddy had brought her from F. A. O. Schwarz in New York—had fallen from the shelf and broken. Not ever . . . And yet, Brian O'Malley had made her cry twice within the space of five days.

Dammit, it wasn't fair. He had been so warm and gentle . . . seemed to love being with her. Kissing her softly and pausing to press his cheek against her breast to hear the beating of her heart as they had made love for the first time. Holding her hand and listening to her bad jokes. Praising the snatch of silly romantic poetry she'd written for him.

And then it had all just stopped.

The thing was, she didn't have the faintest idea what she had done or said to change his attitude toward her. Things had been going so well until . . . Until Tuesday, the day after they had made love on the beach. Something had happened to change him.

Kelly sat up and swiped angrily at the hot tears that were already coursing down her cheeks. Dammit, she *would not* cry! After all, Brian O'Malley was not even really her boyfriend or anything. In fact, she hardly knew him.

She couldn't understand why she was so upset over his sudden rejection of her. And, to be fair, she didn't even think it was Brenda Gaynor. He had told her at lunch on Monday that he couldn't stand the clinging redhead.

But then, the very next day he had very deliberately placed Brenda between them—walking to and from all his classes with the other girl, spending his whole lunch period with her—almost as though he were using the chattering redhead to keep Kelly away from him.

Yesterday she had seen the two of them sitting together on the cafeteria patio at lunchtime again, Brenda jabbering about some dumb rock concert her father was going to get tickets for, and all over Brian like a rash.

Kelly had walked hurriedly past the couple, trying to ignore them, and, for just an instant, Brian had looked up and her eyes had met his. Eyes that were filled with longing, and something else . . . sadness maybe, but more than sadness. Something that Kelly couldn't name, but that had sent an icy chill of foreboding down her spine. What in the hell was happening to her?

Her tears exhausted, she climbed out of bed and wrapped her old terry robe about herself. She padded softly through the darkened house to the kitchen, where she disarmed the blinking security panel by the door, then slipped outside onto the pool deck. Dropping into a chair beside the black, glassy water, she pulled her knees up beneath her and stared out over the dark outlines of the Hollywood hills to the east, waiting for the sunrise.

She sat there like that for a long time, thinking about the brooding, handsome boy who lived up the hill and the intense emotions he had fired within her, emotions unlike any she had ever before experienced. Emotions she felt helpless to do anything about. She knew she couldn't go on like this any longer.

The sun was beginning to tinge the smog-red L.A. skyline by the time she had determined that she must find out what had happened between them. Somewhere deep inside, she was convinced that Brian O'Malley really wanted to be with her, and not with the horrible Brenda. Something was keeping him away, though. Something that he obviously thought he could not tell her.

Kelly smiled, getting to her feet and stretching beneath the brightening red dawn. She would just have to confront Brian head-on and make him realize that there wasn't anything he couldn't tell her.

And if he still wouldn't tell her, well, then she would find out what it was on her own. After all, she was her father's daughter, and John Kovac had always taught her to go after what she wanted in life and grab hold of it.

And she was deeply in love with Brian O'Malley.

Her mind made up, she let the terry robe drop to her feet and leaped into the swimming pool with a tremendous splash.

THE FAINT SOUND of a splash echoed up the hillside.

Billy Quinn pushed himself forward, letting the front legs of his plastic lawn chair drop heavily onto the balcony floor and peering down the canyon at the roof of the silent house below.

He listened carefully for a moment, heard nothing but the far off drone of traffic on the freeway, then leaned forward with his head held between his hands.

What in the fuck was he going to do?

Before he had heard the unexpected sound, Billy had been leaning back against the stuccoed wall outside his room with his eyes closed, smoking cigarette after cigarette and trying to drain the tension from his body before forcing himself into the shower for the beginning of another day. As on the previous three nights since he'd learned of the Major's announcement, sleep had been an impossibility.

He couldn't stop thinking about it.

The Queen!

Somehow, he was certain that Kileen planned to use the old boy's honors invitation to assassinate the Queen when she arrived here in California in just two days for a brief state visit.

Or, worse, the bastard meant to have Billy do it.

"Christ!" He spat the meaningless epithet at the empty brown hills. The man must be completely mad. Even if somebody was willing to murder a helpless old woman, whoever was fool enough to attempt to even get in close enough to the old bat to have a decent chance with a gun, or even a knife, would surely be killed before they made it across the bloody room. Certainly they'd never make it out alive.

It was a suicide mission, plain and simple.

He furrowed his brow, trying to put together all the pieces: After the Major had showed him the announcement naming the time and the place— 7:00 P.M. *in the evening in the Oak Room of the Hotel Beverly, cocktail reception and dinner to follow*—Billy had pored through the local newspapers, all of which he'd found filled with breathless accounts of the impending royal visit to Los Angeles, which was, he had discovered, actually just a one-night stopover en route to a World Health Conference meeting in Hawaii.

The news articles had been long on useless detail, naming the many dignitaries who were to be present at the state dinner, giving flight arrival and motorcade times, even printing the bloody menu of delicacies to be served. They had, however, contained no mention whatsoever of the things that

Billy wanted desperately to know. Things like what floor of the hotel the Oak Room was on, whether the ceremony was to be held in the same room as the reception and dinner, how many security agents would be crawling the corridors and the crowds, what kinds of armaments they carried . . . Nothing that would help him decide if Kileen's insane plan had a chance in hell of succeeding.

"Damn!" He pounded the black wrought-iron railing with his fist. "Damn! Damn!"

Yesterday, in his desperation to know more, he had driven to the Hotel Beverly, thinking he'd casually stroll the corridors like a rich kid looking for his parents. He'd turned the Jag over to a grinning valet and stepped through the ornate lobby doors, only to discover to his horror that the place was crawling with cops, grim-faced men in conservative suits, wearing tiny earplugs and identical lapel pins . . . He had almost shit his pants. And, of course, once there, he couldn't just run back out and hop in the Jag, as every fiber of his being had screamed at him to do. Instead, he had been forced to walk calmly up and down the vast lobby, peering into the windows of the expensive shops, looking at his watch and pretending to be waiting for someone.

After what he thought was a decent interval, he had escaped back into the sunshine, calling for the Jag and waiting nervously while it had been brought up from the underground parking garage. By the time it arrived and he had slipped behind the wheel, his hands had been trembling so violently that he had damn near collided with a taxi driving up to the hotel entrance. The cabdriver had begun blowing his horn at him, shouting obscenities in some thickly accented Mideastern tongue, causing everyone within fifty yards of the main doors to stop whatever they were doing and stare.

Fucking brilliant! He had no doubt whatsoever that had Kileen even dreamed he'd done such a daft thing, drawing attention to himself, the murderous terrorist would gladly put a bullet in his brain for him.

And, as if all of that wasn't bad enough, he'd had to continue the charade of attending classes at Pacific Academy, first managing to convince the grinning track coach he needed a week or two on his own to "loosen up" before going out to formal workouts with the team, then stumbling zombielike across the postcard-perfect campus to sit stupidly through a succession of classes he didn't comprehend, while the daft high school girls in their sexy costumes had nudged and winked and whispered to each other about him, and the tanned, muscular boys all glared openly, though he couldn't imagine how he might have offended the latter, having scarcely spoken to a single one of them since he'd been there.

Not, he'd finally decided, that it made a fucking bit of difference, considering the life-and-death matters that were on his mind. He wondered what the stupid bastards would think if they knew who he really was. *What* he really was.

Christ, they'd all pee their tight, deliberately ripped jeans and run wailing home to their mothers.

And then there was the problem of Brenda Gaynor.

At first, Billy had encouraged her to hang about, anxious to isolate himself from Kelly, who, of all people, he had determined he couldn't allow to be hurt by even a casual involvement in Kileen's deadly game.

And for a day or two it had worked. After his initial rebuff on Tuesday morning, Kelly Huston had stayed away from him, looking hurt, but leaving him alone. And, in his daze over Kileen's mission, having the constantly jabbering redhead on his arm as he'd made his way from class to class had probably served far better than he'd known to keep other people away from him, as well—it seemed that almost nobody liked Brenda Gaynor, certainly not the other girls at school.

By yesterday, however, Brenda had started to become a major nuisance. In the first place, he'd discovered that she really never did stop talking. Never. Billy thought if he heard her remind him one more time about her Mercedes convertible or her father's record company or his gigantic yacht, or his "place in the Springs," that he would reach down her throat and yank her wagging tongue out by the roots. *Here, Brenda, my girl. Take this and stick it in your bleeding Gucci bag!*

He couldn't fucking think when she was around.

But that wasn't even the worst of it. Yesterday, after school had let out, she'd followed him out to the parking lot, jumping into the passenger seat of the Jag and brazenly cocking her legs up so that he'd been staring right up her crotch. "Let's go someplace and screw," she'd suggested lecherously, kicking off one of her expensive sandals and reaching across with her little foot to massage his balls.

He had nearly croaked, although, he decided on reflection, he'd probably have been a lot better off going with her than to the Hotel Beverly, as he'd done. He wondered grimly what it would actually be like to screw Brenda Gaynor. Concluded that she'd probably go right on talking, as though nothing unusual were happening.

The sound of movement in the kitchen below snapped him out of his ruminations, causing him to drop the glowing cigarette onto his bare leg. He peered down over the balcony, saw a shadow against the kitchen window. Just old Ranjee fixing the Major's morning tea before starting breakfast. Billy had never been this jumpy before, not even the night he and Kileen had dropped the bomb at the border crossing. Christ, that seemed like it had been a hundred years ago.

He counted backward, mentally adding up the days. Ten days. That was how long it had been since the night they'd blown up the border post and Kileen had talked him into coming here. Ten days to destroy his entire life. He wished to God he'd never fucking met Michael Kileen, the great bloody hero of the revolution.

Billy pulled himself wearily to his feet, crushing out the cigarette in his overflowing ashtray, hoping ten minutes beneath a scalding shower would clear his head enough to pull him through another day at Pacific Academy. He was about to step into his room when he heard the sound of a car on the canyon road below. He caught a brief glimpse of a dark vehicle moving up through the foliage lining the drive to Kelly Huston's house. The maid arriving for the day, he supposed.

He stood looking down at the roof of the other house, wondering what she was doing now. Wishing he could just sit someplace with her for a quiet hour, to explain, and to beg her forgiveness.

A smile flickered across his lips for the first time in days. "You stupid sod," he murmured wearily, "haven't you done enough? You've got to leave her the hell out of this."

Choking back the hard lump constricting his throat, Billy turned and walked into his room, pausing by the washbasin just outside the bathroom door to strip out of the shorts he was wearing. He was on the point of stepping into the bathroom to start the shower when he caught a glimpse of his haggard reflection in the mirror above the sink. "Oh Christ, no!"

He froze on the spot, then leaned forward to stare in horror at the faint blond line showing at the roots of his raven black hair.

Tears of rage and frustration coursed down his cheeks as he stormed back into the bedroom and ripped Brian O'Malley's expensive suitcases from the closet, rummaging in the cases for the package they had told him was inside.

"IS IT REALLY YOU?"

The curvacious, dark-haired woman in the tight black leather jeans gazed up in wonder at the handsome face smiling down at her.

"It is," said Kileen, reaching up to stroke his newly molded chin. "Do you like it?"

She jumped to her feet from the concrete bench outside the Los Angeles Airport international arrivals terminal and threw her arms around his neck. "Now you're perfect," she whispered into his ear.

Kileen squeezed her briefly, then held her out at arm's length to look at her. "You told me I was perfect before," he said.

"Well, now you're even more perfect," she retorted, bending to pick up one of the two bags sitting on the ground beside him and wrapping her free arm around his waist. "I love your suit too," she said, leading him into a crosswalk and sticking out her tongue at the three cabs that screeched to a halt in order to avoid running them over.

"You could be killed outright for doing that in London or New York," he said, glancing at the cursing cabbies.

"Yeah, well this is L.A., and running down somebody in a crosswalk is the most serious crime on the books." She laughed and threw a murderous look at the nearest cabbie, who was revving his engine threateningly and inching into the crosswalk. "Up yours, pal," she shouted, removing her hand from Kileen long enough to flip her middle finger at the driver.

"Same old Sally, I see," said Kileen.

"Betcher sweet ass," she grinned, leading him into the depths of a huge, echoing parking structure.

"And were you able to obtain a suitable vehicle for my use?" Kileen scanned the long rows of parked cars, trying to guess what she'd picked in response to his transatlantic telephone request for something "expensive but understated."

"How's this, Sweetcakes?" Sally proudly led him around a concrete pillar to the dove gray Mercedes C340 sedan she'd stolen the previous evening.

Kileen nodded approvingly. "I should have known better than to even bother asking."

Sally Hilton basked in his praise. Extracting a set of keys from the pocket of the loose leather jacket she wore, she opened the trunk and dropped the case she was carrying inside. "I know there's another question you're dying to ask," she said, "so I won't keep you in suspense. Yes, the car is absolutely clean. Borrowed from the private garage of a Beverly Hills surgeon who's attending a medical convention in Paris. The license plates belong to a nearly identical gray Merc that's lying up in the back of the dealer's garage in Santa Monica, awaiting the settlement of an insurance claim. You can use this car for at least a week before I return it and the plates to their rightful places." She grinned. "Slicker'n snot, as my poor old daddy used to say back home in Kentucky."

"You really are a remarkable woman," said Kileen, bending to kiss her cheek.

Sally shuddered pleasurably at his touch. "Yeah," she whispered, "and don't forget, I've got a great ass too."

Kileen's face reddened slightly. Though he had been doing occasional business and sleeping with the audacious Sally for nearly three years now, he had never quite grown accustomed to her coarse language, which he found all the more disconcerting because of her sweet, almost delicate looks. Still, he found her exciting to be with and had often reflected that if he were ever to truly fall in love with a woman, it would be Sally. "Yes," he agreed, feeling somewhat foolish. "It's a wonderful bit of ass."

Sally laughed delightedly, opening the front passenger door for him. "Where are you staying?" she asked, not even bothering to suggest he come to her place in West Hollywood. For, although she was desperately in love with the rugged and mysterious Irishman, she had long ago learned that he valued his privacy, and that leaning on him only pushed him away. Michael Kileen always stayed in hotels—pricey but nondescript resort lodgings in Santa Monica that, for the most part, catered to visiting Brits and Irishmen.

"Actually," Kileen said, slipping into the soft leather bucket seat beside her and looking up at her with those deadly black eyes, "I was wondering if I might stay at your place this time, Sally. That is, if it wouldn't be too inconvenient . . ."

"Darlin'," Sally sighed, leaning down and pressing the tops of her lovely breasts to his cheek, "you are not goin' to regret that decision."

"Oh, really?" said Kileen, laying his head back against the cushioned leather rest and allowing her to close the door, enjoying the rare luxury of the feeling of total security that being with her always gave him.

"Really." Sally grinned, opening the driver's door and sliding in behind the wheel. "'Cause mama's gonna take you home and give you a nice, hot bath, then she's gonna take you into that big ol' water bed of hers and fuck your sweet brains out . . ."

"Sounds wonderful," sighed Kileen, who had been traveling almost continuously for more than three days.

"And then, Sugar Booger," cooed Sally, twisting the key in the ignition and expertly backing the big Mercedes out into the aisle. "Then you know what I'm gonna do?"

Kileen closed his eyes and shook his head.

"Then," said Sally, driving out to the exit ramp and pulling the Mercedes into a short line of early morning commuters waiting to exit the airport. "Then, I'm gonna tuck you up for a nice long sleep while I cook you the goddamnedest down-home country meal you ever ate in your whole damn life."

Kileen smiled, for once forgetting the pain it caused him. Everything was going perfectly.

CHAPTER THREE

Late for School

"WELL, MY BOY, how did you sleep?"

The Major sat across the veranda table from Billy, spreading marmalade on a piece of wheat toast.

"Fine, sir," Billy lied. His hair was still damp from the shower, and he kept his hands in his lap, afraid the Major would discern the dark edges rimming the nails of his left hand, where the flimsy plastic glove that had come with the hair dye had torn.

Ranjee fussed silently around the table, laying plates of bacon and eggs before the two of them, then retiring to the kitchen doorway in case he should be needed.

"Wonderful!" The Major smiled, popping a triangle of toast into his mouth and chewing enthusiastically. "And how are you getting on at school? Any problems?"

Billy shook his head, lifting the unstained right hand to pick up a fork, which he poked into his eggs. "I'm still getting used to it," he said evasively, worrying that someone from the school had noticed something odd in his behavior and called the old man. "It's very different from what I was used to at home," he added, hoping to ward off any suspicions.

"Of course, that's to be expected." The old fellow chewed thoughtfully on his toast for a moment. "No doubt you'll do well as soon as you've gotten into the routine," he said, swallowing. "No doubt whatsoever." He squinted across the table at the bedraggled lad. "I daresay you do look a bit tired, though, Brian," he observed. "Sure you're sleeping well in that bed? Not eating either, I see."

Billy nodded miserably, trying to muster up the energy to eat a little something for the sake of appearances. "I'm afraid it's just been a very long week, Major." He glanced down at the handsome watch Kileen's men had taken from Brian O'Malley's wrist. "I'd better go or I'll be late for school," he muttered, anxious to escape the old man's scrutiny as quickly as possible.

The Major nodded sympathetically, but held up a hand to indicate that he should remain where he was. "Takes some adjusting, I'm sure," he repeated encouragingly. "You'll see though, a few more days and you'll be right as rain." He finished his toast and reached into the breast pocket of his spotless navy blazer, extracting a neatly folded slip of white paper and spreading it on the cloth. "Now, I won't detain you a moment, but there are a few details that must be taken care of today, I'm afraid," said the Major, carefully scanning the handwritten list he'd prepared in his study the night before. "You'll need to run down to Armani's in Beverly Hills right after school for a final fitting of your formal togs. They've agreed to rush the alterations so that Ranjee can pick them up tomorrow afternoon when he goes in for my dress clothes. Can you manage that, or shall I have him take you?"

Billy groaned silently, recalling the torturous hour he'd spent with one of Armani's frantic tailors sticking pins into the baggy formal suit they'd draped on him earlier in the week, while Ranjee had watched. "I think I can manage on my own, thanks," he said, casting a sidelong glance at Ranjee, who gave him a grateful nod.

The Indian servant had come up to his room after dinner for the past two nights, to explain in detail how he should conduct himself at the forthcoming state dinner, also discreetly dropping several hints that had helped him brush up on his table manners.

Billy had at first found the visits disconcerting, for, following the incident with the cigarettes, Ranjee's new interest in him had immediately led the boy to believe that the servant suspected something and was spying for the old man. After the first session, however, it seemed evident that Ranjee attributed his slipups at table to poor training, and that the Indian was simply attempting to be helpful.

Still, having him constantly padding about made Billy nervous, even though he had decided the little wanker wasn't a bad sort after all. In fact, he thought, if Ranjee spent very much time on his manners, he was sure he could pass himself off as the bleeding Duke of Edinburgh.

"Good," said the Major, making a tick mark on his list. "You'll see to the clothes yourself, then. Ranjee's got absolutely a thousand things to take care of before Saturday evening as it is."

Billy jumped as a bell rang somewhere at the front of the house.

The Major looked up expectantly. "Ranjee, see to that." The servant disappeared into the house, and Billy heard the sound of voices at the front door. "That'll be the security bloke from the British consulate, I'll reckon," said the Major, making another tick mark on his list.

"The consulate?" Billy felt a sickening wave of black dread welling up in the pit of his stomach.

"Of course, my boy." The Major winked at him. "Got to have your security clearance for the grand festivities, now haven't you?" He poured himself a cup of coffee as footsteps sounded in the corridor running through the house. "They rang up yesterday and wanted you to come all the way down there, if you can believe that." The old man snorted self-importantly. "I naturally told them that would be quite impossible, what with your school and all. Threatened to speak to the consul himself. Told them they'd just have to send their man round here to see you . . . "

Billy stared at him in horror. Not only was he going to have to deal with a Foreign Office security agent, but the old man had started it off by insuring that whoever they sent would probably arrive pissed off. "He's here *now?*" His voice was a tremulous whisper.

The old man saw his stricken expression, mistaking the sheer terror in his bloodshot eyes for concern over being late to school. "Now, now, nothing to concern yourself over, Brian," he said soothingly. "We'll simply give the fellow a cup of tea and send him on his way. Probably some third assistant secretary fresh out of Oxford and anxious to get back to his cubbyhole and his telephone, if I know these fellows. Won't take a minute . . . "

"A Mr. Applewhite to see you, sir." Ranjee stepped clear of the doorway, revealing a skinny young fellow with a severe haircut, a three-piece suit and a school tie.

"Mr. Applewhite!" The Major was on his feet, hurrying across the veranda to grab both the startled visitor's hands in his own and beaming a high-intensity smile into the security man's sallow face. "How very kind of you to drop by. We were just speaking about you . . . "

"Major . . . Pardon me," Applewhite smiled, showing a mouthful of long teeth, "*Brigadier* Queally-Smythe. It's a great honor, sir. A great, great honor. If I may say so, I consider myself your greatest admirer."

"How perfectly wonderful," said the old fellow, clapping his hands together in feigned delight. He winked and dropped his voice to a conspiratorial stage whisper. "I *knew* you must be out there somewhere."

Applewhite looked puzzled for a moment, then he laughed appreciatively. The Major led him to the table where Billy stood with his left hand jammed tightly in his trouser pocket, the other clutching the back of a metal chair, as he tried valiantly to prevent himself from throwing up. "And this," said the Major, "is my grandson, Master Brian O'Malley. A desperate-looking fellow, wouldn't you say?"

Applewhite grinned, extending a thin hand. "A pleasure to meet you, Mr. O'Malley. Sorry to bother you with the visit, but it's required, I'm afraid. Bloody nationalist fanatics still manage to shadow Her Majesty everywhere she goes these days . . ."

Billy firmly grasped the young security man's limp hand, praying the quaking in his knees wasn't being transmitted. His nervousness at standing face to face with an official representative of the hated enemy was exceeded only by his apprehension over the bold gambit he was about to make. "Thank *you* for coming, Mr. Applewhite," he said. "And there's no need whatsoever to apologize for the visit . . . If we'd had better security at home, I believe my parents might still be alive today."

Applewhite stood back to appraise the nervous youngster. "A commendable attitude, Mr. O'Malley." He smiled. "We greatly appreciate your cooperation."

"Well, now, Applewhite," the Major said, waving them to seats at the table. "Any rule against your having a nice cup of tea while you interview this young man?"

Applewhite grinned. "None whatsoever, Brigadier."

"Now, now," the old man wagged a cautionary finger at him. "That's not official yet." He turned toward the kitchen and bellowed, "Ranjee, bring some tea!" When there was no answer, he scowled. "Now where has that heathen little beggar gone off to? 'Scuse me." He stomped into the house, still bellowing for the servant, and Applewhite looked at Billy. "Quite a marvelous old gentleman, your grandfather."

Billy nodded, fighting back his panic. "Grandfather is that." A pot clanged to the floor inside the house, and he forced himself to smile. "I'm afraid he does become a bit agitated with poor Ranjee at times though."

Applewhite followed his gaze toward the kitchen. "Well, that's because he's from the old school, you see. Days of Empire and all that. One was expected to exercise a firm hand with the servants." He chuckled. "You should have heard my old granddad rail at the maids when I was growing up. And of course," he added confidentially, "most of them *were* awfully lazy."

Billy smiled his understanding, letting his eyes drop to Applewhite's pale, manicured hands; hands that had surely never done an honest day's work. *And I bet you were right there beside him in your precious little public-school togs, Applewhite, smiling that smug smile and eating a toffee while the old bastard humiliated some helpless parlor maid,* he thought. An image of his own mother came to him, and he felt his fear being transformed to rage. His stomach was beginning to settle down, and his grin broadened as he suddenly realized that he wasn't in the least afraid of this pompous little wanker. *Come on, Applewhite,* he urged, *find a hole in my story so I'll have a reason to shove that skinny, aristocratic nose right up into your fucking brain!* "I've got to get to school soon," he said, glancing pointedly at his watch. "Were there some questions you wanted to ask me?"

"Yes, of course. Sorry." Applewhite extracted a folded form from an inside pocket of his suit and smoothed it on the table, fumbled in another pocket for a gold pen, which he poised over the paper. "I took the liberty of getting all the pertinent facts from your passport file," he said. "So I have just one or two questions to ask you. Purely a formality, you understand."

Billy nodded, drumming his fingers on the table and trying to look suitably impatient. "Of course."

"Very well, then, Brian." Applewhite glanced down at the printed form. "Do you consider yourself to be a loyal British subject?"

Billy forced what he hoped was a pained expression, for this was a question that Kileen had prepared him to answer, though the questioner was to have been a bored immigration officer, not this arse-kissing consular official. "If the purpose of that question is to determine whether I have any sympathy for the renegade Catholic bastards who left that bomb in the road to blow up my mum and dad, the answer is definitely no."

Applewhite looked embarrassed. "Yes, of course. Sorry. As I said, just required questions . . ."

Growing bolder, Billy reached over to touch the sleeve of the other's tailored suit. "No," he said. "I understand."

Relief showed in Applewhite's face, and he scrawled something on the form. "No recent travel to the Mideast, Cuba, the Balkans, any other war zones, I suppose?"

"Well, I did have a trip to Hollywood the other night." Billy found himself suddenly beginning to enjoy the dangerous exchange, realizing that the whole trick of making himself appear beyond reproach to this wanker was simply to make himself seem a part of Applewhite's snobbish world.

Applewhite smiled appreciatively. "Oh that's very good. Must remember that one for the fellows back at the office." His nasal voice dropped to a confidential tone, and he leaned closer. "Los Angeles can be quite a dangerous place. Why, one of our secretaries had her purse taken at knifepoint, right in the entrance of a very good restaurant just the other evening," he reported in shocked tones.

"I shouldn't wonder," said Billy, imagining what the lads back in his old West Belfast neighborhood would think if they could hear him talking like this. *I shouldn't wonder—I shouldn't wonder they'd kick my bleeding arse all the way down to the gasworks, he thought.*

"Well then," said Applewhite, looking pleased with himself. "Just one more question, Brian." He raised his pale eyes and gazed into Billy's. "What are your personal feelings toward the Royal Family?"

Billy looked thoughtful. "Well, I really did think that Diana and Charles should definitely have stayed together . . . " he began as seriously as he dared.

The security man tried to suppress a smile. "No, Brian. What I mean, is do you wish them any harm?

Billy looked suitably embarrassed. No sense leaving this sod with the impression that he was less intelligent than a mere schoolkid. "Oh . . . oh, I see what you mean," he stammered. "No, of course not. I definitely believe that the monarchy is a sacred institution. I mean, it is really, isn't it, despite all that talk back home about its being useless and decadent and a waste of our tax revenues?"

Applewhite smiled at the daft answer, jotted a final note on his form and tucked it away in his pocket. "Well, I think that'll be quite enough. I think I can safely say you pass muster with the Foreign Office, Brian."

"Found the blackguard!" They both looked up to see the Major striding through the door, his face flushed. "Tea will be right along."

Billy stood, extending his hand to Applewhite. "Sorry, but I've absolutely got to run. I've got a physical education class first period, and the coach is a bit of a bear for punctuality."

Applewhite got to his feet and took the boy's hand. Shook it firmly. "It's been a great pleasure meeting you, Brian." Billy nodded to the Major and started toward the kitchen door.

"Oh, Brian," called the Major. "We'll be dining out this evening, so do try to be back by seven." Billy waved and disappeared into the house.

"Fine boy," said the Major fondly. "Going to be on the track team, you know."

Applewhite bobbed his aristocratic head up and down enthusiastically. "A fine boy," he parroted, noticing the Indian servant approaching with a silver tea service. "Well," he said, looking about reluctantly, "I suppose I'd better be getting back . . ."

"Without your tea? I won't hear of it," boomed the Major, pushing him down into his chair. "After all, it's not every day one gets to meet one's greatest admirer."

Applewhite flushed happily, imagining what the fellows back at the office would say when he casually let it drop that he'd spent the morning having tea on James Queally-Smythe's veranda.

BILLY WHEELED the Jaguar into the Pacific Academy High parking lot, noting that the usual mob of students lounging around the cars was missing. He was late.

He found a parking place at the rear of the lot and leaped from the car, sprinting across the pavement toward the gymnasium.

"Brian!"

He stopped and turned to see Kelly Huston sitting in her Mustang. It was obvious from her eyes that she had been crying. His heart sank, and he looked pointedly toward the school. "Kelly," he said lamely, "aren't you going to class?"

"Brian, I have to talk to you." She opened the door and got out of the car, her golden hair falling about the shoulders of her pink blouse.

Billy edged toward the gym. "I've really got to go," he said apologetically.

Kelly shrugged. "Okay, I just thought it would be less awkward now than tonight."

He looked at her. "What do you mean?"

"My mother said that you and the Major were having dinner at our house tonight," she snapped, "to celebrate their movie deal."

A final bell sounded somewhere within the school, and Billy looked helplessly toward the gymnasium. Kileen had warned him to do everything exactly by the book at school, so he dared not miss the class. Besides, he didn't want to talk now, especially not to her. For, if he allowed himself to fall under her spell again, he wasn't absolutely sure he could trust himself not to blurt out the whole story to her, something that he was certain could endanger her life. "I'm very sorry, Kelly," he said, edging away, "I didn't know about the dinner . . . I mean, the Major mentioned we were dining out, but . . . Well, what was it you wanted to talk about?"

"I guess it will wait," Kelly snapped angrily. She reached back into the Mustang and lifted out a handful of books. "You'd better hurry or you'll miss your class."

"Can we talk later?" he asked miserably.

"Whatever." She slammed the car door shut and stormed away in the opposite direction.

"Kelly!" he called after her, but she did not look back. "Bloody hell!" The ache in his heart at the sight of her leaving made him feel even worse than he had, and he was tempted to run after her. *What for, you damned fool? In two more days you'll be gone and she'll never see you again. It's better this way. Better for both of you.*

Hot tears of loss and frustration threatening to fill his eyes, Billy Quinn turned and blindly ran toward the gymnasium.

CHAPTER FOUR

Dangerous Games

P.E.

Stanley Kinsella hated P.E.

Ever since he'd been in junior high school, it was the only class he'd dreaded, the one part of the academic regimen that prevented him from maintaining a straight A average. For Stanley's thin body, with its sunken chest and rounded shoulders, its myopic vision and weak ankles, had been constructed for hunching over computer keyboards and fascinating science experiments, not for running and jumping and throwing balls with a bunch of stupid jocks. As a result, he was always dead last; last to be chosen for any team, last at the end of every run and last on the list of competitors in every game.

Today was no exception.

Huffing and puffing, his thick glasses steamed with perspiration, his lank hair flopping in his eyes, Stanley wearily plodded through the last of the five torturous laps around the cinder track that Coach Gianelli had mandated every student must complete at the end of the period. Looking ahead, he saw that he was, as usual, alone on the course, which encompassed Pacific Academy's manicured football field. The rest of the class had already finished their laps some time ago and were either sitting out on the bleachers, enjoying a few minutes of rest, or heading for the showers.

Footsteps crunched on the cinders behind him, and he swiveled his head around, surprised to see Brian O'Malley, the good-looking new guy from Ireland, overtaking him. "Hey," yelled Stanley as the other boy drew up alongside. "How come you're still out here?"

"Coach gave me ten extra laps for being late to class," huffed the other, pulling ahead of the skinny boy.

"Oh, too bad," Stanley sympathized, feeling somehow better over the fact that he wouldn't be the last one into the showers for a change. "Well, see ya."

Brian O'Malley waved as he headed into the curve by the scoreboard to begin yet another dismal lap of the long track. His own circuits completed, Stanley angled toward the bleachers and collapsed in a sweaty heap on the bottom row of seats. Most of the others were already gone now, and he knew they were all inside, horsing around and snapping towels at each other's asses in the locker room.

In another minute, he knew, the bell would ring and he would be forced to go inside and shower, then he'd have to run his ass off in order to avoid being late for his next class. Nevertheless, he waited, knowing from long experience that if he went into the locker room while the others were still there, some smart-ass would snap his backside with a towel, or try to take his glasses away. That, more than anything, was the reason he hated P.E.

Out on the track, Brian O'Malley was just rounding the far end of the oval, his black hair flying in the wind, his long, muscular legs effortlessly eating up the distance. Stanley gazed at the distant figure, a sudden pang of jealousy stabbing at his skinny chest. Stanley Kinsella was hopelessly in love with Kelly Huston and, from conversations he'd overheard between her and Samantha Simms, and the scribblings he'd seen in Kelly's notebook, he knew that she felt exactly the same way about Brian O'Malley.

For months now, Stanley had been experimenting with psychokinesis, halfway convinced by a parapsychology text he'd picked up for fun in the university library that if he concentrated hard enough he could use his brainpower to effect physical changes in the people and things about him. Recently too he'd experienced a series of vivid dreams in which he had employed this amazing power to save Kelly Huston from all manner of disasters. Now he focused all the malevolent energy his brain could muster on the boy running around the track, willing the other's legs to grow heavy as lead, forcing him to a stumbling, exhausted halt.

Brian O'Malley pounded past the bleachers, turning to look at him with his sharp blue eyes, and Stanley smiled foolishly and waved. The other boy lifted his hand in acknowledgment of the friendly greeting and ran off again.

Stanley shrugged and got to his feet. Of course he'd known the brain zap wouldn't really work. Besides, he decided, he kind of liked O'Malley. Even though the other boy had been in the P.E. class for less than a week, he was just about the only one of the guys who hadn't shoved Stanley aside or made some stinging remark about his physical shortcomings or his nerdy clothes. And besides, Kelly Huston liked the newcomer a lot.

•

"OKAY, JAKE, Jerry, Cliff, you all in?"

Thad August stood at the end of a row of lockers, surveying the small knot of senior boys gathered around him. The rest of the class had already left the locker room, and these were the guys Thad had grown up with. They had all been sailing and surfing and partying together ever since they were kids. They were guys he knew he could count on.

"Let me get this straight," said Jerry Hoffman, rubbing his damp curly hair with a towel. He was a short, compactly built kid whose father headed a powerful Beverly Hills law firm and, like his old man, he was possessed of a lawyer's quick, analytical mind. "You want us to get this O'Malley guy alone someplace and kick the shit out of him, right?"

August nodded nervously, because he hadn't put it like that at all. "Yeah, Jer," he said, "but like, anonymously. I mean, we'll catch him alone someplace at night."

Cliff Gundersen, a tall, well-muscled guy who looked exactly like his TV Western star father, and who was just about as bright, slowly shook his head. "I don't get it, August. What for?"

"I told you," said Thad, patiently reciting the outrageous story he'd made up to tell them, "the guy's a narc. The cops planted him in school to find out who's using and who's holding." He looked meaningfully at the others, all of whom he knew did grass and coke on a regular basis. "I think the son of a bitch is out to bust us, and he's not any high school kid."

"Sounds pretty stupid to me, Thad," said Jake Conway, a beefy jock who was August's best friend. "I mean, if this guy really is a narc and we get him alone someplace, what's to keep him from pulling his gun and blowing our brains out?"

The others murmured agreement.

"You sure you just don't want to mess this guy up because he's getting into Brenda's pants, August?" Jerry Hoffman grinned knowingly.

"Yeah," said Jake. "I mean if it's just a boy-girl thing, we'll bust him up for you, Thad. But I'm not about to start messing with no narcs."

"How come you don't just pound this O'Malley down yourself, August?" Cliff was looking at him quizzically. "I seen you stomp lots of dudes bigger'n him."

"Wait a minute, Cliff," Jerry interrupted. "I think I'm getting the picture here. Say August calls this asshole out and messes up his pretty face for him. Then Brenda might get pissed at Thad. But if we scare the shit out of the guy and convince him to find himself another lady, August's out of it."

He turned to August, who was looking down at the floor. "That about it, Thad?"

Thad August shrugged. He wished he'd thought of Jerry's explanation himself, instead of the stupid narc story. "Yeah, something like that," he muttered. "But he might be a narc too . . ." *After all, there's three of them,* he was thinking. *Three of them would be able to take the bastard down, no matter how tough he thought he was.*

"You asshole! We'll murderize this prick. What are buddies for, anyway?" Jake punched him painfully on the shoulder and they all trooped out of the locker room together.

"Okay, here's the deal, if we take care of this guy for you, you gotta get us all a case of that booze your old man has flown in from Scotland," laughed Jerry Hoffman.

"So, August, you want us to break his arms, or what?" Cliff Gundersen danced down the corridor behind them, throwing mock karate chops at the walls.

STANLEY KINSELLA pressed himself back against a locker trying to stop his heart from pounding. Hearing the other boys in the room when he first entered, he had sneaked past them to the next aisle and was silently stripping out of his sweaty P.E. clothes when he had begun to catch fragments of the conversation coming up over the tops of the lockers. They were going to hurt Brian O'Malley. Really hurt him bad.

When he was certain that August and the others had left, Stanley grabbed his towel and scurried down to the showers. Carefully setting his glasses and towel on a bench, he turned on the water and stepped beneath the scalding spray, letting it pound down on his head while he tried to decide what he should do.

Stanley knew from hard experience that Thad August and his friends were vicious, and he knew too that if he went to the principal, they would find out. People like them always found out who'd ratted on them.

And then it would be Stanley Kinsella they'd be standing around plotting to get.

On the other hand, he reasoned, maybe he could just warn Brian O'Malley to watch out. Let him go to the principal if he wanted . . .

Stanley smiled. Yeah, that was it. Then O'Malley would owe him a favor, maybe even tell Kelly Huston he'd helped him out . . . After all, the Irish kid didn't seem to like Kelly very much himself, or else he wouldn't have been hanging around all week with that Brenda Gaynor bitch.

"Any hot water left?"

Stanley blinked out into the steamy shower room, turning off the water and fumbling for his glasses. He pushed his wet hair aside and fumbled them on, blinking owlishly at Brian O'Malley, who stood in the doorway, wrapped in a towel.

"Yeah," said Stanley. "Lots." He grabbed his own towel and began blotting himself dry. "Hey, uh, maybe it's none of my business, but I think there's something you ought to know . . ." he began.

The other boy stepped into the room, adjusted the hot water and casually tossed his towel onto the bench. "What's that?" he asked, turning to regard Stanley through bloodshot eyes.

Stanley stared at him for a long moment, then wrapped his towel around himself and stammered, "Uh, well, that is . . . I mean, Kelly Huston really likes you a lot." Stanley blurted out the sentence, unable to tear his eyes from Brian O'Malley's lean, muscular body. Fortunately, the other boy had his eyes closed under the shower, so he wouldn't think Stanley was some kind of a homosexual.

"Yeah," said the handsome Irish boy through the screen of splashing water. "I like her too."

"Well, see ya," Stanley muttered. He turned and fled the shower room, slipping and nearly losing his balance on the wet floor. Back in the locker room, he threw his clothes on and ran outside with his hair still dripping. He was more frightened than he'd ever been in his life.

BILLY QUINN stood under the pounding shower wondering what all that had been about. He knew that the shy, studious boy who had just spoken to him was the butt of the school's jokes. *Christ, did everybody in the world have to find somebody else to feel superior to?* But why had Stanley Kinsella gone out of his way to tell him about Kelly? Had she put him up to it?

Billy's head was buzzing from the debilitating effects of insomnia and worry. He tried to think clearly, but nothing came. He wished now only to have Kileen show up and tell him what in the hell he wanted him to do so they could get on with it and leave this place.

And what if it really is a bleeding suicide mission he wants you to go on? What then, Billy?

"Well then I'll just tell the crazy bastard to get stuffed," he said into the cascading water. Secretly, he was convinced that once he explained to Kileen about Applewhite and the security he had seen with his own eyes at the Hotel Beverly, the terrorist would see the impossibility of carrying out his mad scheme.

•

"WOULD YOU LIKE ME to take another one?" The chubby young woman in the revealing green jumpsuit raised the Nikon, prepared to shoot again. She was standing in the center of a lush green lawn flanked by a corridor of royal palms, aiming the expensive camera at the handsome stranger she'd met by the pool.

"Oh, I think that's enough of me, Bev," Michael Kileen walked up to her and gently removed the camera from her hand. "Now I'll take one of you and Gloria. Suppose you stand right over here with the hotel behind you."

Gloria, Bev's reed-thin friend, giggled behind her oversized sunglasses and hurried out from the tiny patch of shade where she had been sheltering—for she was horribly sunburned after six days in Los Angeles—and joined the other woman on the grass. Bev shot Gloria a withering glance, willing her to disappear, but Gloria seemed not to notice, striking a comic pose next to her plump friend and hiking up the ridiculously large tee shirt she was wearing, to afford the stranger a glimpse of peeling, sinewy thigh.

Kileen laughed and peered into the Nikon's viewfinder. "Wonderful," he said. "But perhaps if you could both move just slightly to the left . . ."

Bev, an electronics consultant from Omaha who had practically maxed out her Visa Gold card to pay for this California vacation, roughly elbowed Gloria in the ribs, regretting her decision to invite her dense friend along. Now, as the two of them shuffled clumsily to the left, she tried again to think of some tactful way to get rid of her obnoxious companion. So far, the trip had been an absolute disaster. For though they were staying at one of the best—and, incidentally, most expensive—hotels in Los Angeles, a place, according to *People*, that was frequented by movie stars and millionaires, Gloria, with her braying nasal laugh and her gross blisters, couldn't have more effectively prevented them from meeting anyone really interesting if she'd hung signs around both of their necks proclaiming them to be lepers.

Until today, their last in L.A., Bev had despaired of anything at all happening. Then, less than an hour ago, she had been sitting glumly at her little table by the pool—the only place where she was finally free of the hideously sunburned Gloria—when the gorgeous stranger had struck up a conversation with her. Within moments he'd bought her a drink, and she'd learned that he was an executive from New York. He'd come to the hotel to meet an investor, only to discover that the other man's flight had been delayed.

The handsome businessman had told her he had the entire afternoon to kill, and Bev was positive that he'd been on the verge of asking her to lunch. And then, of course, Gloria had appeared in her stupid tee shirt and ruined everything. Since that time, the two of them had been strolling the grounds, snapping pictures of each other with his expensive camera and listening to Gloria's inane chatter about the trials and tribulations of her dull job managing the accounting department at the electronics company.

"Stop right there," said Kileen. The two women stopped moving and resumed their pose. The eastern wall of the Hotel Beverly—which completed the circuit of the rambling pink stucco, ten-story building—was perfectly centered in the Nikon's viewfinder as he snapped his final picture. "Terrific!" he said, raising his dark eyes from the camera and scrutinizing the details of the hotel's roofline, noting here, as on the other sides of the building, the absence of outside fire escapes, and committing to memory the position of the window washers working on a scaffold near the seventh floor, the wind sock denoting a rooftop helicopter pad on the southeast corner and the workmen unloading concrete blocks from a truck near the service drive.

Earlier, Kileen had strolled the hotel's elegant lobby with the intention of going up to the floor containing the meeting and banquet rooms. That plan had been frustrated by the early presence of a massive security force, which had already sealed off the stairwells on the ground floor and had posted guards who required guests to show hotel passports before being permitted to board the elevators. Hoping to find an unguarded approach to the upper floors, he had stepped into the open courtyard in the center of the building. There he had spied the corpulent Bev alone by the swimming pool, her gold hotel-guest passport lying open on the table beside her cup of decaf.

Now Kileen replaced the Nikon in its leather case and glanced at his watch. "Gee," he said in his best American accent, "lookit the time. I didn't get a chance to eat yet. Can I invite you ladies to join me for a bite?"

The sunburned Gloria grinned. "Oh, that'd be . . ."

"I'd love to," Bev interrupted, glaring daggers at her doughty companion, "but Gloria has some shopping she just has to get done today. Don't you, Gloria?"

Gloria's face fell. "I, uh, well, yes . . . I guess there were a few things I wanted to pick up."

"Come on, honey," hissed Bev, catching the startled Gloria by one skinny elbow and propelling her toward the hotel. "We'll walk you to the lobby and get you a cab. I bet you'll be gone for hours and hours, won't you?"

Gloria nodded miserably and allowed herself to be trotted back inside the hotel and through the lobby. As her taxi pulled away from the covered portico moments later, Bev turned and beamed her sexiest smile at the handsome stranger. "Well," she asked, "where should we lunch?"

Michael Kileen's low voice resonated deliciously in her ears. "I hear the room service here is something really special," he said.

Bev's head bobbed up and down enthusiastically. "It's absolutely fabulous," she agreed, fumbling in her bag for her hotel passport and handing it to him.

"STANLEY, what on earth happened to you?"

Kelly Huston looked up from the lab table where she had been glumly contemplating the towel-shrouded tray containing the frog corpse.

Stanley, the laces of his black Kmart sneakers flapping loose around his damp socks, scurried onto his stool and dropped his book bag on the floor beside him. Brenda Gaynor turned around to look at the commotion and nudged Thad August, who grinned like a depraved baboon. "Kelly, I have to talk to you," whispered Stanley, leaning over and dripping onto her notebook, "about that O'Malley guy."

"Better not let Mr. Acne too close, Kelly," taunted Brenda. "You might catch some of those zits from him."

Kelly glared back at the redhead. "Brenda, why don't you shut your big goddamned mouth?"

A murmur ran through the class, and everyone turned to stare at Brenda Gaynor, whose mouth was hanging open in shock. No one had ever spoken to her like that. "You are socially dead in this school, Kelly Huston," she retorted.

Kelly began to laugh, "Oh my God, someone call in a network news team quick. Brenda has spoken."

A mild titter ran through the class, and Stanley, who had been following the brief, angry exchange between the girls like a confused spectator at a tennis match, joined in the laughter. Suddenly, Thad August was on his feet. Stanley watched curiously as the bigger boy raced around the tables, realizing only when it was too late to flee that August was heading directly for him.

"What in the fuck were you laughing at, you little pizza-faced bastard?" August grabbed the startled Stanley by his cotton shirt, hauling him up off of his stool.

"N . . . nothing," stammered Stanley, raising a trembling hand to keep his glasses from slipping off his nose. August slapped the hand away, balling up his big fist and drawing it back to hit the quavering nerd.

"Let him go, you brainless, muscle-bound creep!" screamed a voice at his back. August whipped his head around to see Samantha Simms glaring at him. He grinned nastily. "You got the hots for this nerd, honey?"

Samantha stepped closer, sparks of anger flaring in her brown eyes." I said, let him go," Samantha repeated in a soft, sinister voice so low August had to strain to hear her, "or I swear to God that I will tell everyone in this school what happened the night you took me to the freshman dance, Thad August."

August looked at her uneasily, then let his eyes wander around the room. The entire class was leaning forward expectantly. "Better watch who you're laughing at from now on, Stanley," he warned, dropping the startled boy onto his seat and making his way back to his own table.

"Are you all right, Stanley?" Samantha was fussing over the shaken nerd, bending to straighten his rumpled shirt.

Kelly had watched the entire confrontation in stunned silence, unable to believe her eyes. "Samantha!" Her voice was a hoarse whisper. "What are you doing?"

Sam, her eyes still sparkling, turned to look at her. "I'm taking care of Stanley," she said, stroking his pitted cheek like a tigress protecting its cub. "Poor baby," she cooed. "Are you all right?"

Stanley nodded dumbly, gazing up through his thick lenses into Sam's beautiful face.

"Good," she said, squeezing him to her magnificent breast. "Because I don't want anything to happen to you." She pulled away and looked down at him. "Want to come over to my house and listen to some music tonight, Stanley?"

Stanley's jaw dropped. "Sure," he mumbled.

Sam blew him a kiss and pranced back across the room to her seat. Stanley's eyes followed her, and he turned to gaze dreamily at Kelly. "She likes me," he whispered. "Samantha Simms likes me."

Kelly rolled her eyes, unable to fathom what in the hell her best friend was up to. She'd seen Sam's male victims before, and they'd all had the same dazed look that was now on Stanley's pimply face; a "what the hell just happened?" look, not unlike the one frozen on the features of the poor embalmed frog staring up at them from the bottom of the plastic dissecting tray. Confused, she looked toward the front of the room. Now that the excitement was over, most of the other students had gone back to work on their frogs.

Thad August was leaning over, trying to talk to Brenda Gaynor, who was studiously ignoring him.

"Stanley," Kelly whispered, turning back to her stunned lab partner, "what was it you wanted to tell me?"

Stanley tore his gaze away from Samantha and gave her a blank look. "Huh?"

Kelly sighed impatiently. "Right before August grabbed you, you said you had to talk to me, about Brian."

Stanley's eyes darted over to August's broad back, and a shudder ran through his gangly body. "Nothing," he said.

"Nothing?"

Stanley shook his head. "Nothing."

"WHAT IN THE HELL was that all about with Stanley this morning?" Kelly and Samantha were walking toward the cafeteria together, Sam swaying dreamily to the edge of the flower-lined walkway to pluck a blossom from a rose bush, sticking it in her hair.

Sam looked hurt. "What do you mean, what was it all about? Can't I just decide I like somebody?"

Kelly stopped and stared at her. "Stanley Kinsella? Samantha, what is going on? I don't want to see that poor guy get hurt any more. And what happened to Brad, by the way?"

Sam tossed her dark curls impatiently. "Oh, Kelly, Brad is such a child," she replied.

"Right," said Kelly, "and Stanley Kinsella is Harrison Ford."

Sam smiled mysteriously. "Maybe he could be, with the right clothes and a little bit of guidance."

"Samantha, you like guys with Porsches. Have you seen Stanley's car? He drives a Yugo, for God's sake!"

"All of that will change," Sam said confidently. "Stanley just needs a little . . . encouragement."

"Yeah, plus a couple of million dollars in the bank," snorted Kelly.

"I don't think that's going to be a real problem." Sam grinned.

"What is that supposed to mean?"

Sam shook her head in disgust. "Kelly, don't you ever read the papers?"

"No," snapped Kelly. "And neither do you."

"Well, my father does," Sam retorted, "and for your information, Stanley's father was just named the head of Allied Pacific Studios, which is only the single largest movie studio in the entire world. Can you believe it? He used to be an accountant."

Kelly suddenly understood all too clearly where this was going. "And I suppose that little bit of information has nothing whatsoever to do with what happened between you and Stanley in biology lab this morning," she jabbed.

"I've always liked Stanley," Sam shot back defensively.

Kelly gave up. Once Sam had her mind set on snagging a new male she was unstoppable. "Uh-huh," she conceded. "Well, while you're working your magic on poor Stanley tonight, see if you can get him to tell you what he was going to tell me about Brian before you rescued him from Thad August."

"I'll call you." Sam smiled confidently.

"One more thing," said Kelly, "what *did* happen when August took you to the freshman dance?"

Samantha turned beet red beneath her rich tan. "You weren't supposed to hear that."

"Tell me anyway," Kelly demanded, "or I swear I'll tell Stanley you're only after his father's movie studio."

Sam leaned over and whispered into her ear.

CHAPTER FIVE

Lessons Learned the Hard Way

"THE FINAL SEGMENT of our study of Great Britain as a colonial empire brings us to the present day. Can anyone name Britain's remaining colonial possessions?" Horace Wilder, Ph.D., a small man in academic tweeds, scanned the bored class before him, hoping for a response, any response.

At times like this, Wilder, who had once held the chairmanship of the history department at a small but respected Midwestern college, sometimes regretted that he had allowed himself to be lured away to the exclusive private school in Pacific Palisades, where the average attention span of his students was on a par with the shelf life of the sushi they ate. Still, the money was fabulous and his wife adored the climate. "Anyone?"

"Hong Kong!" Henry Wang, one of the recently arrived Chinese students whose families were flooding into L.A. with suitcases filled with money, in anticipation of the imminent Communist takeover of the old Crown Colony, said as he raised his hand.

Wilder smiled. "Hong Kong." He turned and wrote Hong Kong on the board. "Very good, Henry. For a very short while, at least. Anyone else?"

"Bermuda and the Bahamas?" This from a dark, studious girl in the front row.

"Bermuda, yes," said Wilder, happily writing it below Hong Kong. "The Bahamas, however, gained their independence in the 1970s, as did most of the other former British possessions in the West Indies . . ."

"Northern Ireland."

Wilder turned to see Brenda Gaynor beaming up at him. The teacher frowned, trying to remember if the little redhead had ever before volunteered an answer in his class. He didn't think so. "Well, not technically, Brenda," he said, being careful not to discourage her. Brenda was a borderline student whose test grades indicated that her knowledge of history was restricted to the last action movie she'd seen.

He looked at Brian O'Malley, who sat beside Brenda, gazing out through a window. "Perhaps Mr. O'Malley would care to enlighten us on the current status of Northern Ireland," Wilder said in a voice loud enough to snap the new boy out of his daydream.

Billy Quinn blinked up at the smiling teacher. He had been slumped in his seat since entering the classroom, his concentration wavering between trying to keep himself awake and deciding how to avoid the forthcoming confrontation with Kelly Huston. He had just settled on the idea of begging off the evening's dinner invitation altogether, by claiming to be ill, when he had heard O'Malley's name called and looked up to see Brenda gazing proudly at him from the next seat.

"I beg your pardon, sir?"

Wilder smiled indulgently, making allowances for the boy's recent loss of his parents. "We were wondering if you could enlighten us as to the current status of Northern Ireland in the British Commonwealth," he said.

"It's an occupied war zone, isn't it?" said Billy, annoyed at having been interrupted by the stupid question.

Wilder frowned, wrinkling his high, pale forehead at the unexpected reply. "Well, Brian, he allowed with an indulgent smile, I'm sure that there are some elements in Northern Ireland who would still categorize it that way, but I was thinking more of Northern Ireland's official status as one of the several integral parts that make up the United Kingdom's modern parliamentary democracy, as is Scotland." He turned back to the rest of the class, who were gazing up at him in complete bewilderment.

"Well, sir," said Billy, mimicking the teacher's pedantic tone and feeling strangely light-headed, "there've been no British troops wandering around Edinburgh in tanks lately, have there?"

The wrinkles in Wilder's brow deepened. "Of course not, Brian, he spluttered, but—"

"And there've been no secret Scottish societies going about blowing up pubs and school buses and such, have there?" Billy's tone was mocking.

"Well, that has very little to do with the country's status today, I'm afraid—"

"Unless you happened to live there," said Billy, interrupting. "Then it has everything to do with it, wouldn't you say?"

The rest of the class was staring at the raven-haired Irish boy now, their interest engaged, no doubt, both by his willingness to challenge the teacher and by the interesting talk of tanks and explosions, and Billy felt compelled to keep talking. "You see, sir," he said, "you really wouldn't know the difference between a parliamentary democracy and an occupied war zone unless you'd actually lived in a war zone . . . The difference being that if people in a war zone decide to protest the government, the soldiers come out into the streets and shoot them down—"

"Now let's be accurate, Brian," said Wilder, holding up his hands good-naturedly and noticing that the students were staring at the O'Malley boy in rapt concentration. "While, admittedly, it is true that some civil disturbances have in the past been put down by police and British troops firing rubber bullets—"

Billy laughed derisively. "Ah yes, the rubber bullets. Tell me, sir, have you ever seen a *rubber bullet?*"

Wilder shook his head uncertainly. "Well, no, Brian, I can't actually say that I have, but—"

"You see," said Billy, turning to the class, "they're not really rubber at all—that's just something the government thought up to make them sound sort of funny and harmless, like something you'd see in a film cartoon— Boing! Oh my, they're shooting rubber bullets!—but what they really are is chunks of rock-hard plastic about a foot and a half long that they fire from these huge shotguns."

Billy Quinn closed his eyes and a painful scene flashed across his eyelids. "Once, when I was about thirteen, I saw a five-year-old Belfast girl shot in the head from about twenty feet away with a *rubber* bullet . . ."

Billy snuffled convulsively, then wiped his nose defiantly on his sleeve and glared at his fascinated classmates. "The shot fractured her poor little skull into five or six bloody pieces," he said. "And, of course, it killed her. The undertakers tried to fix her up, but it was no good. She looked like a broken doll in her little white coffin . . ."

The class stared at the red-eyed boy in stunned silence. Billy looked out the window, and when he continued, his voice was small and distant. "And then, another time I remember seeing a small boy walking down the street with his mum. They were just coming back from the pictures when a bunch of soldiers ran around the corner, chasing some demonstrators. The soldiers started shooting, and one of them funny little rubber bullets hit the poor little kid squarely in the eye . . . You could see the eyeball hanging right out on his little cheek—"

"Well, Brian, I think the class gets the idea," Wilder, his voice tinged with panic, hastily interrupted. Several of the students were beginning to look decidedly queasy. "And, after all," the teacher stumbled on, "there is peace in Northern Ireland now . . ."

Billy coldly eyed the nervous man by the blackboard. "No, I don't think the class does get the idea, sir," he said combatively. "I don't think any of them really has a fucking clue as to what goes on in the world. They just sit here like lumps in this temperature-controlled classroom, with the palm trees and the flowers waving in the breeze outside the window, and they sort of try to memorize the names of places that you write up there on that blackboard, in case you put them on the exam, and they listen to you talk about parliamentary democracies and the like, but I don't believe they really understand how that relates to some eighteen-year-old British soldier who's pissed off because the girls make fun of him in his armored car kicking down your door in the middle of the night and dragging your mother out into the rain in her nightgown, and maybe taking turns raping her with his mates, if there's not too many people about to see . . .

"And as for the fucking peace—"

"Mr. O'Malley, that will be quite enough!" Wilder's soft voice cracked on the verge of hysteria, and he was wringing his small hands together in desperation.

Billy blinked his eyes and looked around at the other students, all of whom were now openly gaping at him. Several girls were softly weeping, and even some of the boys seemed troubled by what he had said. Brenda Gaynor was staring at him, wide-eyed, and he cursed himself for his emotional outburst, *Jesus Christ, what are you doing, you stupid sod?*

"I'm sorry," he said, lowering his head and massaging the bridge of his nose with his fingers, trying to remember to speak the proper English he'd drilled into his thick brain. "I hope you'll . . . all forgive me," he murmured.

Wilder nodded gratefully. "I'm afraid this is all my fault," he stammered. "That is, I should never have brought up the subject." He turned to the class, lowering his voice to a funereal whisper. "Mr. O'Malley recently lost his parents in Northern Ireland," he explained.

The shaken teacher hurriedly crossed to his desk and fumbled through a textbook, searching for a new subject to discuss for the rest of the class time and frowning to himself over the boy's strange emotional outburst. Strange, he thought, because he distinctly recalled having been told that Brian O'Malley's parents had died in a nationalist bomb blast, yet a moment ago the boy had sounded like a nationalist rebel himself.

Kelly Huston, who had listened in horror from her seat on the opposite side of the classroom to everything that had just been said, wanted with all her heart to get up and walk boldly across the room, to put her arms around Brian O'Malley. To her, his strange behavior of the past week seemed suddenly heartbreakingly explainable in terms of the tragedies he had endured in Northern Ireland; tragedies that she was certain no one else within the sheltered confines of Pacific Academy High could even begin to imagine or understand, but that he must be living with every waking moment of his life.

His bitter tirade finished, Brian had sunk slowly into his seat. Now, he sat there with his eyes cast down at his desk, while Brenda Gaynor looked help-lessly on, and Kelly decided against doing anything, afraid of embarrassing him any further right now. But she vowed to herself that she would make things right between them when they were together this evening.

And she vowed also to discover the dark and horrible secret that she was now completely certain was torturing his gentle soul.

MICHAEL KILEEN sat sipping a cappuccino before a cluster of neon palm trees that rose forty feet to the domed glass roof covering the central plaza of an upscale shopping mall in Santa Monica. Soft music filled the air, and the delicious smells of fresh-baked bagels and croissants wafted across the busy concourse, which at this time of day was filled with prosperous young mothers pushing strollers and smartly dressed matrons hurrying down to their Mercedeses and BMWs in the parking level below, their arms laden with shopping bags emblazoned with the glossy logos of smart shops.

As he waited for the photos he had taken to be developed by the one-hour service near the mall entrance, Kileen idly speculated on the amazing destructive effect that a small package of explosives properly planted be-neath the glass dome would have on the luxury mall. His mind's eye pro-duced a shimmering image of the contented, overdressed women shrieking in horror as a curtain of razor-sharp shards descended without warning and their calm and privileged world dissolved before their very eyes.

Kileen shook his head to dispel the bloody image. In times of extreme stress, he was often distracted by such vengeful visions, and he had to force his mind back to the difficult problem at hand.

The Hotel Beverly had been far better secured in anticipation of the brief royal visit than he had expected. And, although, after leaving the ex-hausted Bev snoring in a heap of sweaty bedsheets, he had easily made his way into an unguarded stairwell, identifying several potential avenues to the upper floors and the roof, he would have to choose his route very care-fully if he expected to penetrate the sealed area where the Queen was to honor the old man, for it was crucial to Kileen's plan that he be close by when she entered the crowded roomful of dignitaries.

A giant wooden clock bonged above the façade of a toy store across from where he sat, and a comical animated cuckoo sprang out to chirp the hour. Getting to his feet,.Kileen made his way through the crowd of passing women, en route to the photo service. Smelling the mingled scents of their perfumed bodies, he thought of Sally, regretting the necessity of having spent so much time at the hotel, because it meant that he would not now have enough time to return to the condo for an early supper, as he had promised her he would do, before going out again for the night's work.

CHAPTER SIX

The Lads

"LET'S GO!"

Dermot Tumelty looked up from the jumble of souvenirs filling the coffee table before the television set to see Duffy hovering over him. The big terrorist already had his baggy leather jacket on, and the L.A. baseball cap was pulled down over his protruding ears. Tumelty plunged his good hand into a giant-sized box of Froot Loops, crammed a dry handful of the brightly colored breakfast cereal into his mouth and selected a white Disneyland sweatshirt from a plastic bag on the table. He carefully unfolded the shirt and began to pull it over his head.

"What the fuck are you doing now?" Duffy growled. His head was splitting from the aftereffects of the monumental drinking binge he'd been on, and his crotch chafed uncomfortably following the ministrations of the three different women he'd brought to the dingy hotel room after dispatching the younger man on a three-day bus tour of Southern California's major tourist attractions.

Dermot, his boyish face glowing like a five-year-old's at Christmastime, had returned to the hotel well after midnight last night, his arms filled with garish plastic bags of mouse ears, plastic mugs, and games and books touting the overpriced glories of all the places he'd visited. Since he'd gotten up early this morning, the little fellow had been sitting cross-legged before the coffee table, dreamily sorting through his treasures and humming the new song that he'd been writing in his head.

"I'm just putting on my shirt," said Tumelty, wriggling his damaged hand into the sleeve of the sweatshirt and turning to expose the giant portrait of Mickey Mouse emblazoned across his thin chest. "Do you like it?"

Duffy squeezed his eyes shut, willing the throb in his left temple to subside. "You can't wear that today, Dermot," he said quietly. He didn't want to start screaming at the youngster, who had, after all, been the one to come up with the brilliant suggestion that they each go their own way for the three days it would take Kileen to arrive in California. And thus having sworn each other to secrecy, each had gone off to immerse himself in his own separate orgy of wish fulfillment—both of them violating Kileen's strict order that they remain together at all times.

Tumelty looked wounded. "What? Why not?" he demanded, looking down and flicking an imaginary speck from the dazzling white cotton.

Duffy sighed. "Because," he said, "in the first place, it makes you look like a right fucking idiot. And in the second place, Kileen would have both our balls if he knew I'd let you spend operational funds on all that shit."

"This shit? What about all the liquor and that whore you had?" asked Tumelty, who had arrived back at the room the previous night to find Duffy still loudly and enthusiastically banging the last of the three women he'd found in the bars he'd been frequenting.

"They didn't leave me with no souvenirs, except this exploding headache," Duffy shouted. "Now, I'm ordering you to take it off, Dermot."

"Probably left you with a good case of the clap," muttered the youngster, reluctantly pulling off the white shirt and folding it neatly back into its plastic bag.

"Come on, then," prodded Duffy, unwilling to argue with him further. He opened a drawer in the cheap maple dresser and rummaged through their week's collection of dirty laundry. "It's nearly half-four. We've got a long drive in the traffic to find the place, and he'll be shit-mad if we're late."

Tumelty shrugged, unconcerned, cramming another massive handful of Froot Loops into his mouth and slipping into a dark blue sweatshirt with a tiny gold UNIVERSAL STUDIOS crest embroidered over the breast. Duffy stopped what he was doing and squinted across the room at him. "What's that you've got on now?"

"Just a different shirt," Tumelty said evasively.

Duffy shook his head, feeling around in the bottom of the drawer for the package that was supposed to be there. "Jesus Christ," he exploded as his fingers touched bare wood, "where's the fucking stuff gone to?"

"I moved it," said Tumelty, walking to the nearest of the sagging beds and lifting the mattress to expose a flat black box molded of some heavy plastic. He picked up the surprisingly heavy container, which was the size of a small book, and displayed it proudly to the big man. "Just in case somebody decided to go through the dresser while we were out . . ."

Duffy, his knees suddenly weak, sank onto the other bed and stared at him in disbelief. "Dermot," he croaked, "I've just spent three days bouncing up and down on top of that bloody bed like a fucking acrobat. What if that stuff had gone off?"

Tumelty looked chastened. "The blacks said it wouldn't go off," he rejoined defensively.

The big man snatched the box containing the explosives out of his hand and shoved it into the safety of his own jacket pocket. "Bugger the fucking blacks," he snapped. "You think they'd care if we get blown up now that they've got our bleeding money?"

Tumelty wiped his nose on the sleeve of his new shirt. "I'm sorry, Francis," he snuffled. "I was just trying to be helpful."

Duffy laid a massive hand on his companion's thin shoulder. "You've got to think about such things as that before you do them, lad," he said quietly. "Else we'll never get home alive."

Tumelty nodded meekly, although, in fact, he no longer intended to go home to the perpetual rain and cold of Belfast. For something had happened to him while he and Duffy had been separated. Something that had led him to believe he might never again have to return to the dreary winters and grinding poverty of Northern Ireland.

It had happened while he was standing on Hollywood Boulevard three days earlier, waiting for his holiday bus tour to begin.

Dermot Tumelty had already wandered through the open-fronted courtyard of Mann's Chinese Theatre, gaping along with the other tourists at the hand- and footprints of famous movie stars impressed into multicolored blocks set in the cement walk, and he was watching a street entertainer who could stand frozen in place for minutes at a time without so much as blinking an eye, so that you started to think perhaps he was a wax dummy.

Glancing up at a neon clock above a souvenir shop by the theater, Tumelty had seen that he still had more than half an hour before his bus was due to leave, and so he had gone inside to examine the glossy postcards and glittering tee shirts and miniature Hollywood street signs.

He was thumbing through a display of maps to the stars' homes and tour books about Hollywood, when he had noticed a small green book—really more of a pamphlet—hidden away at the very bottom of the rack. It was titled *The Immigrant's Guide to Los Angeles,* and he had picked it up curiously, shocked to find when he opened the cover that the publication was actually a how-to book for foreign tourists who had arrived on visitor's visas and who wished to remain illegally in the United States.

His heart pounding wildly, Dermot Tumelty had bought the small book for three dollars. All through the long bus ride south to Anaheim, he had devoured its contents from cover to cover, discovering to his amazement that thousands of English and Irish citizens annually landed in Southern California on holiday, then simply vanished into the giant megalopolis that stretches over a hundred and fifty miles from L.A. to San Diego.

According to the guide, which provided detailed instructions on dozens of subjects, such as how one might legally obtain driving licenses, Social Security numbers and other necessary documents, the overwhelmed U.S. Immigration authorities—who annually dealt with more than two million illegals coming across the Mexican border from Latin America alone—seldom bothered themselves over the relatively minor flow of English-speaking Caucasians entering the country. Seldom, in fact, even bothered to look for them.

So excited had Dermot Tumelty been by what he had read, that he had hardly looked up when his bus finally pulled into the parking lot of the huge motor inn just across the road from the entrance to The Magic Kingdom. Since then, he had committed most of the contents of the pamphlet to memory, including the astonishing fact that, statistically anyway, the chances of an Irish or English illegal encountering the INS was less likely in Los Angeles than of his being run down by an auto, and that even if one were somehow found out, that the chances of being deported were almost nonexistent, especially if one could be classified as an entertainer or an artist.

Dermot had pondered the incredible information all during the course of a deliriously happy day at Disneyland and well into the sleepless night that followed in his room at the Anaheim motor inn. Back on his bus the next morning, en route to an equally delightful day at the Universal Studios Tour, he had made up his mind to stay on in California if he possibly could.

He was, after all, he reasoned, both a composer and a songwriter, which he was certain qualified him as an artist. And, according to the guide, if he could obtain some employment related to his music—something he had spent his whole life dreaming of anyway—then chances were good that a smart immigration lawyer could ultimately obtain legal status for him in the United States.

The guide made it all seem so easy that he had very nearly not gone back to Duffy and the cheap Hollywood hotel at the end of the third and final day of his wonderful tour—which had been spent at a fabulous amusement park called Magic Mountain.

After the tour bus had dropped him back on Hollywood Boulevard late last night, it would have been so simple to board one of the many public motor coaches that stopped on the adjoining corner every few minutes; motor coaches with intriguing destinations spelled out in huge block letters behind the lighted glass plates above their windscreens, destinations with names like ECHO PARK and VAN NUYS and WESTWOOD, that conjured up images of tree-shaded suburbs where Tumelty might wander among tanned and smiling Californians in pursuit of the peaceful life he so desperately sought.

He had come that close to not going back.

But then he had remembered Francis Duffy, and imagined the hulking terrorist sitting there in the sleazy fourth-floor room of the Hollywood Sunset Hotel, alone with the machine gun and automatic pistols and explosives, and his blood had turned to ice water. For Dermot knew that if he did not return to the hotel, that Michael Kileen would know Duffy had let him out of his sight, and their merciless leader might simply put a bullet through Duffy's big, shaved head.

Even worse than that frightening possibility, Dermot knew that Kileen might well send the murderous psychopath out after him. A sudden image of Francis Duffy taking the life of the fearsome biker Hog Mother—snuffing him out as swiftly and with as little concern as most men would swat a fly—had flooded Dermot Tumelty's mind, the bloody recollection reacting uneasily with the three foot-long hot dogs and the strawberry shake he'd consumed for dinner.

And so he had gone back to the Hollywood Sunset Hotel, his mind made up that, as soon as the mission was completed and he had fulfilled his obligation to Kileen and Duffy and The Cause, he would watch for an opportunity to disappear among the teeming millions of people in L.A. Until then, he would remain faithful.

He looked up now to see Duffy standing impatiently by the door, watching him, and he reached under the cushions of the worn settee for his automatic pistol, glad that Kileen had finally arrived so they could get on with their mission—whatever it was to be. The television had lately been abuzz with the news of the Queen's impending arrival, and Tumelty was sure the mission would involve some harmless but embarrassing act designed to protest the British government's continued occupation of Northern Ireland, while the harsh glare of the American media was focused upon the royal visitor. He reached for a spare mag.

"No need for that today," said Duffy, indicating the extra clip. "We're only off to meet with Kileen."

Tumelty's face brightened, and he was sure he was right about the nature of the mission. "Where will we be meeting him?" he asked excitedly.

"Santa Monica, in a restaurant overlooking the ocean," Duffy replied, holding the door open for him. "Perhaps you'll even get to see some of them surfers you've been going on about."

Dermot Tumelty stood in the dimly lit hallway while his companion locked the door behind him, then stretched a tiny piece of cellophane tape across the top corner, an old habit he'd picked up years ago in one of the Soviet-run Algerian training camps the big man was known to have frequented in his younger days. When he was done, Duffy turned and started down the hall toward the creaky elevator, with the younger man at his heels.

"What do you think the mission will be, Francis?" Tumelty deliberately kept his voice low, excited at the prospects of seeing another part of California and proud that he'd remembered to save any talk of their work until they'd left the room—another of Duffy's endless safeguards, this one against the possible presence of listening devices, he had explained on their first night in the hotel.

Duffy came to a halt before the elevator and shoved a thick finger at the old-fashioned call button centered in the polished brass plate. "Kileen didn't tell you?" He turned and squinted down at the eager young face.

Tumelty shook his head. The elevator doors clanked open, and Duffy stepped inside, waiting for his companion to follow. When Tumelty was in the cage, Duffy punched the DOWN button and waited for the doors to slide closed. The elevator started down with a jerk, and the big man leaned forward until his thick lips were within an inch of the youngster's ear.

"Sure, it's Disneyland we'll be after blowing up, Dermot," he confided. "Good thing you saw it before the carnage," he added, his breath still reeking of last night's whiskey.

Tumelty stared speechlessly into the giant's murderous eyes for a long moment. "What?" he finally stammered. "With that little bit of explosive we bought?"

Duffy nodded solemnly, extracting a black cigar from his jacket and biting off the end. "Massively powerful stuff, that," he whispered. "The trick, you see, is placing it in exactly the right place. Now where in Disneyland do you think that might be?"

Tumelty dumbly shook his head, remembering the beautiful, flower-bedecked park he had so happily wandered through just three days earlier. Disneyland, with its thousands of smiling visitors and running, laughing children. He could not imagine a more heinous crime than to plant a bomb in such a place. "The monorail," he breathed, horrified, "or Space Mountain or the Matterhorn ride . . . Duffy, we can't do it," he pleaded."There's families there, innocent children . . . The place could never be evacuated in time . . ."

Duffy waved him to silence. "It's none of those places you named," he said, touching a match to the end of the cigar and filling the tiny elevator with a cloud of acrid blue smoke. His crafty little eyes suddenly darted around as if there might be an eavesdropper in the lift with them. "You see," he continued, "we'll be after planting the stuff right up the dress of that wicked queen they keep in the Snow White's castle." Duffy's thick eyebrows arched dramatically. "Then BOOM, the stuff goes off and all the kiddies will see she's got no knickers!"

Tumelty stared at him in disbelief. "You're having me on, aren't you?"

Duffy's roar of laughter rolled up the elevator shaft as the cage clunked to a stop at the lobby. "Me, having you on, Dermot? I swear on the bones of all the holy saints and martyrs," declared Duffy, "it's the wicked queen's knickers we've been sent to explode, but no harm to the kiddies."

The noisy elevator doors slid open, and Tumelty stumbled out into the lobby behind the psychopath. "Really, Duffy," he whispered, his relief that that target wasn't to be Disneyland evident in his voice. "What do you actually think we'll be after?"

Duffy ignored him as they walked out through the threadbare lobby and past an ancient, snoozing bellboy, stepping through a set of smudged glass doors and into the secured parking lot with its chain-link fence topped with razor wire.

The big man stooped to unlock the rented yellow Toyota, then turned to look at the worried youngster. "Who the hell knows what we're after here, lad? The higher-ups never tell the likes of you and me beforehand—just in case we get caught. So we don't know anything, see?"

He folded himself down into the driver's seat of the little car, then rolled his eyes up at Tumelty, who was still staring worriedly at him. "But I'll tell you one thing, young Dermot." Duffy winked and smiled encouragingly. "If Michael Kileen thought up the target, and the high command approved his plan, as he says, then it'll be something nobody would ever expect . . . And we'll all get away clean as a whistle. So don't you worry."

CHAPTER SEVEN

Rules of Engagement

"Brian?"

Billy stopped, squinting into a blaze of late afternoon sunlight at the attractive woman leaning against the door of the green Jaguar. He had been walking down Rodeo Drive after the fitting of the ridiculous formal suit at the Major's outrageously overpriced clothiers, lost in thought, almost passing the Jag by in his daze.

The woman stepped away from the car now, the skirt of her smart blue designer suit blowing in the light breeze to reveal an extraordinarily good pair of legs. "You are Brian O'Malley," she smiled, tucking an expensive handbag up under her arm.

He nodded, wondering if he was supposed to know who she was. She had the same carefully lacquered look as the two women who'd been hanging about at the Huston house the day he'd gone swimming with Kelly, though he didn't think he'd met her there.

"Come over here and look at this marvelous Lhasa apso," she cooed, slipping her arm into his and propelling him toward a shopwindow.

Billy stared into the window—a pet shop, he saw—at an ugly little dog covered in long hair.

"Isn't he just the sweetest little thing?" She pursed her red lips in a kiss and tapped on the window, sending the little dog into paroxysms of tail-wagging delight. The tiny creature began to hop madly up and down on its hind legs. "Kileen is here," said the woman without taking her eyes from the dog.

Billy stared at her. "He's here?" He swiveled his head around toward the street, almost expecting to see the old warrior leaning against a lamppost.

"Look at the fucking dog," hissed Sally Hilton.

He turned back to the window and gazed in at the little dog, which was now peeing excitedly on the glass.

"Now listen very carefully," said the woman, continuing to tap on the glass and smile at the dog. "He wants to see you. Can you get out without making the old man suspicious?"

"When?" Billy raised his hand to the glass and mimed patting the silly dog, feeling foolish at going along with the elaborate charade.

"Tonight," she said. "About nine."

He nodded. "I think so . . ."

"Good!" She slipped a small piece of paper into his hand, and he pocketed it without looking down, as he had been taught.

"Look," he whispered, "are you going to be seeing him before then?"

She turned and gazed at him. "Why?"

"Tell him it won't work," he said desperately. "I've been to the hotel and it's impossible . . ."

"Tell him yourself," she snapped, stepping away from the shopwindow and spinning him around to face her.

"You don't understand . . ." he began.

"No, honey," Sally Hilton smiled, leaning so close he smelled her musky perfume. "*You* don't understand. I'm just a little errand girl. I don't know what he's doing here and I sure as hell don't want to know."

She took both of his hands in hers and held him out at arm's length, flashing him a killer smile, speaking through clenched teeth. "But I know just enough about this man to tell you that he'd probably kill both of us if he knew you were stupid enough to even hint at his business here to anyone, even me . . . Get it, asshole?"

Billy nodded dumbly, and she leaned forward again, pressing her full, red lips briefly against his cheek, then dropping his hands. "Do say hello to your grandfather," she said loudly. "Such a marvelous man. Well, I have to run now, darling. Bye!"

She turned and clicked away down the street on her smart heels, leaving him standing there alone.

"Jesus Christ," he breathed, knowing that what she had said about Kileen killing the both of them was absolutely true. What had he gotten himself into?

BRENDA GAYNOR lay naked on the satin sheets of her pink-canopied princess bed, staring up at the carved cherubs smiling down at her from the gilded bedposts. She had been lying there like that for more than an hour, ever since she had come home from school and showered.

She was thinking.

Brian's strange outburst in history class this afternoon had thrown Brenda into a state of near shock. For hours afterward, she kept imagining the little dead girl he had described, lying in her coffin looking like . . . a broken doll. Something in Brian O'Malley's impassioned outburst had reached deep inside of Brenda like a cold hand, shattering the brittle protective shell she had so painstakingly built up around herself.

Like a broken doll!

Brenda rolled over, burying her face in the pillows, trying to drive the horrible image from her mind.

But the ghastly mental picture came back to her again; the tiny broken form lying in the little white box . . . Except, that what she saw, the dead child, wasn't some nameless, faceless stranger. It was Jessie, her own little sister, lying in her own little coffin, the victim of the drunk driver who had smashed his speeding pickup truck into the back of their mother's Mercedes five years ago.

Like a broken doll.

Brenda Gaynor felt the bitter tears of loss welling up inside her all over again, and she realized that she really did know how Brian O'Malley felt.

Exactly how he felt.

And Brenda was suddenly sorry for all the terrible things she'd done and said and become since her little sister had died. The little sister who had used to sit in her lap and wrap her soft baby arms around Brenda's neck and tell her she was the kindest, prettiest, most wonderful sister anybody ever had.

And then the drunken bastard in the pickup had taken her away. Her and their mother.

Leaving Brenda with nothing.

Nothing at all except the meaningless gifts her grieving father constantly showered upon her. Letting her do whatever she wanted. Giving her *things*. Giving her nothing.

Nothing at all.

"Shit!"

Brenda sat up, wiping her eyes on her arm and realizing that what she had been doing with Brian O'Malley was all wrong. She had only wanted him as a trophy, excited by his lean good looks and his hard body, and the brooding, dangerous aura she'd detected surrounding him that night in the parking lot of Club Retro. A fucking trophy.

But she hadn't known then that she loved him.

Not until today, in history class.

Not until she'd heard him pour out his heart in almost an exact recitation of her deepest and most secret feelings. Feelings that she herself was incapable of expressing.

She sat up and got to her feet, pulling on a sheer silk robe and walking through the deep rose-colored carpet of her room to the shaded French doors of her balcony. She threw open the doors and stepped outside, gazing into the glorious red sunset that was turning the flat, silvery waters of the Pacific a shade of blue the color of his eyes.

So far, she had only been toying with the handsome Irish boy, making an elaborate game of getting him to sleep with her, not much caring what happened afterwards.

But now it was all so different.

Now she wanted him to be hers.

For she realized that she needed him more than she had ever needed anything in her entire life.

Brenda Gaynor decided she was going to have Brian O'Malley for herself. No matter what.

And anybody who got in her way was going to get hurt. Hurt the way he'd hurt the two robbers she'd seen him disable that night.

Swiftly.

Brutally.

Without mercy.

They were alike, herself and Brian. She was certain of it. Exactly alike.

And she was going to do something about it.

"DO YOU LIKE the view?" asked Kileen.

"It's fucking brilliant," breathed Dermot Tumelty. He and Duffy were sitting at a restaurant view bar set up flush against a broad plate-glass window overlooking the crashing surf of Santa Monica Bay. The setting sun was swiftly sinking into the waters of the bay now, tinting them a brilliant red and radiating violet rays up over the horizon to paint the bottoms of an approaching cloud front an impossible shade that rightly belonged on a postcard.

To their left, beside Duffy, sat Michael Kileen, his eyes masked by wide, mirrored sunglasses. A floppy Western hat was pulled down low over his forehead, casting the rest of his face into deep shadow. The men heard footsteps behind them and turned to see a pretty cocktail waitress with a blond ponytail arriving with the drinks they had ordered.

Kileen waited until the waitress placed the drinks on the narrow bar, then dropped a handful of bills onto her tray. She flashed him a grateful smile and departed into the rear of the busy restaurant. "Cheers," he said, lifting his whiskey and looking down at the others. Duffy raised his own whiskey in silent salute to his leader, and they both waited while Dermot carefully removed the little paper umbrella and pineapple slice from the frothy pink concoction he'd ordered and held his glass high.

"Cheers."

They all drank in silence, gazing transfixed at the disappearing ball of the sun. When it had at last faded to an orange glow on the horizon, Kileen set his glass on the wooden bar and turned to Duffy. "Have you got it, then?" he said in a voice just loud enough to carry over the grumbling sound of the surf beyond the window.

Duffy shot him a conspiratorial grin and patted the side of his jacket. "Right here."

Kileen held out his hand, and Duffy passed him the black plastic box he had purchased from the Double Zeroes. The terrorist leader placed the container on the counter before him and carefully opened the hinged lid, the inside of which contained a stuck-on hazard label filled with warnings and instructions. Below the label, nestled in individual niches cut into a thick liner of dense black foam, a double row of flattened metal pyramids, each not much larger at its base than a postage stamp, gleamed in the dim indirect lighting above the bar.

"Perfect," whispered Kileen, reaching into the deep foam lining of the box to touch one of the deadly pyramids.

Duffy, who had not dared to open the box himself, leaned over to peer down at the tiny explosive charges in their heavily padded and insulated case. "Sweet Jesus," he snorted derisively, "now how could you think we'll really be able to do any damage with something that size? There's hardly room inside one of those little buggers to pack any explosive at all."

Kileen smiled, lifting one of the tiny pyramids into the soft light, turning it like a gemstone between his fingers. "Better read up on your munitions," he said in his low, gravelly voice. "This is M-37-L, the most powerful demolitions payload ever packed into a single warhead."

He held the explosive up to the light so that the highly polished facets glittered. "What you see here *is* all pure explosive charge, Francis," he explained. "There's no clumsy jacketing. No wasted space. Just a single condensed plug of sheer, unadulterated destruction."

"What, that little thing?" Tumelty peered suspiciously down the bar, jumping as Kileen suddenly tossed the pyramid to him. He caught it in his good hand, marveling at its weight. "It feels like lead," he exclaimed, hefting the tiny chunk of metal in his hand.

"Heavier, actually," said Kileen. "The material you're holding, which began as a dry compound similar to TNT, has been compressed under hundreds of tons of pressure, jamming the molecules so tightly together that there's no space left between them. In its normal state, that piece you're holding would be about the size of a large bar of soap."

Duffy whistled softly, gingerly plucking the deadly charge from Tumelty's fingers. "Does it lose none of its power by squeezing it all up like that?" he asked.

Kileen shook his head. "The compression makes it far more powerful. By, say, a factor of fifteen." He smiled and lifted his glass. "All those little molecules are anxious to get out of their jammed-up state, you see."

Duffy bobbed his bald head up and down admiringly. "Fantastic," he whispered, turning the lethal bomblet over and over beneath the light. "But why does it have such an odd form to it?"

"It's what the demolitions engineers call a SHAPE charge," Kileen said, pointing to the mirror-smooth bottom of the pyramid. "In the base is a thin metal plate containing an integral, radio-activated electronic detonator."

He moved his finger to the tip of the pyramid. "When the charge is detonated, the whole explosive force wants to escape by the easiest possible path. The pyramid configuration directs the explosion away from the steel plate, concentrating something like seventy percent of the energy into this one tiny point at the top, radiating the rest of the force out in a star-shaped pattern along the sharp edges at the sides."

Duffy looked dubious. "It can't really be all that powerful though, can it?"

"The American military engineers designed these little buggers to bring down bridges," said Kileen, smiling. "A dozen of them properly placed will take down a four-lane span of reinforced concrete. Just one of them on its own will slice through a six-inch steel girder . . . Is that powerful enough for you?"

Duffy replaced the pyramid in its foam niche with trembling fingers, then raised his glass and took a large swallow of whiskey. "Cripes," he gulped, "what in the hell are we going to blow up with this lot?"

Kileen carefully closed the black case and slid it into the inside pocket of his suit jacket, then lifted his glass in a mock toast. "Her Majesty the Queen," he said.

Duffy looked around behind them to see if anyone was eavesdropping, then he turned back to stare at Kileen. "The Queen?" His voice was a hoarse whisper. "Are you out of your fucking mind, man? How will we ever get one of these things near her?"

"We won't." Kileen smiled, raising his empty glass for the cocktail waitress. Catching her eye, he motioned for a new round of drinks for the three of them, then looked down the bar at Tumelty, who was gaping at him over the top of his pink margarita. "Drink up, lad," said Kileen. "There's work to be done."

Dermot Tumelty noisily slurped down the rest of his sweet concoction and sat staring glumly out at the tumbling surf as the pretty waitress appeared to set fresh drinks before them. The mission was worse even than Duffy's cruel Disneyland joke. Worse than his worst nightmare. He looked over to see Duffy glowering at Kileen.

"It'll never work, man. They sweep her car and every damned place she's going to be for days before," hissed Duffy when the blond waitress had departed. "They've got X-rays and electronic explosive sniffers and trained dogs . . ."

Kileen nodded and sipped thoughtfully at his drink. "Yes," he agreed, "but even the X-rays can't see through this, can they?" He flipped a shiny golden object onto the bar before the big terrorist. It struck the damp wooden surface with a hollow clink and spun around in the light.

The psychopath's skeptical scowl slowly turned to a grin of amazement, and he picked up the round object, holding it reverently to the light in his clumsy fingers.

"You are completely mad, Kileen," he said, meaning it as a high compliment.

Kileen raised his glass and took another drink in acknowledgment of the commendation.

"I don't get it," said Tumelty. He was looking at them over the gaudy paper umbrella sticking out of his second margarita. "I mean, who's going to wear this thing?" he asked, reaching out to take the thick, three-inch medallion from Duffy's fingers.

Kileen laughed. "Now that's where our young friend Brian O'Malley comes in," he said. "You see, by marvelous coincidence, his old granddad's being promoted to brigadier by the Queen herself tomorrow." He grinned, and a bit of stainless-steel alloy shone in the light.

"They told the old duffer to come in full dress, which means he's entitled to wear his decorations . . . All of them." Kileen winked conspiratorially. "And just between the three of us, I'm betting the old fellow is going to be proud enough to bust . . ."

"Fucking brilliant!" Duffy's beady little eyes shone with rapt admiration for his leader.

"But what about the electronic explosives sniffers and the dogs?" Tumelty was gazing at the gleaming medallion now. "Won't they still pick up the smell of the charge the second the old man walks through the door?"

Kileen shook his head. "Not after the little beauty is sealed in epoxy resin and encased inside this solid bronze medal," he said. "In fact, the only real problem we'll have is that all that metal shielding also cuts the effective range of the radio signal used to detonate the explosive, down from fifty meters to about five . . . "

"Less than fifteen feet," Duffy breathed.

Kileen nodded. "Right, so whoever triggers it will have to be in the same room."

Duffy raised his eyebrows. "The kid?"

Tumelty removed the gaily colored little umbrella from his margarita, sucked the sticky liquid off the end and placed the umbrella carefully in his shirt pocket beside the one he'd saved from his first drink. "It'll be fucking suicide," he murmured, suddenly very glad that he wasn't the poor sod they'd chosen for that particular task.

Duffy grimaced. "Look at it this way, Dermot," he said savagely. "The lad'll get his name in all the history books, just like Lee Harvey Oswald." He turned back to glare at Kileen, still trying to accustom himself to the other's smooth new face—or what he could see of it anyway. He supposed that the huge hat and the mirrored glasses were to cover up the scars from Kileen's surgery.

"What's our part in all of this, then?" he asked suspiciously. It was clear from his manner that Francis Duffy didn't like suicide missions, even when he wasn't the one being asked to make the supreme sacrifice.

Glints of stainless steel gleamed at the corners of Kileen's smile. "Now that's the beautiful part," he said.

Duffy's frown of dissatisfaction deepened. "And what makes it so fucking beautiful?" he demanded.

"Relax, mate," smiled Kileen, placing a reassuring hand on his shoulder. "I've got something very special and very safe planned for you and young Dermot. Something I promise you're going to like very much." He turned toward the restaurant behind them, which was beginning to fill with early evening diners. "Tell you what, suppose I buy you lads a meal? I'll tell you all about your jobs while we eat."

Tumelty, who was perpetually hungry, was already on his feet. "Do you think I might order the Maine lobster?" he asked. Duffy rolled his eyes in exasperation.

Kileen laughed out loud and clapped him on the back. "Whatever you like, Dermot," he said, leading him into the candlelit dining room. "Nothing's too good for our lads in the trenches."

"NOT FEELING TOO WELL, are we?"

James Queally-Smythe stood over Billy's bed, looking concerned. "Nothing serious, I hope," he said worriedly.

Billy shook his head. "I'm sorry, Major," he groaned. "I'm just very tired. I think I might be coming down with the flu. They say there's a lot of it about at school," he added, hoping to lend a note of authenticity to his feigned illness. He was, in fact, totally exhausted and hoping to catch a few hours of sleep before meeting with Kileen. "Perhaps if I get some sleep . . ." he said, feeling vaguely guilty for disappointing the old fellow.

The Major nodded. "Suppose that's best," he reluctantly agreed. "Ranjee is out for the evening, or I'd have him fix you something on a tray . . ."

"Oh no, thank you, sir," said Billy, propping himself up on his elbows and trying his best to look ill. "I don't feel very much like food now, but if I'm hungry when I wake up I'll just go out."

Queally-Smythe's bushy eyebrows came together and he looked at him strangely, and for a moment Billy feared that he'd pushed things too far by trying to give himself an excuse for being out, in case anyone checked on him later. "Very well then, Brian," the old man finally sighed. "Just please do try to get over whatever it is by tomorrow evening." He touched the youngster's shoulder and gave it an affectionate little squeeze. "Not every day one has an opportunity to meet the Queen, after all."

Billy smiled and nodded gratefully. "I'm sure I'll be feeling better by then," he lied. "Please apologize to Mrs. Huston about my missing her dinner."

Queally-Smythe harrumphed noisily, turning away to adjust his necktie in a mirror hanging over the dresser. "Have no fear, Brian," he said, smiling at his distinguished reflection, "I shall carry on in the best family tradition."

Billy laughed and watched him leave the room. "Good night, Major, and thank you."

The Major waved over his shoulder and disappeared down the stairs. When he was gone, Billy sat up and fumbled on the bedside table for the package of Marlboros. He lit one and wandered over to the balcony door, stepping out into the cool night air and gazing at the roof of the house down the road. The blue lights beneath the wavering waters of the Huston swimming pool cast shimmering reflections up onto the trees, and he wished that things were somehow different so he could see Kelly.

After a moment, he crushed out the cigarette and reentered the room, throwing himself across the bed and mentally rehearsing the speech he'd been preparing to make to Kileen. He would not, he had decided, be involved in anything that might result in the Major being injured, or that did not present at least a fifty-fifty chance of himself getting away clean. Since he didn't really believe that any assassination attempt on the Queen—no matter how carefully planned—could possibly be carried out under the latter of those conditions, he hoped Kileen would relegate him to some minor supporting role in his scheme, or, better yet, see the absolute madness of it and drop the idea altogether.

On the other hand, he reasoned, perhaps the stress he had been under had led him to jump to wild conclusions about the actual purpose of his mission here. Maybe Kileen had something altogether different in mind for him to do in Los Angeles. He prayed that was it. For, in point of fact, Billy realized, he had very serious doubts about the morality of assassinating a doddering old woman who was, after all, nothing more than a ridiculous symbol of the hated oppressors occupying Northern Ireland, and who, even he knew, wielded little or no actual control over her country's government at that.

If killing the Queen of England was what he had in mind, Billy decided, then Michael Kileen, the great hero of The Cause, could bloody well do it himself, because Billy Quinn wasn't going to be the one to pull the trigger.

His mind firmly made up, he closed his eyes and almost immediately fell into a deep sleep and began to dream. In his dream, he imagined that he really was Brian O'Malley.

KELLY HUSTON sat at the far end of the dimly lighted dinner table, listening to Katherine's shrill artificial laughter. Kelly raised her eyes from her untouched plate and looked down the length of the candelabra-studded table to see her mother reaching across to touch the Major's sleeve. The old man was telling a long and involved story about something that had happened to him when he was a young man in India, and everyone else seemed to think that it was hilariously funny.

Kelly, feeling foolish in the slinky white cocktail dress and heels she had worn especially for the occasion of her dinner with Brian O'Malley, glanced at the empty place that had been set for him next to hers. She felt the tight ache rising in her throat, unable to tell whether she was angry or hurt over his failure to appear.

There was another burst of laughter from the other end of the table as Chuck and Katherine led their studio friends in applauding the end of the Major's story.

Kelly reached for one of the bottles of Italian red wine that had been set out and refilled her glass for the third time. Raising the crystal goblet to her lips, she took a large swallow, feeling the fiery liquid splash into her empty stomach.

Angry, she decided.

Very damned angry.

But hurt too.

Chuck Huston was standing at the other end of the table now, beginning a slightly slurred speech about all the Academy Awards *The Harts of India* was sure to win. Kelly squinted at him through the flickering candlelight, trying to decide whether it was the wine he'd drunk or the buzzing in her own ears that made him sound like he was in an echo chamber.

Deciding that it didn't really matter, she got quietly to her feet, hoping no one would notice. No one did, and, grabbing the half-full bottle of wine and her glass, she slipped silently into the shadows by the dining room door, wobbling dangerously on her high heels.

Once into the darkened living room, she leaned against a wall to pull off the shoes, then padded through the long house in her stocking feet. Inside her own room, she closed the door, flipped on the CD player and curled up in the window seat with the bottle of wine. Billie Holiday's sweet, sad voice filled the room as Kelly pressed her forehead against the cool glass of the window overlooking the pool and settled in to feel seriously sorry for herself.

The phone by her bed chimed, and she raised her head to stare at it, aware that her heart was suddenly pounding. Of course, it was Brian calling to apologize . . . Or maybe just to talk to her.

The chiming sounded again, and she swung her feet down onto the floor, then hcsitated, remembering that she was very angry with him . . . Perhaps she should just not answer. *Let him wait,* she thought, raising the wineglass to her lips and taking another long swallow. After all, she had feelings too . . .

The phone rang for a third time, and she leaped to her feet, sloshing the dark wine on her white dress. "Oh hell!" She set the glass on the corner of her desk and stumbled across the room to the bedside table, grabbing for a towel and dabbing clumsily at the stained fabric with one hand as she snatched up the receiver in the other.

Of course she would forgive him, she had just been acting foolishly because she was disappointed that he hadn't come to dinner.

"Brian?"

"Sorry, honey. I must have the wrong number."

Kelly's heart sank as she recognized Samantha's voice on the other end of the line. "Dammit, Sam," she snapped, dabbing at her stained dress with the towel, "you just made me ruin my dress!"

"Well, pardon me," Sam shouted. "Weren't you the one who practically begged me to find out what Stanley wanted to tell you this morning?"

Kelly flopped down weakly on the edge of the bed, suddenly aware of the wine churning uncomfortably in her stomach. "I'm sorry, Sam," she said softly. "Everything is just all screwed up tonight. What was it he wanted to tell me?"

Sam took a deep breath. "Are you sitting down?"

"Samantha, I think I'm about three minutes away from throwing up," Kelly screamed, "so if you've got something to say, say it quick."

She listened with growing horror as Sam began to relate Thad August's charge that Brian O'Malley was an undercover narcotics agent, and August's cowardly plan to have his friends waylay Brian and beat him up. "Brian, a narcotics agent? That is the most ridiculous thing I ever heard," she said when Samantha had finished her breathless recital.

"Maybe it's not so ridiculous," said Sam.

"What do you mean?" Kelly demanded angrily. Her churning stomach was beginning to ache now, and she wondered if she could even make it into the bathroom before she became violently ill.

"Stanley says that Brian's got scars on his body," Sam excitedly reported. "He thinks they're bullet wounds."

Kelly felt her stomach threatening to turn over on her. She had completely forgotten the slick, shiny scar she'd accidentally touched that day in her room. The scar Brian had admitted came from a bullet.

"Kelly, it's true," Sam insisted when she did not reply. "Stanley saw him in the shower at school today . . . Kelly, are you still there?"

Kelly Huston sat swaying on the edge of her bed, staring at the telephone in her hand. Something hot and vile surged up inside her, and she knew what was about to happen. "Sam, I've got to go," she gurgled, slamming down the phone and running for the bathroom.

CHAPTER EIGHT

Suspicion

SALLY HILTON angrily paced the living room of her West Hollywood condo. Every time she heard a car outside, she paused long enough to step out onto the tiny second-floor balcony and peer down into the alley behind the complex, hoping to glimpse the dove gray Mercedes before it entered the underground parking structure below.

The candles she had lit guttered low in their silver holders on the little dinette table by the kitchen, splotches of yellow wax falling onto the linen cloth set with her best china. And in the kitchen, the meal she had spent most of the day preparing from a book of difficult French recipes was undergoing a final metamorphosis from the succulent gourmet delight it had been to a sad, inedible mass of dried-out poultry and sagging, overdone vegetables.

"Bastard!" She stepped onto the balcony once more and glowered down into the empty alley, willing Kileen to appear in the Mercedes. The Mercedes she had stolen for him! When there was still no sign of the car, she stormed back into the room, where she blew out the candles and snapped on an overhead light. Then she went into the kitchen and began angrily scraping her lovingly prepared dinner into the garbage disposal. The hot tears running down her cheeks streaked her mascara, giving her the look of a sad clown, and she wanted nothing more at that moment than to kill Michael Kileen, who had left more than ten hours before, promising to return "an hour or so before dark" to dine with her before going out to his nighttime meetings.

She had meant to surprise him with the lovely dinner. Perhaps even entice him back to her bed for another quick round of lovemaking as the sun went down.

But it was she who had been surprised.

Now, her little dream of a quiet romantic interlude with the dashing

Irishman had been rudely crushed, and she hated herself for having cooked the stupid meal and lit the stupid candles and dressed in the silly red lingerie she was wearing.

Men did not do things like this to Sally Hilton, and she had always believed that any woman who allowed herself to be debased and victimized so was just plain dumb.

Yet here she was, goddamn his eyes! Crying like an idiot over having done every goddamn silly, stupid thing she had sworn she would never do for any fucking man.

For Sally, who had changed her name to Hilton after fleeing the backward country hollow where she had been born, the last of eleven children, had learned early on about men and their ways. Raped by a neighbor and his two dim-witted sons at the age of thirteen, she had vowed then that any man who had his way with her in the future would pay. She had what they wanted and she would, by God, use it. And from that day forward, no man had ever taken advantage of Sally MacFarland, now Sally Hilton.

No man except Michael Kileen.

She had done things for him she would never have considered doing for any other man. Not even for money.

But Kileen had swept into her life like a goddamn tornado, plying her with expensive gifts and romantic dinners whenever he blew into the city for a day or two, bringing her to his rooms in picture-perfect oceanside hotels and making hard, passionate love to her, staying just long enough to make her want him and ache for more of him before suddenly disappearing for weeks or months, then always waiting until she had convinced herself she was finally over him before showing up again.

The bastard!

This time he had promised it would be different.

This time he had told her he loved her, wanted to be with her. For always.

Then he had gone again, and not returned.

Well, she wasn't going to let him get away with it, by God. Not this time.

She would show him that she wasn't just some dumb bimbo he could drop around and screw whenever he felt like it. Sally knew things about Michael Kileen. Things she could use to make him stay with her for as long as she felt like it. For, despite the stern warning she had given the frightened boy this afternoon, about the danger of Kileen, she was not really afraid of the handsome Irishman at all. Sally Hilton had seen the look in Kileen's dark, fathomless eyes every time they had made love, a gentle, faraway look that had unmasked the stern, forbidding stranger, revealing to her alone the warm and vulnerable human inside.

And, for all her ignorance of the world, Sally Hilton knew all about the masks people wore to hide their true selves, and her knowledge told her that the looks Michael Kileen gave her when they lay together in her bed could never be counterfeited. Deep inside, she knew that Kileen was as much in love with her as she was with him, knew that he needed her as he had never needed any other woman.

He only had to be made to understand that.

Then everything would be fine between them.

A little smile of determination curved the corners of her red lips as it occurred to her that it would strengthen her hand to know exactly what he was planning for tomorrow. It would be easy enough to figure out because, after all, it was Sally herself who, disguised as a clerk from the county Earthquake Preparedness Office, had copied the blueprints of the Hotel Beverly from the county building inspector's files. And it was she who had confirmed the time of the ceremony to award some medal to the old movie director, and who had kept an eye on the Irish kid who'd come to live with the old man, and taken all the other dangerous risks to obtain the many strange articles Kileen had said he needed.

Blowing her nose on a paper towel, she threw the last of the empty pots and serving pieces into the dishwasher and walked back into the living room to examine the thick collection of newspapers, maps and blueprints he'd laid out to study. As soon as she had figured out exactly what he intended to do, she would insist he make her a part of it.

Then he would see how much he needed her and how useful she could really be in the new life she had planned for the two of them.

Either that or she would, she vowed, threaten to expose him.

MAYBE IT WAS ALL TRUE!

Kelly sat in the Yugo, which was parked along a dark side street just off Santa Monica Boulevard, trying to make some sense of what she was seeing. Less than fifty feet away, she could see Brian O'Malley's handsome profile through the window of an all-night coffee shop on the busy corner. He was sitting in a booth, talking earnestly with a dangerous looking man in a dark cowboy hat. One of his police contacts? If Brian really was an undercover narcotics officer, as Thad August had alleged to his friends, then that was the only answer that made any sense at all.

But then nothing else fit together. Because, supposing the story that Stanley Kinsella had overheard in the shower room was true, then the Major would have to be deeply involved in Brian's deception. And even if that was the case, would the famous director have gone to the elaborate extreme of making a movie deal with Chuck Huston, just for the sake of finding out which kids at Pacific Academy were using drugs? It was all too ridiculous.

She reminded herself, with a sinking feeling in the pit of her still-queasy stomach, that at least one element of Stanley's fanciful story was true. Brian O'Malley did carry the unmistakable marks of a bullet wound on his body. Marks he had explained away that day in her room.

"But then," she murmured aloud, "who is that guy he's talking to? And why did he sneak out to meet him tonight when he was supposed to be home in bed?"

After being sick in her bathroom earlier, Kelly had stripped off the silly cocktail dress and changed into jeans and a sweater, still slightly woozy and feeling awful for having made such a fool out of herself with the dinner wine. Despite the way she felt, she had been determined to get to the bottom of the mystery surrounding Brian O'Malley. She was furious with him for having stood her up without even calling to apologize, and at the same time worried that he might really be sick or in trouble, especially after having heard Sam's secondhand version of Stanley Kinsella's bizarre story.

Kelly had called Sam back and, after another brief conversation, left her room, hoping not to be noticed.

Slipping quietly into the kitchen, she had listened to the sounds of the guests, who were still laughing and talking elsewhere in the house, then stuck a note to Katherine on the door of the refrigerator with a magnet shaped like a miniature pineapple. That done, she opened the fridge and found a can of Coke. Drinking it had made her stomach feel a little better, and she had just been leaving when Katherine had come in and caught her at the door.

Kelly had cringed in anticipation of one of her mother's angry outbursts over the way she'd left the dinner table earlier. To her surprise, though, Katherine, who had been verging on ecstasy ever since the movie deal had first started taking shape, had winked happily at her, crossing the kitchen and placing a cool, motherly hand on her forehead to ask if she felt all right.

Kelly had nodded, apologizing for having left the party—which had since adjourned to the living room for after-dinner drinks and dessert. "It's all right, darling," Katherine had bubbled. "The Major is telling us all more wonderful stories about the days of the Raj, things we might use in the film—you'd probably just be bored to death."

"In that case," Kelly had replied, feeling only slightly guilty for lying and placing the note from the fridge in her mother's hand, "I think I'll go over to Sam's house for a little while." She had hesitated before adding, "Maybe I'll even sleep over tonight."

Katherine Huston had glanced at the note, then placed her smiling stamp of approval on the vague plan by kissing Kelly perfunctorily on the cheek and reminding her to call if she decided to stay the night at Sam's place, before hurrying back into the living room to her guests.

When her mother had departed, Kelly, who had something else altogether in mind, had gone out through a side door and hurried down to the canyon road, turning up the hill toward the Major's house.

Slipping silently through the tall iron gates, she had skirted the steep drive and walked around through the deep shadows to the veranda. Backing out onto the lawn, she had peered up at the tower room that Brian had told her was his, expecting to see a light in the window.

The room had been dark.

She had breathed a deep sigh of relief then, assuming that what the Major had told her when he had arrived for dinner was really true. Brian actually was not feeling well and had gone to sleep.

Kelly stood on the dark lawn, wrestling with the decision of whether or not she dared to go up and wake him. After a moment, the ache in her heart had won out and, moving as quietly as possible so as not to startle either Brian or Ranjee, whom she imagined also to be somewhere in the house, she had slowly climbed the winding iron stairs leading to the balcony outside Brian's room, and knocked gently on the side of the open glass door.

No one answered, and she had softly called his name several times before stepping into the room and discovering that it was empty. Brian was not asleep at all! Probably he wasn't even sick.

A thin beam of moonlight shone into the room, revealing his rumpled bed and a nightstand topped by a small lamp and overflowing ashtray. Kelly had felt her anger building anew as she wondered if perhaps he was downstairs somewhere, and she had been on the point of leaving, trying to work up the courage to backtrack around to the front of the house to ring the big brass doorbell and demand that he explain what in the hell was going on.

Then a deep rumbling sound from below racketed through the balcony door, and she had whirled about in the semidarkness, knocking over a wastebasket beside the night table. Rushing to the door, she had looked outside, seeing nothing, but recognizing the distinctive roar of the green Jaguar's exhaust pipes. The sound of the engine had settled to a grumbling idle after a moment, and she realized that the car was still in the garage beside the house.

Kneeling quickly, she righted the wastebasket, replacing the scatter of crumpled papers that had spilled onto the floor. A familiar foul reek assailed her nostrils, and she had lifted one of the pieces of paper and sniffed it curiously. Hair dye! The same odoriferous stuff that her mother's hairdresser religiously applied to Katherine's youthful tresses once a month.

Raising the paper—a page torn from a lined school notebook—into the moonlight, Kelly saw that it was smeared with black dye. As if someone had gotten the stuff on their hands and tried to wipe it off without ruining a towel.

Then the Jag's powerful engine had roared in the driveway, and she raced to the door and down the winding steps in time to see a splash of moving light slowly painting the shrubbery near the front of the house as the car turned around. She ran after it, calling Brian's name, her voice lost in the snarl of the quadruple exhausts.

"Dammit, Brian!" she had screamed, pounding down the driveway after him. "Wait!"

The taillights of the sports car had disappeared around a curve in the canyon road, and Kelly threw herself down the hill at a fast run, arriving before her own house a moment later to find Sam and Stanley waiting at the foot of the drive in his funny little car.

Gasping for breath, she'd had to tap on the fogged window in order to startle them out of the passionate clinch in which they were locked. When they had finally come up for air, Stanley's glasses were tilted crazily on the end of his nose, and Sam was smiling like the proverbial cat that had just swallowed the proverbial canary.

Ripping open the door, Kelly had clambered into the cramped backseat of the Yugo and ordered the astonished Stanley to follow the Jaguar. Poor Stan, who had evidently never done anything more dangerous while driving than making a right turn on red, had turned around and given her a disbelieving look. "You want me to follow *that* in *this?*"

"Stanley, just do it, baby!" The confused nerd had turned his thick lenses on Sam, who was making tiny kissing motions with her lips. A dazed expression filled his eyes, and he had popped the Yugo's pathetic little clutch, eliciting a painful shriek of rubber from the skinny tires as the tiny car cut a perfect U-turn and hurtled down the canyon road like a dropped brick.

Somehow they had managed to catch up with the speeding Jaguar, tracking it all the way here to the sleazy coffee shop in West Hollywood. Since arriving five minutes earlier, they had been gaping in through the window at Brian O'Malley and the strange man in the cowboy hat.

"What do you think they're talking about?" Samantha twisted around in the front seat to peer back at Kelly, whose knees were beginning to cramp in the confined space.

Kelly shook her head miserably, thinking of the spilled hair dye and Brian's lies. "I don't know," she confessed.

"Well, what are we going to do?" Stanley had turned to look back at her, as well. "I mean," he said, remembering the disjointed story Kelly had told them as they drove, about the way Brian had destroyed the two would-be robbers at the nightclub the previous weekend, "what if he looks out and sees us sitting here? He might get really pissed." He hesitated, glancing over at Samantha. "Maybe we ought to get out of here . . ."

"Stanley, sweetie," said Sam, slipping her arm around his shoulders, "Brian isn't going to do anything to us. We could just say we came to warn him about August and his jerk-off friends." She looked hopefully into the backseat. "Isn't that right, Kelly? I mean, he wouldn't hurt us or anything, would he?"

"Of course not," Kelly said with more conviction than she actually felt. She looked out at the coffee shop window again. Brian O'Malley was leaning forward now, gesturing urgently with his hands. The other man sat gazing at him, his face shadowed by the cowboy hat, eyes inscrutable behind the wide, mirrored glasses he wore.

"WELL," SAID KILEEN when Billy had finished his impassioned report on the sequence of events that had transpired in the week since he had arrived in California, posing as Brian O'Malley, "it sounds like you've done a commendable job of fitting right in."

Billy Quinn stared at the terrorist leader, wondering if Kileen had been listening to him at all. "Didn't you hear anything I've been saying?" he asked peevishly. "Having me in that school is a bleeding disaster. Half the time I don't even know what they're talking about in the classes and the other half of the time they're all staring at me like I was some kind of freak, 'cause they can see I'm different from them . . ." He took a deep breath. "And the fucking track coach has been on my ass too," he moaned. "Got me running my balls off, every chance he gets. You never mentioned to me that O'Malley was a champion long-distance runner."

"Your little charade has served its purpose well," said Kileen. He stirred his coffee, and a smile flickered across his handsome new features. "Besides," he added, "the running hasn't hurt you a bit, what with all those cigarettes of yours, and you won't have to sit examinations anyway."

"Right," said Billy, annoyed that Kileen was treating the whole hellish week so lightly. He reached for a packet of sugar and emptied it into his own coffee, which had grown cold while he had been talking. He sipped the dark brew and took another deep breath. This was the part of the conversation he had been dreading.

"So, what's next, then?" He asked the question as casually as he could, hoping against hope that he was wrong about Kileen's intended target.

"What's next?" Kileen repeated the question as though he were thinking it over, then lifted his mug and swallowed some coffee. "Well, what do you think would be next, Billy?" The terrorist carefully set his cup down on the faded Formica tabletop and removed the mirrored glasses, fixing the boy in his steely black gaze.

"Well, uh, I don't know yet, do I?" Billy squirmed at the unexpected turnaround of his question, confused and uneasy over Kileen's stare, and trying not to stare back at the brilliant job the surgeons had done on his previously devastated face.

"Come now," said Kileen. "You're a bright lad, Billy. Why do *you* think we went to all the massive expense and trouble of setting you up here as Brian O'Malley? You tell me what the mission is. Think hard, now. What's the one thing you've been perfectly positioned to do here? The thing that'll hit our enemies right in their guts?" Kileen raised his coffee cup to his lips again, his deadly eyes still staring over the chipped rim.

"The Queen!" Billy's voice was a harsh whisper. "You've set me up to get the Queen."

A slow smile curved Kileen's lips. "See, I knew you could figure it out all on your own."

"It'll never work in a million years," Billy protested. He felt an involuntary shudder of cold wrack his body, despite the coffee shop's steamy atmosphere.

Kileen raised his eyebrows. "Won't it, now?"

The boy shook his head emphatically. "The hotel where she's to be has been crawling with cops for days," he said, glancing nervously about the room. "You couldn't get a weapon inside that place for love nor money."

"Of course not," Kileen agreed. "And by the time she arrives they'll have all those metal detectors, explosives sniffers and the like too."

Billy felt his eyeballs straining in their sockets. "You know all of that, then?"

Kileen laughed, a low, easy sound. "Well of course we know all that, Billy. What on earth did you think we had planned, to knock the old girl off her pins right here on American soil for all the TV cameras to see?"

He shook his head at the sheer frivolity of such an idea, then leaned forward and took the boy's trembling hand in his iron grasp. "Listen to me, Billy Quinn. I'm not saying there's not some of us in the movement as wouldn't love to see the silly old bitch with her brains splattered all over the inside of some fancy hotel banquet room," he whispered, "but we've got to face reality now.

"In the first place, ninety percent of our operational funds have always come from sympathetic Irish Americans who see us as the victims of brutal English oppression. To assassinate the reigning British monarch on U.S. soil would alienate those supporters from us in droves." Kileen's eyes were drilling into Billy like lasers, and his voice was low and urgent. "Secondly," he continued, "there'd be a massive state funeral following such a travesty, hundreds of reporters and television cameras, and public apologies and denials until hell wouldn't have it."

Kileen leaned back wearily against the cheap plastic padding of the booth and shook his head as if he were trying to envision the unimaginable scope of such a disaster. "Before it was over, the whole world would actually be feeling sorry for the fucking English."

He suddenly released the youngster's hand and gazed off into space. "And all the suffering that our poor nation has seen would be as nothing compared to the retribution the bastards would unleash upon our innocent people . . . The false peace they've shoved down our throats would be locked in place forever." Kileen looked back at the boy. The steel seemed to melt from his eyes, and his gruff voice took on a note of heartfelt sadness. "It's we who deserve the world's sympathy, Billy. Not them. Do you understand that?"

A profound sensation of relief was flooding every fiber of Billy's being. So he'd been wrong after all. They weren't going to kill the Queen. He could see now that it made no sense. Cursing himself for his stupidity, he struggled to keep from hugging Kileen, pulling the old warhorse to his feet and waltzing him around the grease-stained restaurant. "Well, I can see what you mean," he said, reining in his emotions and trying to look solemn. "But then I don't understand what it is we're going to do."

Kileen's slow smile returned. "We're going to make them all look ridiculous, Billy," he said. "We're going to show the whole world what a bunch of bloody coldhearted simpletons they are, by proving that we could wipe out the whole lot of them any time we choose." The smile widened into a steel-edged grin. "To demonstrate with one brilliantly executed and spectacular operation both the power of our movement and the rightness and justice of our cause. Do you see now? It's the new way."

Billy leaned forward eagerly. "Yes," he grinned. "Yes I, . . . I see . . ." He hesitated, feeling a bit foolish for not yet understanding. "What exactly are we to do, then?"

Kileen leaned back in his seat. "You're going to love it," he smiled. "It's a plan I've been working on for many years. But I warn you, it'll take all your powers of persuasion with the old man . . ."

Now it was Billy's turn to grin. "Don't worry about the Major," he assured the terrorist leader. "The poor old fellow is absolute putty in my hands. In a way, I hate to use him like this." He thought guiltily about the Major for a moment, then observed, "But when this is all over he'll get his real grandson back, so that whatever has happened won't be a total loss for him at all, will it?"

Kileen nodded agreeably. "That's just the way to look at it, Billy. No harm, no foul, eh? Let's have some more coffee," he suggested. "Have you had anything to eat?"

"I'm starved," Billy admitted, realizing that he really was hungry. "Did I tell you I had to fake a stomachache to get out of going out to a dinner with the old boy and his Hollywood friends tonight?"

Kileen laughed appreciatively. "Ah, the terrible sacrifices we freedom fighters are forced to make for The Cause, eh? Well, let's get you a bit of food, then, and I'll tell you the details of the entire operation."

"WHAT ARE THEY DOING NOW?"

Stanley was squinting toward the coffee shop window, trying to see around Sam.

"They're looking at menus," the dark-haired girl giggled. "Some narcs."

"It's not funny," said Kelly from the backseat. The pain in her cramped legs was becoming unendurable, and she was beginning to feel stupid for spying on Brian. For all she knew, there was a perfectly logical explanation for everything he'd done. After all, she didn't know for certain that the substance she'd sniffed on the smudged papers she'd found in his room was hair dye. People used dye for other things too, leather for example. And the man in the coffee shop with Brian might be a family friend, or somebody he'd met since he came here.

A sudden peal of deep male laughter filled the air and a trio of drunken bikers, their naked arms a gallery of sinister prison tattoos, lurched by on the sidewalk, bending to peer curiously into the interior of the Yugo. "Can we go now?" Stanley was looking back at Kelly with pleading eyes. "Samantha and I didn't get to eat yet."

The bikers halted on the corner of Santa Monica, turning to stare back at the little car and arguing among themselves about something.

"You guys go on," said Kelly, pushing on the seat back for Sam to let her out. "I'm staying here."

Sam stared at her, making no move to open the door. "What are you going to do?"

"Don't worry about it," said Kelly, who had a half-formed idea of waiting for Brian to leave the coffee shop, then trying to talk to him. She reached past Sam and fumbled for the door handle.

"Kelly, you cannot stay here alone," Samantha squealed. "This is *Hollywood*, for God's sake!"

"*West* Hollywood," Kelly corrected.

"Whatever," Sam hissed, jerking her head toward the trio of drunken bikers. "The streets are crawling with weirdos and axe-murdering perverts!"

"Samantha, get out of my way," Kelly warned.

"No fucking way," hissed Sam. "I am not going to have to go to the morgue to identify your body."

They settled into a silent staring match, while Stanley divided his attention between the bikers on the corner and the two beautiful girls inside his car, wondering if this was all really happening to him, or if he had simply dreamed the whole bizarre, exciting day and would soon wake up to find himself back in his gray, uneventful life.

He wasn't sure that would necessarily be so bad.

CHAPTER NINE

Wild Cards

Sexy!

Brenda Gaynor turned around, looking back over her smooth shoulder at the full-length mirror to check the fit of the tight green dress across her buttocks. "If this doesn't get him, nothing will," she whispered. She ran her fingers through her long, glossy mane of red hair, pulling it away from her face on the left side—her best, she thought—and shooting herself a sultry look in the mirror.

Satisfied with her appearance, she slipped her feet into a pair of black-velvet heels and snatched up her purse and keys from the white dressing table with its colorful collection of fanciful perfume bottles, another of which her father bought for her whenever he left the country, then she crossed the room and opened the door.

The soft, melodic sounds of a Mozart piano concerto drifted down the long hallway from her father's study, and she could hear his voice as he talked on the phone, ordering someone to have the company jet ready to fly him to New York in the morning to meet with the managers of a new rock group he was hoping to sign over the weekend. Brenda smiled, knowing that he'd be on the phone with his lawyers next, and confident that when he was finished he'd go right to bed, as he always did when he had an early morning flight.

She stepped out into the hall and walked quickly through the large house to the servants' wing off the kitchen, stopping before a closed door to listen to the theme music from a decades-old rerun of *Perry Mason*. She tapped lightly on the door and waited while the volume was turned down. After a moment, the door opened and Greta Hanson, a rotund, middle-aged woman in hair curlers, squinted out at her. "Yes, Miss Brenda?"

"I'm going out for a while, Greta. It's a school thing," she explained. "My father was working and I didn't want to disturb him," she told the housekeeper.

Mrs. Hanson, a childless widow who got down on her knees every night and thanked God Almighty for having provided her with a beautiful room and a kind, generous employer like Mr. Gaynor—God bless him—who even let her have her twice-monthly Ladies of the Altar Society meetings in the lovely poolside garden behind his magnificent house, understood precisely why the headstrong and—in her own private opinion—wild Brenda was stopping by to inform her of her departure.

Mrs. Hanson and Brenda had come to an unspoken understanding a long time ago, right after the housekeeper had done what she thought was her Christian duty, reporting to her employer that the girl had been sneaking boys into her bedroom when he was off on one or another of his frequent trips. Mr. Gaynor had been suitably outraged—but with the well-meaning housekeeper, not his headstrong daughter—and Greta had very nearly lost her wonderful job.

A practical and devout woman of stolid Scandinavian heritage, Mrs. Hanson had gotten down on her arthritic knees that night and prayed for divine guidance. It had come with the realization that Miss Brenda was going to do precisely what she wanted to do, whether or not Greta Hanson or some other, and probably far less deserving, woman was occupying the Gaynor's sunny housekeeper's suite with its own private entrance, telephone, brand-new cable television and sparkling little bathroom.

The very next day, Greta had set out to make Brenda Gaynor her friend and confidant, baking her a big batch of her favorite Toll House cookies and letting the poor, motherless girl know that, in future, she could always count on Greta Hanson.

In return, Brenda had given Greta the unlisted number of the tiny cellular phone she carried in her purse, and she always checked in when she was going to be out particularly late. Since that time, Mr. Gaynor had always had the false security of knowing that someone knew how to reach his precious daughter, and Brenda always had an airtight cover story for her nocturnal adventures.

Both Greta and Brenda thought it was a wonderful arrangement.

Greta smiled broadly now. "Well, you be sure to drive carefully, dear. And don't you worry about your daddy. If he asks, I'll tell him you're studying late with your girlfriends. My, my, that's a pretty outfit you have on!"

"Thanks, Greta, you're a sweetheart." Brenda leaned over and mimed pecking the housekeeper's ruddy cheek. "Bye!"

"Tomorrow I'm going to make that special yogurt salad you like so much," called Greta, as Brenda clicked away down the hallway leading to the four-car garage at the end of the huge house.

In the bright, fluorescent-lighted garage, Brenda passed her father's black BMW sedan and the two-year-old blue Range Rover he used for his occasional ski trips to the Sierras, and slipped into the familiar leather seat of her red 500SL convertible. She raised the power top against the chill night air, fastened the latches to the windshield frame, being careful not to damage her freshly polished nails, and turned the key in the ignition. The Mercedes's powerful engine purred like a sleepy kitten as she backed out into the circular turnaround before the house, with the headlights off.

At the end of the drive, Brenda switched on the headlights and aimed the car toward the twinkling lights of the hills above Sunset Boulevard. She fiddled with the radio as she drove, tuning in to KOST—Coast Radio—a popular "soft" FM station that played nothing but love songs.

Music spilled from the eight stereo speakers fitted into niches in the Mercedes's black leather upholstery, and the beautiful redhead hummed softly along with the haunting lyrics of Gloria Estefan's old classic, "Anything for You," thinking about how wonderful it was going to feel to make love to Brian O'Malley.

For once, the thought of having sex with a boy did not seem dirty to her.

BILLY QUINN felt clean and good.

He knew that he was going to be able to sleep tonight, secure once again in the knowledge that what he was doing was right. Certain that no innocents would be hurt by his actions. When tomorrow's mission was complete, he would leave California for a well-deserved rest at an isolated villa in the Canary Islands, there to begin work on the second stage of the campaign that Kileen had assured him would finally bring genuine freedom and democracy to Northern Ireland.

Kileen had explained it all so clearly while Billy had wolfed down a double order of ham and eggs in the little coffee shop: The Queen's visit to Los Angeles and the coincidence of Brian O'Malley's coming to California to live with his famous grandfather following the tragic deaths of his parents had been just the sort of opportunity the tired old warrior had been seeking ever since the brilliant plan had come to him years earlier. An opportunity to strike a frightening but nonetheless completely nonviolent blow for peace and reason while the world's media looked on.

Billy grinned as he hopped into the green Jaguar and gunned the big V-12 engine to life. So simple, Kileen's plan. He wondered why nobody had ever thought of it before.

Of course, he realized the plan was no less dangerous for all its simplicity and ultimate harmlessness. For the legions of trigger-happy security men surrounding the royal visitor would surely interpret the opening stages of the action as a deadly attack on the Queen and, for the few critical seconds until they were neutralized, Kileen had made it clear that Billy's life would be in extreme jeopardy. The fierce freedom fighter had even surprised him by giving him a chance to back out if he wished.

Billy had assured his brave leader that he would do no such thing. This, after all, was the work he had been born to do. The reason his mother had given him over to The Cause as a small child. And, anyway, he could see now that the whole plan depended entirely on him.

As he engaged the Jaguar's heavy clutch, easing the sleek machine away from the curb and accelerating down Santa Monica Boulevard with the cold night wind in his face, he only regretted that Kileen's plan was going to disrupt the Major's long-awaited honors ceremony, as well as causing the poor old fellow some minor physical discomfort. Billy swallowed hard, pushing away the painfully certain knowledge that, after tomorrow, he would probably never see Kelly Huston again. Not for a very, very long time anyway.

"WELL, WHAT DO YOU WANT me to do now?"

Stanley Kinsella watched Brian O'Malley's green Jaguar pull out into the river of evening traffic streaming west on Santa Monica, then turned to look questioningly at Kelly, who had remained crammed in the Yugo's tiny backseat after Samantha had refused to leave her on her own.

"Follow him, I guess," Kelly said dejectedly. They had waited in the darkened car for more than half an hour while Brian had eaten, watching him as he had listened attentively the whole time to the man in the dark hat. And, when finally he had stood and shaken hands with the other, she knew no more than when they had arrived. There was nothing to do now but hope he was returning home, where she prayed she could talk to him in privacy.

Stanley obediently started the Yugo's buzzy little engine. He was reaching for the plastic headlight switch when Sam grabbed his hand. "Look," she said, pointing to the coffee-shop window.

Kelly followed her gaze to the booth where Brian had been sitting opposite the man in the black cowboy hat. The man was still there, looking up from his cup of coffee at two new arrivals; a tall, simian brute with a baseball cap pulled down tightly over his ears, and a slightly built boy, not much older than herself, who seemed to have an injured hand. As she watched, the pair slipped into the side of the booth where Brian had been sitting, and the three men began talking.

"That first guy might be an old family friend of Brian's," whispered Sam from the front seat, "but those two look like refugees from *America's Most Wanted*. I'll bet the big one majored in kicking ass at San Quentin."

Stanley's head bobbed rapidly up and down in agreement. "We are getting out of here—now," he squeaked, reaching for the light switch again.

"I thought you said you were hungry," Kelly said.

"Yeah," he replied. "And I know a really good place for pizza over on Wilshire . . ."

Samantha's head whipped around, and her flashing dark eyes met Kelly's. "Look, the booth next to theirs is empty," she said, interpreting her best friend's meaning perfectly. "We could just go in here for something to eat . . . and maybe listen to what they're saying. We could probably even find out if they're actually cops or not."

"Are you crazy? Those are *not* cops," groaned Stanley.

"Come on, Stanley," ordered Sam, snatching the keys from the ignition and opening her door to step out onto the street. "We'll get you something nice to eat."

"I'm not hungry anymore," he retorted.

Kelly painfully unfolded herself from the backseat and got shakily out of the Yugo to stand beside Sam. "Come on, Stanley," she coaxed, bending to peer back into the car. "It's perfectly safe. These guys don't have any way of knowing who we are."

Stanley did not budge.

Samantha placed her hands on her exquisitely rounded hips and somehow managed to look both sexy and stern at the same time. "Stanley, you promised me you were going to change," she reminded him.

"Samantha, I promised I'd ask my dad for a cooler car and get contacts and some new clothes," he whined.

Sam shrugged. "Okay, if you want to go through life being afraid of every little thing that comes up, I guess that's your decision." She rolled her eyes at Kelly. "I tried," she said. "I really did. Come on, Kelly. I guess we're on our own."

"Crap!" Stanley opened his door and got out of the car, tucking his shirttail into his baggy corduroys. "Okay," he muttered, "but don't blame me if we get killed." He looked up to see the girls almost at the entrance of the coffee shop. "Wait up," he called, hurrying after them.

They stopped to let him catch up, and Sam planted a kiss on his ear. "All right now," she whispered excitedly, "remember, we're just a bunch of dumb high school kids stopping by for a bite after the movies, so everybody act completely natural."

Stanley pushed open the door, and they stepped into the coffee shop, ignoring the amused stares of a couple of footsore hookers who were resting on stools at the counter. "Oh look, there's an empty booth by the window," Sam said a bit too brightly, considering the fact that all of the booths in the place but one were unoccupied.

The three men by the window stopped talking and turned to stare at them.

"We are all going to die," whispered Stanley.

"DID YOU GET the special tools that I asked for?" Kileen had stopped talking as the three teenagers passed and slid into the booth directly behind him. Now he returned his attention to Duffy, whose eyes were still fixed suspiciously on the newcomers.

"We got it all," said Tumelty, passing a dictionary-sized box across the table, "but we had to go all the way up into the other end of Hollywood to find a building supply, and it was hugely expensive."

Kileen was already opening the box, ignoring Tumelty's breathless explanation and lifting out the compact electric model builder's drill and the plastic case of carbon-steel bits and tapered grinding tips. "Good," he murmured, hefting the precision tool in his hand, then rummaging through the box to examine the assortment of odds and ends they'd purchased and packed around the little drill. "Very good."

Tumelty blushed with pride, then lifted the coffee shop's thumb-worn laminated menu to the light, turning directly to a page illustrated with slick color photos of idealized desserts.

Duffy glowered at the trio of kids in the next booth, who were all intently studying menus of their own, then fixed his flat gray eyes on Kileen. "What about the kid?" he asked in a low voice. "Is he going to go through with it?"

Kileen nodded. "He'll go through with it."

"Ballsy little bastard," Duffy grunted in grudging admiration. "Do you think there's really a chance of pulling him out afterwards?"

Kileen turned his palms up in a gesture that said the chances were iffy. "Still, we've got to try our damnedest to save the lad, haven't we?"

Duffy nodded. The answer was too obvious to require comment. Of course they had to try. Die trying, if necessary. His enthusiasm for Kileen's plan had returned in full force only after it had been explained to him that the primary role he and Tumelty were to play in the assassination concerned the safe extraction of young Billy Quinn afterwards. And the more he had been told since, the more he was coming to believe that they might even pull it off. "And the car?" he asked, finding it difficult to believe that Kileen had actually managed to lay hands on the vehicle he'd described to them over dinner, much less all the other bits and pieces.

"All set," Kileen assured him. "Parked in a private garage east of the city right now, along with everything else you'll need . . ." The terrorist leader looked up as an energetic blond waitress with a bit too much flesh showing through the sheer fabric of her stained white uniform walked over to the next booth and took the orders of the three teenagers.

When she had finished, she returned to look down at the men. "Get you gents anything?" she enquired around the pink wad of gum she was busily chewing.

"Coffee, black," said Duffy, eyeing her large breasts and mentally comparing her shape to that of the smashing little dark-haired bint in the next booth. "Coffee, black." The waitress turned to Tumelty and smiled down at him. "What about you, honey?"

Dermot Tumelty blushed and looked at Kileen, who indicated with a paternal nod that he was free to order what he chose. "I'll have the banana split, then, please, miss," grinned the youngster.

Duffy rolled his eyes at the waitress. "Bloody bottomless pit, this little bugger," he said with a trace of affection in his voice. "Never stops eating."

The waitress winked at him. "Got a boy about his age from my second marriage," she confided, patting Tumelty's bony shoulder. "They can sure put away the groceries, can't they?"

Duffy grinned back at her, wishing he'd known enough to come here during the week instead of blowing all his money on the indifferent whores. He was certain that the buxom waitress—whose name, according to the little plastic tag on her uniform, was Ruby—was bombarding him with sexual signals. Kileen gave him an impatient look, and he turned sheepishly back to the leader. Ruby looked puzzled, then sashayed back to the counter, where she handed the teenagers' order to a Mexican cook behind a little window, then began making Tumelty's banana split. When she was out of earshot, Duffy cleared his throat and laid a hand on the box containing the drill. "You can do all this tonight?"

Kileen smiled. "Not much to it. A few hours' work at most. It'll be delivered to the boy at his school tomorrow, along with his transmitter. You'll have a far more powerful transmitter of your own, set to a different frequency, to cover his extraction, as we discussed."

"When will we be able to pick up the car and . . . all the other things?" Tumelty had discarded his menu and was looking intently at Kileen.

"Tomorrow, at around dusk. You'll drive out to the garage and park your rental there until you've finished. I'm going to tell you how to get to the place now. Can you memorize the directions, Dermot?"

Dermot Tumelty flashed him a boyish grin. "They say it's one of the things I do best." Tumelty smiled, proud of his unique talent, the photographic memory that had enabled him to deliver complicated messages to the troops back home without the necessity of ever carrying incriminating documents on his person.

CHAPTER TEN

Dreambreakers

JAMES QUEALLY-SMYTHE'S house was still.

The glare of headlights across the front of the tall, stuccoed walls glittered back from lightless windows as Billy drove the Jaguar past the shadowed porch, then activated the electronic door opener with the tiny remote unit attached to his key ring and backed into the garage. He shut down the Jag's engine, noting with relief that the Bentley's parking space was vacant—meaning that Ranjee had not yet returned from his evening off.

From the blaze of lights he'd seen as he'd passed the Huston house down the canyon, he guessed that the Major was still there, entertaining the Hustons' studio friends with his seemingly endless supply of adventure stories. Relieved that he would not have to offer explanations to anyone regarding his whereabouts for the past hour and a half, Billy sighed wearily and hoisted himself up out of the Jaguar's low bucket seat.

Entering the silent mansion through the same interior garage entrance by which he'd earlier left, he traversed the long corridor to the opposite end of the house and climbed the steep flight of steps to his room. Exhausted as he was, he could feel the tense muscles of his shoulders bunching painfully about the base of his neck, and so he walked directly through the dark bedroom, pausing only to peel off his shoes and shirt by the closet, then stepping into the attached bathroom and switching on the lights. Squinting against the glare of the fluorescents on the tiled walls, he reached around the glass side of the double-sized shower stall and turned the taps.

As he waited for the hot water to fill the pipes, he stood critically studying his reflection in the wide mirror above the marble washbasin. His eyes were still red from lack of sleep, and the dark circles beneath them seemed, if anything, more prominent than they had just this morning, despite the few hours of sleep he'd managed to squeeze in prior to his meeting with Kileen.

Deciding that a good night's rest was all he really needed to improve his haggard looks, he lifted one hand to his face and pushed back the shock of black hair falling over his forehead, examining the hastily touched-up roots at the hairline for some sign of the blondness beneath. He thought the hair still looked a little lighter there, but determined there was nothing more he could do about it now, as the risk of bringing another bottle of hair dye into the house and—as he had discovered when he had gotten some of the stuff on his hands in this morning's clumsy attempt to fix things—experimenting with the unfamiliar process was far more dangerous than the slight chance that someone might notice the light roots.

Besides, he wearily reminded himself, he only had to pass himself off as Brian O'Malley for one more day.

One more day.

Billy allowed himself a small smile at the grim countenance of the dark stranger peering back at him from the rapidly steaming mirror. One more day and he could stop being the stranger, stop having to analyze every word he uttered beforehand, stop having to force himself to affect the strained upper-class English accent he'd dredged up from a thousand boring gram-mar lectures by the nuns who'd been his teachers, stop pretending he un-derstood a thousand things that baffled him, liked a thousand more that he held in utter contempt.

Tomorrow he would say good-bye to Brian O'Malley forever. "Good-bye, asshole," he grinned.

Dropping his pants onto the floor, Billy opened the shower door and stepped into the cottony clouds of steam boiling up from the splatter of hot water against the cold tile. Scalding needles of spray pounded down onto his head, and he gratefully turned his face up into the powerful stream from the showerhead, squeezing his eyes shut and opening his mouth to let the pulsing water batter his teeth and tongue.

After a few minutes, the soothing effects of the shower began to take hold and some of the tension drained from his taut muscles. As he began to relax, a funny thought occurred to him. What if, after he had gone and the real Brian O'Malley was returned to his rightful place, everyone discovered that they had liked the substitute better?

A picture of the miserable boy he'd last seen trussed up on a dirty mat-tress in the dank upstairs room of the tumbledown farmhouse north of Belfast filled his mind, and a broad smile creased his handsome features. "Well, Brian, old boy," he muttered into the cascading water, "by this time tomorrow night you'll be free as a bird. Now how do you feel about that, you little wanker?"

The conjured image of the pathetic prisoner on the mattress looked up helplessly, his pale features strangely devoid of hope.

"ARE YOU SURE this is the right place?"

Kelly was standing beside the Yugo, looking down a long, narrow driveway of crumbling concrete that ran into the shadows beside a darkened ranch-style house with a badly overgrown lawn. The dilapidated structure was located on a winding street of only slightly better looking houses in the far-out Los Angeles suburb of West Corona, an arid place that had flowered briefly during Southern California's halcyon post–World War II boom, when anybody with a hundred dollars and proof of military service could buy a cozy "ranchette" out among the citrus groves that had once surrounded Los Angeles on all sides.

Kelly shivered in the chilly night air, wanting nothing more than to go home and get under her down comforter. Of course that was not possible now.

Not after the broken snatches of conversation she had overheard from the three men in the coffee shop—two of whom had spoken with exactly the same rough Irish accents she had heard Brian use the night he had beat up the two parking-lot muggers. She was sure that the men were planning something. Something dangerous that depended entirely on Brian O'Malley's cooperation.

She had known then that she had no choice but to find out what it was. Find out and confront Brian with it before he got himself into serious trouble.

Except for the fact that it had seemed that what they were planning was both illegal and dangerous, the address of the garage in West Corona that the man in the dark hat had given the others was her only clue as to what that might be. Kelly had waited until the three men had left the coffee shop, then talked her friends into bringing her out here.

Neither Sam nor Stanley had ever heard of West Corona before tonight, and Kelly only vaguely recalled having seen a sign somewhere along the road on the hundred-mile drive to Palm Springs, remembering the name because she had thought it strange that there had been no sign for a Corona, only a *West* Corona.

Tonight, driving toward the desert for close to an hour via three different freeways, she and Stanley and Sam had managed to get themselves hopelessly lost in the barren industrial wastelands fringing the vast eastern edge of L.A. Unable to find West Corona and nearly out of gas, they had finally turned off the San Bernardino Freeway and driven into the notorious Latino community of El Rancho—a place they had all heard of as the result of its numerous gang wars and drive-by shootings.

The Yugo's gas gauge was hovering below the empty mark, and all three of them were verging on panic when they had chanced on an all-night Arco station tucked away among the shuttered taco stands and wrecking yards along El Rancho Boulevard. Seeing other cars in the lot, the two girls had sighed with relief as Stanley had guided the sputtering car into the station, only to discover that all the other vehicles they had seen were low riders and that they had evidently interrupted an impromptu gang meeting.

Their little car was immediately surrounded, and a tense moment had followed, during which seven or eight dangerous-looking youths in turned-up baseball caps, and outrageously baggy pants held up with bright suspenders over sleeveless undershirts had stared the three lost teenagers down.

"What in the hell kind of a fucking car jou call this, man?" a slender Mexican youth with a CUT ON DOTTED LINE neck tattoo had demanded of Stanley.

"It . . . It's a Yugo," the terrified nerd had stammered, his voice squeaking comically on the *Yu*.

"Jou-go!" another of the heavily accented gang members had howled, throwing down his cigarette and gleefully pounding the glistening bronze metal-flake fender of his lowered '67 Chevy Impala.

"Yeah," laughed the first boy, picking up on the other's hilarity. "First they get the money for this piece-of-shit car, then they say, 'Okay, now *Jou-go* fuck yourself, 'cause we got the money.'"

For some reason, all of the gang members had found the childish joke uproariously funny, and they had spent several seconds laughing and repeating it among themselves. Meanwhile, Stanley, his knobby knuckles white on the steering wheel, had smiled weakly.

"Hey, guys, can we get some gas and directions to West Corona," Sam had called, taking advantage of the *cholos'* seeming good mood to flash them a dazzling smile.

The boy with the neck tattoo—who, it turned out, was named Rico, and who was also the leader of the group—had returned her smile with a roguish grin, brusquely ordering someone named Paco to fill the Yugo's tank while he pulled an ancient street map from the glove compartment of his customized Buick Riviera.

Leaning in through the passenger window to brazenly brush his arms against Sam's breasts, the darkly handsome Rico had pointed out West Corona on the map—they hadn't gone far enough on the freeway—then graciously presented the many-creased map to Sam, in return for her telephone number.

They had been back on their way within minutes, the strained atmosphere inside the little car melting away as Samantha happily informed the distraught Stanley that the telephone number she had given the amorous homeboy belonged to none other than Brenda Gaynor. They had all broken up laughing over that, and fifteen minutes later they had pulled up in front of the abandoned house.

"I'm sure this is it." Stanley sat behind the wheel now, squinting at the homie's tattered street map by the beam of a penlight. He ran a nail-bitten index finger across a spidery network of lines representing streets, bending closer to make out the minuscule letters spelling out the name. "Los Flores Street," he read, "six blocks south of Lincoln Avenue. This has to be it."

Sam, who was standing outside the car with Kelly, pointed to the black-and-gold stick-on letters spaced unevenly across a warped strip of wood beside the faded eviction notice that someone had taped to the paint-peeling front door of the house. "Six thirty-nine. This is definitely the place," she whispered.

A dog barked somewhere down the street, and a deep voice hollered through an open window, telling the stupid son of a bitch to shut the fuck up unless it wanted to have its balls ground up for cat food. The unhappy mutt let out a final mournful yelp and fell silent, and Sam began to giggle at the unlikely threat. Kelly angrily elbowed her in the ribs. "Be quiet, for God's sake. Somebody will call the police."

Sam cynically surveyed the scruffy neighborhood with its yards full of junked refrigerators and rusting automobile carcasses. "We should be so lucky," she laughed.

Kelly shot her a withering glance, then reached into the car and snatched the penlight from Stanley. "What are you doing?" he asked.

"The garage is back there," Kelly said, pointing down the driveway.

"You're going back there?"

"Well, we're not going to find out what's inside by standing out here," she snapped defiantly before turning and walking away into the shadows.

"I'm going with you." Sam fell into step beside her.

"No, stay here with Stanley," Kelly said. "Get back in the car and pretend you're making out with him."

Sam pouted. "Do I have to *pretend?*"

Kelly stopped and glared at her. "Dammit, this is no time for jokes. Beep the horn twice if you see anybody coming."

"Kelly!" Sam protested, but the other girl had already walked away, disappearing into the void of darkness beside the house.

The broken driveway terminated in an oil-stained concrete apron at the front of a sagging double garage. Bright metal flashed in the penlight's weak beam, revealing a shiny new brass padlock at one edge of the door. Swinging the penlight across the front of the building, Kelly saw that one side abutted a cinder-block wall covered with thick tendrils of ivy. She walked across to the opposite side of the garage, which faced a dirt yard containing a broken swing set. A sad doghouse fashioned of unpainted plywood and tarpaper was set against the wall of the garage.

There was a warped door beside the doghouse.

Walking carefully to avoid twisting an ankle in the rutted yard, Kelly moved to the door, placed her hand on the rusted knob and tried to turn it. The door was locked, and its single dusty window was papered over from the inside with an old drag-racing poster. Frustrated, she walked around to the back of the garage, pushing past a stand of overgrown shrubbery to flash the light onto the rear of the building. A dull reflection shone off another small square of dirty glass set high up on the wall.

Looking around for something on which to stand, Kelly settled on the doghouse. Grabbing it by the edge of the roof, she dragged the heavy contraption through the dirt and past the shrubs, feeling the rough wood biting into her fingertips. She paused for breath, examining her fingers—two of which were bleeding. "Dammit, Brian, there had better be a good reason for all this crap," she whispered angrily, licking the blood from her fingers and feeling the end of a jagged splinter with her tongue.

"Come on, damn you!" She angrily attacked the doghouse again, shoving it up to the wall beneath the window with an adrenaline-charged burst of energy and climbing awkwardly up onto the sloping roof.

The Yugo's high-pitched horn beeped twice from the front of the driveway.

Dropping into the dirt, Kelly felt a sharp stabbing pain in her left ankle. She hobbled across the yard to the house. Reaching it, she edged along the wall to the corner nearest the driveway and peeked around to see Stanley standing beside the Yugo, his pale skin illuminated in the brilliant glare of a spotlight mounted on the windshield post of a black-and-white police car.

The nerd was gesticulating wildly with his hands as a tall police officer in a dark uniform stood listening with crossed arms. After several minutes, the cop finally got back into his car. Kelly ducked as the spotlight suddenly stabbed down the driveway, bathing the front of the garage in a dazzle of white light. Her heart pounding, she pressed her back against the stained wall, expecting at any second to hear sirens and a command to freeze.

Instead, the bright light was suddenly extinguished, and she heard the sound of a departing engine. She remained frozen against the wall for several more seconds before daring to peek around the corner again.

The street in front of the house was empty.

Her mouth dry and the blood still pounding in her temples, Kelly debated her next move. Reasoning that the cop had simply told Stanley to move on, and praying that he and Sam would have the nerve to come back for her, she limped back to the rear of the garage and clumsily boosted herself up onto the steeply angled roof of the doghouse. Even from her precarious perch on the peaked ridge of the roof, the streaked garage window, which looked as though it had never been cleaned, was still two inches above eye level. Inside, she could see only the dark outlines of rafters and what looked like a few pieces of loose lumber propped against an unpainted wall.

Her turned ankle was killing her now, and she had to grit her teeth in order to force herself up onto the tips of her toes. With both hands braced against the rough stucco of the wall, she managed to peer down into the depths of the dark garage. The bulk of a large car filled the shadowed space below. Cursing under her breath, she balanced herself with one hand, raising the penlight to the glass and shining its feeble beam down into the garage. What she saw made her gasp in fright and surprise.

Beneath the dirty window, its shiny paint and wide plastic roof bar gleaming in the dim light, sat a brand-new LAPD squad car. A number of plastic-wrapped packages containing what looked like police uniforms, hats and badges were neatly laid out on the hood.

Kelly Huston felt as though she were going to throw up again.

BILLY TURNED OFF the shower taps and fumbled through the mist-filled bathroom for a towel. Rubbing his hair to remove most of the water, he roughly patted the rest of his body dry and wrapped the damp towel about his waist.

He opened the bathroom door and switched off the lights, then stood peering out into the darkened bedroom while his pupils adjusted to the pale glow of moonlight spilling in through the balcony doors. After a moment, the outlines of furniture began to take shape, and he crossed the room to sit on the edge of his bed. He fumbled on the night table for cigarettes and matches, found them and struck a light to a Marlboro.

The sudden glare of the match illuminated a small form hunched in the shadows before his desk. He had a fleeting impression of a cloud of coppery hair above white shoulders. A pixielike face smiled at him as the match went dead between his fingers.

"Hello, Brian!"

Billy Quinn blinked in the sudden darkness, not certain for an instant whether he was dreaming. Reaching for his book of matches, he struck another and gazed into the mischievous eyes of Brenda Gaynor. She sat on his desk chair with her knees pulled up to her chin, waiting for him to speak. The second match flickered and died. "Brenda," he whispered, "what are you doing here?"

She smiled mysteriously, reaching across to take the dangling cigarette from his fingers and placing it between her lips. The orange tip glowed in the darkness, painting her face with an ethereal light, then she held out the smoke for him.

"I came to see you," she whispered. "I've been waiting here for hours."

He looked toward the dark bathroom. "You mean you've been here the whole time I was in there?"

"Uh-huh. I was sitting right here at your desk when you came in, but you went into the bathroom and turned on the shower before I could say anything." She made a pretty little gesture of biting her lower lip. "I almost came in and joined you . . ."

"How did you get in here?" he breathed, suddenly acutely aware of his nakedness beneath the towel.

Brenda smiled slyly. "There was nobody home when I knocked, so I walked around by the veranda and came right up that cute little wrought-iron stairway to your balcony. You really ought to lock your doors around here." He heard the wheels of the chair squeaking across the floorboards, and a slender hand snaked out to touch his cheek. "Or some pervert might sneak into your bedroom . . . Don't worry," she added. "I parked down the hill so no one would see my car."

Billy felt a sudden charge of electricity tingle through his body at the feathery touch of her fingers. "Brenda," he asked hoarsely, "what do you want?"

Brenda's expression grew serious as she leaned forward and pulled him to her, and he felt her breath on his skin as her lips touched his ear. "I want you, Brian," she sighed. "I love you."

"Oh, Christ!" Billy moaned as she stood and leaned over him. Her silken tongue fluttered in his ear, and she pulled her slender body close to his in the moonlight. Getting clumsily to his feet, he pressed his damp body against the sheer fabric of her clinging dress. He immediately felt himself becoming aroused beneath the towel, and cursed his weakness. *What in the hell are you doing, you stupid sod? You can't fucking stand this little bitch.*

Billy pulled away to look at her. Adoring eyes gazed up at him from her angelic face. *And what goddamn difference does that make now?* his exhausted brain screamed back. *She's beautiful and she's here . . . And after tomorrow you're never going to see Kelly Huston again anyway . . .*

CHAPTER ELEVEN

Fatal Flaws

IT WAS LATE.

Kileen huddled over the antique writing table before the window in the living room of Sally Hilton's West Hollywood condo, pausing to wipe a dribble of perspiration from his forehead with the back of his hand.

He had waited until the woman had finally fallen into an exhausted sleep in the adjoining bedroom before carefully spreading a layer of newspapers across the polished surface of the valuable writing table—which she had once proudly boasted of having stolen from a film star's estate in Brentwood—and laying out the items that Duffy and Tumelty had delivered, alongside the pair of nearly identical gilded medals he had purchased in London and the assortment of minor electronic components he had selected at a nearby Radio Shack earlier in the evening.

The tantrum that Sally had thrown when he had finally returned to the condo after his meetings with Billy Quinn and the others had delayed his getting started on the delicate work for hours. First, he'd had to calm the hysterical woman down, and then she had insisted upon a protracted round of sweaty lovemaking on her water bed in order to seal the uneasy bargain she had forced upon him with her threats. Now, while she slept blissfully in the next room, he still had a great deal left to do.

Sighing at the prospect of the exacting work that lay ahead, he gingerly prodded the cone-shaped hollow he had drilled into the back of one of the heavy medallions, pleased at least that he had gotten the difficult task right the first time and would not need the spare, which bore a different year on its face than the medal he had selected. The bed of acrylic dental cement with which he had lined the space in the center of the heavy bronze award was already beginning to take on the consistency of window putty.

His eyes burning from the volatile fumes being given off by the cement, Kileen opened the black plastic case containing the powerful explosive pyramids and peeled the paper label from the inside of the lid, holding it up to the light to squint at the long list of printed instructions and cautions. When he was satisfied that he fully understood how to arm and detonate the devices, he folded the paper and placed it in his shirt pocket for future reference. Then he carefully pried one of the tiny charges from its foam niche in the case and pressed it gently into the doughlike bed of acrylic cement in the hollowed out medal, positioning the tiny pyramid with its deadly tip pointed directly to the front.

Working quickly now—for once the chemically activated cement began to set, nothing would stop it—he used a screwdriver from an eyeglasses repair kit to turn a tiny screw set almost invisibly into the bottom of the explosive charge, thereby activating its self-contained radio sensor. He layered over the exposed plate with another thin coat of cement, so that the pyramid was entirely encased in acrylic, smoothed the excess from the back of the medallion with the flat edge of a kitchen knife and set the piece aside to dry. Later, when the cement was completely hard, he would polish the new surface smooth with the buffing attachment on the tiny model-maker's drill kit, then blend a thin layer of wax-based gold gilt over the repair, making it invisible to all but the closest inspection.

In the meantime, however, he had several other exacting tasks to attend to.

Pulling three remote electronic signaling devices from the plastic Radio Shack bag, and checking to be certain that their battery compartments were empty, he laid the first—which was also the smallest of the three—on the corner of the table beside the drying medallion.

The two larger, and far more powerful, radio control units—modified from standard garage-door openers—he set next to the three heavy automatic pistols and the Uzi that he had insisted Duffy turn over to him for his personal inspection after they had left the coffee shop earlier tonight.

Placing one of the pistols in the desk drawer, he picked up another and ejected the long magazine from its butt. He set the pistol aside and carefully removed a second explosive charge from the black plastic box, holding it up against the base of the metal magazine and judging by eye that it would just fit beneath the bottom of the spring steel mechanism that fed bullets up into the firing chamber of the pistol.

Satisfied with the approximate fit of the pyramidal charge, he went to work to remove the spring from the magazine with a large screwdriver, taking great care not to scratch the dull metal finish.

As he worked, Kileen felt a great sadness building in his heart; sadness that Duffy and Tumelty, the two brave lads he had secretly recruited to bring Northstar to life, would, like young Billy Quinn, never live to see the free and united Ireland for which they had spent nearly their entire lives fighting.

As late as this afternoon, Kileen had still toyed with the idea of letting the loyal pair live—he had long ago deemed that Billy Quinn's death was completely unavoidable. But, after serious reflection, he had determined that the risks of letting the others live were also unacceptable.

Both Duffy and Tumelty had seen his new face. And, too, both of them were wild and unpredictable lads who, as Duffy had made clear tonight, would never willingly go along with the deliberate sacrifice of young Billy Quinn's life, no matter how noble the end. Kileen shuddered to think what the vengeful Duffy would do if he actually knew the full nature of the sacrifice demanded by their mission.

The big man, whose prison experience had left him seriously deranged at best, Kileen considered to be dangerous in another way as well. For, despite his unquestioned loyalty to The Cause, Kileen had seen, in the way Duffy had looked at the teenage girls and the coffee-shop waitress, that the madman might be readily enticed to reveal what he knew under the influence of a woman's wiles.

And so, in the end, he had concluded that it was far better for Francis Duffy and Dermot Tumelty—both of whom were, after all, rough-and-tumble street fighters born and bred, and not much given to analyzing political strategies under any circumstances—to die as shining martyrs to Northstar and The Cause. For neither of them, in Michael Kileen's view, stood much chance of surviving in a normal world anyway.

A weary smile flickered at the corners of his mouth as the black steel spring popped out of the magazine and dangled above the newspapers. He carefully pulled the yielding metal the rest of the way out of its hollow housing, inserting the tiny explosive charge sideways down into the magazine in its place, and delighted to see that it nestled perfectly at the bottom of the empty case. From that point, it was a relatively simple matter to arm the second explosive charge, affix it to the inside of the case with a drop of epoxy and reassemble the magazine.

His head was beginning to throb now—as it regularly did ever since the explosion, whenever he was under a great deal of stress—and he forced himself to concentrate on the work still to be done, laying out the components he would need and going to work on the magazine from the second automatic.

Michael Kileen did not resent the pain, which he had come to equate with the price he must pay for the inspiration that had brought about his plan for Northstar. He smiled through clenched teeth, popping the stiff spring from the next magazine. Somewhere in a dark recess of his mind, it occurred to him that the explosion that had placed him in that London hospital—and which the know-nothing English surgeons claimed had resulted in permanent damage to his brain—had actually jarred the wonderful scheme loose from its secret hiding place inside his head. The scheme whose entire details he had shared with no other living human. For no one else would understand that snapping the centuries-old chain of British power that had held his people hostage for more than three hundred years was the only way to permanently end the never-ending horror that had obliterated Ginnie Keenan's innocent life on a cold Belfast sidewalk and thrust young Michael Kileen forever into the solitary and dangerous existence of a terrorist.

The hated existence that had made him a legend and a folk hero to supporters of The Cause, but that was in reality nothing more than a living hell.

No one else *could* understand.

"I'M SORRY."

Billy Quinn looked down at Brenda Gaynor. Her head was resting lightly on his shoulder, her arms clasped tightly about his waist. He didn't know what else to say to her.

"It's all right," she whispered, seeming to read his thoughts. "You don't have to say anything."

She had caught him at a vulnerable moment, appearing in his room as she had, when he was so tired and confused. And, he remembered guiltily, his first instinct when she had pressed her hard, satiny body against his had been to pull her down onto the bed with him, peeling the slick, shiny dress she wore up over her long legs, and surrender to the eager, insistent explorations of her bold hands. Because at that moment, he had wanted nothing more than to drown his own excruciatingly impossible yearning for Kelly Huston in the taste of Brenda Gaynor's hot and hungry mouth.

But his pain had stopped him for just that one moment, and he had peered into Brenda's feverish eyes, seeing there, a desperate, unspoken need that had frightened him with its intensity, a need that went far deeper than the ephemeral sex she was so blatantly thrusting at him.

"What is it, Brenda?" he had asked quietly, holding her away at arm's length and forcing her to look directly at him. "Why are you so unhappy?"

And, for the first time since he had met her, Brenda Gaynor had had nothing to say. She had made no smart retort, delivered no breathy, insinuating reply. Instead, the beautiful girl's lips had begun to quiver as the tears welled up in the corners of her blue eyes. She had suddenly sagged in his arms, and he had pulled her close, feeling the crush of her small breasts against his chest, holding her tight as she began sobbing uncontrollably, blurting out the poignant story of her lost baby sister and mother.

Billy, who understood all too well the desolation of such losses, had tried to comfort her as best he could, awkwardly patting her heaving shoulders with trembling hands, telling her it would be all right, when, of course, he knew it wouldn't. Billy Quinn, of all people, knew that losses like the ones he and Brenda Gaynor had experienced were not so easily made right, and that there was really nothing anyone could ever do for them. All the same, he was sorry for her, and he had said so. But he had other things to worry about now, his own losses to mourn. And so he had brushed the tears from her pale cheeks and held her.

After a while, he had gently disengaged himself from her grasp, ducking into the bathroom to pull on his jeans. He had stepped back into the darkened bedroom to find her sitting in the chair at his desk, pulling on her shoes.

"I guess I made a complete fool of myself," she sniffed, brushing ineffectively at her tear-stained cheeks with the back of her hand. More like the old Brenda he had come to know, he thought.

"I really think you should go now." He said it quietly, leading her to the balcony door.

She nodded silently. Then, pausing to touch his lips with the tips of her fingers, stepped onto the balcony and crossed to the head of the winding stair. "Tomorrow?" she asked hopefully. "Can we maybe just talk?"

Billy smiled. "Yeah. Tomorrow," he promised, anxious for her to go so that he might sleep.

When she had gone, vanishing like an image in a dream, he sank wearily onto the chair outside his door and gazed at the twinkling lights of the vast and dangerous city spread out at his feet, wishing that he could somehow walk down into them and stop being who he was, by simply disappearing into the trackless urban sprawl.

His eyelids grew heavy, and he willed himself to stand, wanting nothing more now than to go inside and fall onto his rumpled bed, there to sleep and dream of another, better life. A life in which he and Kelly Huston were still driving north on the endless seaside highway, the sound of the Jag's exhausts rumbling around them, insulating them from all the pain and ugliness of the real world.

But still he did not move. Instead, he stood there teetering above the glittering landscape, watching dully as a pair of headlights detached themselves from the carpet of lights, moving steadily up the winding canyon road and disappearing behind the thick screen of hedges surrounding the Major's property.

Then a car door opened and slammed shut at the foot of the drive, and he blinked, wondering if he had only imagined the sound and the lights coming up the canyon. A moment later, halting footsteps crossed the veranda below, whoever it was staying close to the wall of the house, remaining hidden in the inky shadows.

Billy's muscles tensed as the intruder below in the dark hesitated. He shuddered in the cold breeze as the footsteps began moving again, slowly mounting the circular iron stairway at the end of the balcony. Turning, he saw a slight figure emerge from the shadows.

"Brian?"

He took an awkward step toward her, a hot rush of blood rising to his ears. "Kelly!"

Her blond hair was tangled about her face, and there were dark spots on the torn sleeve of her white sweater. "I have to talk to you, Brian." She blurted out the demand, then stood shivering miserably in the cold night air. "Can we please go inside?"

"Jesus Christ, Kelly . . ." His words were an anguished whisper that rose above the small night sounds of the canyon and the distant hiss of traffic on the rushing freeway, and he took a step toward her, every atom of his being aching to enfold her in his arms.

And then he remembered Kileen. Remembered the terrible trouble that was coming, and that it would bring her nothing but pain and disappointment.

"Not now!" he hissed angrily.

"Brian, please!"

She moved closer, her arms extended, ready to enfold him, and he knew that one touch from her could seal their doom. For the great swell of passion he had denied the pathetic Brenda was surging up within him, and he wanted Kelly as he had never wanted anyone or anything in his life, but if he once more let himself lay his hands upon her, he knew that he could never let go.

"I said not now!" he repeated brusquely, hating himself for it.

Still she did not move, but stood there, uncomprehending, her eyes pleading for some explanation.

He averted his face, looking back into the empty bedroom, seeing the white glare of the fluorescent light shining beneath the bathroom door, remembering how he had come out of that same door to find Brenda waiting for him. "There's someone else here," he said, grasping for a reason that would make her leave.

Kelly's hands flew to her mouth, and her eyes darted from his bare feet and shirtless chest to the closed bathroom door. "Oh my God! I'm so sorry," she whispered. She lurched away from him, grasping the iron railing and stepping onto the stairs.

"Wait," he called miserably. "It's not what you think."

Billy Quinn watched helplessly as she disappeared down the spiral stairway like Brenda before her.

"I'm sorry, Brian," she wailed as her feet touched the ground and she ran away into the darkness. "I'm so sorry . . ."

He forced himself to let her go, clutching the cold iron railing of the balcony until his knuckles turned white and he was certain that the bones of his fingers would break.

RANJEE SAT in the driver's seat of the silver Bentley parked at the side of the canyon road, fifty yards below the iron gates flanking the driveway.

He had been driving up the canyon following a pleasant evening spent at an Indian restaurant with several friends when he had seen the strange little automobile parked at the foot of the Major's driveway. Curious about the late visitor, but anxious to avoid another embarrassing incident like the one at the beginning of the week, when he had surprised young Master Brian and the blond girl from the house down the canyon, he had pulled over to the side of the road and extinguished the Bentley's lights.

Now he watched in amazement as the Huston girl—who was very obviously weeping—hurried down the drive and got into the small car, which immediately backed around to face down the hill and sped toward him.

Ranjee waited until the Yugo had passed, surprised when it stopped but did not turn in at the Hustons' drive. He watched the girl get out, then raised his eyes to the Major's dark mansion, certain now that something was dreadfully wrong, a premonition that had been growing within him throughout the week.

It had begun with small things; the cigarettes, and young Brian's awkwardness with certain words and phrases—as though he had to think through what he was about to say before uttering the smallest sentence. Then there was the boy's propensity to discard his clothes wherever he happened to shed them, and his seeming ignorance of the uses of certain items of silverware at table. And, though none of those things was in itself important, together they did not at all bespeak the habits of a young man who had spent several years in the disciplined atmosphere of an exclusive boarding school, or even a lax boarding school as Ranjee had at first tried to convince himself was the problem . . . It was all very strange and disturbing. For although he would never say so to the Major, Ranjee could not dispel the feeling that Brian O'Malley was something other than what he pretended to be.

It was, he thought, all most incredibly odd, and he determined to put himself on his guard, lest some harm come to his beloved Major.

SALLY HILTON walked into her living room, blinking in the glare of the lamp on her antique writing table.

She had awakened moments before to find herself alone on the water bed, the first gray traces of the coming dawn illuminating the tangle of sheets where Michael Kileen had been when she fell asleep. Pulling on a sheer black robe, she had come out of the bedroom in search of him.

He was at the desk, asleep, his head cradled atop his folded arms on the covering of old newspapers he had laid out to protect the glossy surface.

Smiling softly, she walked up behind him and placed a gentle hand on his neck. "Hey, fella, you coming back to bed with me?"

Kileen moaned in his sleep and arched his neck against the comforting hand. Sally made no further attempt to wake him, but stood there, looking fondly at him in the gray light and wondering what it was about this dangerous and mysterious man that stirred such passion and tenderness in her, long after she had given up the hope of ever experiencing such feelings.

Certainly he was not good for her. Not in any accepted sense of what was supposed to be good for women. His present business in Los Angeles, for instance, had exposed her to incredible risks, risks that she now understood made even the theft of the brand-new, fully equipped LAPD patrol car— the theft that she had been so worried about—seem minor by comparison. Because, while she didn't know the precise penalty for having taken the police vehicle, she assumed it was harsh.

But still, in her mind—a mind trained by years of poverty and abuse to gloss over the finer points of morality concerning larceny—the theft of the police car had been an understandable thing. And, even though the danger of being caught—a danger that had really existed only during the fifteen minutes it had taken her to locate and remove the vehicle from the city storage yard where it had been awaiting its license plates and the installation of a new computer system, along with twenty identical cars just delivered from the factory—was very real, it had been calculable and thus acceptable.

Acceptable because she had done it for him.

Done it for love.

What he planned to do with the police car—that and all the other items of contraband that she had thus far obtained for him—was far harder for her to deal with, because, on its surface at least, if Kileen was planning what she thought he was planning, the risks against his succeeding seemed astronomical. And she could not even begin to imagine what the penalties might be.

Sally closed her eyes, listening to the steady rhythm of his breathing in the still morning air and remembering the slow, delicious lovemaking that had lulled her to sleep hours earlier; lovemaking that had been even more glorious than their first unbridled coupling of the previous morning. Only Michael Kileen could make her think of sex in such superlative terms.

But things had been different tonight too. For the lovemaking had come only after Sally had confronted him with the suspicions she had confirmed by poring through all the maps and blueprints and the dozens of news clippings that he had amassed, clippings containing detailed descriptions of the movements and protocols and security surrounding the Queen of England.

Frightened by the sheer scope of the crime she felt sure he was contemplating, and irate over Kileen's casual treatment of her love, she had demanded that he abandon his insane plan. She had expected him to be furious with her for prying, because, before she had examined Michael Kileen's papers, she had still naively believed that he was planning some sort of clever robbery while the luxurious Hotel Beverly was filled with wealthy guests and the primary attention of the city's police forces was focused on providing security for the visiting dignitaries in the public rooms.

Sally felt her face reddening as she realized just how pathetically blind her feelings for Michael Kileen had made her. Because, until tonight, she had actually believed him when he had told her he was a fucking jewel thief, that his face had been scarred in an accident. She had conjured up in her head a suave, jet-setting character, a character she now realized that she had wholly pieced together out of scenes from old romantic adventure movies.

"Jesus H. Christ!" Sally whispered the epithet in the chilly silence of the darkened room, shivering as she remembered the look that had come into in his eyes when she had confronted him with her discovery of what he was really up to and demanded that he stop because she loved him so terribly and didn't want to see him killed or imprisoned.

There had been a split second when all traces of the emotion she had been so certain he held for her had fled those hard, black eyes of his, a tiny fraction of eternity when she had been absolutely positive that Michael Kileen was going to kill her.

But then the shock of that awful instant had passed and Kileen had taken her into his arms, gently pulling her down onto the brocaded sofa and stroking her long, dark hair as he explained in a soft and reasonable voice exactly why he must go through with the thing he had planned, expressing his love for her and promising he meant to kill no one.

Shaken by the hypnotic sincerity of his words, Sally had agreed not to interfere, making him promise, however, that he would give up the dangerous life he lived, when this one thing was done, telling him too of the money she'd saved, and confessing the dream she had of the two of them taking it to a new place and starting over afresh.

And, miraculously, he had agreed.

But she must let him finish what he had started, he'd begged. Perhaps she would even even help by doing one more small favor for him.

Sally Hilton smiled now, looking down at the strange assortment of objects on the tabletop beside the sleeping man. She glanced distastefully at the stacked weapons, reaching past them to run her fingers across the golden surfaces of the two gleaming medallions he had laid out on a fold of newspaper, noting curiously that they differed from one another only by the different years inscribed on their faces.

She lifted one of the medals, surprised by its weight, and then the other, turning them both over to examine their smooth, burnished backs and wondering what he planned to do with them. After several seconds of close examination, during which she noticed that the second medallion was appreciably lighter than the first, she set them both softly back on the table, and shifted her attention to the black plastic box beside them. Reaching for the lid, she hesitated, knowing he would be angry if he suddenly awoke and caught her snooping again. Resisting the urge to open the black box, she touched his head again instead.

Letting her fingers trail through the thick crop of chestnut hair curling down the back of his neck Sally prayed that the work—his mission, he had called it—really was not as dangerous as it seemed to her. In truth, she could not understand why anyone would deliberately place themselves in such danger for some hazy political ideal like the one that he'd patiently tried to explain to her last night.

She didn't care about any of that crap.

She only knew that she loved him.

Sally gently squeezed his neck, then turned and went into the kitchen to make his morning coffee. Kileen had something very important for her to do today, and she did not want to disappoint him. Because when he left the city this time, she was going to go with him.

Sally Hilton found herself humming a snatch of a popular song as she ran cold water into the coffeemaker and, for the first time in her entire life, she realized that she was truly happy.

CHAPTER TWELVE

Foreign Objects

MICHAEL KILEEN pulled himself from beneath the rear bumper of the police car and snapped off the portable light he'd been using. It was dark in the cramped garage, and he waited for his eyes to adjust to the gloom before getting to his feet and brushing the worst of the grime from the dirt floor off the back of the grease-stained coveralls he was wearing. Crossing to a small workbench by the door, he unplugged the work light from a cracked wall socket, neatly coiled its frayed cord and hung it back on the hook where he'd found it.

The empty black explosives case, all eight of its pyramidal foam niches now empty, lay open on the bench beside the tube of quick bonding adhesive he'd been using. He gathered up those items and walked around to the open trunk of the car, reaching inside to place them beneath the thick rubber mat covering the floor. That taken care of, he slammed the trunk lid shut and walked back to the bench for the two heavy automatic pistols, which he placed beneath the front seat of the car.

The lightweight Uzi, which Duffy had been at such pains to obtain from the motorcyclists, lay on the bench with three spare mags, its dull black finish gleaming in the weak spill of light from the dirty window set high in the wall. Kileen expertly snapped the loaded magazine from the weapon and examined it with a critical eye. Then he took a tiny tube of epoxy cement from his coverall pocket and carefully applied a drop of the clear liquid to the open end of the magazine. The liquid disappeared between the two topmost bullets, and he applied another drop, then another, raising the magazine to the light and watching critically as the invisible bonds fused the forty shell casings inside into a solid mass. When he was absolutely certain that the weapon could not be fired, he replaced the magazine in the Uzi and repeated the process with each of the three spare magazines. Finally, he wrapped the gun and mags in a plastic trash bag and laid them on the backseat of the car.

His work completed, Michael Kileen stripped out of the coveralls and the thick latex gloves he wore. The coveralls he hung on a peg near the work light. The rubber gloves—one of two pairs he had purchased at a nearby hardware store—he tucked into the pocket of his denim work shirt, to be reused later. Then, whistling a tuneless melody, he left the dark garage, locking it behind him and climbing behind the wheel of Sally Hilton's innocuous old Cadillac.

As he drove along the quiet West Corona street toward the busy freeway leading back to L.A., he noticed for the first time that it was turning out to be another beautiful sunny day in Southern California.

"CUTE KID. You banging her, or what?"

Billy Quinn stared at the familiar face of the dark-haired woman behind the wheel of the gray Mercedes.

He had been walking out of school with Brenda Gaynor, who had latched onto his arm the instant he'd left his last class, clutching him possessively and talking in a soft, dreamy voice about how much better he had made her feel the night before, telling him how meeting him had changed her entire life. Billy had been trying to think of something to say that would not hurt her feelings when he had spotted the woman, who Kileen had told him would be delivering the things he needed for the evening's work.

Billy had gotten rid of the strangely subdued Brenda with the lie that he had to run some errands for his grandfather, promising to call her later tonight, then he had sprinted away across the parking lot to the Mercedes and hopped inside.

"Well?" Sally Hilton raised her eyebrows, watching approvingly as Brenda climbed into her red convertible and drove away, blowing him a kiss.

"It's none of your fucking business," snapped Billy. "You got something for me?"

"Ohhh, touchy, touchy." Sally smiled, reaching into her purse and extracting a slightly worn, blue velvet jeweler's box. He took it and opened the lid. The bright gold of the medallion Kileen had placed inside gleamed in the afternoon sunlight streaming down through the windshield.

"Okay." He snapped the lid shut and tucked the box into his jacket pocket, looking out impatiently through the windows. The parking lot was clearing rapidly as students poured out of the school, laughing and chattering, jumping into their cars and departing for their carefree weekends at the beach or the shopping malls, or just hanging about and going to the films. He spotted Kelly's distinctive yellow Mustang three rows up, but, thankfully, saw no sign of her. "Where's the trigger?" he asked.

Sally Hilton opened the Mercedes's glove box and removed a miniature garage-door remote unit nearly identical to the one that Ranjee had given him along with the set of keys to the Jaguar. Billy reached for it, but she slapped his hand away. "Now you listen very carefully," she said, suddenly all business. "This little booger contains the transmitter that sends the radio signal to the medallion, releasing the gas inside . . ."

He nodded his head wearily. "Right. I know all of that. Kileen told me last night." In fact, Kileen had badgered him about the workings of the remote, how its coded chip had been substituted with another, explaining how he must wait until exactly the right moment before activating the device. He must be absolutely certain that the Queen was in close proximity to the medallion. And that he himself was no farther than fifteen feet away from her . . . After he had explained it, the terrorist had made him repeat it all back to him. Twice.

"Fine," said Sally, tossing the remote transmitter at the impatient youngster. "You know it all."

Billy caught the transmitter and looked down at the single button control. "So I just press this when I'm ready?" he asked.

The beautiful woman glared at him from behind her flawless mask of makeup. "You can if you want to," she said huffily. "Of course the fucking thing won't work."

Billy felt the hot flush rising in his cheeks. "Oh." He turned the unit over in his hands, searching for another control. There was none. He swallowed, feeling suddenly young and foolish. "How does it work then, please?"

Sally shook her head and retrieved the unit from him, prying open the battery case with a bright pink fingernail. "First, you remove the battery," she said, dumping it on the plush velour of the seat and turning the case up so that he could see the metal contacts, and pointing to the bottom one, a flat copper strip pop-riveted into the plastic. "Then you turn this contact all the way around, so that it points toward the top of the unit instead of the bottom. That arms the device. Got it?"

Billy nodded sheepishly, accepting the remote transmitter back from her and fitting the tiny AAA battery back into its niche between the contacts. "I'm sorry," he murmured. "I'm a little nervous today."

Sally patted him on the cheek. "That's okay, Sweetums," she said indulgently. "Kileen has that effect on people." She reached into her purse again, removing a small, tissue-wrapped packet from a side pocket and unfolding the tissue to reveal a pair of dark gray cylinders of soft plastic foam.

"These are your nose filters," she said, handing the foam plugs to him. "Insert them as far up your nostrils as you can get them, just before you leave to go to the hotel. When you activate the charge in that medallion, it's going to blow out a single cloud of gas that'll knock everybody within a fifty-foot radius flat on their asses."

She grinned, secretly thrilled that Kileen finally trusted her enough to have confided the smallest details of his plan to her. Another very good sign, she thought, that his love for her was the genuine article.

"And don't forget to keep your mouth closed," she stressed. "Or else, Kileen says you'll wake up in about twenty-four hours with a killer headache, trying to explain all of this shit to some extremely pissed off Secret Service and British Intelligence agents."

Billy grinned at the pretty woman, suddenly realizing that he liked her. "I'll remember that. And thanks."

Sally acknowledged his gratitude with a little smile. "Just remember," she said, "the minute everybody's down, you start screaming bloody murder. The security people in the corridor will run in to see what's happening, and the gas should take them out too. As soon as there's plenty of confusion, then you get the hell out of there. And no heroics." She winked confidentially. "Kileen says you're a smart kid and he wants you back alive.

"There'll be two men dressed as cops waiting just outside the main lobby entrance in an LAPD police car to cover your escape. It'll look like they're arresting you in all the confusion. Don't resist. Just let them put you in the car and you'll be outta there. Any questions?"

Billy looked down at the bulky foam filters in his hand. "Yeah," he quipped, "how do I get this bloody lot out of my nose when it's all over?"

Sally punched him playfully on the shoulder. "Go on now, get out of here, kid. And good luck."

He stepped out of the car and watched her drive away, then turned and walked across the nearly empty parking lot to the green Jaguar. Christ, he was really going to do it. Him, Billy Quinn. He wondered if there'd really be as many television cameras there as Kileen had said.

As he reached the Jaguar he noticed that Kelly Huston's car was still parked near the front of the lot. He felt a sad lump building in his throat as he wondered what she would think when she saw him on television, putting the Queen of England and all her attendants to sleep.

KELLY SAT on the cafeteria patio poking listlessly at a cup of strawberry yogurt she hadn't eaten at lunch, trying, as she had all day, to keep Brian O'-Malley out of her mind.

The image of him on the balcony last night, with some girl—the sluttish Brenda Gaynor, no doubt—hiding behind the door in his bathroom had burned itself indelibly into her brain. She had deliberately cut two classes today in order to avoid seeing either of them, but still the maddening, hurtful image would not go away. She wanted to go home and take a hot bath and sleep, and she regretted having promised Sam she would meet her here after school to discuss the situation.

Kelly didn't want to discuss it. She simply no longer cared what Brian O'Malley was or what he did, nor even, for that matter, whether Thad August's brainless friends were planning to catch him in a dark place some night and beat him senseless.

As a matter of fact, she almost wished that they would.

"How's your ankle?"

She looked up to see Sam standing over her with an armload of books and a banana. Without waiting for her reply, the dark-haired girl dumped the books onto the table, dropped onto a bench and began peeling her banana.

"My ankle still hurts, thank you." Kelly looked down at her left foot, which was swollen beneath her sock from the sprain she'd gotten last night. Actually, Sam and Stanley had tried to force her to go the emergency room at Cedars, but that would have meant a call from the hospital to Chuck or Katherine, as she was still technically underage until her eighteenth birthday.

So, instead of going for an X ray and a lot of clumsy explanations, she had sneaked back home and picked up her car, then gone to Sam's house, where she had spent an hour soaking the ankle in a scalding bath, along with the rest of her bruised and aching body—for she had gotten more than a twisted ankle before it was all over.

After she had sneaked out of the backyard behind the dilapidated West Corona house, she had been chased by a slobbering dog. And then she was forced to hide in the bushes for almost half an hour before Stanley and Sam had returned to pick her up—good old dependable Stanley having gotten lost in his haste to distance himself from the suspicious cop. Then, later, running across the Major's veranda in the dark, she had tripped and fallen . . .

"Have you decided what to do yet?" Samantha's mouth was unattractively crammed full of banana. "About what we found out last night, I mean?"

Kelly shook her head, annoyed. "I just want to forget the whole thing, Sam. Besides," she added, "we didn't find out anything. Not really."

Samantha stared at her. "What are you talking about? Stanley says those guys were planning *something* . . . And they have a police car stashed in that garage in West Corona, for God's sake."

"Well, it's just a wild guess, but I would say it's painfully evident that they actually are undercover policemen," Kelly replied petulantly. "Wasn't that Stanley's *previous* brilliant theory, by the way?"

"I'm sure." Sam tossed the banana peel into a KEEP PACIFIC ACADEMY GREEN basket and dropped her voice to an excited whisper. "*Four* undercover cops, every one of them with a heavy Irish accent?"

Kelly shrugged. "Well, it works in Boston," she said, fighting to dismiss the terrible hurt and anger that had been nagging at her all day.

"Kelly, this is not Boston . . ."

"Why Samantha, you notice everything," Kelly spat back nastily. "Look, frankly I don't care who Brian O'Malley's friends are or what they're doing, okay? If I never see him again it will be too soon."

Sam looked around the deserted patio, then leaned closer, her breath reeking of banana. "Kelly, Stanley thinks they're probably Irish terrorists," she said.

Kelly began to laugh. "Stanley thinks? Samantha, get real. Stanley is a poor, dopey idiot who likes to cut up frogs and drives a Yugo. Brian O'Malley may just be another horny asshole, just like Thad August and every other macho jerk at this school, but if there's one thing he is definitely not, it's an Irish terrorist. Irish terrorists killed his parents . . . Do you really think he'd join up with them?"

"Never," said Sam, shaking her long, dark curls emphatically. "That is, if he really is Brian O'Malley. I mean, the *real* Brian O'Malley."

Kelly felt a sickening wave of dread clutch at the pit of her stomach. "What do you mean?"

"Think about it, Kelly." Sam's voice was filled with excitement now. "Brian dyes his hair. And he doesn't seem to know anything at all about any of the classes he's in at school. He sneaks out late at night to meet a bunch of mean-looking Irish guys who have a police car hidden away in a garage out in the Tulies . . . What if he's not really Brian O'Malley at all, but some imposter the Irish terrorists sent here to take his place?"

"No way! That is absolutely the most ridiculous thing I ever heard!" Kelly laughed, but she felt her disbelief in the nerd's radical theory crumbling as huge blocks of logic clicked into place in her mind. *Yes, Kelly, and what about that old, scarred bullet wound he made you promise to keep secret from the Major? Or the way he seemed to turn into another person when he got into the fight with those two muggers—not just because he somehow took them both down, but the way he did it—even his voice changed, his whole way of talking. And then there was that weird, hauntingly sad speech he made in history yesterday . . . almost like he was . . . one of them.*

"Well?" Samantha was impatiently tapping her long nails on the scarred redwood tabletop.

"The Major!" said Kelly. "What about the Major? In the first place, he's English, not Irish. My God, Sam, he's going to be decorated by the Queen herself. Do you think he'd let Irish terrorists replace his own grandson?"

"Maybe the Major doesn't know," Samantha postulated. "When was the last time he actually saw Brian before he came here?"

The weight of Sam's logic was devastating. Kelly tried desperately to think back to the day they'd all had tea with the Major. Hadn't he told them it had been years and years since he had last seen Brian? Her head was beginning to throb with all the twisted strands of information. She couldn't remember what the old man had said.

But most of all, she didn't want any of it to be true. For if it was, she knew they would have do something about it. Tell someone. The police. The government. Someone.

"What are we going to do?" Sam was staring at her.

Kelly shook her head helplessly. She didn't want anything bad to happen to Brian.

Even after last night she still believed she was in love with him. Though she desperately didn't want to be.

It hurt far too much.

Love.

LOVE.

Brenda Gaynor turned the soft, strange word over and over in her mind, remembering the night before, trying to recapture in her mind the warm security of Brian's strong arms wrapped tightly around her, protecting her, his hand softly stroking her hair as she had poured out her anguish. And then, today at school, blushing at his first sight of her, walking quietly by her side with a dreamy, faraway look while she had told him all the things she was going to do to make him happy.

She sighed, remembering the gentle way he had squeezed her hand just before he'd had to leave to take care of something for his grandfather.

Love.

Brenda Gaynor loved Brian O'Malley.

She had left school in a daze, driving down to the Beverly Center—her favorite place in the whole world—and parking the red Mercedes in the vast garage, then riding one of the gleaming, neon-trimmed escalators up into the huge, eight-story mall to wander the marble corridors in search of something extra special to wear for him tonight. She smiled a little secret smile, thinking about all the trouble she'd gone to with her clothes last night; clothes he'd barely seen at all.

Brenda had shopped for more than two hours before she had found the perfect outfit, a dazzling black velvet pants suit that fit her size three figure like a glove. When she wore it tonight, Brian O'Malley would be proud to have her on his arm, knowing that every other male they passed would be jealous.

Exhausted from her mini–shopping spree, she sat now in a far corner of the glittering Food Fair up on the eighth floor by the cineplex, sipping a Venetian ice decorated with a sprig of mint, and wondering if she had time to get her nails done at the Japanese salon down on four. Brian hadn't said exactly what time he would call her tonight, but she thought it would be late, since he had to go somewhere first with his grandfather . . .

"Hey, Brenda."

She looked up to see Thad August standing over her, hoped he wouldn't start in on her again. She had made it perfectly clear yesterday that it was over between them, had already suffered his angry accusations once.

"Hi, Thad." Brenda kept her voice deliberately neutral, wary of his volatile temper.

"Can I sit down for a minute?" he asked.

Surprised, she nodded. "I've got to go in just a minute, Thad . . ."

"Look," he said, pulling out a chair, sitting and resting his elbows on the table, "I just wanted to say I was sorry for the way I acted yesterday . . . I mean, calling you names and things. I didn't really mean it." Thad August smiled abashedly. "You know my dumb temper."

Brenda frowned. She had never seen this side of August before. Hadn't even known he had such a side. Always when they'd been together before, he had been demanding, sullen . . . "It's okay," she said warily. "Sometimes things just don't work out."

He looked genuinely relieved. "Thanks, Bren. I mean, I didn't want there to be any hard feelings or anything."

Brenda smiled generously. "No hard feelings."

August seemed to relax. He leaned back in his chair, looking around at the passing parade of chic Asian and Arab shoppers in their one-off designer outfits. "So, you just catching a little shopping on your own?" he asked innocently.

Brenda smiled with relief. "Yes, want to see?" She opened her bag and held up the new outfit.

"Yeah, that's great. Something special?"

Brenda wrinkled her nose. "I've got a date later."

August smiled. "Let me guess. Brian O'Malley, that new English guy?"

"Irish," she corrected. "He's from Northern Ireland." She leaned forward, confident now that Thad really wasn't going to make any trouble. "I think I'm really in love with him, Thad. I mean, the real thing." Brenda hesitated and tried to look solemn. "That's why I can't go out with you anymore. I mean, you and I had some really good times together, but this is, like, totally different." She smiled. "Besides, half the girls at school are hot for you. Now you can give some of them a chance."

Thad August stood and leaned across the table to kiss her cheek. "I understand, Bren. And I'm really happy for you. You're a great girl."

Brenda's face lit up. "Are you really? I mean I didn't want to hurt you . . ."

He winked and grinned. "Hey, Bren, you know me. I mean, shit bounces off of me. And if it's true love . . ." He shrugged helplessly. "Well, you know. Be happy."

"Thanks, Thad. I mean, really."

Thad August turned and walked away from her, trying to keep the murderous rage from boiling up inside of him until he was out of her sight.

He'd show her true fucking love.

Now that he knew for sure that Jake and the guys could find that cocksucker when he came out for his date tonight, Brian fucking O'Malley was dead meat.

And after that, after they had turned the bastard's face into five pounds of bleeding ground round, the little bitch would come crawling back to Thad on her goddamn knees.

CHAPTER THIRTEEN

The Judas Kiss

"WELL, WELL, BRIAN, I must say you look quite the handsome young fellow this evening."

Billy, who had been leaning against the mantelpiece pretending to examine a portrait of a languid lady in a lacy Victorian dress, turned to see the Major entering the high-ceilinged living room. The old fellow was turned out in black tie and tails, a row of miniature campaign medals hanging from colorful ribbons over his left breast.

"You're the one who looks splendid, Major." Billy looked down at his own stark black suit, which was stiff and uncomfortable, making him feel like a waiter in a fancy eatery. "I'm afraid I feel a little strange in formal dress," he confessed.

The Major beamed, crossing the room to a wooden cart and carefully filling two tiny glasses from a crystal decanter of amber-colored liquid. "Well, it'll soon grow on you, my boy. A mark of civilization," he harrumphed. "When I was serving in India we all dressed for dinner every evening. Set us apart from the natives, you see. Beastly hot at times, though. I expect the poor woggies thought we were all off our heads."

Billy forced an appreciative laugh as the Major returned with the glasses, holding one out to him and sniffing the other appreciatively. "Lovely sherry. Lovely." He raised his glass. "To your first suit of evening clothes, young man. May you wear them in good health."

Billy nodded, sipping the sherry and finding the taste far too sweet for his liking. Nevertheless, he raised his own glass. "May we drink to your promotion, Brigadier?"

The old man flushed with pleasure and they drank together. "Well," said the Major, setting his glass on the mantel and digging into his coat pocket for a round gold watch. "Suppose we'd better be on our way." He winked enormously. "Don't want to keep Her Majesty waiting, eh? Ranjee should be round with the car by now, I imagine . . ."

"Major, before we go, may I ask a favor?"

Queally-Smythe, who was already moving toward the door, was stopped by the sudden seriousness of the youngster's tone. "Why certainly, Brian. What is it?"

Billy Quinn took a deep breath. "Well, sir," he began, repeating verbatim the speech that Kileen had made him memorize, "I know from my studies that one is entitled to display all of one's honors on occasions such as this evening's ceremony and dinner . . ."

Queally-Smythe flushed. "That is correct," he said, tapping the military medals pinned to his chest. "Damned nuisance, of course . . ."

"Well, the thing is," Billy continued, reaching into his pocket and extracting the blue velvet case that Sally Hilton had given him, "my mother was awarded this before her death . . . And I thought you might wear it for her this evening." Billy cast his eyes down to the floor. "She'd hoped to be presented at court someday herself, but she'll never have the opportunity now, you see."

The old man took the box with trembling hands and opened it to reveal the handsome gold medallion nestled on a shimmering blue ribbon. Tears filled his pale eyes as he read the inscription. "Best All-Around Horse-woman, Northern Ireland Equestrian Society, 1993 . . . I don't know what to say, Brian." He sniffled. "I'm simply overcome."

"I know she would have wanted you to have it, sir," said Billy, despising himself for having to play with the old man's emotions this way. "I realize it would be a bit unusual to wear another person's decoration," he continued, "and that it's not actually a military award, but I was hoping that, just for tonight—"

"Say no more," said the Major. He lifted the heavy medallion from the box by its ribbon and carefully hung it around his neck. "I shall be honored beyond words to wear this before Her Majesty, and damn the man who calls it improper." He winked and clasped the boy in a tight, emotional hug. "After all," he chuckled, "I'm just an old duffer anyway, eh?"

Billy, his heart thumping wildly, bowed his head, not daring to look into the old man's face, for Kileen had made it clear that everything depended on this moment. "Thank you," he murmured, praying the old fellow wouldn't notice his quaking voice.

"I'm afraid your mother and I weren't as . . . close as I would have wished," said the Major, stepping back and dabbing at his eyes with a handkerchief.

"She thought very highly of you, sir," Billy said. "In fact," he added unnecessarily, "I believe she had planned to invite you for a long visit."

"God rest her soul, and that of your poor father too, Brian." James Queally-

Smythe blew his nose into his handkerchief and dug out the watch again.

"My word, look at the time. We must go." He turned and strode proudly toward the door with the huge gold medallion bouncing against his thin chest.

Billy Quinn paused to wipe a tear from the corner of his eye, telling himself it was caused by the irritation of the foam plugs he'd jammed into his nostrils. Then he marched boldly out of the room behind the Major, the shape of the tiny remote transmitter in his trouser pocket burning against his leg.

"DO YOU HAVE TO GO so soon?"

Kileen smiled, straightening his tie in the mirror above her dressing table. "I'm afraid so, love," he said.

"But you promise you'll come back for me?"

He saw the look of concern in the pretty face floating above his own reflection in the mirror. "Yes," he smiled. "I will come back." He turned to face her, thinking how beautiful she looked in the sheer black dressing gown she had pulled up around her shoulders. "Come and give us a kiss, then. For luck."

She hurried into his arms, raising her lips eagerly to his. He kissed her for a long moment, savoring the feel of her ripe body against him, regretting that she was never to be his.

Sally Hilton sighed softly as he pulled away, then reached up to take her chin in one strong hand, cradling the back of her head in the other. Her eyelids fluttered open as she realized what he was about to do, and she looked at him like a wounded bird that knows it is beyond salvation and must be put out of its misery.

Kileen moved his hands quickly, breaking her neck painlessly and mercifully, catching her limp body against his chest, then effortlessly lifting her in his arms, marveling at how light she felt as he laid her on her water bed.

Poor Sally, he thought as he straightened his jacket and left the silent bedroom. So many, many things would lead directly back to her, once the massive manhunt was underway. What else could he have done?

It occurred to him as he stepped out into the hallway and locked the door of her condo behind him that anyone who had just seen the act he had committed would think him mad. She had reminded him so much of Ginnie Keenan.

CHAPTER FOURTEEN

Killing Ground

THE SILVER BENTLEY'S engine was a whisper as the big car glided through the unusual evening traffic jam on Wilshire Boulevard, slowing at the police barricade blocking the entrance to the Hotel Beverly. Ranjee opened a window, and a bullet-headed man in a dark suit leaned into the car and scrutinized the occupants. "Your names, please."

The Major told him their names, adding importantly that he was one of the evening's honors recipients, and handing the guard his invitation. The security man nodded noncommittally, then stood and walked to a makeshift desk set up on the hood of an unmarked black sedan. He checked the invitation against a list, then returned and passed it back into the car. "Thank you, Brigadier, and congratulations." He smiled, touching two fingers to his forehead in salute. Then, turning to Ranjee, he pointed down the hotel drive and said "You may drop these gentlemen by the front entrance and then follow the signs to the reserved parking area on the right. If you intend to wait for your passengers, please remain with your vehicle at all times."

Ranjee nodded, and the Bentley crept forward past a barricaded sidewalk area filled with a crowd of jeering onlookers, several of whom carried crudely lettered signs demanding unconditional freedom for Northern Ireland.

Billy felt a shiver of pride shoot down his spine as he looked out at the demonstrators, knowing exactly what they were thinking about the privileged toffs arriving in their limos for an opulent evening with the Queen; an evening paid for with the sweat and blood of people like the rabble on the sidewalk. *Don't worry, my friends,* he thought, *they'll all soon be laying about on their noble arses!*

"Quite a show, eh?"

Billy turned away from the window to see the Major beaming at him.

"Yes, sir," he murmured. *But nothing compared to the show that's to come. Sorry you won't be able to see it, Major. You're really an okay geezer.*

The car proceeded slowly to the end of the long drive, passing through a larger crowd of cheering spectators. These were smiling, and many were waving tiny Union Jacks, and Billy wondered how the police had managed to separate them out from the protestors. His palms were damp, and he wiped them on the legs of his formal trousers as the Bentley pulled into line behind a string of limousines. Ahead, he could already see the glare of television lights and a nearly continuous sparkle of strobes from the cameras of press photographers. *By God, Kileen hadn't been lying. There must be hundreds of reporters here.*

"KELLY, we'll never get through this."

Sam sat in the Mustang's passenger seat, looking down Wilshire at the tangle of stalled and honking cars in which they were stuck. They had been in this same spot for a good fifteen minutes now, and they were still more than three blocks from the Hotel Beverly.

"We've got to get through," breathed Kelly. Not knowing for certain the exact time or location of the state dinner, she had finally gone up to the old mansion at the top of the canyon, taking Sam along, to explain Stanley's terrorist theory to the Major. But Queally-Smythe's house had been empty when they'd arrived. Returning to her own house, she and Sam had found Chuck and Katherine and their friends gathered around the giant-screen television set in the playroom, drinking Dom and gushing over the fact that their distinguished new business partner was about to be decorated by the Queen herself.

Then the TV screen had filled with pictures of the Queen's arrival at Los Angeles International, showing her stopping before a line of dignitaries. Pausing for several seconds to talk to one man, moving down the line to address another . . .

Kelly had stood silently in the doorway with Stanley's stupid terrorist theory running rampant through her mind. The television picture had changed to a different angle, and she saw the nervous men in dark suits hovering behind the monarch, their restless eyes darting about helplessly. She saw clearly that the woman they were guarding was incredibly vulnerable. For, if any one of the men she was talking to had suddenly decided to reach out and do something, nothing the nervous security men could do would stop it . . .

And suddenly Kelly had known for certain. Known why Brian O'Malley had been sent to Los Angeles. Known she had to stop him. Before he did something horrible.

Her voice trembling, she had asked what time the Major was to be decorated, but no one had known exactly. She had run into her bedroom, with Sam trailing behind her, asking stupid questions she'd had no time to answer as she ripped through the contents of her closet in search of something to wear.

The traffic was not going to move any time soon.

Kelly stood and looked out over the top of the Mustang's windshield, then she opened her door and stepped out onto the street. Samantha stared at her, dumbfounded. "Where are you going dressed like that?"

"I've got to find Brian," she said. "Take the car back to your house and wait for me."

"Kelly, you can't even walk in those heels," Sam protested.

"I'll manage," Kelly said. She slipped off the satin evening pumps, gathered up the skirt of the pink prom dress she'd hurriedly thrown on back at the house and started down the sidewalk in her stocking feet.

"They're not going to let you in there," Samantha yelled over the traffic noise. "Stanley said you have to have an invitation or something."

THE FILTERS in Billy's nose were driving him mad, and he fought the urge to sniff, as each previous attempt to do so had simply pulled the foam plugs higher into his nostrils. He couldn't imagine how he was ever going to get the damn things out.

The Bentley was waiting on the drive behind a white Lexus carrying a miserable-looking couple who had driven themselves and now obviously wished they'd hired a limo. There was an embarrassed commotion on the carpeted walkway as a red-jacketed valet was summoned, and the couple finally started for the hotel entrance. The woman elbowed her husband sharply, and they both smiled for the cameras.

The Lexus was driven away, and the Bentley moved forward once more, stopping beneath the blaze of the TV lights. A uniformed attendant hurried to open the door, and Billy Quinn stepped out and blinked in bewilderment at the mob of media reporters lining the walkway. Then the Major was beside him, taking his elbow and propelling him toward the open doors to the hotel's glittering main lobby.

Inside, a crowd of several hundred splendidly dressed and bejeweled people were standing around, sipping champagne and talking too loudly. Billy nervously scanned the room, picking out at least a dozen dark-suited secu-

rity agents circulating at the fringes of the crowd. The entrances to the hotel's outdoor patio, he saw, had been barricaded with an unbroken line of
tables draped in white linen, which extended to the nearest elevator. Uniformed guards stood at every doorway leading into the lobby.

As he and the Major passed through a set of airport-style metal detectors,
someone stepped from the crowd, and Billy recognized the long, equine
face of Applewhite, the priggish Foreign Office official who had inter-
viewed him the day before.

"Brigadier Queally-Smythe, so good to see you again." Applewhite nearly
tripped over himself in his haste to attach himself to the Major. "Do allow
me to escort you directly up to the Oak Room while I explain how the ceremony is to be managed," he gushed, leading the old fellow away.

Billy, who had seemingly been forgotten in the rush, stood blinking at
their departing backs. He felt a hand on his elbow and turned to see
Michael Kileen smiling at him, a glass of champagne in his hand. Billy's
mouth dropped open, and he stared at the terrorist.

"Don't tarry too long, Brian," Kileen said pleasantly. "You'll want a place
in the front row to watch your old gramps getting his decoration."

"Jesus Christ!" Billy's knees were suddenly trembling. "How the fuck did
you get in here?" he whispered.

Kileen grinned, sticking a thumb under a hand-lettered self-adhesive label stuck to his lapel. "Aw, gettin' inta this shindig was a piecea cake," he
said in a thick New York accent. "My name's Joey Krampton, import-ex-
port. We do a helluva lotta business with the Limeys; mostly plastics and
small appliances right now, but we're lookin' inta athletic equipment . . ."

Kileen gestured at the crowd of drinkers, a few of whom were already
drifting toward the heavily guarded elevators. "Acourse guys like me don't
get invited ta the big fancy doin's upstairs," he said. "For that ya gotta have
heavy connections, like your gramps." Kileen held up his glass in a mock
toast. "They just give us bums down here in the bleachers a coupla watered-
down drinks and a few cheese crackers." He jerked his chin toward the line
of banquet tables, adding, "If we're real lucky we might get ta see her royal
nibs for about ten seconds when they hustle her through from the garage
behind that line of tables, then it's the old heave-ho."

Billy stared at the narrow corridor formed by the flimsy looking tables,
and Kileen leaned closer, lowering his voice to a confidential tone. "They
got a solid wall of concrete blocks laid four deep under them tables," he
whispered. "Ain't that a pisser?"

The terrorist straightened and looked across the lobby. "You'd better go
now, Billy," he smiled. "They're waiting for you."

Billy nodded dumbly and stumbled away after the Major and Apple-white, who were waiting in a short line before an elevator. As he got closer, he saw that two alert security men with hand-held electronic wands were efficiently scanning the suit and gown of a glittering middle-aged couple.

"Now this will all be quite simple, really," Applewhite was explaining to Queally-Smythe. "Those to be honored will be lined up before the podium. Her Majesty will approach the honorees with an aide who will be carrying the decorations, certificates and so forth. When she stops before you, your name will be read out, and she will present your decoration." The aide smiled knowledgeably. "It is, of course, proper at that time to bow. Please do not speak to Her Majesty unless she first addresses you . . ." Applewhite smiled, showing his long teeth, "which she will most certainly do in your case, Brigadier. The proper form of address at that time is, as I'm sure you are aware, Your Majesty, and thereafter ma'am."

Queally-Smythe's silver mane was bobbing up and down excitedly. "Yes, yes, of course . . . Understand completely . . ." The elevator doors sighed open, and the waiting couple were allowed to enter. The short line moved forward, and the Major turned to look back at Billy, who stood frozen to the richly patterned carpet ten feet away. "Come along now, lad," called the Major. "Mustn't be late for Her Majesty."

His heart thundering in his chest, Billy stepped forward to join the old man. The elevator doors closed, and the security men began scanning the next couple in line, a tanned and handsome man with a pouting blonde in a skimpy cocktail dress in tow. Billy stared at the tanned man, who he suddenly realized was a famous film actor.

The nearest of the security men, an expressionless six-footer, glanced over at the gawking youngster, his cynical gray eyes seeming to burn through the boy's flimsy disguise. Billy felt a drop of perspiration sliding down his forehead, and he was absolutely certain that the security man was staring at his clumsily dyed hair. The actor asked a silly question. His girl-friend giggled, and the agent turned back to smile at her.

A BLOCK from the hotel drive, Kelly Huston leaned heavily against a news-paper vending machine. Her feet were burning from having walked so far, and her sprained ankle was beginning to swell.

From where she stood, Kelly could see that the boulevard in front of the hotel had been blocked off by police cars with flashing roof lights. Two uni-formed cops were diverting all but a few cars in the slowly moving traffic stream down a side street. Her heart sank as she saw, just beyond the road-block, the yellow crowd-control barriers lining the sidewalk, making it clear that it was not going to be possible for her to simply walk up to the hotel and go inside, as she had planned.

"Dammit!" Cursing her own stupidity, Kelly tried to force her mind to work, despite the threatening flood of tears welling up in her eyes. She had envisioned herself breezing into the hotel lobby in her expensive dress, just as she and Chuck and Katherine had done two months earlier when they had attended a television awards banquet there.

On that occasion, no one had challenged them until they had actually reached the doors of the mezzanine-floor banquet room where the dinner was being held.

Tonight's security at the Hotel Beverly was obviously far different from what it had been at the cable awards banquet. But, if she could only get inside and find Brian, she believed, she could talk him into leaving with her, before something terrible happened.

Before she was forced to tell someone what he and his friends were about to do.

A car horn blared almost in her ear, making her jump. She looked up to see a black BMW sedan attempting to edge through the traffic along the curb. A bespectacled, red-faced man in evening clothes stuck his head out through the open driver's window and waved angrily at the taxi blocking his way.

For a long moment, Kelly stared at the man's slightly familiar face. Then, bending quickly, she stuffed her swollen feet into the satin heels and ran into the street. "Mr. Kinsella," she called, hurrying up to the black car.

Stanley Kinsella, Sr., turned to squint through his thick accountant's lenses at the pretty young girl standing in the gutter in her pink evening dress. "I . . . I'm sorry," he stammered nervously. "Do I know you?"

"My name is Kelly Huston," she said breathlessly. "I'm a friend of Stanley's, from Pacific Academy. I saw you there last month, on Parents' Day."

The elder Kinsella squinted harder, furrowing his shiny brow. Then an attractive dark-haired woman in a shimmering blue cocktail dress leaned across the BMW's front seat and looked through the window at Kelly.

"Of course, Kelly. You're the girl from biology. Stanley talks about you all the time," said Doris Kinsella. Her smile faded as she took in Kelly's reddened eyes and pained expression. "Is something wrong, dear? Why on earth are you standing out there in the street?"

Without waiting for Kelly's reply, Doris Kinsella elbowed her husband sharply in the ribs. "Well, don't just sit there gawking like an idiot, Stanley. Let the poor girl in here."

Kinsella mumbled an apology and pushed a switch and the BMW's back doors unlocked. Kelly tumbled gratefully onto the soft leather seat, and a moment later the car began to move. "Thank you," she whispered.

"Now," said Doris Kinsella, swiveling around to regard the distraught girl, "What happened to you, dear?"

Kelly stammered out a disjointed story about meeting her parents at the hotel, and a flat tire, as the car made its way to the police barrier. "Well, don't you worry about a single thing," said Doris Kinsella, producing a thick envelope from her handbag. She leaned across the car and kissed Kinsella's ear. "Now that Stanley's the president of the studio, everyone wants us at their cocktail parties. You'll just be our guest until we find your parents."

"THIS WILL JUST take a moment, sir," said the security agent, in a polite Yorkshire accent. Applewhite and the Major had already been scanned and admitted to the waiting elevator. Now it was Billy's turn. The agent raised the electronic wand and scanned downward from the boy's left shoulder to his knees, started back up along his right trouser leg . . .

Beeeeeeppp!!!

Billy nearly fainted as the wand emitted a shrill electronic tone and a blinking red diode began to flash on its handle.

The Major and Applewhite, who had been explaining some detail about the ceremony and the state dinner to follow, looked out from the elevator.

Fucked! Billy's mind screamed at him. *I'm fucked!*

"Got something in your pocket, have you, sir?" The security man was staring down at his trousers, and from the corner of his eye Billy could see the second agent edging nearer, his sharp eyes suddenly alert.

"K . . . keys," Billy stammered, fumbling in his pocket. "Just my keys." He held up the silvery Jaguar key ring with the tiny transmitter attached.

"I'll just have those for a moment, then, if you don't mind, sir." The agent's flat, businesslike tone made it absolutely clear that the politely worded request was not a request at all but an order. Billy handed over the keys, feeling another greasy drop of sweat roll down his forehead.

The security man passed the set of keys to his partner, a squat, balding man with the ugly face of a pug boxer. The second man turned the key ring over and over in his hand, then held the radio transmitter to his ear and shook it vigorously.

Jesus Christ, don't press that button. Please, keep your fat fucking finger away from it! Billy, his eyes fixed in terror on the agent's pudgy hand, was vaguely aware of Applewhite and the Major watching him from the open elevator door, their conversation momentarily suspended, the golden equestrian medallion gleaming like a beacon from the old man's starched shirt front.

"Now, then, anything else in your pockets?" Billy ripped his terrified gaze from the keys to find the first agent closely scrutinizing him. He shook his head dumbly, and the man squatted and resumed his scan, expertly running the electronic wand up between Billy's legs, then down his back. "Thank you, sir," he said, straightening.

The tall security man nodded to the second agent, who reached across and pressed the keys back into Billy's damp palm. The shorter man's ugly countenance split into a broad grin and he winked at the boy. "Now, then, nothing to be nervous about, my boy," he whispered jovially. "They tell me Her Majesty hasn't bitten anybody's head off for years."

The little man clapped him solidly on the back, and Billy stumbled into the waiting elevator, his knees wobbling so badly beneath him he felt sure they might give way. Applewhite and the Major were once again engaged in earnest conversation as the metal doors hissed closed.

Billy looked down at his clenched fist, willing his fingers to relax, and staring at the tiny black box dangling from the shiny ring. *Fucking Kileen!* his benumbed brain whispered inside his skull.

Bloody fucking brilliant Michael Kileen!

MICHAEL KILEEN was in a tight space. With the jacket and trousers of his conservative blue business suit turned inside out to protect the fabric from the grime, and his hands and the toes of his shiny oxfords capped incongruously with the pink rubber gloves that both protected them against scuffing and allowed his feet and fingers to grip the sides of the metal conduit, he looked comically like a ragged beggar's monkey as he slithered inch by painful inch up the narrow ventilation duct from the lobby to the sealed mezzanine floor above.

Reaching the horizontal branch that was his goal, he levered himself up onto his belly and flopped panting into a rectangular tunnel of cold metal that stretched away into the darkness ahead. The new passage was even smaller than the one he had just left, forcing him to keep his arms extended before him as he mentally reviewed the maze of branching tunnels that lay ahead. The glow of numerals from his watch was the only light in the pitch-blackness of the duct, and he twisted his wrist around awkwardly to gaze at the dial. Ten minutes. Fifteen at the most, if he was to be in position.

The omnipresent roar of the building's powerful air conditioners thrummed all around him, making it hard to think clearly. Cold, pressurized air crushed in on him from all sides, making his head throb, numbing his fingers and toes and draining the heat from his legs and torso. Driving the claustrophobic thoughts of the consequences that would follow if he took a wrong turn or encountered a section of ducting smaller than specified in the builder's blueprints, he forced himself forward into the darkness, for there was no other way.

As he inched along, Kileen allowed himself a tight, painful grin, picturing the bewildered expression on the faces of the smug government types as they tried later to reconstruct how he had penetrated their "sterile" security floor. Actually, it had been quite simple, after he had determined that the impossible forty-foot ascent up the narrow ventilation duct was really quite possible using elementary rock-climbing techniques. It had simply been a matter of substituting the sticky rubber gloves on his hands and feet for the metal crampons used on rock. And, of course, of getting past the idea that there were no ledges or safety ropes to break one's fall, should the worst happen.

Following his last-minute reconnaissance of the Hotel Beverly the previous day, the terrorist had briefly considered several other options, all of which had included making his way to an upper floor and then coming down onto the sealed mezzanine from above—the stairwells on the higher floors had to remain accessible in case of fire. But he had found the doors to the desired floor all heavily guarded, making such an approach unfeasible for a lone man.

Because, even if he could somehow manage to overcome one or more guards, Kileen knew that any disturbance whatsoever in the stairwells would bring the whole security force down on him. Similarly, he had toyed with the idea of coming down the outside of the building on the window-cleaners' scaffold. But the presence on the roof of sharpshooters armed with high-powered rifles had quickly ruled out that possibility as well, leaving only the ventilation duct as a viable route for entering the mezzanine floor undetected.

So, disguised as Joey Krampton, an identity verified by several months' worth of friendly correspondence between the British Trade Delegation in New York and several large orders of British goods sent out from temporary offices set up in Boston and Los Angeles by his millionaire financier in Spain, Michael Kileen had arrived at the cocktail reception on the hotel's ground floor armed with a proper invitation.

From there, it had been a relatively simple matter to slip into the janitor's closet in the lobby men's room, fix his clothes and boost himself up through the false ceiling to an inspection panel leading into the air-conditioning ducts.

A shimmering reflection flickered against the metal walls ahead and slightly to his right, just beyond the point where the duct branched off into two more channels. Kileen breathed a bit more easily and shoved himself ahead, for his greatest fear had been that there would be no light burning in the room he had chosen as his entry point to the sealed floor.

FRANCIS DUFFY, his stomach straining against the buttons of the dark blue uniform shirt, sat behind the wheel of the black-and-white police car, which was parked halfway along a line of official vehicles across the street from the driveway leading to the hotel entrance. No one had noticed as they had pulled into the space, although he had been instructed to say that they had been sent along for traffic and crowd control, if they were challenged. That and the sergeant's stripes he wore, according to Kileen, should be more than adequate to deter anything more than casual scrutiny, as LAPD units had been drawn from all over the huge city to cover this event.

Earlier, Duffy had seen Kileen drive by in the gray Mercedes and, just moments ago, he'd watched the old film director's distinctive silver Bentley pull up to the hotel entrance. The big man looked at his watch, surprised to see that it was almost time. He closed his eyes, running down his instructions once more. According to the primary plan, sometime within the next fifteen to twenty minutes, he should hear a loud explosion from the hotel. At that instant, Duffy was to drive the police car directly across the lawn to the front door and pick up Billy Quinn as he ran outside. Then, with the boy safely in the car, he would activate the remote transmitter clipped to the sun visor above his head, setting off the charges Kileen had strategically placed in the lobby. As the explosives went off, he would turn on the police car's lights and siren and speed away in the ensuing confusion.

Simple enough . . . if everything went as planned.

On the other hand, if the carefully laid plan went bad—and wasn't that usually the way of it?—then things would get very dicey. For, although there was a backup plan, Duffy didn't think it had a whore's prayer of succeeding.

"I still don't see how he's going to blow up the Queen without getting himself blown up as well," said Tumelty.

Duffy looked over at his young companion, who was staring out the window at the mob of people and the television cameras. "I told you," he growled. "He'll drop to the floor the instant before he triggers the bomb. With any luck at all, the blast will leave him untouched and he'll run out in the confusion."

Tumelty looked doubtful. "It's daft, if you ask me."

"I didn't hear anybody asking you," Duffy said.

"Yeah, Francis, but what if the security grabs him as he runs out?"

"That's what we've got this for." Duffy pointed to the garage door opener clipped to the sun visor above his head. "If the lad isn't out within two minutes, we're still to drive directly up to the front doors and detonate the charges that Kileen's laid about in the lobby and among all the TV trucks . . ."

"It stinks," said Dermot Tumelty. "Who knows if another blast will give the boy-o a chance to go free? What if he's running through the lobby as one of them bombs goes off?"

Duffy sighed. "I suppose you've a better idea."

"Why not just run inside and get him? After all, we're dressed as cops, ain't we?"

Duffy shook his big head. "Kileen said absolutely not."

Tumelty spat out through the open window. "Well then, I say fuck Michael Kileen. It's not his ass they'll have in there, is it?"

Duffy stared at his slight young companion. The little wanker might have more balls than brains, but when he got right down to it, he thought, Dermot Tumelty might have been the son he'd never had. "We'll just see what happens," said the big man, glancing again at his watch.

CHAPTER FIFTEEN

Last Chances

BECAUSE THEY WERE INVITED only for the low-security consular reception in the lobby, and not the state dinner, the Kinsellas encountered no difficulty whatsoever in bringing Kelly Huston into the hotel with them.

As they entered the lobby, a jolly fat woman wearing a straw hat with little British flags stuck in the band took them in charge, leading them to a table manned by two smiling embassy secretaries. After glancing at the invitation proffered by Mr. Kinsella, the women used a red marking pen to write each of their names on a paper name tag, then pointed them to the bar and tables laden with drab English canapés.

Kelly was the last to get her tag, which said HI, MY NAME IS KELLY. She stuck it to the bodice of her dress and turned, intending to tell Doris she was going to look for her parents. The couple, however, were surrounded by a little cluster of Hollywood people. The men were all stepping up to pump the slightly bewildered ex-accountant's hand, the women oohing and aahing over Doris's dress. And so the girl slipped into the milling crowd in search of Brian O'Malley.

After two hurried circuits of the crowded room, she determined that Brian was not there. She asked a passing waiter where the honors ceremony was being held. Her heart sank as he pointed to a bank of elevators guarded by a phalanx of stern-looking men in dark suits. To her great relief, the waiter informed her that the Queen had not yet gone upstairs, but that she was expected to be passing through the lobby in a few minutes.

Snatching a glass of ginger ale from the waiter's tray, Kelly drifted closer to the elevators, gauging her chances of talking her way past the guards, wondering desperately how much time was left until the Queen arrived, and whether the ceremony would take place before or after the dinner.

Her thoughts were interrupted by a sudden commotion at the rear of the lobby. The noisy buzz of conversation in the room suddenly died. Kelly looked around to see everyone crowding toward the long line of tables flanking the far wall, the backs and shoulders of the mob blocking her view.

Then a knot of tall security men swept down the narrow aisle behind the tables, their heads all that could be seen over the crowd, and people began to clap. Shifting her eyes back to the elevators, Kelly caught a momentary glimpse of a smallish woman in green, framed in the open doorway between two men with darting, suspicious eyes.

The woman smiled, raising her hand to the applauding guests, then the elevator doors closed.

BILLY QUINN was perspiring in his stiff, formal suit.

The Oak Room was stuffy, crowded with many of the people from downstairs, plus, it seemed, the majority of the security agents. They had all pushed forward to one end of the room, where a blue velvet rope separated them from the rank of mostly old men waiting to be honored—although one or two women and a well-known English rock star were also included.

The honorees stood anxiously awaiting the entrance of the Queen. The Major, standing a few spaces from the far end of the line, was braced at stiff military attention, his rounded shoulders pulled back, which made him look even taller than he was.

Billy, who was pressed right up against the rope opposite him, searched James Queally-Smythe's face and was rewarded with a quick wink from the old man, who, he suddenly realized, was fighting to suppress a proud smile.

There was a sudden flurry of activity around a door at the side of the room, beyond the line of honorees, and a recorded trumpet fanfare blared out of tinny speakers hidden somewhere in the ceiling. An expectant hush fell over the crowd, and the old men braced themselves.

Billy felt the remote device in his pocket pressing against his thigh as a booming voice announced the entrance of the Queen, reciting the long list of titles and places she ruled, ending, of course, with Northern Ireland.

Northern Ireland, my bleeding arse. Billy felt the familiar anger he'd known his whole life rising within him like a pent-up glut of lava in the throat of a volcano. *By what fucking right does she call herself ruler of Northern Ireland? Ruler of half a million imprisoned, ragged have-nots like me and me ma, whose lives were a living hell of poverty and abuse before their fucking peace.*

And nothing has changed for us since . . .

He slipped his hand into the pocket, palming the tiny rectangle of plastic, slowly pulling it out and dropping the hand to his side. Sweaty fingers closed about the little box as a slightly frumpy woman in a shocking lime-colored dress walked through the doorway, followed by two attendants.

Jesus, she looks like somebody's ma!

The assemblage broke into warm applause and the old men stiffened as the Queen stepped up to the first of them, took a small box from an attendant, who whispered into her ear, then turned and pressed it into the trembling hands of a profusely sweating bald man. She said a word or two to him, then moved to the next in line.

It's not as if the stuff will really hurt her . . . A long sleep and a bad headache. Kileen said that's all it'll do . . .

Billy took a deep breath as another award was presented, another word spoken. She moved on.

Just two more to go . . .

He looked at the Major. The old man's watery blue eyes were fixed on the Queen now. His pride shining out from them like a beacon.

It'll kill the old fellow. The shame of it. Letting himself be duped by the likes of a West Belfast brat . . . Him blamed for being the one responsible . . .

His fingers tightened about the remote.

One to go. Just one more . . . He'll be mortified. His great shining moment turned to shit . . .

He exhaled.

Took another deep breath.

Held it.

The Queen was standing before James Queally-Smythe now. Pinning a decoration of some sort to his breast beside the row of colored ribbons.

Do it, you daft fuck! There'll never be another chance like this again. Never.

His aching finger poised above the knurled plastic of the button that would send the signal to the medallion around the old man's neck, blasting a cloud of immobilizing gas right into her face. Hesitating. Now the Queen was peering myopically at the gold medallion hung round the old man's neck. Leaning forward to read the inscription. Raising her eyes to question him about it. Smiling at the whispered explanation.

Do it, you stupid, sodding fuck!

And then she was gone on to the next one.

And Billy Quinn knew he could never do it.

Not to the old man.

Hot bile rising into his throat, he pushed his way blindly through the crowd, seeking the door at the far end of the hall.

Kileen! What about Kileen?

A figure in a dark blue suit stepped away from the wall to intercept him. He looked up to see a familiar face frowning at him. "Something wrong?" The question whispered.

"Not feeling well . . . " Mumbling. Anxious to get out of the room.

Applewhite nodded, leading him to a side exit. "Sorry. You'll find a men's room right through there. Need any assistance?"

Billy shook his head, rushing out through the door and into a carpeted corridor. A dark-suited security agent glared suspiciously from his post by the stairwell door, started forward. Applewhite waved the man away, pointing Billy to another door down the hall, then ducking back into the banquet room.

Billy rushed through the indicated door. Found himself in a gleaming tiled restroom. He started for a stall, saw a pair of legs in blue beneath the locked door and, oddly, a pair of pink rubber gloves lying on the tiles. Stumbling, he barely made it into the adjoining stall and leaned over the commode, fearing he might faint at any second.

"PLEASE, I've got to get upstairs."

"And why is that, miss?" The ugly security man by the lobby elevator door was scrutinizing Kelly with hard, suspicious eyes.

"I, uh, my grandfather is getting an award," she stammered. "I mean, I'm supposed to be up there, but I had a flat tire," she lied.

The guard nodded and pulled a typewritten list from his coat pocket. "And your name?"

"Smythe," she said. "Kelly Smythe."

He flipped over several sheets until he found the one he wanted, then began tracing down the list, his thick finger moving from name to name with agonizing slowness. "Well, I'm afraid you're not on the list, Miss Smythe," he said after a moment.

"He didn't know I was coming. I just got in from New York." Kelly blurted out the hastily contrived story in desperation, realizing almost before she'd finished that it had been a mistake. The security man's eyes narrowed perceptibly and he lifted the lapel of his sharply cut suit to reveal a tiny microphone. "A for Albert," he whispered, "William is orange. Repeat, William is orange."

Almost immediately, another security man materialized behind Kelly, grasping her firmly by the elbow. "Please, miss, if you'll just walk quietly with me, I'm sure we can sort this out," he said pleasantly.

"Let me go," demanded Kelly, snatching her arm free. The startled agent reached for her again, but she backed away. "You don't understand," she shrieked, all pretense gone from her voice. "They're going to kill her."

BILLY HUNCHED MISERABLY over a commode, his forehead pressed against the cold tile of the wall. He was vaguely aware of the restroom door slamming open, and of someone hurriedly walking in to stand outside the stalls.

His stomach finally let go with a rush, and he doubled over the porcelain bowl, heaving uncontrollably until there was nothing left but the sour taste in his mouth. He was suffocating because of the fucking plugs in his nostrils, gagging until he blew them out into the toilet.

Then at last it was over and he stood, gasping for breath. Leaning weakly against the metal stall, he felt the panic slowly filling his brain.

Kileen is going to fucking kill me! What'll I do?

Run. Run, screamed a voice in his head, *Run as fast and as far as you can. Then run some more.*

His guts aching as though he'd been kicked in a back-alley brawl, he straightened, wiping his mouth on the sleeve of the black tuxedo. Turned around.

"You stupid little fuck!" Kileen glared at him from the open door of the stall. There was a stubby automatic pistol in the terrorist's hand, and his black, murderous eyes drilled into Billy Quinn's very soul.

"I . . . I'm sorry," Billy stammered, his eyes on the gun, unable to fathom how the terrorist had managed to smuggle it into the hotel through the seemingly airtight security. "I just couldn't do it."

"You've got to fucking do it," hissed Kileen. "You've got no choice. Now go back in there . . . It's not too late. There's still the dinner."

Billy shook his head. "I can't . . . do this. I . . . want to get out . . . Before any innocent people get hurt."

The terrorist's laugh made his blood run cold. "Innocent people, is it? Do you know how many 'innocent people' have died for this opportunity?"

Billy stared at him.

"There's Brian O'Malley, for starters. He died in a Belfast explosion dressed in your clothes."

"O'Malley? But you said—"

"And his mother and father," Kileen sneered.

"That was a fucking accident!" Billy was shouting through his tears.

"Was it, now?" Kileen's voice was mocking. "Or was it because they had to be eliminated so their poor little orphaned son could be sent for by his dear old grandfather who'd not seen him in years and was soon to be deco-rated by Her Royal Fucking Majesty in there?"

Kileen laughed. "And then there've been a few more died here, as well. Not exactly innocents, but at least ignorant . . ."

"You bastard!" Billy threw a fist at his smooth, handsome face. Kileen moved his head aside with a fighter's grace and slammed a devastating punch into the boy's solar plexus, doubling him over.

"Shit," sighed Kileen, taking a square plastic box from his pocket and aim-ing it in the direction of the Oak Room. "I suppose this will just have to do."

Billy gaped up at him from the floor. "You said the transmitter had to be close-in to trigger the gas."

Kileen shook his head in amusement. "The gas? You've been reading too many comic books, Billy. There's no magical gas. There's only the explosive charge in that medal you gave to the old man. I can set it off from fifty feet away with no trouble." Kileen gave him a vicious grin. "I only wanted you close-in because it would've been far better if it had gone off while he was standing right in front of her—turned her to a cloud of bloody pink vapor. They wouldn't have been able to find enough of her to fill a matchbox." He shrugged. "But this'll do almost as well . . . Blow the whole damn lot of them to hell anyway . . ."

Billy dived for his legs too late. Kileen stabbed at the remote button, brac-ing for the explosion.

They fell to the hard floor together, Billy striking his head against the cold tiles. He rolled out through the door and looked up groggily, expecting a renewed assault from the terrorist. Instead, his eyes caught sight of the se-curity man he had seen guarding the stairwell in the hotel corridor. The man was slumped grotesquely against the side of a metal toilet partition, his flat, dead eyes staring into space above the bloody slash of his throat. His dark suit jacket had been pulled open, exposing the empty shoulder holster beneath his left armpit. The holster Kileen had taken the automatic from!

Swiveling his head around, Billy saw Kileen sitting on the floor, still gaz-ing transfixed at the transmitter in his hand. Stabbing the impotent button over and over again. "Sally," he whispered in disbelief, "you stupid goddamn bitch! You fucked around with the medals while I was sleeping, didn't you? You switched them on me, Sally! You fucking switched them . . ."

Scrabbling to his feet, Billy crashed out though the restroom door and ran down the corridor. Two running security men rounded a corner, raising their guns to fire. Shots exploded behind Billy, and both men fell. He looked back to see Kileen standing in the corridor, swinging the muzzle of the pistol around toward Billy's head. The boy dived for the open doors of the elevator.

"SOMETHING'S GONE WRONG." Duffy was staring at his watch. More than twenty minutes had passed, and still there had been no sound of an explosion from the hotel. Then, a moment before, a pair of dark-suited security men had left their posts and hurried into the hotel.

He looked back across the street at the hotel entrance. The TV lights had been turned off once all the dignitaries had gone inside, and many of the sidewalk onlookers had drifted away.

"What are we going to do?" Tumelty was fidgeting in the passenger seat.

"Get behind the wheel, Dermot." Duffy opened the car door and stepped out into the street.

Tumelty slid over behind the steering wheel and stared out at the big man, who was adjusting the policeman's hat on his head as he gazed at the hotel. "I thought Kileen said we were to stay here . . ."

Duffy turned back to look at him. "Stuff Kileen," he said. "The kid could be trapped in there. I'm just going to have a look." He reached down and casually unstrapped the top of the holster containing the powerful automatic pistol. "If anything happens, you drive in and pick me up as planned."

"Francis . . ."

The hulking psychopath glared at his frail partner.

"Good luck," Dermot Tumelty whispered.

Francis Duffy gave him a yellow-toothed grin, then he plucked a black cigar from his shirt pocket and clamped it between his teeth. "Watch your ass, young Dermot," he said, lighting the smoke with a match and sauntering away across the hotel lawn, trailing a cloud of blue vapors.

KELLY STOOD BY the elevator, her elbow still held loosely in the grasp of the remaining security man. His partner had gone up minutes ago, leaving this one to watch over her. There was a gun in his other hand now, though the same hand was pressed to the side of his head, as he tried to make sense of the urgent babble of conversation pouring into the tiny receiver plugged into his ear.

Then the elevator door slid open, and Billy Quinn, his suit jacket ripped across one shoulder, his white shirt front stained, stood there, staring wide-eyed at the girl in the pink prom dress. Their eyes locked for an instant before he looked down and saw her elbow gripped in the security man's big fist. "Upstairs," Billy gasped to the startled agent. "They're trying to kill the Queen! They've shot the guards!"

"Stay here!" ordered the security man. He dropped Kelly's arm and leaped into the elevator. The doors hissed shut on him.

Kelly Huston and Billy Quinn gazed at each other. The cocktail-party guests were milling about behind them, and somewhere a woman began to sob loudly as Billy's words to the agent spread through the crowd.

He reached for Kelly, but she shook him off, her eyes filled with shock and horror. "The Queen's not hurt," he murmured. "I stopped it."

Kelly, her heart filling with joy, grasped his hand.

There was more shouting, and he looked up to see people crowding toward the main doors. "You've got to stay away from me!" he said, jerking his head toward the escaping crowd. "Get out with the others!"

She shook her head, grabbing his hand. "No!" she said fiercely.

"I've got to run," he grunted, dragging her along toward the doors. "They'll be wanting to kill me now."

She stared at him, uncomprehending. "But you saved the Queen's life. We can explain to the police . . ."

He shook his head in frustration, trying to free himself from her deathlike grip. "Not the police or the government, the ones that sent me here," he said angrily. "There's no explaining to them."

"Brian," she pleaded.

"My name is Billy Quinn," he breathed, pulling her to him and crushing his lips against hers in a brief, painful kiss. He pulled abruptly away and gazed into her eyes. "And there's been nobody else but you. Nobody!"

A stairwell door slammed open near the elevators and Michael Kileen stepped into the lobby. "You traitorous little bastard," he screamed, loosing a shot that plowed into the back of a matronly woman in a long satin gown.

Billy Quinn shoved Kelly Huston into the shelter behind a metal planter and dove into the stampeding crowd.

DERMOT TUMELTY sat at the wheel of the idling police car, trying to decide what to do. A moment before, there had been a disturbance at the hotel doors, followed by a sudden glare of television lights. Then people had started spilling out onto the walkway before the entrance.

Duffy was more than halfway across the broad lawn, moving steadily toward the milling crowd.

Then a lone figure broke from the mob and ran straight toward Duffy, pursued by a man in a blue suit. The man in blue raised a gun and fired two shots.

Francis Duffy froze in his tracks, unholstering his gleaming silver pistol and tracking the running figures.

Confused by the unfathomable activity, Dermot Tumelty unholstered his own pistol, laying it on the seat beside him, then turning the steering wheel to angle the front wheels of the police car away from the curb. He was about to press the accelerator down when he recognized the fleeing figure as Billy Quinn, the man in blue as Michael Kileen. Uncertain what was happening, Tumelty hesitated, watching dumbfounded as Duffy took aim at Kileen.

Michael Kileen saw Duffy standing before him, aiming the deadly pistol at his head. The terrorist leader let his eyes wander from Billy Quinn long enough to raise the multicircuit electronic garage-door opener he held in his other hand and press the second of its three buttons.

Across the lawn, Dermot Tumelty shrieked in horror as Francis Duffy disappeared in a flash of white-hot light. The shock of the explosion knocked Kileen down and rocked the police car on its springs. And then Kileen was picking himself up off the ground, standing unsteadily to aim his automatic at Billy Quinn, who lay on his face thirty feet away. People were screaming and running away from the killing ground as Kileen stalked toward the boy with the dead security man's gun held out at arm's length.

"You fucking bastard!" Dermot Tumelty slammed his right foot into the police car's accelerator. The powerful V-8 engine spun the rear end around on smoking tires, and the car leaped across the street, jumping the curb and plowing into the manicured hotel lawn.

Michael Kileen heard the roar of the approaching engine. Lowering the automatic to his side, he raised the deadly transmitter a second time, again poising his finger over the button and watching the speeding vehicle close the distance between them.

The police car was racing across the soft grass. Dermot saw Kileen's arm coming up. The youngster's eyes darted to the chromed pistol lying on the seat beside him, and he suddenly knew what the bastard had done. That he'd intended for none of them to live, had planned all along to blow them up to cover his own escape. Tumelty let go the steering wheel, grabbed the automatic pistol from the seat with his good hand and tossed it out through the open passenger window.

The chrome pistol exploded ten feet behind the onrushing police car, blowing out the back window and peppering the trunk lid with hot metal fragments. The car veered hard as Tumelty fought for control, sliding harmlessly past Michael Kileen, who stepped nearer to the boy on the ground and raised his pistol to fire a shot point-blank into his head.

Billy Quinn looked up at Kileen from the grass. His forehead was bleeding, and the torn black tuxedo was covered in dirt. "Why?" he asked miserably as the black mouth of the stubby automatic centered on his heart.

Kileen shrugged apologetically. "This is the way of it, Billy." He smiled sadly, then his mad eyes darted to one side as a strange whisper of sound filled the air and a ghostly shadow grew in his field of vision.

The speeding Bentley sedan caught Michael Kileen from slightly behind, its massive, square radiator slamming into his left hip, tossing his body high into the air. The three-ton car plowed into a stand of manicured shrubbery and came to a sudden halt as the terrorist's body dropped headfirst into the concrete drive and lay unmoving beneath the glare of the television lights. Ranjee looked out from the driver's seat of the Bentley, his dark eyes fixing Billy Quinn's startled blue ones in their gaze.

Ranjee made no move toward him, and Billy scrambled to his feet, looking frantically around the littered lawn. Stunned security people were slowly standing. Drawing guns. Suddenly, he heard the roar of another engine, saw the battered police car backing toward him, its rear wheels tearing up great raw clods of turf. It chewed its way across the lawn and spun to a halt facing the street.

"Get in!" An ashen-faced Dermot Tumelty was screaming at him from behind the wheel.

Billy nodded slowly, then looked back at Ranjee. "Tell the Major . . . " he began, choking back a sob. "Nobody was supposed to be hurt . . ."

People were running across the lawn, and he saw Kelly Huston's pink gown flying out behind her as she ran through the hotel doors and down the carpeted walkway toward him.

Tumelty gunned the engine. "For Christ's sake, get in!" he screamed.

Billy opened the passenger door, holding it until Kelly leaped into the police car. He dived in behind her, and the car sped off toward the street with its lights flashing and siren screaming. The converging cops moved aside to let it pass.

CHAPTER SIXTEEN

Lovers

"I'm sorry. It's time."

Kelly Huston looked up into the gloom to see the strange little man bending over them. Dermot Tumelty had exchanged his policeman's uniform for faded jeans and a spotless white sweatshirt with a grinning portrait of Mickey Mouse on the chest, the new clothes making him seem even more frail and childlike than before. "It's dangerous for us to stay here any longer," he whispered apologetically. "We've got to go."

Kelly nodded, and Dermot withdrew to finish stowing the few items they would be taking with them in the yellow Toyota, which was squeezed into the garage beside the battered police car. When he was out of sight, she leaned over Billy Quinn, who was sleeping cradled in her arms.

The long black hair was gone, sheared close with a pair of drugstore clippers and roughly colored with a can of brown hair spray, both of which Tumelty had bought when he'd left them alone to venture out in the Toyota for food.

Billy's features were soft in the glow of the shaded battery-powered lantern they'd set up in the corner where they'd withdrawn for privacy, and she gazed at him for a long time before gently reaching to brush his lips with the tips of her fingers. He opened his eyes, looking up at her accusingly. "You let me fall asleep."

"You needed to rest," she answered.

He did not reply immediately, turning instead and pressing himself closer in the nest of dusty blankets they'd fashioned for themselves a few hours before, atop a pile of sagging cardboard boxes.

"I didn't want to waste a single minute with you," he whispered regretfully, laying his cheek softly on her breast.

She held him tightly, struggling to keep her voice from cracking. "We'll have lots of time when you come back to me." She smiled. "You will come back?"

"I will," he promised. "If you're sure."

A single tear, sparkling like a dewdrop in the lantern light, fell from her cheek to his.

"I'm sure," she said.

CHAPTER SEVENTEEN

Aftermath

IT WAS VERY LATE.

Brenda Gaynor sat in her parked Mercedes convertible, looking up at the dark Spanish-style mansion beyond the iron gates. When Brian O'Malley hadn't called by eleven, she had driven here to wait for him. Strangely, she was hurt but not angry at having been stood up. She simply wanted to be with him again.

She had already been waiting here outside his house for more than twenty minutes. It didn't matter, she thought. She was willing to wait all night if necessary.

A car door opened somewhere behind her, and she looked back down the canyon to see a figure emerging from the front seat of a vehicle pulled over to the side of the road. She thought it was strange that she had not noticed the other car there when she had driven up the canyon.

The figure walked slowly up the hill, and as it drew closer she recognized Thad August, his shock of sun-bleached hair shining in the glow of the lights above the iron gates. He walked to the Mercedes and looked down at her. "Brenda . . ."

She wiped her wet cheeks with her fingertips, unable to understand what he was doing here.

"He's not coming back, Bren," August said softly.

She gazed at him as though he'd spoken in some ancient, indecipherable tongue.

"It was on the radio," he said, jerking his head back toward the other car. "He was involved in some kind of terrorist attack . . ."

"Is he dead?" Her voice was a monotone.

August shook his head. "I don't think so. They say he got away with a couple of other people . . ." He shrugged, slapping his hands against his legs. "Well, I just thought you ought to know . . . I'd better go now."

"Why were you parked down there, Thad?" Brenda's shining eyes locked on his.

"I followed you," he confessed.

"I thought I saw somebody else in the car when you got out."

"Just Jake and Jerry and a couple of the guys."

Brenda sniffled. "Do you want to drive me someplace for a cup of coffee or something . . . I need to talk."

August nodded. "Sure, Bren."

Brenda Gaynor slid across to the Mercedes's passenger seat, and Thad waved at the other car, then got behind the wheel. "Where do you want to go?" he asked.

She shook her long, coppery tresses. "Someplace loud," she said as he started the engine.

KELLY HUSTON was propped up among the pillows in her bedroom. She had turned off the television a while ago, and now she was staring out at the shimmering waters of the swimming pool, thinking about everything that had happened.

The television reporters had already labeled Brian O'Malley "The White Knight," claiming that he had saved the lives of the Queen of England and at least a hundred other people. Nobody knew who he was or where he had gone, though it was rumored that both the CIA and British Military Intelligence were claiming him as their agent and that a major television producer had already announced plans for a Movie of the Week.

She prayed he was all right.

She did not doubt that Billy Quinn would keep his promise to her.

THE YELLOW TOYOTA sedan rolled across the vast wasteland of the Mojave Desert, its headlights drilling a clean, white cone of light into the black night.

"So, where are we going to go?" Billy was at the wheel, the cold, dry air through the open window riffling the half inch of brown fuzz atop his close-cropped head. The L.A. radio news shows had faded to static fifty miles back, and he knew only that he and Dermot Tumelty were wanted by everyone. The news reports had made him happy because the authorities had no more clue to the identity of the mysterious "Woman in Pink" than to his own identity.

Tumelty grinned up from the can of Coca-Cola he was drinking and pointed to the glow of lights on the far horizon. "We'll stop in Las Vegas for the night," he said. "It's America's top tourist destination. We can just leave the car in one of those huge auto parks by the hotels and get a plane in the morning . . ."

"A plane to where?" Billy was astonished by Tumelty's almost festive demeanor but said nothing. After all, he owed the little fellow his life.

Dermot Tumelty grinned. "Where? Anywhere. We could go to Montana and become cowboys, or to Nashville and start a country band with my music . . . Don't worry. We'll fit right in. I know all the tricks."

"And what'll we use for money?" Billy asked impatiently. "What little I had I left back at the Major's house with the false passport . . . and you said you dumped everything else back at the garage."

Tumelty reached into the blue nylon Disneyland bag at his feet and held up a great handful of bills. "Everything except this," he said. "Kileen's operational fund."

Billy stared at the money for a moment, then turned his eyes back to the arrow-straight highway. "Do you think you'll ever go back to Belfast, Dermot?"

Tumelty shook his head. "Can't now, even if I wanted to. Not for years and years anyway. And you?"

Billy shrugged helplessly. "I don't know," he said. "Kileen told me 'Billy Quinn' was killed in Belfast. So I guess I'm dead to all of them there . . ."

Dermot nodded. "The bastard wanted all of us dead. He rigged that police car for us to blow ourselves up. Fixed the machine gun so it wouldn't fire . . ." He stared out the window at the rushing desert landscape. "Was he completely mad, then, do you think?" he asked.

Billy's grip tightened on the Toyota's steering wheel, and he cut his sharp blue eyes across the darkened passenger compartment. "Don't you get it yet, Dermot? They're all completely fucking mad, the bloody terrorists and the politicians and everybody that sits on their arses in front of the telly and lets them keep on doing it. All of them."

Dermot Tumelty nodded and looked ahead toward the brightening glow on the horizon. "They say there's a grand hotel in Las Vegas that's built to look just like an Egyptian pyramid," said Dermot. "Let's stay there tonight if we can."